HIS WIFE WAS BARELY
IN HER GRAVE.
BUT
EVEN THEN,
MARGARET KNEW
HE WAS HER FUTURE.

"I am going to help Lewis Fleming." Louisa's perplexed frown only stiffened Margaret's intent. "I know it sounds insane to be saying a thing like that today, but dear Louisa, it's true."

"What's true? Whatever are you talking about?"

"I'm—going—to help him. Oh, I know I can't anytime soon. But I'm going to wait for Lewis Michael Fleming if it takes all the years until I'm an old woman! Even if I'm an old, *old* woman by the time I manage to wipe that stricken look from his face, I'll do it." She paused for the merest instant. "No. Don't say anything. You are my friend. The only close friend I have outside my father. I wanted you to know that however long it takes, I'll wait ."

Bantam Books by Eugenia Price
Ask your bookseller for the books you have missed

THE BELOVED INVADER
MARGARET'S STORY
MARIA
NEW MOON RISING

Margaret's Story

Eugenia Price

BANTAM BOOKS
TORONTO • NEW YORK • LONDON • SYDNEY • AUCKLAND

For Dena Snodgrass

This low-priced Bantam Book
has been completely reset in a type face
designed for easy reading, and was printed
from new plates. It contains the complete
text of the original hard-cover edition.
NOT ONE WORD HAS BEEN OMITTED.

MARGARET'S STORY

A Bantam Book / published by arrangement with
Harper & Row, Publishers, Inc.

PRINTING HISTORY
Harper & Row edition published October 1980
Bantam edition / October 1982

ISBN 0-553-22583-9

Published simultaneously in the United States and Canada

Bantam Books are published by Bantam Books, Inc. Its trademark,
consisting of the words "Bantam Books" and the portrayal of a
rooster, is Registered in U.S. Patent and Trademark Office and in
other countries. Marca Registrada. Bantam Books, Inc., 666 Fifth
Avenue, New York, New York 10103.

PRINTED IN THE UNITED STATES OF AMERICA

H   0 9 8 7 6 5 4 3

PROLOGUE

For a long moment, as the lean, robed priest from St. Augustine searched for his place in the service for the Burial of the Dead, there was only winter silence around the open grave in the tiny cemetery at Hibernia plantation on the St. Johns. The well- and warmly dressed group of mourners stood nearly motionless, even the children, as though the uniquely vibrant life of Augustina Cortez Fleming, so suddenly gone just before Christmas in the year 1832, had left them lifeless, too.

A pod of bright crimson seeds from the ancient magnolia, which stood beside the open grave, fell to the ground. Crashed. The familiar sound seemed a crash, so deep was the silence in the cupped clearing that formed the Fleming family plot, hemmed by dense woods, as the mourners—relatives and friends from Fernandina and St. Augustine—were hemmed by the stillness that followed the interruption. The priest cleared his throat and began to chant the ancient Latin phrases.

Nineteen-year-old Margaret Seton, her light, curly hair half hidden by a beaver bonnet tied against the north Florida winter chill, stooped to pick up the brilliant, velvety seed pod, which had fallen at her feet. Mourners turned to look at her, but she was not embarrassed. There was life in that seed pod and she meant to remember life even here in the face of death.

All eyes riveted again on the open grave as Margaret tucked the pod into her muff, wondering how long the priest would drone on. An Episcopal priest would at least have read in English so that some comfort might come.

He needs to be comforted, she thought. Major Lewis Fleming needs to understand that priest! Let the others stare into that grave—I can't take my eyes off Major Fleming's tortured face. Strong men seldom faint, but he could. Oh, God, notice him and let someone help him. . . .

Involuntarily, she took a step toward the tall, grieving

1

man. Louisa Fatio, her best friend, slipped her arm through Margaret's. Louisa, fifteen years older and a head taller, did not glance at Margaret. She merely restrained her without once shifting her own gaze from the cedar coffin still visible in the freshly dug grave.

I can tell that dear Louisa's worried most about his children, Margaret thought. But it *has* to be worse for him—for Lewis Fleming, holding a baby daughter in his arms, his eight- and ten-year-old sons pressing hard against him on either side. Lewis Michael Fleming, near Louisa's age, was to Margaret the most beautiful man she'd ever seen, including her own father, Charles Seton. Her handsome father was standing now beside her mother, Matilda, both staring down into the hole as though their fixed gaze could reveal just once more the fine Spanish features, the flashing, laughing eyes of Augustina Cortez Fleming, the woman Lewis loved. The young woman whom everyone, including Margaret, had considered such a perfect mate for gentle, strong, reserved Lewis Fleming.

Margaret pulled her heavy, dark blue woolen mantle closer about her, allowed her slender back to rest for a moment against the gray trunk of the big magnolia and prayed fervently for Lewis Fleming. Help him, Lord! This minute, help him stand there until it's over. Help him when he'll have to walk away and leave her lying in the cold. Help him learn to live without her. Lord, I know how much You must love him. I've adored every glimpse of Major Fleming since the day he first walked with that quiet confidence through our front door at Fernandina beside my father—dwarfing even Papa—as he bent to shake the hand of a small girl whose eyes must have shone with admiration even then.

Her dark eyes still on Lewis's face, Margaret marveled that throughout the long service he had scarcely moved a muscle, had not shifted his gaze from the oblong hole in the sandy earth, as though memorizing even the grain in the wood of the coffin that held Augustina's body. Only once had he forced a long, sob-broken breath into his lungs, then nothing.

At last, the droning ended and the gravedigger reached for his shovel.

"Papa?" The voice of eight-year-old Louis Isador was thin, frightened. *"Papa!"*

Lewis Fleming tightened his arm around the small boy, but said nothing as the first shovelful hit the wooden lid.

Margaret heard Louisa sob once, softly. Then the silence closed in again, so dense it seemed to hold even the gravedigger motionless. A wren shouted nearby and the shovel scraped up another load of dirt. The digger held it poised in midair as though waiting for the answering wren call. It came from somewhere over by the river. The second shovelful was emptied and again the gravedigger waited. Pity for the lone man with his three motherless children seemed to numb him, too.

When at last another and then another spade of dirt fell heavily into the open grave, Lewis Fleming buried his face in the thick blanket protecting baby Augustina and wept. On impulse, Margaret again started toward him. Louisa pulled her back.

"Wait," Louisa whispered. "Only God can help him now."

Not until the last shovelful had been firmly mounded did Lewis Fleming move again. Her heart pounding, Margaret stood with the others, watching as his red-rimmed, deep gray eyes moved slowly toward his small sons and then back to the mound, as though for one last time, he must make sure that everything was in order for Augustina. Margaret saw his shoulders straighten and the slender fingers adjust the baby's heavy cap. With his free hand, he touched one and then the other son. Together they began to trudge heavily away across the winter-browned stubbly grass toward the sandy lane that would take them to their beloved home, Hibernia, standing silent and empty now of Augustina's laughter under its giant trees over by the wide St. Johns.

The knot of friends and neighbors and cousins broke up slowly and straggled after him. Louisa started, too, but stopped when Margaret did not move.

"I know what you're thinking, my dear," Louisa said softly. "Christmas is almost here. It's going to be so sad for the children. Sophia and I will have them all with us across the river at our house. Come, Margaret. You must be chilled to the bone. I am."

"Because you're wearing only that short fur tippet," Margaret said absently, still making no move toward leaving the cemetery.

"My dear, we'll be needed at Hibernia." Louisa's kind, open face was puzzled. "As Lewis's eldest cousin, I'll be expected to manage the servants. Folks will need hot coffee and tea and food."

Still standing beneath the huge magnolia, Margaret turned her gaze enough to follow Lewis Fleming as he walked, only enormous effort forcing him to take each step away from the grave now covered with palmetto fronds and glossy-leafed orange branches.

"Margaret," Louisa whispered sharply.

"Yes, it *is* sad for the children, Louisa—but what about *him?* Who's going to help Major Fleming through Christmas?" Her voice firmed. "Who's going to help him through—all the years ahead?"

She could feel Louisa Fatio's wide-set hazel eyes studying her.

"Margaret Seton, you've been dear to me since you were a little girl—an infant, really. I think my heart went out to you the minute I set eyes on you at age eight months, but—"

"I know, I know, Louisa." Margaret struggled to soften the edge of annoyance in her voice. "I know how long we've been friends. You're dear to me, too, but what does that have to do with—right now?"

Louisa's slow, warm smile came. "Simply that after nearly nineteen years, you don't stop surprising me. You're really behaving very strangely."

Margaret turned away.

"Margaret, my dear, are you crying?"

"I don't know. Am I?" There was no hint of weeping in her voice. She felt strong and sure. Suddenly, very strong and very sure.

"Oh, I shouldn't be surprised if you wept," Louisa was saying. "No death could be sadder than Augustina's. Eleven short years together. It's all making you so sad because—well, you're only nineteen. And this is undoubtedly the first time you've seen such deep grief."

"Yes, but that has nothing to do with—anything right now."

"It must have."

"You're wrong. It's *his face*, Louisa. That broken, helpless pain in—Major Fleming's beautiful face . . ."

"Death scars our faces. It scars our hearts."

"For—always? Don't the scars ever leave?"

Louisa was silent a moment. "No. The scars don't leave. My Roger has been gone for nearly seventeen years."

"And—you still grieve for him? Even though he died before you could be married?"

Louisa nodded. "I had him to love for only six months."

Margaret stared at her. "Poor Louisa. You've had—too much death! First, Roger, then your grandmother Fatio, who was more like your own mother, really. Your grandfather is gone, too, now. Early this year, your father—oh, Louisa, and just last month, your brother, Louis!" Embracing her friend suddenly, Margaret whispered, "I shouldn't have said a single thing—to remind you. Please forgive me." A quick frown intensified the depth of Margaret's dark eyes. "But, I do have to talk to you just a minute longer. You see, Louisa, I know something no one else on earth knows. I don't want to be the only one to know. It's too—big to know all alone. It's—about Major Fleming. That look on his face."

"I think I know, my dear. His heart is broken."

"No, you don't know. There's no way you could know."

"I am acquainted with grief," Louisa said on a long sigh. "Enough so that I can tell you firsthand that only God and time can help Lewis Fleming."

"No!"

"What?"

"*I am going to help Lewis Fleming.*" Louisa's perplexed frown only stiffened Margaret's intent. "I know it sounds insane to be saying a thing like that today, but dear Louisa, it's true."

"What's true? Whatever are you talking about?"

"I'm—going—to help him. Oh, I know I can't anytime soon. But I'm going to wait for Lewis Michael Fleming if it takes all the years until I'm an old woman! Even if I'm an old, *old* woman by the time I manage to wipe that stricken look from his face, I'll do it." She paused for the merest instant. "No. Don't say anything. You are my friend. The only close friend I have outside my father. I wanted you to know that however long it takes, I'll wait. I've—loved Lewis Fleming since I was a little girl. I haven't known all the ways I loved him, but I know now. And I mean to see to it that someday, he'll laugh again. Be happy again. *Happy*, Louisa."

"I believe you mean that!"

Margaret lifted her chin so abruptly that the tawny curls on her forehead bobbled. "I do mean it. I'm young. I hate waiting, but I can wait."

Part One

1832–1836

1

On a mild, late November afternoon almost a year after Augustina's death, Lewis Fleming sat alone in the Hibernia parlor—a cherished copy of Plato's dialogues open, but unread, on his lap. His eyes moved vacantly from the sun streaks along the wide board floor of the sturdy country house his father, George, had built, out toward the gleaming expanse of the St. Johns River. The house on Fleming's Island and the thousand acres of good Hibernia land belonged to Lewis now. George Fleming, for whom the island had been named, had been dead for nearly twelve years. All that had happened during that period made his father's death seem a lifetime ago.

For all but one of those years, Lewis had known joy and comfort and ecstasy and laughter and love. At their home, Hibernia, which Lewis loved as his father had loved it, the days with Augustina had been filled with the brightest hope, confidence in the future and daily expectancy. His satisfaction had run deep because the children would grow up on the dear, familiar banks of the St. Johns River, their very roots in the sandy soil, their characters molded by the love and guidance of both parents as the wind molded the shapes of the oaks and cedars and sweet gums and cypress that nestled densely along the river's banks.

And then death had come again; this time, bringing the end of hope for Lewis Fleming. The end of hope and the beginning of the first gnawing guilt which he had experienced in all the thirty-five years of his life. Reason told him that he should not lose hope: Augustina had not left him alone. She had given him a tiny daughter bearing her name and two fine sons. Reason had never deserted him before, but now, the very lives of the children so dependent on him formed the ugly guilt. Outwardly, he went about his daily life as master of Hibernia; he taught his sons—George, now almost twelve and L.I. (Louis Isador), nine—with mechanical regularity. They were interesting boys—George, dark-eyed and slender, with his mother's Spanish coloring, was sensitive, moody, and so tenderhearted that he used to cry when his younger brother, L.I., shot a bird for sport. L.I., who looked like Lewis, the same heavy, rusty brown forelock hanging in his eyes, the same deep gray eyes, was all boy. If he faced it, Lewis knew that the boys themselves caused his guilt—merely by being there. By needing their father to be stronger than he found it possible to be without their mother.

How he wished his sons had known their Grandfather Fleming, but even Augustina had missed knowing Lewis's father by a year. George Fleming had fallen dead from his horse as he galloped toward Hibernia from his south field in 1821, the same year in which Lewis, along with his relatives and friends, had renounced their Spanish oaths and sworn allegiance to the United States. Numb from the loss of his adored father, Lewis had scarcely thought about the change in government. Only when he married Augustina in Havana a year later and was teaching her the history of Florida did he begin to take any interest in the future of his new country. For that matter, the government in Washington seemed to take little interest in Florida. Lewis still felt as he'd always felt—a man who belonged to a possession of a distant country—Spain, and then the United States. There was talk that Florida might someday become a state. It was Lewis Fleming's state now, when he thought about it at all. The affiliation of its central government meant little. This oldest, most colorful part of a new, awkward nation—lush, lake- and river-streaked Florida—merely contained his beloved thousand acres, and in them, the tiny plot which held the remains of dear Augustina.

Lewis closed the book and sank deeper into his armchair, exhausted as he had been for nearly a year by the ongoing grief. "Augustina," he whispered, "there is no harder work—than grieving."

No one needed him at this hour. The servants were occupied, the boys fishing, little Augustina asleep. It was the time of day when he and his wife would have been together in this room, or walking hand in hand along the river path, Augustina hunting, as she did every late autumn, for red, velvety seed pods from Hibernia's magnolias. "I must find more seeds because I will never have enough blossoms," she would declare in her thick Spanish accent. "I want so many trees that I can fill our house with fragrance!"

Lewis tried not to notice the still painful beauty of the westering sun as it turned the thick trunks of Hibernia's trees a luminous, gold-brown. Tried not to picture her running from window to window so as not to miss one change of sky color.

He did notice. Her presence was, after nearly twelve long, agonizing months, everywhere he turned or looked. At times, comforting him. At other times, as today, tormenting him because his mind dwelled on her body lying cold and waxen and still in a wooden box just down the lane from where he tried to live his life without her.

In an effort to break the bleak mood, he began to pace the room. Then, he heard Maum Easter's steady footsteps in the hall and with no coherent thought except that he could bear to talk to no one—not even Maum Easter—Lewis bolted from the room, crossed the river porch and ran down the path to the dock where his small sailboat lay at anchor.

Handling the sheet and the tiller from habit, he had sailed halfway across the two miles of river which separated Hibernia from New Switzerland, the Fatio home, before he realized that he was hurrying to the only person on the face of the earth—including his mother in Jacksonville—with whom he could talk freely. With whom he could be himself in such a hopeless state of mind. He was running, like a frightened child, to his first cousin, Louisa Fatio.

"She'll know," he said aloud as he adjusted the small sail to prevent being stalled in the center calm of the wide river. "Louisa will know."

He shivered in the damp wind off the water. He had forgotten a jacket.

"Louisa will find a way to—help me."

Gratefully, Lewis took the small glass of claret that Louisa handed him. He had been right. The quiet, perceptive woman had merely greeted him warmly, invited him into the parlor and, after pouring the wine, seated herself across from him now—without a single question. Her strong hands resting on the arms of her father's favorite wing chair, Louisa simply smiled at him and waited. Not the bright, cheerful smile his children loved, but a smile which told him that for as long as he needed to remain silent, she would wait—just being glad to have him there.

"Louisa," he began at last. "I'm relieved to find you alone. I—need you."

"The children must be all right or you'd have told me right off. Is it—the darkness still, Lewis? Still the darkness all around?"

He sighed heavily. "I'm—not doing well at all—without her. I don't seem to learn how." He frowned, glancing toward the hall. "Will we be alone for a while?"

"Oh, I think so. Sophia and Margaret Seton are down at the quarters making a wedding dress for Scipio's bride. You remember Miss Seton, don't you?"

"Yes, of course." He spoke absently. "I'm fond of her father, Charles Seton. Fine man. Did he and Mrs. Seton come down from Fernandina, too?"

"They'll follow for a Christmas visit. Only Margaret is here now."

"I see." Then, "Louisa, I—don't do well at all with the boys. Oh, I pretend courage when I'm with them, but—"

"And do you think that's the right thing to do, Lewis?"

He only frowned.

"I'm sure you mean to be shielding them from your grief," she went on, "but, it might help them both if they knew some of what you feel. You might find them quite eager to share their grief with you."

Lewis buried his head in his hands.

"Lewis?"

"Yes?"

"Do you and the boys talk about—their mother often?"

"I seldom mention her name. It's usually L.I. who speaks of her. George's eyes are simply so full of sadness, I think I can't bear it. L.I. does talk about her—some."

"Then L.I. has more wisdom than his father. At least, where grief is concerned. It helps to speak as naturally as possible about the one gone away, Cousin. It helps everyone. I know. I was able to talk about my Roger so long ago with Father. In fact, Papa urged me to talk about him all I needed. I did—for years."

His shoulders slumped. "It's my nature to keep pain to myself."

"I know that. But, Lewis, you're human. Your needs are the same as mine were."

"*Were*, Louisa? Does one—ever pass by—grief?"

"In a way, no. I'd still like to be able to talk about Roger as he was when we were both young and in love. Oh, now and then I do talk to Margaret Seton. I find her always ready to listen. I find myself talking to her more and more, in fact, with each visit. Much as we're talking now. Even though she's only twenty, she's quite mature." Louisa laughed affectionately. "And you know how Sophia is. I love my little sister dearly, but she waxes so dramatic about anything and everything—exaggerates so, I can't really share myself with her much. Frankly, for her own sake, I hope she marries soon. That is, if she can find a young man who can fit her flowery ideal."

"You'd be alone, Louisa."

"Yes. But I'd manage. As you will. You're blessed to have your children."

Lewis tried to smile. "No one knows that better than I. In fact, I'm a little ashamed to have—run to you today, Cousin. Not very ashamed. Just a little. I felt I was failing the boys. Little Augustina won't even remember her mother. The boys will—always." He got up. "I was feeling lost and—scared. Wishing, frankly, for my own father. As I'm sure you wish for yours."

"Are you wondering, Lewis, if George Fleming might have shown more courage than you feel you're showing—had he lost your mother?"

Lewis nodded. "And I'm sure Mother wonders why I don't take a boat to Jacksonville more often to visit her."

"I'm sure she does wonder. But I don't."

He grinned. "You don't?"

"No one respects and loves your mother more than I. She's a brilliant woman. Lovely to look at, charming and courageous. A truly courageous lady. Your handsome, red-haired father was not an easy man to lose. Sophia Fleming weathered it like a good frigate. Still, I sense, Lewis, that her advice to you now—is more of a burden than a solace. I can just hear her urging you to—hold your head high, forge ahead."

He bent to hug her. "What would I do without you, Cousin?"

"You have me. Always just across the river."

"I must go. Pompey and the boys will be back from fishing. I don't want George and L.I. to find me away from the house."

Louisa stood, too, both hands out to him. "And you aren't up to the silly chatter of two very young ladies who might also be back soon full of talk about Scipio's bride and her wedding gown."

"No, I'm not."

"You won't believe me now, but times does eventually help. And, don't let anyone badger you about finding another mother for the children."

"How did you know Mother started on that the first time I went to Jacksonville after—Augustina went away?"

"Because I know dear Aunt Sophia and I also know other people a little. 'You're still young,' they'll say. 'Be patient. You'll find someone else.' " When she saw Lewis's eyes fill with tears, Louisa embraced him. "Perhaps you will—someday. But I'll never urge you to it. It's been nearly eighteen years now since Roger died. I'm still *Miss* Louisa Fatio. I accept it as God's plan for my life. He has a plan for you, too, Cousin."

As he untied his boat at the Fatio dock, Lewis heard chatter and laughter and glanced up to see his younger cousin, Sophia, and Margaret Seton hurrying toward him. His impulse was to push off and head back across the river, but they were so obviously trying to hail him, courtesy won out. He did jump into the boat, though, hoping to make his haste evident.

Sophia, shrilling, "Cousin Lewis! Cousin Lewis!" was running toward the dock as fast as her long, full skirts allowed. Young Miss Seton, in spite of a bright yellow apron filled with something they'd been gathering, was even faster.

"Good afternoon, ladies," he called.

"Cousin Lewis, would you dare visit this side of the river without seeing me?" Sophia rushed up behind her friend, already standing on the dock. "Oh, Lewis—this is Miss Margaret Seton from Fernandina. I'm sure you know her."

From the boat, Lewis bowed. "Of course. How do you do, Miss Seton?"

"Very well, thank you, sir. I've told you over and over, Sophia, that Major Fleming and I met first when I was four years old!"

"I believe I remember the day," Lewis said. "Actually, that was my first meeting with your father, Miss Seton. How is he?"

"Quite well, Major—except that his old wound bothers

him at times. For a man in his late fifties, he's doing splendidly." She laughed easily. "And to me, Papa grows more
handsome with the years."

"Your mother is well too, I trust?"

"Yes, thank you." Then, with scarcely a beat, she asked:
"How are you—managing, Major Fleming?"

Lewis felt strangely trapped. Not repulsed by her question.
Almost glad of it, but not at all certain how to answer. "Well,
I—the children and I are well cared for. Our servants almost
smother us with kindness, I'm afraid." He pushed the boat
away from the dock. "I do apologize for my haste, ladies, but
I have to ask to be excused." After another brief bow, he sat
down. "I trust your visit will continue to be a pleasant one,
Miss Seton." He maneuvered the sail to catch the breeze.
"Good-bye. Good-bye. Sophia. The boys and I will be over
for Christmas. Maum Easter is keeping little Tina."

"I was wondering," Margaret called, "if you have a lot of
magnolia pods over at Hibernia."

"Yes," Sophia joined in, "we've decided to make a wreath
of them for Polly's head for her wedding. Lewis, can you
believe Scipio wants her dressed in red? Margaret thought of
red-seeded magnolia pods. Could we come over and search
your yard?"

Lewis let the sail go limp and stared at Margaret for just an
instant. Her lovely face, framed by the tawny, windblown
curls, was too appealing for resentment. But all magnolia
pods belonged to Augustina! He could still see her in the
twilight, flying about their yard gathering them, laughing
back at him as he watched and adored her.

"What's the matter, Lewis?" Sophia frowned. "Surely, you
know a magnolia pod when you see it!"

"Yes. I'll—look around when I get back. If there are any,
Pompey can bring them over to you tomorrow."

"That's such a lot of bother," Margaret called. "We can
easily come ourselves—"

"No! It will be no bother at all, Miss Seton. Now, you
ladies must excuse me."

He drew the small sail taut into the wind and skimmed out
over the choppy water, gray now, because clouds had begun
to scud across the sky where the sun was about to set. "No
one else is going to gather magnolia pods at Hibernia," he
said aloud to himself, gripping the sheet more tightly than

necessary. "I'll just not mention it to Pompey. The Seton girl and Sophia will assume there are none."

That night Margaret waited until Sophia was asleep and tiptoed to Louisa's room.

"Come in, my dear. I'm still reading."

"Louisa, I did a stupid thing today—with Major Fleming."

"I saw that you and Sophia caught him as he was leaving."

"I asked if I could go over to Hibernia to gather magnolia pods for Polly. Sophia did the asking, but I maneuvered her into it. I'm ashamed and I feel stupid. The day of his wife's funeral, I told you I could wait. Instead, I jumped headlong. I tried a trick and I don't want to do that."

"No one who is really a trickster admits it, Margaret. So, you're not one. But, you're right about waiting. Lewis Fleming is far, far, far from being able to be more than courteous to—any woman."

"I vow I'll never do a thing like that again!"

"I believe you. Besides, with all he has on his mind and in his poor, broken heart, I doubt that he even noticed."

"Oh, I'm sure he did notice. I wouldn't be worried if I didn't think so. You see, I care too much about him ever to insult him by—mere flirting." She leaned down to kiss Louisa's forehead. "I want everything to be very aboveboard between Major Fleming and me. Don't forget, I'm going to be his wife someday."

"Stranger things have happened."

Margaret smiled wistfully. "Oh, I'm so sure, that none of it seems a bit strange to me."

2

A few days later, L.I. and George, with their dog, Buster, attempted to break for the woods after breakfast. Lewis corralled them, an arm around each and headed them for the parlor—minus the little brown dog—for their final history lesson before they all went to the Fatio's for the Christmas holidays.

"Time for a review," he said. "I want you both to be able to converse intelligently while we're across the river. A gentleman I admire very much—Mr. Charles Seton of Fernandina—will be there. I expect to be proud of my sons."

"Will Grandmother Fleming be *up* from Jacksonville?" L.I. wanted to know.

"Unless her rheumatism is too bad for winter travel on the water." He smiled at L.I. and tousled the boy's rusty brown hair. "I heard what you said. And I'm proud of you."

"Just because I remembered the way our river flows? I know a lot more than that." Standing very straight, L.I. began to recite: "We live twenty miles south of Jacksonville, which to most people is *down*. But the St. Johns River flows backwards—north and not south like other rivers and so, when Grandmother Fleming visits us, she goes *upriver* even though Hibernia is *down* south from where she lives in Jacksonville."

George gave his younger brother a shove. "Dummy. Anybody knows Jacksonville is downriver."

"L.I. is no dummy, George," Lewis said firmly. "He merely has an analytical mind."

"What's *analytical?*" L.I. asked suspiciously.

"A mind that has to figure out everything. A lawyer has an analytical mind. You may turn out to be one, L.I."

George made a scoffing sound. "Who wants to be an old lawyer buried in dusty law books?" he snapped.

Lewis, noticing again the surprising shrillness he'd heard more and more often in his oldest son's voice, was suddenly sure, since his talk with Louisa, that the growing spats between the boys were due to buried grief. He studied George closely. Indeed, the dark eyes were brimming with tears. Attempting not to have observed this, Lewis said calmly, "The law is one of our most honorable professions, George."

"Sure," L.I. growled. "Now, who's dumb?"

"My mind is an *intuitive* mind," George said, his voice cracking. "Mama said so! I think she said that's the best kind of mind to have!"

"Papa, I know Mama didn't say that," L.I. wailed. "I never heard her say that!"

"And I've never heard the two of you act quite this cross with each other before, either." Lewis was aware of more sternness in his voice than he intended. Louisa was surely right. They had not spoken often enough of their mother. Tears burned her own eyes. "George," he said quietly, "look at me. Not out that window—at me. You must have misunderstood your mother, who knew perfectly well that one type of mind is no more desirable than another. She may well have called your mind intuitive. But both are of equal value and—" Lewis broke off, forced to wipe his own tears with the back of his hand. For a time there was no sound in the room except the clock ticking and the snap of the pine splinters and oak burning in the fireplace. George stood staring at the carpet, L.I. at his father.

Finally, L.I. asked in a voice just about a whisper, "Papa? Are you crying?"

Lewis reached both arms toward them and they ran quickly to him. The three clung together. "As I was saying," Lewis went on, still holding them, "one kind of mind is as worthy as another."

"An intuitive mind like mine," George said through his tears, "is quick. It catches on fast. Mama said it was—instinctive—like the birds."

"Like snakes and alligators, too," L.I.'s muffled words came from somewhere in the folds of Lewis's jacket.

"Here," Lewis said, reaching for his handkerchief. "Let's all three blow our noses and get down to some history."

"I thought maybe you had a cold, Papa," L.I. ventured.

"No, son. I—cry sometimes over Mama."

"I—I guess we both feel much better that you do, Papa."

Lewis sighed heavily.

"I imagine that you do, George. So do I. You see, grown men often try to act as they *think* grown men should. It—doesn't always work. Hearts don't hurt any less because a man is older."

"Papa?"

"What is it, L.I.?"

"How do you think we're gonna—live through a lot of—real *years* without Mama?"

Lewis waited, then said softly, "That's one question I simply cannot answer."

The boys exchanged glances; then, after a long silence, George said, struggling to make his voice firm, "God—will help us. We'll—get through it. Agreed?"

Seeing George extend his hand as though to clinch a bargain, Lewis grasped it quickly. "Right. By some means and with God's help—we will."

"Am I too young to shake hands, Papa?"

Taking his youngest son's grimy hand, Lewis said, "Why, not at all, L.I. At nine years? I should say not!" He drew in a deep breath and said on another sigh, "Now, I have no way of being sure about this, but since we've shed some tears together, I have a hunch the two of you are not going to spat quite so much." He saw them give each other self-conscious smiles as they settled themselves on the floor for the lesson. From his teacher's seat on the sofa, Lewis began, "Now—who wants to give me a succinct coverage of the changes of government in Florida to this date—1833?"

L.I. brightened. "Spain was first. Florida was discovered in 1513 by Mama's people, the Spanish. Then in the year 1763, Spain traded Florida to the British. They stayed for about twenty years and turned it back to Spain. Then the year before you and Mama got married, 1821, the United States of America finally got their hands on it."

"Our Fatio grandfather came to Florida," George put in, "during the British period in 1771 and our Fleming grandfather came right after the Spanish got it back and they both stayed on through all the changes of government."

Lewis laughed. "I'd say you've both managed to put a lot of facts into the proverbial nutshell."

"Oh, we forgot to say that when Ponce de Leon came back eight years later to start the colony of Florida, he brought orange trees with him," L.I. offered. "And both our grandfathers got land grants. Hibernia was named by your father, our grandfather, George Fleming, because he loved his boyhood home in Ireland, and New Switzerland was named New Switzerland—across the river—because Cousin Louisa's grandfather, Francis Philip Fatio, loved his homeland of Switzerland."

"Good idea to tie in the family history with the history of our country, L.I. That's clear thinking."

"The part I like," L.I. said, "is that our grandfather Fleming picked out Hibernia because he fell in love with the land along the St. Johns from spending so much time across the river at New Switzerland because he was so sweet on our grandmother, Sophia Fatio. I guess none of the three of us would be here today if George Fleming hadn't fallen in love with Sophia Fatio *and* the land along the St. Johns."

Lewis smiled. "A very astute observation, L.I. My father married into one of the truly prominent Florida families. The first Don Francis Philip Fatio was a magnificent gentleman."

"Yes, sir," L.I. said with some awe. "He spoke six languages. I only speak pretty bad Spanish and—"

"Not such perfect English," George teased.

"Grandfather Fatio had a whole wall full of books, too," L.I. went on, ignoring George. "I wish all our lessons could be history. I hate arithmetic and Latin."

"Then I'm not making them interesting enough," Lewis said.

"Oh, no, Papa! You're the best teacher I ever had." George's dark eyes filled again. Their mother had been their only other teacher. "I mean, you're the best one I've had—this year."

Lewis reached again toward the boys, who scrambled up beside him on the sofa. "I know what you meant, George. L.I. and I both know, don't we?"

The older boy broke suddenly from his father's embrace and ran from the room.

"Don't worry, Papa. Ol' George is probably gonna—go cry again. He cries an awful lot about Mama—and he's two years older. But he didn't love her one bit more than me!"

Lewis tightened his arm around L.I.'s sturdy shoulders. "That should be—'not one bit more than I,' son. We're all different, one from the other. Even members of the same family. I know neither George nor I loved your mother more than you loved her. Do you—try not to cry?"

"Yes, sir, I reckon."

"So do I. Maybe we're wrong. Miss Louisa says we should all act more the way we feel."

L.I. thought a minute. "I—I'm sure glad we're gonna be at Miss Louisa's for Christmas again this year."

"So am I."

"I guess there'll be a lot of people there, huh?"

"If the weather holds, yes. Miss Sophia, Miss Louisa, the three of us—and the Setons and perhaps Grandmother Fleming. Maum Easter will keep Baby Augustina."

"Are the Setons rich?"

"Well off, certainly."

"How old is Miss Margaret?"

"Why, I have no idea, son. Nineteen or twenty, I suppose."

"Good."

"Good? Why?"

"Well, she *might* be young enough to want to play with George and me some. And Miss Sophia might go fishin' with us. But she talks a lot. Papa? Could I ask you a question about women?"

"About women? Why, yes, of course."

"Do you think a lot of Miss Margaret Seton? Like I do?"

Lewis stared at the boy. "I scarcely know her, son! I remember her more clearly as a little girl back when I first came to know her father. I—scarcely saw her when she came to—be with us—a year ago."

"Well, I saw quite a lot of her—then."

"You did?"

"Yes, sir. After—they buried Mama, Miss Margaret was with me a lot."

"I see."

"I don't mean she fussed over me like women do. She was—well, she was really kind of *with* me—that day."

"That—was good of her. I'm grateful."

"And you know something? You're not the first person to tell me about my lawyer mind."

"Is that so?"

"Yes, sir. Miss Margaret thought I was good at trying to figure things out that day, too. And I was only eight then."

"She must be a very perceptive young lady."

"I think she's awful pretty, too, don't you?"

Lewis laughed. "Why, yes, I'm sure she is. I recall that she was a very appealing little girl. Rather like her father, I'd say. Same coloring. Looked quite like him, even as a child."

L.I. sighed. "Well, I'm sure glad I'll get to see her again. She talks to me like I'm as smart as she is!"

3

Christmas was warm and sunny. Clear winter light filtered softly down through the dense, glistening foliage of the Fatio orange grove. A blanket was spread over the soft, sandy earth and Margaret Seton, in a blue and green woven woolen dress, sat between two male escorts: Louis Isador and George Fleming. The three had walked for more than an hour—a good enough way, Margaret thought, to keep the boys' minds off the delectable Christmas dinner being prepared in the

Fatio kitchen. Wild stuffed turkey, venison, hams, oysters, every conceivable vegetable—including Irish potatoes and yams—and for dessert, Polly's famous syllabub, laboriously worked over for hours on end yesterday, minus the supervision of even Miss Louisa. "Me an' my syllabub needs solitude," Polly had repeated every Christmas for as long as anyone could remember.

The blanket on which the three friends sat had, for an hour or so, been a battlefield. Soldiers, long columns of them (closely resembling dark-husked hickory nuts), had been expertly drilled by a sergeant named L.I., and because the boys' father was inspector, with the rank of major, on the staff of the Second Regiment of the state militia, one extremely sturdy hickory nut had marched up and down the lines of troops at attention, relaying orders.

Then, at Margaret's suggestion, the battlefield had been transformed into a series of corrals for fine strong cattle, driven by L.I. and George into stick stockades.

"Don't you like to play soldiers, Miss Margaret?" L.I. asked.

"Well, if I played soldiers with anyone, I'd like it with the two of you," she answered thoughtfully. "But, I hate the idea of killing. Don't you?"

"Yes, ma'am. I hate it, too," George said.

"Aw, not when there's a real battle on," L.I. sneered at his brother. "Or when it's wild deer or turkeys. Do you even hate to kill fish, Miss Margaret?"

"Even that. But we do need to eat. It's the kind of killing war brings that I hate. My poor father will go to his grave with an injury from one small skirmish. War not only kills, it maims."

"What skirmish?" L.I. wanted to know. "I didn't hear anything about Mr. Seton bein' in a war!"

Margaret laughed. "You weren't even born yet."

"Was old George born?"

"No," she said. "I was barely three months old. The skirmish happened at a place called Waterman's Bluff. Get Miss Louisa Fatio to tell you about it. She was nearly sixteen and her father, Francis Philip Fatio, Jr., was in the same small boat with my father. She'll remember hearing all about it when her father got home that evening."

"Home? Here at New Switzerland?"

"Oh, no. This all took place while the Fatio family lived at St. Mary's in Georgia."

"Sure, dummy," George said. "The first Fatio house here was burned back then by Indians. The same as our Grandfather Fleming's first house at Hibernia was burned by Indians! Seminoles. In the year 1812."

"He thinks he's so smart about dates. I knew both houses were burned, George. I'm not so dumb as all that!"

"The Fatio family lived at St. Mary's for a time and then, until this house was rebuilt, Miss Louisa's father rented a big place near ours in Fernandina. Actually, I met Miss Louisa for the first time when I was all of eight months old!"

"And you remember it?" L.I.'s eyes widened.

"No, I can't honestly say I remember it," Margaret laughed, "but Miss Louisa does. She vows that our friendship began that very day. I'm so fond of her now, I'd never argue."

"I haven't heard a lady with such a pretty laugh since—our mother died," George said in a solemn voice. "I hope you laugh a lot, Miss Margaret. Like you have today. Do you?"

She patted George's knee. "Why, yes, I suppose I do."

After a moment, L.I. said, "We're sure glad. We miss our mother."

"Of course, you do. Of *course*, you do."

The three sat for a long time in silence, the stockade only half full of cattle. Now and then an orange dropped from a tree, but none near enough for anyone to reach. Neither boy seemed inclined to move.

Finally, L.I. said, "You sure are better to be with than most women, Miss Margaret."

"Oh? And what on earth makes you say such a thing?"

"You don't talk at the wrong times and you don't talk to us like we didn't have any sense. Neither does your father. He's good to be with too."

"I'm sure he is."

"We're both sorry our grandmother Fleming wasn't well enough to make the boat trip from Jacksonville, but I expect it's better for an old lady to be inside in the winter." L.I. paused. "She's a fine lady, but she does kind of act like George and me are—dummies."

"What L.I.'s trying to say, Miss Margaret, is that a while ago when he said he—missed Mama—you just said 'Of course, you do.' You didn't try to tell us we'd see her again in heaven or to be brave, the way Grandmother Fleming does, or that what would make Mama happy would be for us to study and wash our necks and stuff like that."

"Yeah," L.I. agreed warmly. "You're just—kind of with us in all this, ain't you?"

"*Aren't* you," George corrected.

"Aw, pipe down! That's another good thing about you, Miss Margaret. You don't always correct me."

"Well, if you saw more of me, I just might." She looked at the delicate gold watch that hung on a velvet ribbon about her neck. "Do you boys know how long we've been away from the house? Nearly two hours. No, two hours and fifteen minutes, to be exact."

"That's a pretty watch, Miss Margaret," George said, still sitting contentedly beside her. "I think it looks especially pretty against that blue and green stuff your dress is made of."

"Well, thank you, sir."

"Seems like that dress makes your eyes even blacker. Are they really black?" L.I. wanted to know.

"Oh, I'd say they're just plain dark brown."

"I like your curly hair, too. It's so light and shiny." L.I., like George, had made no move toward getting up. "It isn't a bit like our mother's. Hers was black. Almost jet black. But yours is—awfully beautiful, too."

Margaret got lightly to her feet. "If we don't go back to the house this minute, I'm going to be so vain, no one will be able to bear me at the Christmas dinner table!"

Still neither boy moved.

"We know we're supposed to stand up when a lady does," George said softly. "But I guess this is one time L.I. and I agree. We'd rather stay right here with you."

"Than eat Christmas dinner? I don't believe it!" Margaret clapped her hands sharply. "On your feet! I'll race you to the veranda!"

After dinner, the ladies went upstairs for their customary naps, while the only men present, Lewis, Charles Seton and the two boys, went for a slow, leisurely stroll by the river.

"I'm truly sorry my in-laws, the Sibbalds, had to miss this day," Charles Seton said.

"So am I," Lewis answered. "Business must be good at Panama Mills. You say your father-in-law couldn't take the time?"

"Business would be even better if he had the right kind of management. He couldn't spare the time to join us because someone with authority had to be there. Millhands are never easy to handle. Some of them never heard of moderation. Wouldn't understand the word. It's too bad, because many of those men are really skilled workers."

"Miss Margaret has hair just like yours, hasn't she, Mr. Seton?" L.I. was staring up at Charles Seton's wavy, shoulder-length light hair. "It looks pretty on her."

"What a dumb thing to say," George snapped.

Seton laughed. "Not at all, L.I. I agree that it does indeed look prettier on my daughter."

"What L.I. meant," George went on, "is—well, sir, I think you're a very handsome gentleman."

Charles Seton bowed elaborately. "I return the compliment, George. So are you."

"What I mean, it's a good thing for Miss Margaret," George stammered, "that you do have such fine features, sir, because I'd guess even if I didn't know, that she was your daughter."

Lewis laughed "If I might be permitted to enter this discussion, I think I'll put an immediate stop to it. Before my sons get more tangled up. They do mean well, sir. They're both extremely fond of Miss Margaret."

"We sure are!" L.I. exclaimed.

"Does she always take a beauty rest in the afternoons—like other women, Mr. Seton?"

"George," Lewis said. "That's enough."

Seton laughed heartily. "It's quite all right, Fleming. I'm flattered that your sons like my daughter. As for a daily beauty nap—no. Not Margaret. Perhaps her mother insisted. I imagine Margaret is merely being congenial. After all, she was out with you boys most of the morning."

"You don't limp from your wound at the Battle of Waterman's Bluff or anything," L.I. said.

"And how did you know about that?"

"Oh, George and Miss Margaret and me talked about a lot of things—for over two hours."

"No, I don't limp. The ball went into my body. Fleming, I'm sure you were there in Fernandina at the time the so-called Patriots caused the Spanish all that trouble."

"I recall it well. I was visiting my uncle Francis Philip Fatio. He was in the same boat with you when you were wounded. I remember indeed. I was nearly fifteen at the time."

"Papa, do you know what I just thought of?"

"I have no idea, George."

"If, as you taught us in history, Florida didn't become a Territory of the United States until 1821, I was almost born a Spanish subject!"

"You missed it by a little under a year, son."

"We *are* part Spanish, though, Mr. Seton," George went on, "because of our mother. Papa met her in Cuba when he was there on business once. She was the daughter of Don Dimas Cortez, our Spanish grandfather. But we never saw him. He was descended from Don Hernando Cortez, the conqueror of Mexico!"

"Yeah," L.I. chimed in. "We're half Spanish because of our mother."

There was a moment of strained silence. Then Charles Seton filled it. "Your friend, Miss Margaret, was born a Spanish subject."

"Say, that's right! Sure!" The boys chorused.

"I've lived under four flags, Fleming. The flag of the colony of New York; then, when I came down here, the British Jack; then, the Spanish flag and now American."

"How many has Miss Margaret lived under?"

"Just two."

"Well, your daughter and I have that in common," Lewis said. "Spanish and American."

"Oh, I really think you've got a lot in common, Papa," L.I. said seriously. "Both born Spanish subjects and all. But mainly, you're both good to be with for George and me. I mean, Miss Margaret is the only lady we know like that."

"What about Cousin Louisa Fatio?"

"Aw, you know we love Cousin Louisa for good and always. But, well, she does try to give us advice and stuff."

Margaret stepped from behind an enormous oak tree not ten feet away. "Good afternoon, gentlemen," she said, making a deep curtsy. "Or is it evening by now?"

George and L.I. reached her in long leaps and each grabbed a hand.

Lewis and Seton bowed, greeted her and then Lewis said, "I fear I must apologize for my sons' exuberance, Miss Seton. Are they too much for you?"

"For Miss Margaret?" L.I. asked, scorning his father. "The trouble is, Papa, you just don't know Miss Margaret the way we do!" He stopped abruptly and looked up at her. "We're *not* too much for you, are we?"

In answer, she hugged him, then George.

"There. Does that answer your question, Major Fleming?"

Lewis flushed. "Yes, I suppose it does. I'm grateful to you. More grateful than you know."

Again, Margaret curtsied slightly, still holding the boys' hands.

"We're not going back home to Hibernia tomorrow, are we, Papa?"

"I'm not sure, L.I. Cousin Louisa is certainly urging us to stay."

"My family is staying for at least two more days," Margaret said.

"Papa, Papa, can we stay, too? Please?"

Lewis smiled. "Well, L.I., if you form that question correctly—I'll consider it."

"Aw, all right. *May* we stay, too?"

Charles Seton laughed. "You're in a trap, Fleming. The boy has met your conditions."

"Very well. Two more days."

Near bursting with joy, L.I. shouted: "Come on, Miss Margaret, we'll race you to the dock!"

When the three raced off, Lewis and the older man stood for a long time looking after them.

"I'm glad you're staying, too, Fleming. You'd be stranding me in a houseful of women."

Lewis didn't answer at once. Finally, he said, "Seton? I—hope you'll tell Miss Margaret again for me, of my gratitude for the patient way she puts up with my boys. They—need a pretty, playful lady right now."

"I will, Fleming, but I assure you that patience is *not* one of Margaret's virtues. She doesn't need patience with them. She's doing exactly what she wants to be doing."

4

The year 1834 passed a bit less painfully for Lewis. As much as his plantation work allowed, he filled the time with activities to include the boys: fishing, hunting and short trips. He told stories galore to Tina, now almost three, a pretty, cheer-

ful child, unscarred by the grief he and his sons carried. Tina
not only talked incessantly, her ears seemed to miss nothing.

"Do you think she might be some kind of genius?" George
asked.

"No, son. She's just a bright little girl, very influenced by
everything we say in her presence. For that reason, I want
you and L.I. to promise me that you'll never discuss anything
we learn about the Indian situation where she can hear you. I
don't want her damaged by any kind of fear. The three of us
do quite a bit of traveling about. Whatever you hear that
worries either of you, come to me with it. Don't even mention it to Maum Easter."

Lewis had heard rumblings of fresh Indian trouble in the
spring and again in the fall when he and the boys made the
river trip to St. Augustine for supplies needed at Hibernia
and New Switzerland. Louisa Fatio was a superb manager,
but without a man on the place, she did need Lewis. He and
the boys went as often as possible to Jacksonville too—at
times for goods not available in St. Augustine and to visit his
mother, Sophia. Also, while there, Lewis could learn of any
possible new Indian trouble.

When the Treaty of Payne's Landing had been signed back
in 1832, Lewis was scarcely aware of it. Through that entire
year, every waking hour—even the hours of sleep—had been
permeated by Augustina's weakening heart and then her
death. Of course, he knew of the treaty, knew that James
Gadsden, who had managed the earlier Treaty of Moultrie by
which the Seminoles agreed to be confined on a four thousand-
acre reservation on the peninsula, had been the guiding spirit
of the more recent Treaty of Payne's Landing. Lewis knew
also that the Seminoles had not only refused to stay inside the
four thousand-acre reservation, claiming lack of food, but that
white crackers likewise refused to stay off it. Some crackers
had even been so brazen as to establish homes and farms
inside the Seminole territory. Now, the more recent Treaty
of Payne's Landing would force the Seminoles to move all the
way west beyond the Mississippi. Older chiefs had actually
agreed, but not the young braves. It was then that the name
Osceola began to be talked about. A dynamic, striking-looking
young Seminole, Osceola had acquired the influence to gather
about him a band of other young braves—all of whom rebelled
at leaving the Florida land. Lewis understood Osceola's
rebellion—he loved his own land, too—but mere understand-

ing could not keep down trouble. Daily, he grew more concerned and anxious.

During an October trip to militia Colonel John Warren's home in Jacksonville, Warren heightened Lewis's fears. "Without the apparently very real friendship between Osceola and the Indian Agent, General Wiley Thompson, at Fort King," Warren told Lewis, "there would have been trouble far sooner. I respect Thompson's opinion too much to believe Osceola is a bad Indian. But even a good man can act rashly if he feels mistreated. Many of the old chiefs who agreed to move west have died during the past two years. I'm afraid Osceola and his band have no intention of moving anywhere. Except for Agent Thompson, Osceola trusts no white man."

Lewis thought a moment. "Too bad that both the British and the Spaniards seemed to get along better with the Indians than do the Americans. Too bad for us here in Florida, that is."

"For Georgia, too," Warren said. "All along the southern coast, in fact. As stirred up as the Indians are now, it isn't hard to see why the white man wants them all out. They've stolen or helped to freedom innumerable slaves. Stealing slaves and cattle, firing homes." He shook his head. "I predict that history will one day record the dire consequences of both slavery and our treaties with the Indians, Fleming. For now, we've having skirmishes, burned homes and an occasional scalping. Beyond that, at least so far, things are fairly quiet. But I can tell you, as your commanding officer, that I'm glad you're with me in the state militia. The Regular Army may need us. Our motley volunteer crew does know the terrain and they aren't cowards. So much of Florida has not been mapped; if we do have to fight again, the knowledge of our Florida Horse volunteers will be invaluable. Stay in touch, Major Fleming. In case of emergency, I'll get word to you at once."

While in Jacksonville, Lewis visited Sophia Fleming, his mother, who, in spite of her rheumatism, was still in full charge of her household there. Her niece, Susan Fatio, Louisa's half-sister, had been her companion for years. "I will always love Hibernia," his mother had said often since Lewis's father's death, "but it's too wild and isolated for me now. Susan and I do fine. When she marries, it's agreed that there will always be a place for me."

Lewis loved, even revered his handsome, intelligent moth-

er, but it had always been easier to let her set the tone of
every conversation. On this visit, prodded by his own desperate loneliness, he asked: "Did you leave Hibernia, Mother, because of your grief when Papa died? I—need to know."

"Of course you need to know," the genteel, somewhat
portly lady answered. "I'm sure you're seeking ways to assuage
your own grief. No, Lewis, I did not leave because I missed
your father more at Hibernia. I missed him just as much here
in Jacksonville. Soon after your father died, you married.
With me there, your wife would not have had a home of her
own. But I left mainly because I like the activity in a city. I
loved my own family home at New Switzerland and, of course,
I loved Hibernia. But I have never preferred isolation. I left
because it seemed best for me. You must do what you need
to do—for you."

"I can't imagine living anywhere else," he said. "I need
what I can of Augustina there."

"Each person handles or mishandles grief in a different
way. I know my way. You know yours. I only hope you will
get hold of yourself soon and find another mother for those
children!" When he said nothing, she pressed on. "You *are*
considering a second marriage, aren't you?"

"No, I most certainly am not."

"I see." She studied him a moment. "You've lost a wonderful wife, Lewis. But she—is gone. Courage is your work now.
Your principal work. Daily, hourly courage, for the sake of
the children. Never forget—courage is your absolute duty."

He sighed. "I don't forget, Mother. Sometimes I wish I
could. It's exhausting."

"Of course being courageous is exhausting. Life is never
easy. It isn't even fair. If it were, courage would not be
required." She was silent a moment, stirring a breeze with
her old painted silk fan. Finally, she said, "You haven't
mentioned the Indian trouble. I hear things, you know. Does
this not worry you? Surely, as an officer in the Florida Militia, you're highly informed—and deeply concerned for the
children in the wilds at Hibernia." Giving him no time to
respond, she went on. "There's one Indian, Lewis. Not a true
chief, but a powerful leader—Osceola. A real troublemaker."

Lewis grinned. "If you were his mother, you'd be proud of
him. He's a very brave young man."

"Fiddlesticks. Bravery without law and order can be
devastating."

"Osceola is going to defend his home—as I would. We need to worry also about pigheaded white men who feel the very color of their skin gives them the right to barge onto Indian land and build homes. Without those fellows, the whole thing might not be so incendiary."

"As long as there are Indians hereabouts, it will be incendiary. And don't tell me they were here first. Someone was everywhere first. History will show you that all lands are occupied lands, Lewis."

"I'm sure each side inflames the other." He stood, then bent to kiss her. "Take care of yourself, Mama. It's time I gathered up my sons and headed for home." He grinned. "Back to the wilds of Hibernia."

She returned his kiss warmly. "Courage, son. Courage."

"I—try, Mother. I do try."

"I'm sure you do. And I count on it."

Reluctantly, because it was growing dark, Louisa and Sophia agreed to let Lewis and the boys leave New Switzerland after delivering their mail.

"Seems such a pity they couldn't stay at least a few minutes," Louisa said, as they waved them off across the river.

"But they did bring us two letters," Sophia said. The two sisters walked up the riverbank from the dock arm in arm. "Oh, Louisa, I did want them to stay, too. I get so lonely these days!"

"So do I, Sister."

"Sometimes I think I really hear all the voices calling from room to room—the way it used to be. I guess I don't. But such a big old house for—two women." Sophia turned to peer at Louisa's face. "You look so sad! I must cheer you up. I'm not much help to you beyond my needlework, I know, but I do try to be cheerful. And just think, we have two letters! If we read both only once this evening, they will still be fresh for a week or so—*if* we don't reread them too often. News, Louisa, from two places—Jacksonville from Aunt Sophia Fleming and Fernandina from Margaret. Which shall we read first?"

"One seems to be addressed only to me," Louisa said gently. "You read Aunt Sophia's news while I scan my— personal letter from Margaret."

"I don't think that's one bit fair! Margaret Seton is my friend, too. She's even more my age."

"I know. But I'd never ask you to share a personal letter—
addressed only to you."

"As shut away as we are, I don't think formalities matter at
all," Sophia snapped, flouncing off with their aunt's letter.

"You don't need to leave, Sophia," Louisa called after her,
knowing full well she'd not be answered. Poor, flighty Sophia,
she thought, breaking the seal on the letter from Margaret.
Indeed, a letter from anyone was such an event, she fully
understood her sister's chagrin, but Margaret had confided
her love for Lewis to Louisa. She intended to keep that
confidence.

Back in the house, she sank into her father's chair and
began to read—slowly, to make it last.

28 October 1834
Fernandina

Dearest Louisa,

It is my hope that this letter just to you will not hurt
Sophia's feelings. As always, I trust your judgment in sharing
it with her. Parts of it, that is.

The days go by here without incident. Mother and Father
are well as are my grandparents, the Sibbalds. You were so
gracious to invite us all again for Christmas and, weather per-
mitting, we will be there. Unless, of course, my grandfather
has to stay here again over some trouble between his hotheaded millhands and the Indians. Grandfather does so need
a strong superintendent at Panama Mills. Even the water trip
from Fernandina to the Mills grows harder for him. I suppose I hear more here than you, dear Louisa, but most of the
time I simply put all talk of Indian trouble out of my mind.
One feels rather secure living in a town with neighbors.

I have written only to you because my heart is so heavy
over Lewis Fleming. I dreamed of him last night. He was looking to me for help which I could not give. Do you know of
any particular danger he might be in? How I long for Christmas at your house when I shall see him again! My love grows
stronger with the passing of every day. I spend time on a regular basis with God, seeking to better myself, to strengthen
myself for whatever Lewis will need of me for always. He is
so much a part of my life that I may have difficulty being
merely social with him when at last I see his face again. I miss
his children, too. In my thoughts, I am with them all constantly, so that I marvel that my parents have not guessed.

Perhaps Papa has. I am close enough to him so that now
and then I imagine he is giving me a quizzical look, as though
he just may have some idea of my encompassing love for
Lewis.

After scanning the remainder of Margaret's letter—mostly
about social events in Fernandina—Louisa sat staring at the
flames in the parlor fireplace. I can read parts of the letter to
Sophia, she thought, and if she gets peeved that I don't let it
out of my hands, she'll just have to get over it. Poor Margaret. Lewis Fleming is not only blind to the sight of any other
woman, the very thought is beyond him. Margaret's hopes
are so high! What a heartbreaking Christmas this could be for
her. Unless—unless Margaret Seton is much more mature
than a girl her age has a right to be.

5

Louisa persuaded Lewis and the children to stay on at New
Switzerland until after the new year, 1835, began. The day
after their return to Hibernia, Margaret, too, went home.
Sophia, after all the laughter and cheer of the holiday season,
was bereft. Day after day, she cleaned out drawers, pulled
dresses in and out of her clothes press, started new needlepoint pieces, then cast them aside. Try, as she certainly did,
repeatedly, to convince Sophia that they both must accept
their lonely, uneventful lives, Louisa made no impression
whatever. Sophia's restlessness only grew worse.

On a cold, windy day in mid-January, Sophia caught up
with Louisa, bundled in a warm cloak, headed for the Fatio
barn.

"Louisa, wait! Don't walk so fast, wait for me," Sophia
called breathlessly, running after her. "I know Scipio is fuming about the scale on our oranges, but he can wait a minute,
can't he?"

Louisa gave her a puzzled look. "What on earth is so
urgent?"

Looking at the ground, Sophia gasped, "I did something—

awful. But, it's all so marvelous, so romantic, I'm glad I did!"
She looked up defiantly. "Did you hear me? I'm glad!"

"I heard, but what did you do?"

"I—read all of that October letter from Margaret addressed
to you. The one you hid. You've known all along, haven't
you, Louisa? You've known for a long, long time that Margaret is in love with Lewis and you didn't tell me!"

"I was told in confidence," Louisa said sharply and turned
to walk away. "I'm too angry with you to say more now."

Shivering in the cold wind, Sophia picked up her long skirt
and hurried in pursuit. "But I can't wait till later, Sister! I
swear I didn't catch on to a thing when Margaret and Lewis
were here all that time at Christmas! If she's so devastatingly
in love with him, how does she keep from showing it?"

Still striding ahead, Louisa said firmly, "Because she's not
like another young woman her age—one it is my misfortune
to have as a sister! Margaret is mature. She needs neither to
pry into other people's business *nor* flaunt her every emotion
to the world."

Sophia caught her arm, stopping her. "You can scold me
later. I'm too excited about all the glorious prospects for
Lewis and Margaret to listen now anyway. Louisa, don't jerk
away from me. Don't you like my being so happy about all
this? We have such a solitary life—can't you be just a little bit
glad for *me*?"

After a long sigh, Louisa smiled at her. "For you, yes. For
Margaret—I hope it will work out. Lewis Fleming is as far
from wanting another wife now as a man can possibly be."

"But—it's Margaret who loves him! That makes everything
different. There's no one on earth—like Margaret Seton. Oh,
Louisa, I have one of my hunches!"

"Don't count on this one," Louisa said, walking again toward
the barn.

"I'm going to count on it," Sophia called after her. "I'm
going to count on it fully. After all, Margaret has already
turned down five Fernandina suitors—any one of whom I'd
have married!"

As Maum Easter served Lewis breakfast before the children were up the next morning, she watched him more
carefully than usual. "That all you gonna eat, Mausa Lewis?"

"Not hungry, Easter. That good biscuit and honey will do
fine." He smiled up at her.

"Don't be tryin' to get past me with that grin. For a while it look like you was eatin' like you used to. You feel all right?"

"Fine."

"Didn't touch my ham," she grumbled, clearing the table except for his coffee. "Ham won't go to waste. Them boys be down soon. You warm enough?"

"Fine."

"Can't you say nothin' but 'fine'?" It's cold! That wind off the water go right through me while ago. You sure you don't want me to build up the fire?"

She watched him lean back in his chair, smiling again, trying, she thought, to fool her into thinking he wasn't worried about anything.

"I wish I had a penny for every time you've asked me—in all the years of my life, Maum Easter—if I'm warm enough."

"You be a rich man that way."

"I would indeed."

"One thing I knows," she mumbled from across the room where she placed the uneaten ham on the sideboard. "I ain't never ask you once when I didn't *care* whether or not you was cold."

"If I could be as certain of anything else in this life as I am of that, I'd be a peaceful man."

She returned to the table. "The Lord knows that if I could do anything—just anything—to give you back your peace, I'd do it." Brushing imaginary crumbs from the tablecloth, she asked, "You sure they ain't somepin' new stirrin' your mind, Mausa Lewis?"

"I would like a straight answer to something," he said. "You and Pompey are free. You have been ever since you ran away from that Georgia plantation and crossed the St. Mary's River into old Spanish Florida—when we were all young. Do you ever think—you might want to—leave Hibernia? Have a little farm of your own?"

She stopped brushing and fussing about to stand squarely across the table where she could watch his face. "What's goin' on in that mind of yours, anyway?"

Not once did she take her eyes off him as he folded his napkin slowly, thoughtfully, and slipped it back into the wide silver napkin ring. "Maum Easter, your people and the Indians have a fairly dependable grapevine. Have you heard of any new burnings or—well, anything I haven't yet heard?"

"I knowed it! I knowed something was scratchin' your

brain. You worried that you might have to go fight and you got to know me an' Pompey be here. That we ain't got no notions of leavin'. Mausa Lewis?" She waited until he had to look her in the eye, then went on in a voice as starchy as her apron. "Your chillern be mine, too, the same as they always been. Even if I ain't promised Miss Augustina, I'd never leave 'em; Pompey an me, we's here to *stay*. I'd fight till I couldn't fight no more to save all three chillern. You done hurt my feelin's, sir, by askin' a thing like that."

"It's—just that from what I hear, we could well have more Indian trouble ahead."

"I knows, I knows," she said, her voice suddenly gentled. "But they ain't no use worryin' now. Easter's tol' you an' tol' you that worryin' is always worse than what's up ahead. Your mama, she tol' you that. Miss Augustina, she tol' you, too. Over and over and over."

He took a deep breath. "I know. But you were here when they burned Hibernia a little over twenty years ago. So was I. Even having my father to look after me didn't keep me from being so scared I—didn't sleep well for a year afterward. Those bloodcurdling whoops frightened me more than the flames. Even with Papa here—and a very strong mother to comfort me. What if I'm—called for militia service? My children would have neither."

She stood to her full height—an ample five feet or so. "Your chillern got Maum Easter an' Maum Easter got good, thick shoulders. Comfortin' is—my gift from the Lord."

"One of your greatest gifts," he said simply. "But, Indians on the warpath have been known to steal—or kill Negroes. You know that as well as I. Have you heard—*anything* by the grapevine?"

"Well, not to worry 'bout."

He stood up. "You have heard something! What?"

"Nothin' to do with us here, but you know Pompey an' Little Jim an' Big Owen, they went down to Jacksonville to bring back that lumber for you last week an' they seen Little Jim's cousin. She be married to an Indian named White Tail. Little Jim, he tol' Pompey when they was on the river comin' back here that night that the Indians is starvin' on the reservation they makes 'em live on. They say the land the white man done put 'em on ain't worth spit."

"I know all about that problem," he said. "Did Little Jim find out something else?"

"Nothin' to worry us. Just that some of them Indians—White Tail's in the middle of 'em—is well, ready to make trouble south of here. But that land ain't close to us."

"You're sure that's all you've heard?"

Suddenly, she took after him, shooing him off with her big apron as though he weren't a grown man. "When Easter tell you somepin', it be the truth, Mausa Lewis! Now—git. Out to the warehouse with Pompey. That good man need you to 'splain how to sort all them oranges he done pick off our trees!"

Laughing, Lewis went for his coat, Easter giving him a parting shot: "Ain't no sense worryin' to me 'bout trouble that ain't come an' might not never come. What you needs to do, Mausa Lewis, if you's just got to worry—is worry 'bout them orange trees an' that freezin' cold weather outside!"

Striding down the sandy lane toward the orange ware-house, Lewis smiled to himself. Again, as through all the years since his boyhood, just by being herself, Maum Easter had lifted his spirit. He could depend on her and Pompey. They would live out their lives at Hibernia. Neither would really think of leaving, nor would Louisa's Scipio, also a free Negro. Scipio's new bride, Polly, was not free, but if she were, she would no more think of leaving Louisa than Easter would think of leaving him. Lewis's commanding officer, militia Colonel John Warren, was not an alarmist. There would undoubtedly be trouble ahead. No question but that Lewis would have to go. But he could do nothing about it today. Easter was right.

Nearing the big warehouse, he heard the still unfamiliar sound—the whistle of the new steamboat making its way downriver toward Jacksonville. The whistle blew again—three short, cheerful toots. Lewis waved. His spirit lifted a bit more. Steamboats could navigate the St. Johns carrying his oranges in good or bad weather—with or without a breeze. As Easter had exclaimed in wonder the first time the new *Florida* had churned its way past Hibernia last month: "There ain't a sail on that boat nowhere!"

He walked faster. The day's work lay ahead.

Before the freezing, icy morning of February 5 dawned clear and crystalline over the St. Johns, Lewis knew that his losses were great.

L.I. had caught a deep cold and only George and Pompey and the little dog, Buster, walked with him through the ruined orange groves. From the look of his own crop, every citrus tree in the area would be dead. For an hour, the three walked from one frozen grove to another, one tree to another—now and then touching a ragged wind- and frost-blighted limb. Lewis was relieved that neither George nor Pompey talked much. He needed time in the silence to sort out what had happened. Would need more time to accept it. By all indications, this would have been a good year for oranges. Now, except for those already picked, they were gone. Not only for this year, 1835, but for most of a decade to come. Orange trees grew slowly. Seedlings took fifteen years to begin to bear. Budded trees, five. He would collect from the crates of fruit that he and Pompey had already sent to Savannah—if they had beaten the freeze there. After that, nothing. In six years or so, George would be old enough for college. That would require money. Cash. Oranges had been his main cash crop, even over cotton.

Standing in the midst of the wasted trees in the farthermost grove, he sighed deeply. "Well, son," he said, "we've still got each other. Pompey—you've still got your family."

George said nothing. Pompey took another long look at the devastation—lines and lines of withered trees stretching away toward the woods and the river. "Yes, sir," he said uncertainly. "We all still got each other—but how you gonna *spend* any of us?"

"What about our new wagon, Papa?" George seemed on the verge of tears.

"Yes, sir, Mausa Lewis—the new wagon an' another horse I was plannin' on an'—you needs a new boat. Leastways a new sail. I can't patch that old one many more times."

"Our garden is gone, too," George moaned. "My special artichokes, the English peas, the celery I helped Little Jim transplant, the potatoes and beets and carrots—"

When Lewis saw his son's eyes fill with tears, he put his arm about him. "Now, both of you listen to me. We've lost more in this freeze than any I can remember, but it's only February. We can replant the vegetables. You'll just have to patch that old sail, Pompey. These trees are our biggest loss from the freeze, but—" he sighed again, "they're *not* our biggest loss. We're already weathering the biggest loss we'll

ever have—your mother." He hugged the boy. "We'll handle
this, too. You wait and see."

George buried his face in Lewis's rough, heavy coat. "Will—
anything ever—be the same again—for us, Papa?"

Buster whined softly, his brown eyes fixed on George.

"We still have Hibernia," Lewis said. "That sustains me.
Keeps me willing to get up out of bed every day. Land is one
thing no one can change. Hibernia belongs to us. If we care
for it, nothing can cause us to lose our land, George."

The boy lifted his head, wiped his eyes on a jacket sleeve.
"Yes, sir. I'm going back to the house now, Papa. L.I.'s
gonna want to know about our groves. And—" he began again
to cry. "—well, I'm just goin' back to the house."

Pompey and Lewis watched the boy walk away, Buster
circling him, obviously upset because George was.

"Mausa George already thinkin'," Pompey said. "Tryin'
like a grown man to—figure things out. He even *walk* like a
man—thinkin'."

"He is growing up. I didn't expect him to take our losses so
to heart."

"Miss Augustina, she'd have cried, too, at the sight of these
poor trees."

"He's very like her. He doesn't laugh as much as his
mother did—but, he has her sensitive, tender heart."

Pompey gave his easy chuckle. "That little Tina, *she* make
up for everybody not laughin' enough roun' this place!"

The thought of the merry, appealing child eased Lewis's
heart. He clapped Pompey on the shoulder. "Thanks, old
faithful, for reminding me of that daughter of mine—right
now. Right this minute."

6

The vegetable garden was replanted and Pompey and Lewis
spent four days on horseback supervising the cutting back of
the apparently dead orange trees, just in case a branch here
and there might bear next year. No one was hopeful. Louisa
had lost all her trees, too, and with Scipio riding beside him,
Lewis had seen to their trimming as well. There was money

in both the Fleming and Fatio families, but even so, budgets would have to be trimmed to the bone.

On a warm, windy June afternoon, four months after the freeze, Lewis and Louisa relaxed together on the Fatio veranda after going over their accounts.

"You took your losses in a better spirit than I," he said. "They were even greater, since your groves were larger."

"I don't have children to educate, Lewis."

"True. But I admire you, Cousin, not only as a human being—as a business woman. Not many women would be able to run an enormous plantation like New Switzerland without a single male member of the family alive to help."

"I have you, Lewis." She laughed a little. "And, actually, I think more women could do it if forced, as I am." For a time, they sat in silence, then, apprehension in her voice, Louisa asked, "Any news, Lewis? Did you see Colonel Warren on your visit last week to Jacksonville?"

"Yes. There's been another bad incident at Hog Town, not far from Fort King."

"I want to know everything. Don't spare me any of it."

"I know only what Warren told me. It seems that late last month an express arrived at St. Augustine with word of trouble between Hog Town whites and some Seminoles. An Indian was stealing. They caught him in the act. Rashly, foolishly, they took the law in their own hands, tied him to a tree and flogged him almost to death. The Indian's cries brought his friends out of the thickets and they fired point-blank on the Hog Town settlers."

"The settlers fired back?"

He nodded. "One Indian was killed, another badly wounded. Colonel Warren thinks it might have touched off real trouble."

"What does Colonel Warren mean—'real trouble'?"

"I don't know, Louisa. I honestly don't know. But he is sending out expresses to inform more than a hundred Florida Horsemen to be on the ready."

With a quick intake of breath, she said hoarsely, "And you're—a brigade inspector in the Florida Horse."

He nodded again. "For now, that's all there is. I've begun instructing Pompey—and your Scipio—where the crops are concerned. You can believe I'm also taking perfect care of my horse, Cotter."

"Thank heaven for Cotter," Louisa said helplessly. "I suppose that sounds silly at a time like this. But—nothing is as important to a cavalry officer as his horse."

Lewis gave her a smile. "Now, look here, we've only that small warning. There've been hundreds of incidents like the one at Hog Town."

"You've never heard Colonel Warren send out a call to be ready before, have you?"

"No, Louisa. I haven't."

During the third week in November, Lewis went again to Jacksonville—this time without his sons and directly to Colonel Warren's house. If there was definite news, he would need to hear of it before visiting his mother.

"In a way, I'm sorry so much time has gone by without word from me," Warren said, seating Lewis across from him in his home office. "But word from me these days would be unwelcome at best. You'll have your orders as soon as I have mine."

"On the steamer this morning I heard rumors that Clinch is in a flurry of military activity at one of his plantations," Lewis said. "Is that true?"

"Indeed, it is. As Commander of the U.S. Florida Regular Army, General Duncan Clinch is under pressure to prepare for action. On orders from his superiors. At least, it seems some federal attention is being given us here in Florida. Early this month, General Clinch began to concentrate his forces at his Florida plantation, Auld Lang Syne, about ten miles from Micanopy."

"That's the general's working plantation, right?"

"Yes. He has two others in Georgia. Auld Lang Syne is one of the hardest-working sugar mill plantations anywhere, as I understand it. I've never been there, but I hear it's pretty primitive. Still, it's well located for Clinch's purposes right now in our Seminole trouble. There are plenty of roughly built huts where troops can be billeted, another which can be used as a field hospital, and the entire place is being fortified."

"Fortified—already?"

"In my opinion, not a day too soon. The word is," Warren went on, "Captain Gustavus Drane marched sixty men safely along the King's Road from St. Augustine to Mandarin, then across the St. Johns River to Fort Heilman—"

"Why, that's very near my home!" Lewis interrupted.

Warren nodded. "At any rate, after a brief rest there, these men stopped again at Fort King and then slogged through the swamps and creeks and palmetto thickets twenty-six more miles—unharmed—to General Clinch's plantation near Micanopy. They were not only courageous, they were lucky."

"They encountered no Seminoles?"

"Evidently not. But Drane is understandably boastful of his feat, in spite of the fact that, like most Regular Army officers, he holds the Indians in low esteem as fighters. He's wrong, of course. You and I—no one in the state militia would be so foolish. We know them too well."

Lewis frowned. "They've done my family too much damage in years past for me to underestimate the Seminoles for a minute. Are Drane's men stationed at Clinch's plantation now, sir?"

Warren nodded. "In fact, the plantation has been dubbed Fort Drane. Gustavus Drane is directing the building of the picket fortifications there."

"What else, Colonel? I hope you aren't holding anything back. If I have to leave my own place, the more I know the better prepared I can be to go quickly."

Warren stretched his long legs. "Oh, Fleming, I could keep you all day recounting the gruesome details of scalpings and murders from ambush of both whites and Indians. One very well liked young man named Dalton, who carried the mail, was murdered, scalped, embowled and thrown into a pond. The Seminoles were so out of control, they even shot his good mule. Normally, a good mule's a prize to them. It's all getting out of hand, Major. Another expected problem—supplies. You probably haven't heard, but settlers are swarming into almost every small military fort throughout the region—scared for their lives, needing food because they can't operate their farms in safety. As usual, the federal government sends short supplies. I heard that soldiers at Fort King, themselves underpaid or unpaid—are turning down three dollars for one biscuit!"

Lewis thought for a long moment. "That—brings it right home, doesn't it?"

"It *is*—right at our doors. I'd be unfair to you if I didn't spell it out. The time for action is almost at hand. I suggest that you visit your mother and tell her on this trip. You may not get back to Jacksonville for a while. Then prepare your family. I know that won't be easy, even though service time for those of us who volunteer in the state militia is only three weeks. You'll be notified as quickly as I get my orders from militia General Call. As brigade inspector, you'll have a man-sized job collecting and checking on our motley militia troops. Those farmers and shopkeepers will turn up in every manner of clothing and with every manner of arms. But, you'll know what to do. Unless there's a dire emergency somewhere, I'm sure my orders will send you first to St. Augustine. We have some good men near there. Between now and then, we can only hope that General Duncan Clinch will have great good fortune in moving his various detachments from wherever they are now to Fort Drane." He grinned wryly. "I might add that we'd better hope that the fortifications going up now at Fort Drane are adequate."

Telling his mother was not easy, but for once Lewis was grateful that she revered the human quality of courage. Sophia Fleming showed all the courage a woman could show at the news.

"You will be all right," she said. "I know you will be brave and you may count on my prayers daily for your safety, Lewis."

"Thank you, Mother," he said simply, "for being—such a strong woman. You've made it less hard for me to tell you good-bye."

"These are trying times," she said, an edge of sharpness in her voice. "What manner of mother would I be to add to a son's burden?"

Telling the boys, which he would not do until at least early December, would not be so simple. Barring a miracle, he would be gone through Christmas, and the children had never spent a Christmas without him. Louisa, when he had broken the news to her immediately upon his return from Jacksonville, promised to do all she could to help the Fleming children through the difficult time and if anyone could help, Louisa could. He was relieved, too, to learn that Margaret Seton and her parents would again spend the holidays at New Switzerland. Miss Margaret held his sons captive to her lighthearted charm and friendliness. Tina, almost four, would join the boys at the Fatio house this year. He had no doubt that the little girl would love—not only Margaret Seton, but her gentle, sensitive father, Charles, as well. Mrs. Seton had always struck Lewis as a bit remote, but if anyone could stir her, Tina could. Good people—all of them. Kind people, who would do their best for his children.

Louisa agreed that it was wise not to tell the boys anything until near time to leave and that Tina would be told only that her father had to be away through Christmas on important business. His period of enlistment as a militia officer would last for only three weeks, but travel time would keep him away longer and December 1 had come and gone without orders from Colonel Warren. His nerves were on edge. Any word would be better than more pretense with his children, all three of whom seemed to be talking and planning even more excitedly than usual about what they would all do at Cousin Louisa's at Christmas. If word did not come soon, Lewis would have to confide in his sons. They were too smart not to catch on, and more than that, he needed them.

Lewis was riding Cotter across the boundary of the west cornfield, which Pompey was preparing to plant, when a small boat sailed in toward his dock. Wheeling his jet black horse, Lewis galloped in the direction of the river, but L.I., George and Buster, in their excitement at the unexpected arrival of a boat, were out on the dock when he reached it—Buster barking vainly at the strange young man in the boat.

"Important letter from Colonel Warren, Major Fleming," the militiaman called. Standing to salute, he stretched to hand the message directly to Lewis, adding, "My orders are to return at once to Jacksonville as soon as I see the letter in your hand, sir."

"Very well and thank you. You've performed your duty." Lewis returned the salute and the tiny craft moved out from the dock. "My regards to Colonel Warren. I'll follow his orders to the letter."

For an awkward moment, the boys stood looking after the boat. No one spoke. Even Buster was quiet. Then Lewis broke the seal on the message and scanned it. He was to leave the day after tomorrow, December 7. There were detailed instructions enclosed, but he would study those in the privacy of his room.

Finally, his dark eyes wide with apprehension, George said, "Is—it—trouble, Papa?"

"Yes, George. Indian trouble. I might just as well tell the two of you now."

L.I. stared at him. "Are there bad Indians near us?"

"Not so far as we know. The trouble is to the south. There are orders from Colonel Warren direct from General Call, who heads our state militia. I'm to be ready to leave day after tomorrow and the three of us have a lot of planning and work to do." Noting their stricken looks, he felt it best to go on briskly, giving them a chance to regain their control—to behave as men—the way he knew they meant to behave. "I'll ride Cotter to the stable, then meet you in the parlor." He smiled. "I'll have some orders for *my* good soldiers, too. By the way, if you see Tina, don't say a word. Not to Maum Easter or Pompey either. For the moment, this is just among the three of us. Understood?"

The boys nodded, still unable to speak, and broke for the house, their dog racing after them. Lewis reminded himself firmly that with Maum Easter, Pompey, Louisa and her house guests, the children would be in good hands. I can count on Louisa always, he thought—*and* her friend, Miss Seton, to help all three through the Christmas season. But— who will help me?

After the first night, George and L.I. set to work with a will. Tina cried very hard when he told her, but his promise to be back in a little over three weeks and to let her go with her brothers to visit Cousin Louisa dried her tears.

"You'll get to play with a very pretty young lady, too," he promised.

"Miss Margaret Seton?"

"That's right! How did you remember her name?"

"Oh, we sang a song together a long time ago."

"Did you indeed?"

"Miss Margaret has bouncy curls."

"She has? And do you like them?"

Tina frowned. "Yes, but I couldn't have them."

"Why not?"

"Because my hair's black and hers is yellow."

He laughed. "Well, not exactly yellow, but you're right. She does have light hair. Dark hair curls just as well, you know. Your mother had black wavy hair—like polished silk."

"Did my mother have curls like Miss Margaret?"

"I think you and Cousin Louisa had better discuss that." He held her to him. "You and Cousin Louisa will have lots of time to talk about all sorts of things interesting to little girls like you."

He saw her lips begin to tremble, her big, dark eyes fill with tears. "I don't—want—anybody—but you."

"And you have me. All fathers have to leave on important business now and then." He wiped the tears coursing again down her rosy cheeks. "When you learn not to cry at those times, then you'll know you're almost a grown-up lady."

Maum Easter served breakfast to all of them the morning Lewis was to leave. The boys helped mightily in carrying on an almost casual conversation as they ate Easter's fluffy wheat cakes running with butter and cane syrup. Maum Easter left them only long enough to bring more cakes and by the time the meal ended, she had Tina's attention so completely diverted that giving the child a last hug was not as hard as Lewis had anticipated.

After he finished dressing in his brown officer's uniform, Easter and Pompey met him to say their good-byes on the veranda.

"You ain't to worry none," Pompey said. "Me and Easter'll see to everything." The skinny, quiet, middle-aged Negro kicked at a dried leaf blown onto the veranda floor, then said in a choked voice: "Easter says I get to tell you, Mausa Lewis. Me an' her's got a surprise we hope will help—your heart."

"That's right, Pompey," Easter nudged him as though he were a backward child. "Go on, go on—if you're gonna tell him, tell him!"

"Yes, Pompey. What is it?"

"Me an' the chillern—our chillern, Little Jim an' Betty, has decided we wants Easter to go with Miss Tina over to New Switzerland for Christmas."

Lewis looked at them both with relieved gratitude. "I—I don't know what to say. Being with their mother at Christmas means as much to your children as—" He broke off. "Are you sure?"

"Ain't nobody kin make Miss Tina be at home an' safe in her little innards like Easter can," the short, sturdy woman snapped.

"Oh, I of all people know that," Lewis said quickly. "It—will be more comfort to me than I can tell you, Easter. You're—like Tina's mother. She—doesn't remember her own mother,

I'm sure. I find it hard to admit—but I know it's true."

"No, sir," Easter said tenderly. "She don't remember."

Lewis turned to Pompey, his hand out. "I know it's going to be hard for you, too, Pompey, being away from Easter. I do thank you. I do thank you both—from my heart."

The two boys were waiting for Lewis in the parlor. For once, they were quiet, just standing before the mantel, waiting.

So as not to appear to rush them in their good-byes, Lewis sat down in his favorite chair. "We'll now, the three of us have a big responsibility."

They nodded. Then, L.I. blurted, "You sure do look good in your officer's uniform, Papa!"

"Thank you, L.I. I've had it for years. Glad I can still get into it."

With careful deliberation, Lewis began to talk to them man to man, giving them as little advice as possible—wanting them to feel his trust. He explained as much as he knew of troop movements, of his own orders to collect the volunteers in St. Augustine and take them to Fort Drane. That, with luck, he expected Colonel Warren and his militia volunteers from Jacksonville to join them on the way. He joked a bit about the often funny happenings any time a group of volunteers—independent-minded private citizen soldiers—got together to fight for nothing beyond love of the land they meant to protect.

"I expect they'll be a ragtag crowd," he laughed softly. "Part of my work as brigade inspector will be to persuade them to leave behind over half the trappings they'll undoubtedly want to bring along."

The boys laughed a little with him; then standing very straight, George said abruptly: "I wish I could go too, Papa. I'd like to be with you."

"Aw, that's dumb," L.I. jeered. "You're not even going to be fourteen for three more months! Anyway, you hate guns." Turning to his father before George could respond, he bragged: "Guess I've sure done my part to help you get ready, Papa. Me an' Little Jim's got Cotter all set. He shines like his hide was black satin!"

Then, without warning, L.I. threw himself into his father's lap and buried his face.

"I've—got your musket clean as a whistle, Papa," George said. "Just because I don't like to shoot at everything I see doesn't mean I don't know how to clean a gun. And your ammunition is packed so it fits right in your saddlebags."

"Thank you both. You've been a big help."

Hoping to hide the fact that he had begun to cry, L.I. said brokenly, his face still buried, "I—bet you'll be riding—the best mount—in the whole Florida Horse!"

"You know I will, son. There isn't a horse anywhere as good as Cotter. And I'm sure he's in top-notch shape, thanks to you."

There was only silence in the room as Lewis smothered his youngest son's tousled head. George, still standing almost at attention, said nothing. Then, as quickly as he had tumbled into his father's lap, L.I. got up and stood ramrod straight beside his brother.

"You said you had to go—before noon, Papa," he managed. "I—think it's time—we all shook hands."

Quickly on his feet, Lewis extended his hand first to L.I. and then to George.

"Good luck, Papa," L.I. whispered.

"God—will look after you, Papa," George said. "We'll pray—all the time."

Lewis hugged them both, saluted—took one last long look as the boys returned his salute—and hurried out across the veranda toward the stables where Little Jim held Cotter's bridle—waiting.

There had been no need to ask the boys not to accompany him to the dock. They sensed too that a quick good-bye was best. His orders had said that the steamboat *Florida* would reach the Fleming dock just before noon. Mounted, he waved once in the direction of the house, where he knew everyone was watching, and rode down the sandy lane and across Hibernia's tree-shaded yard to the river. With relief, he saw the small white bulk of the steamer making its way toward him. Close enough, he was sure, for the captain to see him, too.

Still not looking back at the house, he waved in the direction of the boat. His wave was answered by three short blasts of the steam whistle.

There was too much sun glinting off the water for him to make out the Fatio place across river, but Lewis had no doubt that Louisa and Sophia were on their dock, too—waving him off.

Riding ahead of the three mounted militiamen sent from Jacksonville to assist him, Lewis galloped Cotter along the narrow path toward St. Augustine, east from Picolata, where

the *Florida* had docked. The sixteen-mile bridle path over
which he rode had been cut long ago through dense wilderness and ran on an almost straight line between overarching
stands of gum and oak and pine, their lower trunks half
hidden in thick tangles of vine and palmetto. The eleven
miles upriver from his dock at Hibernia had been covered
quickly over almost glass-smooth water. Until now, he had
entertained no thought of danger. The time spent on the boat
was noisy with jokes among the Jacksonville militiamen, loud
laughter and outrageous boasting that the Florida Horse needed
the Regular U.S. Army in order to handle the Indians in
exactly the way they needed horses with three legs! Riding
now through thick shadow which stretched between the walls
of wilderness, Lewis's skin prickled. Any Florida wilderness
made a perfect hiding place for Seminoles.

His orders, once he reached St. Augustine, were to report
directly to the old Castillo de San Marcos, which the Americans had renamed Fort Marion. With luck, some of the
mounted volunteers from the St. Augustine area would already
be there. By day after tomorrow, he hoped, they would all
have arrived from their farms and shops and fishing boats. At
any rate, Lewis was to leave St. Augustine within a week.
General Call would today have men riding from several points,
Lewis knew, even as he rode now toward his first duty. No
journey would be as dangerous as that of the men with Major
Francis Dade, who would be moving straight across the Seminole Nation through forests and open grassy plains from Fort
Brooke on Tampa Bay to Fort King, then north to Fort
Drane.

Slowing his horse as the small party neared the west bank
of the San Sebastián River, which they would ford in order to
reach the city proper, the young Seminole leader, Osceola,
flashed into Lewis's mind. Where was Osceola today? It had
been rumored that the young brave had done some deed so
obstreperous that his white friend, Indian Agent Wiley Thompson, had been forced to throw him into irons. One of the
militiamen now riding with him vowed that he'd heard a later
rumor that Thompson had weakened, because of his regard
for Osceola, and released him. Either way, a worthy prayer,
Lewis decided, would be—"Dear God, let that friendship
hold!" Without doubt, Osceola was the Seminole's most influential leader.

*   *   *

Riding through the narrow streets of St. Augustine, the San Sebastián River now behind them, one of the devil-may-care militiamen with Lewis shouted: "Out of our way, St. Augustine pigs and citizens and cows and carts! The Florida Horsemen are just about to wipe out the Seminoles for good and all!"

Lewis allowed the big-mouthed volunteer to gallop past him along King Street and slowed his horse in order to look at the old city where he had been born. The thought struck: What if a Seminole spy had heard that foolish young Horseman's boast? Then with a start, he realized that in all his thirty-seven years, he had never seen a St. Augustine street without a few idle Indians. Today, there wasn't even an ancient squaw in sight! Harmless, friendly Indians had always been as much a part of the old city as the crumbling fort toward which he now rode. His father had built Hibernia while Lewis was still a young boy, but since George Fleming owned St. Augustine property too, visits were frequent. Lewis had spoken with one industrious squaw on every visit, always admiring and sometimes buying her reed baskets.

Even she was nowhere to be seen today.

Up ahead, he could hear the fort's wooden drawbridge rattle down into position. He urged Cotter ahead. As the officer in charge of the new volunteers, he would be the first to cross the ancient moat and enter Fort Marion.

The earnest faces of his two sons—as they stood at attention—came before him while Cotter clattered across the wooden bridge.

He breathed a prayer of thanks that his enlistment would be for no more than three weeks.

7

Once a week, on Wednesdays, a small local steamboat named the *Puckett* had begun to run the inland waters from Amelia Island, where Margaret Seton lived with her parents at Fernandina, as far south as Picolata.

"My parents have agreed that should my poor father not feel up to the trip to New Switzerland this Christmas, I may come alone," Margaret wrote to Louisa early in December. "I shall be perfectly safe and cared for, since Captain Bill Morehead of the *Puckett* is Father's friend. Father suffers acutely this winter from his old wound and it breaks my heart to see him trying not to let us know. He looks older, Louisa, and, indeed, he will be sixty next year—which year is practically upon us as I write. Today is December 11 and within eight days I will be on my way to spend heavenly hours with you and Sophia. My heart nearly bursts with joy at the thought of seeing you and your neighbors across the river."

Louisa looked at Sophia, then back at the letter.

"Is that all of it, Louisa?"

"Just about. Poor Margaret . . ."

"Yes, poor, *poor* Margaret," Sophia agreed warmly. "Now, don't you see how fortunate it is that I snooped, Sister? What if I didn't know that she loved Lewis as she does? What then? How could I possibly comfort her when she gets here and finds he's—gone to war!"

Louisa shuddered. "You make it sound—so horrible, Sophia!"

"War is horrible, Sister. But I know Lewis will be safe because I can't bear the thought of—of Lewis, our beloved Cousin Lewis, being shot—or *scalped*. Oh, Louisa, not Lewis's handsome head! Such beautiful, heavy, wavy brown hair he has, and—"

"Sophia! *Stop it!* That's quite enough."

"They do it, Sister. You know those Seminoles scalp people—just for the pleasure of it. And sometimes they do—even worse."

"I said—stop it! What we don't need right now is one of your imaginary flights."

"But doesn't it all just give you—goose bumps? Just think of the—sheer drama of that beautiful, golden-haired Margaret Seton happily making her way up the river, her heart welling with joy at the thought of seeing her loved one—and we, you and I, will be the sad messengers of tragic news."

"Sophia, I've had enough. My heart does ache for Margaret. But, there is no tragic news yet. And on this day, the same as on any other day, the Lord God is in charge of His universe. His entire universe, Sophia, and that includes Margaret and it also includes Lewis, wherever he is—right this minute."

"Well . . ." Sophia gave in reluctantly. "At least, we're safe here. Can you just imagine the filth and discomfort and agony those poor settlers around Newnansville are suffering? You remember what Aunt Sophia Fleming's letter said yesterday. They're pouring into Newnansville, living in great distress anywhere they can find a place to lay their weary heads. And just think—oh, I can't bear to think, but maybe you can, Louisa—twenty-two homes have been burned to the ground in Alachua County!"

"Did you lie awake dwelling on all these horrible things last night?"

"Oh, I did—practically all night long. Did I snore?"

"Yes. The same as usual."

"What is the date today, Louisa?"

"December 14, Sister. Why?"

"Oh, I was just thinking about the happiness and excitement in our house last year before Christmas. Now, it's sad, so terribly sad."

"Nevertheless, God still came into the world that first Christmas as a human baby. And we will celebrate as usual— the best we can."

"You know how much I love you, Louisa, but sometimes the way you talk makes me want to scream a good, long scream."

"I'm sure."

"I agree with you, of course. But you do sound more like Margaret Seton every day."

"Because we both choose to believe that God is in charge of human affairs?"

"Not because you *believe* it. Because you both act as though everything will be just beautiful!"

"I didn't say that at all. I'm sure Margaret doesn't feel that way, either."

"But, she's so sure she and Lewis will be married and the thought has never crossed Lewis's mind."

"Can't you find something, Sophia, to busy your hands? Margaret and I simply believe that the Almighty's timing is never wrong."

Leroy Black, a small dirt farmer with a place on the outskirts of the city, mumbled about Christmas as Lewis and his men rode away from the city toward the boat landing at Picolata.

"Yep," Leroy would say, "my pore wife'll have it tough. Them kids of mine jist don't think it's Christmas lessen their pa's home."

Lewis liked Leroy, a simple, strong young man who loved his forty acres as Lewis loved Hibernia. Leroy Black seemed fond of Lewis and when the bridle path was wide enough, rode beside him back through the dark tangle of wilderness to Picolata, where they and their horses would be ferried across to the west side of the St. Johns.

The road south through the stretch of woods and thickets and swampy forest to be covered from then on until they reached the crossroads where Lewis hoped they might connect with Warren and his volunteers from Jacksonville was long and difficult. There was a road, but it was so infrequently traveled the men often had to hack their way with machetes through cat briars and snarls of rope like vines. As they rode, mile after mile, Lewis breathed a prayer for their safety—for the safety of all their loved ones back home. The road was long. There was plenty of time for praying.

So far, they had seen no signs that Indians had been anywhere near the trail they traveled, but no one in their party doubted that danger would increase the closer they came to Micanopy, just ten miles from Fort Drane, their destination. It would be reassuring should they actually meet Warren and his men, but if not, Lewis, once he and his troops reached Fort Drane, could report to Regular Army General Duncan Clinch that his volunteers were as much at home in the unmapped Florida wilderness as most children on their mothers' laps. Not as safe, but as familiar.

"It's my opinion," another young man offered as they rode along, "that we could handle this alone. The militia doesn't have to bother with all those fancy war games the Regulars play at. We don't need 'em."

Lewis grinned at the man, Stoney Pitts, a well-to-do farmer from south of St. Augustine. "I like that kind of confidence, Pitts," he said. "But we're in for only a short time. After that, we can all go home if we choose. My hat's off to the Regulars. They have to stay until ordered to leave."

"You say they got 'em a little fort at Micanopy, too, now, Major Fleming?" Leroy Black wanted to know.

"Yes. Fort Defiance," Lewis answered. I understand supplies are scarce there though—scarce almost all over."

"That daggone Congress up there in Washington," Stoney grumbled. "What do they think soldiers soldier on down here, hot air?"

"Well, if things can be put right, I feel General Clinch will do it," Lewis said. "His reputation is the best. He lives and fights with his men. They call him the Spartan General, you know."

"How does a general from Sparta know anything about the Florida wilderness?"

"That ain't funny, Stoney," Leroy scoffed.

"And it has no bearing whatever on General Clinch," Lewis added. "The man's been fighting Indians and their Negro allies down in these parts since he was a colonel—back in 1815 and 1816."

Leroy Black snickered good-naturedly. "Hear ye, gentlemen, the major's givin' us a whackin' good history lesson!"

After a few more unfunny jokes and some laughter—more to relieve tensions than from humor—there was quiet. The jays quarreling, the uneven thud of hooves and an occasional pileated woodpecker blowing his tin horn from the depths of a thick stand of trees filled the silence their talk had left. As always, when activity ceased at any time—Lewis's thoughts raced back to Hibernia. He actually harbored an infinitesimal hope that, since boats now went more often to Jacksonville from the St. Johns plantations, General Warren might have a bit of news about his family—a longed-for reassuring word that no one was ill or injured. Thank heaven, there had been no news of Indian trouble within twenty miles or so of Hibernia. To the south—the direction in which he headed, yes. But, he had heard of nothing of imminent danger in all of Duval County.

They were traveling through what a man would normally call beautiful country. Not good traveling country, but Lewis had always found spiritual energy in the singular Florida light. Even now, as their horses forded a small, twisting creek, its tea-brown water as quiet as death until they churned through it, he glanced upward toward the slender shafts of golden sunlight knifing through a thick roof of ancient trees. So much tangle, so much green, twisted leaf growth, so much shade—too much for a chilly day. And yet, the light seemed to be forcing friendship down upon them. A reminder. That they were being watched over? Are we being watched over? he asked silently, as he left the difficult path to Cotter and looked up again.

The narrow road had moved them into a veritable forest of tall magnolias and, high up on one branch, the sun causing its seeds to gleam brilliant crimson so that Lewis at first thought it was a cardinal—he saw one late-turning magnolia pod.

Augustina. *Augustina*. . . .

The sun no longer drove its brilliance overhead. It was late afternoon and they had covered nearly twenty miles. But they would not make it to the crossroads that night. An early start, Lewis thought, should bring them all the way to Micanopy before noon the next day. Fort Drane would then be only ten more miles. In the distance he could see a large stand of pine. Large pine standing beside large pine with no room for branches down their trunks made for a good night's stopping place. The dense branches, reaching high into the air for light, formed a roof. A pine forest floor, unless it was too thick with palmettos, would be clean. The season's change of smooth brown needles, comfortable.

A few of the men had begun to sing now. He was glad. It helped dim the spectres that always appear on the trail with night.

Glancing out the dining room window, Louisa Fatio saw the Fleming plantation boat with its passengers, Tina, L.I., George, Pompey and Maum Easter, just as it pulled toward the Fatio dock. Hurrying as fast as her full skirts would permit, she nearly bumped into Sophia, heading also in the direction of the yard.

The women were greeted with shouts of "We're here, Cousin Louisa! Cousin Sophia, we came early!" as the boys scrambled out of the boat in the face of strong admonitions from both Pompey and Maum Easter, who held firmly to Tina's hand.

"It's all we could do, Miss Louisa," Easter called, "to keep 'em over on the other side till this mornin'. Wasn't nothing for 'em but they come—today."

"Why, I think that's marvelous, Maum Easter," Louisa laughed, embracing the boys, who in turn embraced Sophia. "And look at you, Tina," she said, holding out her arms to lift the child up onto the weather-worn dock. "How pretty you look and I declare you've grown an inch since I saw you at your house just last week!"

"We came for Christmas," Tina announced. "We came for Christmas. But—my papa isn't here."

Sophia grabbed the child in her arms, murmuring consola-

tion, her voice suddenly tearful. "Your poor, poor little thing!
You—poor little girl!"

"Sophia!" Louisa scolded. "Stop that this minute. Not another
word. We're together and we're going to have a good Christmas. A cheerful Christmas."

"I hope so," Sophia wailed softly. "I hope so."

"Well, I know so. Maum Easter, you've got Tina looking
like a lovely little doll. What good care you take of her."

"We're not *all* here yet, are we, Miss Louisa?" L.I. asked,
his face troubled. "I mean everybody who's gonna be here
isn't here yet—is she?"

Louisa laughed and Maum Easter and Pompey joined
heartily.

"Never in my days did I see two boys so partial to a lady as
they be to Miss Margaret Seton," Easter said. "That what
they wanta know. They wanta know—is *she* here yet?"

"Why, no. We're not expecting her until tomorrow, L.I.
But she is coming. Alone, I'm afraid. Her dear father is not at
all well."

"Tomorrow!"

"That's what I tell 'em," Maum Easter said. "I tried to hold
'em back till tomorrow, Miss Louisa—Miss Sophia." She held
out her hands in a helpless gesture. "I couldn't hold 'em."

During all the talk, no one noticed that George had wandered off up the riverbank, until L.I. said, "Look at ol'
George. He's always doin' that."

"Is that true, Maum Easter?" Louisa asked.

"You mean does he drift off all by hisself much these
days?" Easter's smile had turned into a look of deep pity. "He
do it all the time. Ever since his papa went away."

"He makes me sick," L.I. said. "You'd think Papa wasn't
my Papa, too!"

"No one would think any such thing," Louisa said. "You
and George are just very different people."

"I'm a lot better to get along with."

"Shame on you, L.I.! That ain't no way to talk 'bout your
own brother." Pompey gave the boy a big, wide grin. "Now,
is it?"

Pulling Louisa to one side, Maum Easter whispered, "The
boys is havin' a special hard time without their papa."

"Do they worry a lot about him?"

"They don't say much. They just cut up and pout or scrap
somepin' awful."

"Well, don't you worry, Easter. I have a feeling that—this time especially, Miss Margaret and the boys will draw even closer to one another. She'll help them."

"You think so?"

"Yes, I do. I'm not at liberty to tell you why, but I do think so. They'll all—need one another now, more than ever."

Easter peered into Louisa's eyes, her round brown face perplexed. Training preventing any more questions, the only thing she said—and she said it doubtfully—was "Yes 'um. I hope somebody kin help."

Margaret sat alone in the cabin of the squat, little steamer, *Puckett*, as it chugged along through the inland waterway from Fernandina toward the vast St. Johns. Rusty winter marsh and little hammocks of high land studded with scrub pine and myrtle broke the monotony of the flat landscape as she watched the startling flights of white seabirds—enjoying it all as only a young woman in love and going to her beloved can enjoy. For her, the sun glanced more brightly off every green leaf and every white wing—danced more merrily off the water, blue, blue reflecting the cloudless sky.

To his face, she had called him only Major Fleming. In her heart, for three long years, he had been Lewis. Lewis. Her whole being sang his name. *I'm coming to you, Lewis. If this time you can be glad—glad in the way I long for you to be glad, I may perish with joy. If not, if not yet, I can wait.*

When the steamer passed the mouth of the Trout River at Panama, where her grandfather's steam-mill stood, she waved. Once more, the press of business—the lack of a good mill superintendent—would keep her grandparents, the Sibbalds, away from the festivities at New Switzerland. Something must be done, she thought. *Grandfather is too old to be so overburdened.*

For weeks, Margaret had been giving much time to her Christmas wardrobe, some of which she made herself of fine fabrics ordered from Philadelphia. Her travel costume, the outfit in which Lewis would see her first should he and the children precede her to Louisa's house, was of light blue wool, cut and fitted by Fernandina's best dressmaker. Blue gave her dark eyes a startling depth and picked out every light in the mass of tawny curls piled on her head. The curls blew wildly now under a matching bonnet tied beneath her chin. She felt—right. Four changes of costume lay packed in her small, rounded trunk in the hold of the boat—one, a cheerful everyday green cotton; another, a dark green velvet for what could be a special evening. There was a pert, simple plaid and, of course, a warm, practical brown for time outside in the winter chill with Lewis's sons.

The *Puckett* docked for what seemed an eternity at the relatively busy little city of Jacksonville. Margaret passed the time pacing the cramped deck, only ten or twelve feet of it not stacked with barrels and boxes for shipment farther up the St. Johns. In her effort to fill the endless minutes, she studied everything in sight. Before Captain Bill Morehead climbed back at last into his pilothouse, she could give a detailed description of every one- and two-storied unpainted wooden building along the Jacksonville waterfront—residence or warehouse or shop.

When the little white boat moved out into the swift current of the St. Johns, Captain Morehead signaled for her to join him. She went gladly. He was a powerfully built, warmhearted man, very careful of her, she knew, because he so respected her father.

Nimbly, she climbed the rickety ladder and stood beside him as he twirled the wooden pilot wheel. Once settled on course, he leaned back in his worn chair and grinned. "Mighty good to see you smile, Miss Seton. Seemed like everybody on the Jacksonville dock was frownin'. Worried half to death over the Indians, I guess."

"Indians? Is there new trouble?"

"Just heard about it. Don't know why word hadn't reached us in Fernandina. Colonel Warren and sixty-some volunteers left Jacksonville four or five days ago. But I wouldn't worry. Ain't no reason to be scared at the Fatio place. I oughta keep my mouth shut. You're off on a happy trip and—"

"No! I want to know—everything. Were militiamen sent from any other place but Jacksonville? Anywhere else on the St. Johns?"

"Sounds like they're headin' toward Micanopy to the south from all over—marchin' today, I'd think." He frowned. "Rumor has it even Major Dade's marchin' a big force straight through the worst part of the Indian nation. Don't see how them fellers will make it—"

She shook his shoulder. "Captain Morehead, were militia officers sent from anywhere else near her? You must tell me! What of Major Fleming? He's an officer in the Florida Horse."

Morehead frowned. "They tell me Major Fleming left days
ago. Headed for St. Augustine to collect volunteers. By now,
he must be almost to Micanopy. They're meetin' at U.S.
Army General Clinch's plantation near there. It's bein' fortified, I hear. Callin' it Fort Drane now."

Without a word, Margaret turned and hurried down the
ladder onto the deck.

"Miss Seton? Miss Seton! You all right?"

She didn't answer.

"Miss Seton! I can't turn loose of this wheel right now—
you all right?"

Still she didn't answer. She couldn't.

8

At the crossroads near Micanopy, where Lewis had hoped to
make connections with Warren's men riding from Jacksonville, the roads were empty. Meeting Warren would have
been little short of a miracle, and for that reason, Lewis
hadn't even mentioned the possibility to his own volunteers.
Responsible for their safety, he had only hoped. There would
have been safety in numbers, since they were now near the
northern boundary of the Indian Nation. More than he wanted
anything, except to be at home with his children, he wanted
to deliver his St. Augustine militiamen safely to General
Clinch of the U.S. Army and to his own militia commander,
General Call, at Fort Drane.

After a short rest stop, they remounted and moved steadily
toward the makeshift fort a few miles beyond Micanopy.
They had been fortunate so far. Lewis remained hopeful. The
road took them through a handsome stand of bald cypress,
their high crowns bare, then across an open space where the
tall grasses grew in such profusion that Lewis could not help
wishing he had time to examine them. Riding past, he could
catch their massed beauty—singular, he was sure, to north
Florida grasses. Some grew in deep purple clumps; others,
waving in a rising wind, were as yellow as ripe oranges. The
stems of some, he knew, would be as tough and bright as
polished wire. He and his son George loved the Florida

grasses. The boy had brought huge bunches to his mother each fall and winter for as long as she lived. Great graceful bouquets—carefully arranged by Augustina—once stood in almost every room at Hibernia. *Hibernia.* Such vivid memories of home must be conquered—kept under firm control. He would hold Tina and L.I. and George deep in his heart. Uppermost in his mind and thoughts must be the safety and competence of the fifty men who looked to him for personal guidance as well as military orders. He was actively *Major* Lewis Fleming now, Brigade Inspector of the Florida Horse.

He urged Cotter to a gallop. The men followed. The sooner they reached Fort Drane, the less effort it would be to focus his thoughts on the work at hand and away from the place called Hibernia.

"Louisa," Margaret shook her sleeping friend gently. "Louisa, it's Margaret. And—it's Christmas morning."

Louisa sat up sleepily, rubbing her eyes, straightening her nightcap. "Margaret, what on earth? Is something wrong?"

Margaret walked away suddenly, her back to Louisa. "Yes. Yes, Christmas makes—everything worse." She hurried back to the bed, forcing a smile. "No, forget I said that! I—I haven't slept at all. And it's almost time for the servants to come—for me to wake the children so they can give them their gifts." Tears began to slip down her cheeks. "I'm—not ready for merriment. I need you, Louisa. I wouldn't have awakened you if I didn't need you. I'd planned to go through with the Christmas gift party with the children myself and let you and Sophia sleep, but—"

"Come here, my dear. Come here to me."

Margaret fell sobbing into Louisa's arms. "If—if only we knew—something about Lewis! When I said—I'd wait, I—didn't count on *this* kind of waiting!"

Louisa was patting her, giving her time to control the helpless weeping. "The children will hear you," Louisa whispered.

"I—know. And I'd hate myself." Abruptly, Margaret stood. "I'll stop crying now. I can stop standing up—better than feeling your arms around me. Don't comfort me anymore. Scold me. That's what I need."

Louisa took a deep breath. "Our worry doesn't help Lewis or us. Our business today is—his children and Christmas."

"And—even if Lewis never learns to love me, his children

do. That won't be enough, but I will always have—that." She gave Louisa a small smile. "Merry Christmas, you wonderful woman! Now, where did you put our small first gifts for the children? They'll be tumbling in here any minute. I promised them you and I would 'Christmas gif' ' them even before the people get here for theirs."

Louisa threw back the covers and sat up. "Hand me my robe on the back of that chair. Christmas is going to be just fine. I know it is. The little gifts are in the bottom drawer of that big chest in the corner." She caught Margaret's arm. "And—a good Christmas to you, my dear. Neither of us will ever forget this one, will we?"

The sixty men whom Captain Gustavus Drane had safely brought through the Seminole Nation were about to finish the hurried fortification just before nine o'clock when Lewis and his weary men rode into General Duncan Clinch's plantation the next morning. Over a tin cup of strong camp coffee, Lewis found he liked Captain Drane at once.

"The place is primitive to say the least," Lewis said, "but you've done a magnificent job fortifying it on such short notice, Captain."

"The part I like best is having the camp named for me," the young man laughed. "Course, my men really dubbed it Fort Drane, but old General Clinch is a good sport. He went right along with the name." The sparsely bearded captain grew serious. "I was just lucky, Major Fleming. My men and I came through some dangerous country; but it's all dangerous these days. Colonel John Warren and his troops were ambushed not twelve miles from here this morning."

"Colonel Warren?" The color drained from Lewis's face. "Was—Warren killed? He's a close friend!"

"No, no, nothing like that. But he lost six of his men. The colonel can give you all the facts himself. He'll be here soon. Sent a rider ahead to report his losses." Drane packed tobacco into a pipe, his face thoughtful. "You haven't met General Clinch yet, have you, Major?"

"Not yet. What do you think of him?"

"Never liked a man better," Drane said, gesturing with his unlighted pipe. "I happened to escort Warren's messenger to the general's hut. You'd have thought he'd just lost six of his own best Army Regulars. I don't know anybody who doesn't like him. He and your militia general Richard Keith Call

don't always see eye to eye, but they respect each other."
Gustavus Drane held a dry stick in the small fire that kept
the coffee hot and puffed until his pipe was lighted. "Of
course," he went on, "General Clinch underestimates the
Seminoles' ability to fight."

"How do you know that?"

"Young Bemrose told me. He's the British fellow. Surgeon's steward, Regular Army. Interesting boy. He's taking
down dispatches for Clinch now. Seems to know the general's
thoughts. Of course, it's no secret that the general's a good
fighter, a real leader. Really lives with the men." Drane
pointed toward one ramshackle log hut near the blacksmith
shop. "Sleeps there with holes in the roof and between the
logs as big as in any other hut here. Rats chase in and out
freely—all night long." He grinned. "Auld Lang Syne belies
its fancy name, you know. In all ways. It's one of the most
profitable *and* brutal working plantations. No big house. No
one lives here with the slaves in peacetime except a mighty
mean driver." He shook his head. "Glad I'm a soldier. I
wouldn't want the burden on my conscience of being the
owner of a working plantation like this."

"Clinch is pretty rough on his slaves, eh?" Lewis asked.

"And yet, I've got to say he's a fine Christian gentleman at
the same time. He may be the only man around here with any
religion." Captain Drane stood up. "Got to check on the men
finishing off my fine log pickets down by the blockhouse, Major."

Lewis looked at his watch. "And I have an interview with
General Clinch at ten-thirty. Why do you suppose he wants
to see me? After all, I'm under the direct command of militia
general Call."

"Clinch is going to commend you for getting your men
here all in one piece. That's one of his aims in life. He never
misses a chance to make a man feel good."

Lewis grinned. "How do you know that?"

"Young Bemrose again. I hope that boy's half as good at
patching up wounds as he is as an informant. He's my source
for believing we might have some friction between my general and yours. See you later, Major Fleming." Drane turned
back, a sad half smile on his bearded face. "By the way,
Major. This is Christmas Day. Merry Christmas to you, sir."

His pride at having been commended by colorful General
Duncan Clinch was not the reason Lewis slept little that first

night in camp. Nor was it the full moon in a cloudless sky, which kept the ugly little hut almost as light as day. On the trail he had been able to lay pine branches for his own pallet away from the others. Now, admittedly, he was bothered by the four officers sprawled close by on their pallets along the dirt floor, snoring, coughing, occasionally cursing softly. It seemed that everything made him nervous. Outside the flimsy hut, the night itself intensified the wild sounds—a panther's scream, a distant screech owl, the cry of a nighthawk, a startled marsh hen. All disturbing reminders of the strange day just ended. Christmas Day, 1835. Beyond Captain Gustavus Drane's almost sardonic "Merry Christmas," not a word had been said of it. The thought was more than the men could stomach, he knew. Most, he was sure, were longing for home, their longing too painful to mention. He tried to quiet himself by thanking God that the children were safe with Louisa. Again, as on the trail, he prayed that his friend Charles Seton had been well enough to go to New Switzerland. Without Seton, there would be only women and children in the isolated Fatio house. Had Miss Margaret gone? He hoped so. In a way Lewis didn't understand at all, she seemed to help his children—in their hearts.

He arched his back to remove a pine cone that felt like a rock. Now, maybe I can fall asleep, he thought. Undoubtedly, the boys, at least, cottoned to Miss Seton because they had come to know her so soon after their mother went away.

"Lord," he whispered. "Watch over us all. And—and will you give Augustina my love tonight? Please?" Tears burned his tired eyes. "Ask her to watch over *me*—too."

December 26 passed and December 27, with no orders for troop movement of any kind. Lewis was responsible only for keeping his own fifty St. Augustine militiamen from growing too restless, but he felt for General Call, who could do nothing until General Clinch of the Regular Army said the word. Call could do nothing but meet time and again with the volunteers to quiet their growing complaints for action, as Lewis and Colonel Warren met with their contingents.

Throughout the day of December 28, General Duncan Clinch strode about the fort: tall, thick of girth, ruddy, pleasant and altogether confident. But he said nothing except to reiterate that the men in the Regular Army, along with

General Call's volunteers, were more than a match for any gang of Seminoles.

"Sounds good," Leroy Black grumbled, "but whata' we waitin' for? Don't he know we only enlisted for one campaign?"

"He knows it," Stoney Pitts complained. "I'm signed up only till December 31. After that, I plan to start ridin' for home."

"I'll ride with ya, pardner," Leroy said. "Besides, we ain't got no guarantee that either the guv'ment of the Florida Territory *or* the army's gonna pay us."

Lewis listened until they fell silent, gave them each a long, disappointed look and walked slowly away. He had said all he knew to say by way of calming them. He would try this one last tactic—an appeal to their personal loyalty to him.

Lewis had walked about fifty feet when Leroy called after him: "Hey, Major Fleming, you knowed we wuz just talkin', didn't cha'?"

The tactic had worked. Lewis, a big smile on his face, threw Leroy a salute, but kept on walking straight for General Clinch's hut, past the odious corncribs, past the barns and storage sheds and blacksmith shop. The big sugar mill loomed ahead to the west on its hill—the source of Clinch's good income from the oddly named Auld Lang Syne. A great winter-red sun-ball eased down slowly behind the sugar works. Tonight, even the sky looked ominous. The smell of boiling pork and coffee from the cooks' shack stank. Lewis shuddered. The long wait was getting to him, too. He meant to learn the reason for the delay from Clinch himself.

Nearing the general's hut, the sight of two strange horses tied outside stopped him. He could hear voices from within, low, tense, not understandable. He waited, moving near enough so that through the one, small, square window, he could see two Indians in conversation with General Clinch. Obviously, the horses belonged to them; friendly Seminoles, Lewis was certain, and in the gloom of the hut he could see that the Indians were in war paint—a precaution against any accidental meeting with a warring tribe.

The talk went on and on, then Duncan Clinch's huge bulk filled the doorway. "Ah, Fleming, I'm glad you're here," he said. "I saw you from inside. Gather your men. Pass the word. There's been a strike some thirty-five miles to the south. On the other side of the Withlacoochee River. Don't know the name of the town where the whites were attacked, but it was vicious. The red monkeys have tipped their hand at last. Now we know where they're gathered. Across the Withlacoochee—*and*," he rubbed his thick hands energetically, "my two trusted Indian scouts tell me the river is easily fordable. They've just given me full directions to a fordable spot. We go first thing tomorrow morning!"

9

Before dawn on December 29, Lewis was summoned to General Call's hut. His heart pounded as he strode across the encampment, *this* morning, of all times, longing for a hot bath and a change of clothes. Since the day he left Hibernia, he'd tolerated himself without either. He shrugged off the idea. Battle nerves gave a man crazy thoughts. He would be heading for battle today.

At the door of the wretched hut, he saluted General Richard Call, who returned the salute, his normally calm, refined face dark with anger.

"Come in, come in, Fleming," he said. "We're in real trouble. I've failed to convince General Clinch that it is madness to travel with every supply wagon in the camp, every mule and broken-down horse. Clinch is of the Regular Army. With all his experience fighting Indians, he still insists upon ordering us *not* to travel lightly. He is in command, so we obey. It may mean our defeat—but we obey."

"I see."

"I hope you do. I also hope you can convince your St. Augustine men that I did my best to dissuade him." Pacing the hut, Call went on to explain the dangerous campaign. "We know, with as much certainty as anyone ever knows about Seminoles, that they are gathered on the other side and some distance south of the Withlacoochee River. Haste, in my opinion, is of the essence. It could be suicidal to encounter them as soon as we cross the river. Once across, we'll bog right down. With that cumbersome retinue of supply wagons, horses, mules—even a pack of pet dogs—" He shook his head. "Can you and Colonel Warren manage to fire your volunteers to action under such clumsy battle conditions, Major Fleming?"

"When do we leave, sir?"

"As soon as the men can eat, pack four days' rations and ready the horses—and, of course, that infernal train of wagons."

"My men will be ready, General. And—I'll urge them to keep their opinions of our—uh, method of fighting—to themselves."

"I hope you succeed. Those frazzlin' supply wagons slowing us down every time we hit soft ground will cause all the unnecessary dissension we need." He and Lewis exchanged sympathetic looks. "At least we have decent weather. Not too cold. Clear sky. We'll need every advantage, heaven knows. I only wish the Regular Army knew half as well as heaven does, that Indians can—in their own habitat—be shrewd and deadly fighters. What we need is speed, silence, mobility. What we'll have is noise, clatter, wagons to pry out of mudholes—and pet dogs yapping after every stray coon and rabbit."

"For certain we can't depend on a surprise attack," Lewis said with a wan smile. "We'll all just have to fight—harder, once we find them."

By 8 A.M., orders had been called and the awkward, noisy movement began. Army Regulars were flanked on either side by Call's mounted volunteers. General Clinch and his staff were to keep roughly fifty yards behind the right flank of the infantry. Lewis, now a part of Clinch's staff, as were General Call and Colonel Warren, could not resist an occasional glance at Call's genteel face—far easier to picture behind a desk in his law office at home than inching along on horseback through the Florida wilderness. He could almost read Call's thoughts. Call had predicted correctly: Besides the combined forces— some two hundred eighty Regulars on foot and five hundred volunteers on horseback—there rattled and clomped and creaked along every cart, wagon, mule and old horse Clinch could find on his plantation. The Army Regulars laughed and joked and sang bawdy songs, as unmindful of the noise they made as of the yelping of their pet hounds running alongside or leaping hither and yon in and out of the dense woods.

After two valuable hours lost in late morning while foot soldiers lifted and shoved and grunted and swore at two heavily loaded wagons mired in nearly two feet of muck, the

lumbering caravan again moved ahead. By noon, when they
stopped to rest and eat, they had covered only seven miles.

"We should be at least fifteen miles further along," Call
whispered to Lewis as they remounted to continue until dark
or for as long as the men could hold out.

Within the hour, two wagons were stuck again—axle-deep.
And only minutes after the weary foot soldiers freed them
and began to slog once more over the sodden ground, they
came to a wet morass that slowed the march miserably for a
distance of at least three miles. Once out of the boggy area,
Lewis caught Leroy Black's eye and smiled. Leroy scowled in
disgust over what to every volunteer militiaman with experience in the Florida terrain was sheer madness.

"We ain't never gonna ketch up to them Injuns at this
rate," he whispered when Lewis rode alongside.

Lewis said nothing. He didn't need to. His men had already
been warned. But no matter what any volunteer thought
about Clinch's orthodox army ways, they would all obey
orders. Especially loyal little Leroy Black.

When darkness fell, they had covered only five more miles.

That night the weary men joked, laughed, watered the
horses, cooked, ate, cleaned up and then sank to the ground
for a sound sleep. Lewis, who had given up his small officer's
tent to Bemrose for the care of two sick men, lay on his back
looking up at the now waning bright moon. He had been
away from Hibernia for nineteen nights and days—nights
dreaded far more than days. It was at night that his hard work
began. The hard work of battling inevitable nightmare anxieties over the safety of his children. Each time darkness fell,
he braced for it. The too realistic pictures of his sons' faces,
Tina's face—even Augustina's haunted his night hours. Tonight
seemed the worst yet. His mind did not drift restlessly from
one worry to another, it raced. The Seminoles—at least Osceola's men—were known to be somewhere just across the
Withlacoochee River. How far toward the St. Johns had some
wild band of them strayed? How far east and north? *As far as
Hibernia?*

Stiffly, he got to his feet and picked his way through the
rows of sleeping soldiers, past the carts and wagons and
horses to the edge of darkness spread by the tangle of woods
that surrounded their campsite. If only they had traveled

light, he thought and promptly suppressed the thought. They had not and that was that.

A branch snapped nearby. Lewis froze.

"Major? That you?"

"Leroy! Why aren't you getting some rest?"

"I jist couldn't shut my eyes, Major. I ain't skeered—least no more'n the rest. But well, I—got them kids back home, ya know, an' one of Clinch's men said he heard the Injuns was burnin' south of St. Augustine. My ol' woman an' my kids is south of St. Augustine!"

Plainly, Leroy needed to talk. Lewis took his arm and led him still farther away from the sleeping men.

"Look here," Leroy said, embarrassed, "I didn't mean to dump all my worries on you, sir. You've got enough already."

"Never does any harm to try to bear one another's burdens," Lewis said. "You and I both have a few."

"Oh, mine ain't nothin' to your'n. I still got my wife. But I—laid there wide awake on the ground, Major—the same as seein' my wife an' kids there in that house all by theirselves. Not a white man in more'n five mile."

"I know. My three children are in a house with—perhaps one older man visiting for the holidays. Otherwise, only women. Don't you have a Negro on the place?"

"Aw, yeah. A free nigger. Good feller an' he's right partial to my two boys. But he lives off at the boundary of my farm."

"Two sons, eh?"

"Yeah. One nine, one seven."

"I have two boys. And a little girl who'll be four at the end of this year."

"I got two little girls," Leroy mused tenderly.

Lewis threw an arm around the thin shoulders. "These two proud fathers need some sleep, Leroy. Come on. Let's try harder this time. Only one more day on the march—if we don't spend most of it in the mud somewhere. Then—" he stopped. The next day surely they would fight. "Then, well— then, we'll know a lot more than we do tonight about many things."

Leroy Black didn't answer right away, but walked in silence beside Lewis. Finally, nearing the bivouac, he whispered: "Maybe we kin ketch a few winks yet tonight if we keep tellin' ourselves that day after tomorrow—December 31 at sundown, you an' me's free to saddle up an' go home to them young'uns—if we're still both alive an' kickin'. Day after

tomorrow, *our time's up*. We kin both ride on home, Major.
Let's think about that—nothin' else. Then maybe we kin
sleep."

For most of the next day, they made their way across a dry
barren where nothing grew but stunted pines and palmetto.
Soaked with sweat and blistered red under the sun, they were
tired enough by now to be more orderly, less racous, and the
progress was faster. That night, the last bivouac before they
reached the Withlacoochee River, Dr. Weightman, the army
surgeon, and his aide, Bemrose, slept little. Five of the men
were ill now with ague and intermittent fever, but in spite of
painful sunburn and insect bites all around, by ten o'clock the
camp was fairly quiet. Quiet and dark. They were only three
short miles from the Withlacoochee River and dared not light
a fire. Not one man had grumbled at the cold, fat meat and
dry bread washed down with water.

Even Lewis had far less trouble falling asleep. He prayed
for his family and for himself, rehearsed the battle plan until
he expected to dream about it. The Seminoles would be just
across the Withlacoochee to the south, but friendly Indian
scouts had assured General Clinch that the river at the point
toward which they headed was easily fordable—very shallow
at the point where they would cross. In one quick rush, the
eight hundred men would wade or ride through the shallow
water and make directly for the Indian town.

Pine branch pallets scratched burned necks and the men
coughed from the dust they'd breathed for most of the long
day, but they slept until 2 A.M., when loud, crisp commands
roused them.

Lewis scrambled to his feet as did the others all across the
sprawling bivouac. Every man in the march was shivering,
Lewis knew, as he shivered both from the frosty night air and
from fear. An upcoming battle brought fear even to the
courageous, unless a man was not in his right mind. Full,
white moonlight, which had illumined the flat earth when
they went to sleep a few hours ago, was dimmed now as the
moon sank, lengthening the shadows in the woods through
which they would march. Again they gulped down cold,
smoked meat and bread, some making feeble jokes, most silent.

Their horses saddled, Lewis and Leroy Black stood drinking a last cup of brackish water. Leroy lifted his tin cup to
Lewis. Lewis returned the good wishes.

* * *

At 4 A.M., leaving the wagons and pet hounds behind, the final march began. Two by two, they entered the dense woods, military scouts ahead searching out the best path to the river's edge. Silence now was of the essence. Almost no one spoke. Then, within a mile of the Withlacoochee, chaos broke loose as the pack of dogs escaped from the guards back at the bivouac and filled the forest with wild yelping.

Leroy turned in his saddle. "Well, at least we ain't gonna surprise 'em, Major," he said.

"I doubt that we were anyway," Lewis said grimly.

After another hour of snakelike movement, the force was halted at a hammock while the last stand of woods separating them from the river was checked out. Within minutes, the scouts rode back with the heart-stopping news that the friendly Indians had been wrong—or had lied. The river was not fordable! It was deep, and one hundred fifty feet across!

Because there was no alternative, Clinch ordered them forward and as they reached the bank of the Withlacoochee, the sun's first rays of the new day poured through the moss-draped trees.

In silence, Lewis sat with the others as General Duncan Clinch paced the riverbank, debating what they should do.

Militia General Call rode up beside Clinch. "I'm sure you've seen that half-sunken canoe on the other side of the river, sir."

"Yes," Clinch mumbled. "I've seen it. But any man who swam for it would be dead before he made it halfway. My instinct tells me they're hiding straight across the water!"

As the generals conferred, Lewis quickly began to strip off his filthy shirt and uniform jacket. Clinch might be right, but he also might be wrong. Lewis Fleming, from the time he was a boy, had been able to swim the two miles of the wide St. Johns from Hibernia to New Switzerland at will. Surely, he could cover a measly one hundred fifty feet without detection. At least, while the two generals weighed matters—Clinch still pacing up and down—there was a chance to try.

About to jerk off the second boot, Lewis heard Clinch bellow: "Halt, Major Fleming! You are under orders to halt. I command you to get back into that uniform."

More angered than humiliated, Lewis obeyed and the generals returned to their discussion, not seeming to mind that the men overheard their confusion and anger that the scouts had misled them.

"We've got to get across," Call insisted. "Once we're over, we've got them dead to rights, General."

"Of course, we have," Clinch said between his teeth. "But, even with paddlers at the bow and stern of that flimsy canoe, no more than five men and their weapons could be ferried across at a time! I've got more than seven hundred men to get across."

Lewis, dressed again, turned his back on the arguing generals and stared across the black water at the splashing figure moving swiftly under thick, overhanging branches at the far side of the river. "General Clinch," he called softly. "Look! Leroy Black has done it!"

Leroy was unable to resist a triumphant wave. Lewis waved back and watched intently as Leroy began to bail out the canoe with his hands.

"General Call, that's one of your volunteers," Clinch snapped. "How did he get away to do that?"

Call said nothing and Clinch did not press the issue. Lewis admired him for that. There was, in fact, no room for argument. Clinch had no choice. Any of Call's five hundred volunteer militiamen was free to leave at sundown when their period of enlistment ended. Without them, Clinch's two hundred eighty Regulars would be slaughtered. To hesitate, to turn back to Fort Drane would only strengthen Indian resistance. To divide the forces as he would have to do in order to make the painfully slow crossing entailed a risk Lewis knew Clinch despised, caring about his men as he did. But the risk had to be taken. The soldiers now were all agitating for action. Not one man would question a command to advance.

Once Leroy Black brought the rickety old canoe to their side, Clinch gave the order and load after load of Regulars began to cross the river. The paddlers worked feverishly and by a little after noon, all the Regulars and twenty-seven volunteers, Lewis and Leroy Black among them, were on the south side of the Withlacoochee in Indian territory. General Call and most of his men remained behind planning a way to construct a crude bridge. In the last canoe load of Regulars to cross the river was General Duncan Clinch.

Together, both on their hands and knees, Lewis and Clinch began to examine the moccasin tracks plainly visible on the wet sand. Lewis felt his spine tingle. The tracks were fresh!

"We need more of Call's men over here and we need them now, Major Fleming," Clinch grunted as he stood upright again.

"I know, General," Lewis said just above a whisper. "But these tracks are so fresh, we'll never have time to throw up even the flimsiest bridge."

He had no sooner spoken than cries of "Indians!" rang through the tangled forest from the direction of their advance guard. "Indians! Coming this way!"

"Ready—fire!" Clinch shouted.

Within seconds after a few Regulars let go their muskets blindly into the trees, the woods erupted with shots, cries, wild whoops and screams.

Lewis saw little Leroy Black pitch backward not ten feet away. Then, except for the searing pain in his own leg, he remembered no more beyond the nightmare sound of those savage whoops, coming closer.

10

On January 1 of the new year, 1836, Margaret, in the Fatio parlor, watched L.I. and George struggle to force split oak pieces under the huge Yule log Scipio had dragged in for their holiday festivities.

"Scipio would be glad to help us turn this big old log, George," L.I. grumbled. "Why do we have to do it by ourselves?"

George gave a mighty heave and the log turned—just the way he wanted it. He straightened up, brushed off his hands and answered, "Because we're not little boys any longer, L.I. That's why."

"I know I'm not," L.I. boasted. "In fact, I could've got that log to move all by myself."

"What makes you say a stupid thing like that?"

" 'Cause I'm stronger than you! You're older, but I'm stronger."

"What does that prove?"

Margaret longed to take them both in her arms and comfort them. Instead, she stepped between them just as they began to shove each other. "Here, here. How safe do you think it makes me feel to have my two protectors fighting?" An arm about each, she walked with them out onto the veranda. "Look what a beautiful day it is. Hard to believe darkness will ever come again on a day like this, isn't it? Last night, after the moon went down, I honestly would have been terribly frightened if the two of you hadn't been in the house."

"You're teasin'," L.I. mumbled.

"You're *not* teasin', are you, Miss Margaret?" George looked at her, his dark eyes solemn.

"I certainly am not. After all, you two are the only men in the house."

She felt L.I. watching her now. "Would you really be scared?" he asked.

"If Louisa and Sophia and I were here alone, I would be."

"Why? Indians?"

She hadn't expected this and tried to think of a way to evade an answer. These two dear ones had more than enough to burden them. There must be a way to pretend that she had never given a thought to an Indian raid on New Switzerland.

"We're scared too," George offered.

"I'm not!"

"Yes, you are, L.I. You admitted it last night in bed."

"Aw, I musta' been talkin' in my sleep."

His eyes searching out Hibernia, barely visible across the wide expanse of water, George said anxiously, but keeping his voice down: "Scipio told us when we went to the woods with him to cut wood yesterday that his grapevine told him the Indians had burned every sugar plantation south of Augustine! Scipio's grapevine knows about Indians."

"Aw, how can a grapevine talk?"

Ignoring L.I., George looked at Margaret. "L.I. and Tina and I—we don't wanta be anywhere you aren't, Miss Margaret. But what if—they fired our house? What would we do all the way over here?"

Margaret thought a minute, then said, "It's true, the Negroes do hear a lot we don't hear, but we really don't have any reason to think the Seminoles are coming this way." She held out a hand to each boy. "You see, I figure it like this. Your father trusts you both. He'd want you first of all to protect little Tina. Next, Louisa and Sophia and—me. So, our part right now is to stay here at the Fatio place close together—and be brave and calm."

Her words hung flatly in the sun-filled air. George shuddered.

"My, we'd better get back beside that big warm fire you've built," she said quickly. "You're shivering, George."

"Not from the cold. I just—tried for a minute to think—what I'd do to protect anybody—if they came."

"Men always know what to do when the time comes," L.I. said, not very convincingly.

"We'd all know," Margaret said softly. "And—God is here with us. He's at Hibernia right now, too."

L.I. looked at her, thinking hard. "Is—God really here with us—this minute? Right now?"

"Sure, He is," George said. "He's—wherever Papa is, too."

"Do you honestly, cross your heart and hope to die—believe that, Miss Margaret?"

"Cross my heart and hope to die, L.I. I do believe it. And so do you."

He thumped the veranda post with the toe of his boot. "Yeah, but—"

"But what?" she asked gently.

"Can't God let us know some way that—Papa is all right—if He's really there with him, too?" He broke suddenly into tears and threw himself into Margaret's arms. "I'm not—so scared—of Indians here. I'm—scared—they—might—kill Papa!"

George, weeping too, pressed against Margaret. She held them both, smoothing their hair, saying nothing. Her own anxiety was too deep. Her own fear for Lewis, minute by minute—too sharp.

Sophia burst out the door, saw the sobbing boys, gasped, "Oh, my—!" ran back into the house and slammed the door.

"What on earth's the matter, Sophia?" Louisa demanded as her sister rushed into the parlor.

"Those two big boys! They're out there on the veranda sobbing in poor little Margaret's arms like they were three years old! You've got to tell them not to do that. Not to impose on Margaret like that. She's worried half to death about Lewis as it is."

Louisa leaned her head against the high back of her father's chair. "Sophia," she said quietly, "let the boys cry. It will help. And understand once and for all that Margaret Seton is doing exactly what she needs to be doing. Consoling Lewis's sons. There's only one other place she'd rather be—where she could help Lewis himself."

Sophia sank onto the sofa. "I declare, sometimes it's all just too much for me. Just think of beautiful, charming, Margaret Seton—in love with—a man who may at this very minute, be lying dead in the bushes somewhere! Heaven knows, I'm worried about Lewis, too, but—"

"That's enough, Sister!"

"Oh, I don't mean anything disrespectful of the danger Lewis's in by what I said. It's—just *so hard* on me. I'd like time to—revel in Margaret's great love. And I have to stay scared to death about the Seminoles and Lewis."

Back across the Withlacoochee, the Seminoles gone, the battle over, Colonel John Warren knelt beside Lewis as he lay on a blood-soaked blanket. In an hour's time, it would be dark, but darkness did not—could not this night—mean an end to the day's work. The dead had yet to be buried, the wounded given emergency aid by Dr. Weightman and young Bemrose.

Fleming, Colonel Warren knew, had for a short time regained consciousness. Now, watching the handsome, bearded face contort with pain, he could only wonder how much good the laudanam had done. At least, Warren thought, the only severe wound is in his leg—his left leg about three inches above the ankle was shattered. Before Bemrose's hastily applied bandage covered the wound, Warren had seen the splintered white bones piercing bloody muscle and skin. Lewis groaned constantly, but Warren made no effort to speak to him. He would merely be there should his friend open his eyes and ask for anything.

The setting sun was filling the woods across the river with roseate light as those hideous war cries had filled it a few hours before. He would hear those cries, Warren knew, for as long as he lived: beginning deep in the savage throats with low, ugly growls which burst finally into fiendish yells and screeches. No panther's scream had ever so chilled his blood. It had seemed an eternity as he waited with Call back at the point of crossing, but the furious fighting had raged for only one hour when the last Seminole fled into the dense woods. Now, there were the groans and cries of their wounded and the scrape of metal on earth as graves for their dead were dug with the only tools at hand—tin cups.

"How is Major Fleming, sir?"

Warren looked up, then got to his feet. "Oh, Bemrose. I don't know, but I'd like to stay right here with him tonight, unless you need me elsewhere—"

"No, sir. Thank you," the young aide said wearily. "I think we've done all we can do tonight, except to keep hot coffee and plenty of water ready and repeat the laudanum dosages as needed."

"By the sound of the cries and groans all around us, I'd say more laudanum is needed now."

"Too much can't be given at once. I'm just thankful Dr. Weightman wasn't wounded." The boy smiled, "I wouldn't be up to all this alone."

"You'll become a man overnight, Bemrose."

"I hope so, sir. If I need you, I'll call you. I'll be working all night. We have fifty-nine wounded. Send for me if Major Fleming gets worse."

Warren looked at Lewis's dirt-and blood-streaked face, as still as death except when convulsed in agony. "He has three motherless children. They need him. They need him."

"We'll do our best, Colonel. Both General Clinch and General Call think highly of the major."

Bemrose hurried off and Colonel Warren knelt again beside Lewis, wishing with all his heart that they had already made the ghastly long march back to Fort Drane. An ugly wound would certainly be even more painful after three nights on the damp ground. Stiff and sore and infected. Bemrose and Weightman had only the barest medical necessities.

Slowly, Lewis opened bloodshot eyes and tried to turn his head to look around. The thick brown hair was caked with blood. His head had struck a tree when he fell.

"It's all over, Fleming. John Warren here. We're all right. We drove them off—Osceola with them." Reading the question in Lewis's eyes, he went on, "Our losses were bad enough. But not great. We lost four men—two volunteers, two Regulars. Fifty-nine wounded. Some far worse off than you." When Lewis tried again to look around, Warren explained, "That scraping sound is—tin cups digging graves. Can you rest some now, Fleming? You know, the first hour we're back in Fort Drane, I'll write to your family. You mustn't worry."

With enormous effort, Lewis began to move his parched
lips. "Lou—Louisa—Fatio," he whispered.

"Yes, yes, I know. She'll break the news to your children
carefully. Our Florida volunteers are leaving soon. Their
time's up. No trouble at all to find someone to hand deliver a
letter to New Switzerland. He felt Lewis's forehead. It was
hot with fever. Warren stood up. "I'll be right back, Fleming.
You need some cold water."

At the wooden water tank, Warren again met John Bemrose.

"His head's hot, you say, Colonel? I hope that doesn't
mean infection. If so, that leads straight to amputation."

The word struck Warren like a knife. "Always?"

"Almost always. A one-legged man's better off than a dead
man."

11

Waiting for Louisa to finish the boys' Spanish lesson downstairs, Margaret sat alone by a window in her room at New
Switzerland, a letter from her father open on her lap—her
whole being flooded with relief. They had all worried a little
less for the last two days about Lewis. After all, his term of
enlistment had ended three days ago. She and Louisa had
convinced themselves that if anything had happened to him,
surely they would have heard by now. He could come home,
in fact, any day. The sun hadn't set yet. Lewis could even
return this evening. Still more relief had come in Margaret's
loving letter from Papa: "It now seems the right time to tell
you," he wrote, "that your old father has long known of your
love for Lewis Fleming and you have my complete blessing.
And, lest you worry, I have not told your mother. My dear,
proper wife would surely think you forward, but your devoted
father knows you far better than that. I am sure the waiting is
the hardest job you've had in your short life, but you are
doing it with grace and courage."

Dear, liberal, loving—*perceptive* Papa! He was biased,
though. She had not waited with any grace and very little
courage, but she had waited. And she would go on for as long

as it took for Lewis Fleming to find out that he could love her, too.

Her room at the Fatio house faced the west. Across the expanse of the St. John's, turning color now under a setting winter sun, a bit downriver, she could see Hibernia. Could barely make out the gabled roof of the two-storied frame house, a corner of the tall barn among thick stands of live oaks and magnolias. During summer visits to Louisa, because of the thick deciduous leaves, the house was almost obscured. On this winter evening, she could see it. Hibernia was not grand. Not as large as the Seton town house in Fernandina, but there was a safe, sturdy permanence about it which became Lewis Fleming. A sheltering quiet feeling of peace pervaded all of Hibernia plantation even when dogs barked and servants shouted; when the carpentry shop was busy and hammer rang against anvil in the blacksmith's lean-to down by the big barn.

Did Lewis Fleming really possess this same serene quiet within himself? Had he possessed it in the midst of whatever had happened to him during his time of enlistment with the Florida Militia? Was his quiet strength—such a magnet to her—in evidence away from the land he had loved for all his life? She was certain of it. She counted on it. She had counted on it for Lewis himself while he was at war. Yet, she had seen his shattered, helpless face at Augustina's grave. Night after night, during his absence, she had felt his anxieties, his fears for his life—for the children. But, if at times his serenity vanished, she would stake her life on its return. To her, Lewis Fleming was very like Hibernia—his sorrow, his burdens streaking the light of his nature as shadows streaked the light that fell among the great Hibernia trees.

Straining now in the gathering dusk to see the outlines of his house, she thought with an inner smile: "Lewis Fleming, Major Lewis Michael Fleming, I not only love you and your children—I love your roofline! Please be safe this minute. Please come home!"

The gold watch on its black ribbon around her neck showed nearly five o'clock. Louisa and the children would be free soon. Before the square, walnut-framed looking glass, Margaret tucked in some stray wisps of hair, pinched her cheeks and bit her lips to bring up their color. It was important that she appear her best for L.I. and George and Tina. She would play the mellow, old Fatio harpsichord this evening and they would all sing. The children were excitedly expecting their father, too. Margaret helped them all when she kept thinking up things to do, herself included.

Back at the window, still waiting for the burst of voices that would signal the end of the Spanish lesson, her gaze went again to his house across the wide river, dimming now in the quick-falling winter twilight.

Her musing look became a stare—her hand flew to her mouth.

"No! Dear God, no!"

In a frantic effort to be sure she wasn't imagining what she saw, Margaret jerked open the window, her eyes fighting the dusk. Black smoke was pouring heavily down and across the top of the trees as though pushed by an unseen force.

When hideous red flames broke clear against the darkness, she rushed out into the upstairs hall and screamed for Louisa.

Immediately, she could have bitten off her tongue. This was no time for her to be screaming. If Louisa heard her, so did the boys and little Tina.

L.I.'s heavy footsteps pounded across the downstairs hall. "Miss Margaret," he shouted. "Miss Margaret—you all right?"

Staring up at her now—speechless, stood Louisa, Sophia and all three children.

"I'm—all right," Margaret gasped, trying to control the panic in her voice, as she went quickly down the stairs. "It's—it's your house, L.I.—George. There's no way not to tell you—it's on fire."

"God help us!" Sophia shrilled and burst into tears. As did Tina.

Louisa swept the child up into her arms and tried to quiet her. The boys raced out onto the veranda.

"Indians!" L.I. screamed. "It's gotta be Indians!"

George ran back inside, stood for a long moment staring at Margaret, his face white, then, without a word, hurried from the house.

"Where's he going?" Sophia demanded. "That boy might get in a boat—and go over there! Louisa! What will we do? You know if Indians are burning Hibernia, they'll be here next! Louisa, you know that, don't you?"

They were all on the veranda now, looking helplessly across at the columns of dense smoke billowing out over the water—and at the flames soaring on the rising wind.

"The Fleming people," Louisa said, almost to herself. "We

must pray for Pompey and Betty and Little Jim—for all of them."

"Someone should find George," Sophia moaned. "What about George? Louisa, where did that boy go?"

At that moment, they could barely make out a light moving in the darkness over at the Fleming dock. Margaret ran inside for the Fatio long glass. Back on the veranda trying to focus it, her hands trembled almost too much to hold its weight.

"The people, Margaret? Do you think it's the people—trying to get over here?"

"I can't tell, Louisa. I can barely make out any figures. It's so dark. If it is the Fleming people, can they all get into those three small boats?"

"I demand to know where George is," Sophia wailed. "Doesn't anybody care about the boy?"

"He's down at your dock," Margaret said, "with Scipio. They're already in your plantation boat, Louisa. Oh, dear Lord!"

L.I. began to cry—out of control. "I—don't want nothing to happen to George, Miss Margaret! I—love—my brother! We fight, but—I love my brother. I—don't—want—him—to be—killed!"

"He won't be," Louisa said firmly, her voice almost cross. "George is doing what he has to do as the oldest son, L.I. He and Scipio will be all right. They're going to meet your father's people. They may need help."

Margaret put both arms around the frightened boy. "George is almost fourteen, L.I. He's doing—what your father would do—if he were here. And you must, too."

"What? What?" the boy sobbed. "I'd do—anything, but—I don't—know what I'm supposed to do!"

"Look after Tina," Margaret answered. "Take her with you, run to the kitchen and tell Polly and Maum Easter we'll need lots of hot coffee and tea. George is going with Scipio to meet the people in case they need help crossing the river. Your job is to—do as I say. And, it's very important."

L.I. wiped his eyes with his sleeve, took his sister's hand when Louisa put her down and started for the kitchen. Then he turned back, his face stark. "Miss Margaret?"

"What is it, L.I.?"

"Where—will my papa go—when he—comes home? Will—our house—burn all the way to the ground?"

"I—won't lie to you, L.I. We'd better be prepared for the—worst." She lifted her chin and gave him a shaky smile. "As for your father—he'll be where we are. We'll find a way to get word to him. Don't worry for a minute. Sooner or later, we'll all be at my house in Fernandina."

"We will?"

"Oh, Margaret," Sophia moaned, "I wish we were there now! I—I think—I—might—faint. *Louisa!*"

"No, you won't! There isn't time. March! *March, Sophia.* Right to the kitchen with the children, do you hear?"

Alone, Louisa embraced Margaret. "I declare, those children will do whatever you tell them to do," she whispered.

"I—try to remember that," Margaret said. "Oh, Louisa! Poor Lewis! Poor, poor Lewis." She stepped back and faced her friend. "Louisa, we'd better leave here—tonight. As quickly as possible."

For the first time, Louisa's eyes filled with tears. "Yes. Yes, Margaret." Suddenly weak with fear, she sank onto a straight-backed bench. "I've—lived through this twice, you know. They burned our first house here when I was about young George's age—Scipio remembers. He was just a boy. He and old Dublin, who warned us, were the only people who escaped when we did." She shuddered. "After all these years, Margaret, I can still hear those Indian bullets whistling past—hitting the water all around us—on our way to St. Mary's."

Louisa's usually quiet eyes were an agony of dread. "We *will*—have to run again, won't we? And—without a man left in the family."

"Dear Louisa, let it help—some—that I'm here." She focused the long glass again. "Oh, I can see them better now. Enough to be fairly sure it's at least some of the Fleming people—in three boats. They're halfway across. There'll be plenty of room at Fernandina for everyone. Papa will see to the Negroes who come, too." She put down the glass. "Louisa, can you take a few orders for a change. Will you go into the parlor and rest and let me see to the packing? Can you just—rest, even for the little time we have left?"

"Oh, Margaret, my dear, how can I? Sophia's so little help. She's all to pieces and she'll stay that way. How can I rest?"

"Because you've already lived through two fires and I'm a big girl now!"

Margaret could see Louisa's courage begin to return. She

took two or three deep breaths, smiled and got up. "I'm fine. I—think the shock made me a little dizzy. I can rest some other time. Come on, we'll get ready together. We've got to be on that river within the hour. Not a minute later."

From 6 A.M. until nearly noon on the first day back at Fort Drane, young Bemrose assisted aging Dr. Weightman as he worked his way from one tent to another, extracting lead balls from the wounded and amputating legs and arms. Some bore the excruciating pain bravely, most screamed and struggled from the first incision through the last stroke of the saw. A few fortunate men fainted. By the time Weightman quit from exhaustion, Bemrose was reeling from all he had been forced to watch as he struggled to hold men quiet, staunched blood and applied bandages.

"I will hear the sound of that knife ripping and hacking through good flesh—for all the days of my life," he said to the surgeon as they stretched at last on the floor of the plantation driver's house. "And don't mention food. I couldn't face it."

"Give yourself time, son," Weightman said. "Food will revive you. I owe you a debt of gratitude, but we're not finished yet."

"You mean Major Fleming?"

On a sigh, the doctor said, "Yes. Another amputation. Both bones in his lower leg are so shattered I see no other way." He sighed again, heavily. "But, I—just can't do it—quite yet. The strength's gone from my right arm." For a moment, both men were silent. "I—also think," Weightman finally said, "that I'm having trouble—facing that one in particular. The wound's just above the ankle. Perhaps only his foot."

Young Bemrose's respect, near reverence, for the doctor ran deep, but he could not wipe from his mind what General Clinch had told him only yesterday: *Army surgeons are too quick to amputate. Even Weightman.* "Uh—have you talked with General Clinch today, sir?"

"Not much conversation, but I've been aware of him all morning. As you have seen. That big-hearted gentleman following us from tent to tent, down on his knees on the ground by the men after we'd left them, I hear—comforting them, praying for those who won't live. He's not only a great general, he's a kind human being."

A voice boomed from the open door of the hut where they lay. "Weightman? Bemrose? You in there?"

Both men scrambled to their feet, saluting. "Yes, General."

Inside the door, Clinch thundered, "Lie back down! I've brought you hot coffee." The warm smile came. "Didn't you hear my order? Lie down!"

Stretched again on the floor, the two gratefully took the steaming cups.

"I've come to see what I can do for you, gentlemen. And to get your report on the men. Will more than those three wretches down near the end of the tent row die?"

"I hope not," Weightman said. "It's—early to say. There are a few cases where gangrene could set it."

"Which ones?"

"Two are your Regulars, sir. The other one is Major Fleming, brigade inspector, Colonel Warren's Second Regiment."

"Do you think I don't know who Fleming is? In fact, I've thought a lot about him this morning. I don't want you to amputate his leg, his foot—or anything. Is that understood?"

Weightman sat up. "But, General, if gangrene—"

"Bemrose? Are you awake?"

"Oh, yes, sir!"

"Good. If I talk to Fleming, get him to agree to stay here for as long as is needed, will you do as I say?"

"Yes, sir!"

"I regret having to speak so, General," Weightman interrupted, "but if amputating Fleming's leg or even his foot will save his life, I—"

"I examined your fine work this morning, Doctor. In the case of each amputation, part of the leg or arm had been nearly torn off. Fleming's wound is ugly—splinters of bone plainly visible to the naked eye—but the leg is still there. Can't we put forth added effort and at least try to save it?" He cleared his throat. "You see, I happen to think very highly of the man. I give him full credit for not only seeing to the supplies and the safety of the militiamen he brought safely here but also for their courageous behavior. They all but worship Fleming. And, when you consider what an outlandish lot they are in the main, I declare the major to be a man not to be taken lightly." The general's voice grew tender. "Anyway, I hear he has three motherless children."

Weightman thought a long time, then said, "All right, sir. If Bemrose is willing. It will surely take long months of attention."

Young Bemrose jumped up, saluting Clinch. "I'm more

than willing! In fact, I was—hoping, just before you walked in here, sir, that we might at least try to save Major Fleming's leg. I'll do anything—*anything* for as long as it takes!"

After promising that he and the other servants who escaped would wait at the Fatio place until it was safe to go back across the river to Hibernia, Pompey, with white folks present, kissed Maum Easter shyly, then waved them all off into the darkness. There were two overloaded boats. The large New Switzerland plantation boat, manned by only three Negroes and loaded with extra clothing, food and water, moved out into the center of the St. Johns first, to what was hoped would be a safe distance from shore. Then followed the Fleming sailboat bearing the children, Maum Easter, Margaret, Sophia and Louisa.

From the crowded sailing vessel, Louisa called back to Scipio, her faithful servant for all his life: "Please, you and Polly and all the others sleep tonight as far from the big house as you can!"

"Louisa, sh!" Margaret whispered. "Did you forget?"

"Mercy, I guess I did. I'm just—so tired."

The two boats had gotten only as far as Mandarin Point downriver, when L.I. first, then George, handling the sheet himself, saw the New Switzerland house literally burst into flames.

Out in the swift current on the blackest of winter nights, huddled together, they all heard the eerie, bloodcurdling shrieks of the Seminoles putting the torch to New Switzerland for the second time in Louisa's thirty-nine years.

12

Daily, for more than two weeks, young John Bemrose was up at 4 A.M. to prepare dressings and to begin attending the wounded still unable to leave Fort Drane. Dr. Weightman had been ordered back to St. Augustine, where a measles epidemic had struck prisoners and soldiers at Fort Marion. Bemrose was left in complete charge. He was exhausted, but he had become a man, more willing and more able to handle his heavy responsibilities. One of the reasons for his new growth, he felt certain, was his daily contact with General Duncan Clinch, with whom he shared a hut. His admiration for the Spartan General soared.

Toward the end of January in his carefully kept diary, John Bemrose wrote:

The general and I—he so highly ranked, I, so low—are friends. He is a great man. So plain and so simple are his habits that he is never a clog to the army. Unlike General Winfield Scott, who demands a special chair in the field and his own musicians and servants in battle, a camp stool is all General Clinch requires; he eats with his men and sleeps in the same hut with me, a surgeon's aide. He shows much interest in my work and concern for the men. Especially does he show deep interest in the painfully slow progress of Major Lewis Fleming. A word here about Fleming: I have never known a braver man. I know I hurt him intolerably each morning when I remove large and small splinters of bone from his leg. We cannot know yet, but he and I remain hopeful that the leg will heal in nature's course. Colonel John Warren, who left with his volunteers on 6 January, has written Fleming that his home was burned and that his children are now in Fernandina with a family named Seton. I feared for a time that the tragic news would be too much for Major Fleming in his weakened condition. He wept. I see the strongest men weep under these conditions, but his resolve to get well and return someday to his beloved Hibernia held him steady. He is a widower and his children and his plantation are his life. I wrote to Mr. Seton in Fernandina. He knows of Fleming's wound from Colonel Warren. Fleming will improve once he has had a chance to hear from his family. Conditions here at Fort Drane are the worst. The encampment is crowded with civilian refugees and many are ill. Daily, we wonder about Major Dade and his detachment who were marching through the Indian Nation before we fought at Withlacoochee. I fear great tragedy has come to them.

The tragedy became known the next day. Dade and all but two of his men had been massacred. Only one survived his wounds to talk about it. Murders were rife throughout north Florida. Even the kind, patient Indian Agent, Wiley Thompson, had been murdered—by Osceola himself—the young Indian leader he loved. On February 1, Bemrose wrote.

We are in a hornet's nest here at Fort Drane, in constant danger of attack—too far from the seaboard. No one is safe anywhere except along the coast. A stark tragedy for Fleming that his beloved home was burned, but at least his children are safe. General Clinch has requested a promotion for him from major to colonel. Perhaps that will lift Fleming's spirit. To his credit, he is in no way sorry for himself. If only he would get a letter from his cousin!

Margaret's father, Charles Seton, and the Fleming boys became instant friends. Seton, unwell from his old wound, had welcomed the half-frozen travelers to his spacious two-storied frame home on Calle Amelia in Fernandina, and from the day of their arrival, his health had seemed to improve.

"Well, I'll tell you what I think, Mr. Seton," George said as the two walked together one crisp February day. "I imagine now that your own son, George, has moved to the North, you just needed some male companionship." The boy smiled up at him. "I try to supply it, sir." His voice broke. "Not knowing about Papa, you—help me a lot, too."

"Do I now? That pleases me. And do you know, we might be lucky today. Even my aging bones feel lucky. If I were a betting man, I'd wager we'll find some word about your father this very day. That would help you more than anything in this world."

George ran ahead to the lean-to post office and within minutes ran out again waving a letter. "Your bones were right, Mr. Seton! There's a letter for you from Fort Drane!" He frowned. "But—that's not my father's handwriting!"

Examining the letter, Seton said, "Well now, the man's probably just not up to writing yet. We'll know soon. I'll open it."

They crossed the sandy, shop-lined street and sat down on a wooden bench. One steadying arm about George, Seton broke the seal and began to read:

" 'My Esteemed Mr. Seton,

I am John Bemrose, the medical aide at Fort Drane, in charge of the case of Major Lewis Fleming, who was wounded in the fighting at Withlacoochee. Colonel Warren wrote the major that his home was burned and of his children's whereabouts. He has taken it well, grateful that his children are safe. I am caring for Fleming daily and have good news. He is weak and cannot put weight on the injured leg, but it has been decided that we will not amputate.' "

His face white, George gasped: "*Amputate*! Mr. Seton—Papa—almost lost his leg, didn't he?"

"Evidently so," Seton said, "but he didn't. And he's alive."

"What else, sir? What else did that man write?"

" 'I cannot promise good results, but we are hopeful and I am doing my very best.' " Seton scanned the remainder of the letter. "Oh, yes, George, there's this. 'My time is short, and I am very busy with both sick and wounded. Please tell Major Fleming's children that he loves them tenderly and sends his deepest thanks to you, sir, for taking them into your home. I beg you to write to him soon, giving him all the news, directing your letter to Fort Drane.' Well, that's about it," Seton said, getting to his feet. "Our part right now is to hurry home so that the ladies can read this for themselves."

"Yeah," George said shakily, as he fell in step with Seton. "And old L.I. I wish old L.I. had come with us. He's a good brother these days. He's not such a kid anymore. And he's been awful worried about Papa."

Tears of relief still streamed down their faces after Seton took Margaret and Louisa off alone to his office "to make some decisions," as he tactfully explained to the children.

"I know we have things to decide," Margaret said, "but, oh, Papa, Lewis—is going to be all right. If he were going to get gangrene—he would have it by now. He doesn't! That medical aide didn't say a word about that. Oh, Papa, Lewis isn't—going to die! Louisa—he's all right!" The women embraced. "And—I'm sure he'll be right here with us—soon."

"Don't get your hopes up too high, Margaret," Louisa said. Then, turning to Charles Seton: "Have you read us everything in that letter, Mr. Seton?"

"Uh—as a matter of fact, no. There is a postscript I felt only the two of you should hear first."

Margaret stared at him, her eyes wide with fear.

"Now, my dear, he's undoubtedly going to be all right, but Bemrose says it will take at least four or five more months."

Louisa shuddered. "He must have—a dreadful wound! And—well, that's *too long*. We can't all stay here for that length of time. Your house is full to overflowing. Sophia and I will find a place to take the children and—"

"And nothing," Margaret snapped. "You can stay and you will stay until Lewis comes back—and that's the end of that." She sank into a chair, her face white, but her voice growing stronger by the minute. "I don't need to pretend with the two of you. You both know I love him. And if you love me, Louisa, you'll stay. My heart is going to be helped—oh, so much by having all three of his children—here. *With me.* For as long as we all have to wait. You're staying, too, Louisa. I—can't possibly wait all that time—without you to help me."

Part Two

1836–1838

13

"You must be sick of the sight of that ugly leg of mine." Lewis said to young Bemrose on a soft March morning.

Bemrose laughed. "At least we don't have to mess with those charcoal linseed poultices anymore, sir. The infection is gone—and the smell." He pressed hard all around the healing wound, feeling for loose bone fragments. "I'm sick of—hurting you, Colonel, but I'm afraid there's one more piece of loose bone in there."

Lewis braced himself. "Go ahead."

The scalpel dug into scarred flesh and with his fingers, John Bemrose worked out a tiny fragment. "There. Not as bad as it used to be, eh, Colonel?"

Still breathing hard from the pain, Lewis said, "I'm—not used to that 'Colonel' business yet."

"You deserve that new commission for your bravery alone. I'm sure glad it came through before General Clinch lost his command of the Florida forces. Meaning no disrespect for President Jackson, but I'd think after his own years as an Indian fighter, he'd know a superb military man like our general."

"I take it you don't think much of Winfield Scott."

"If you think he won't bring his musical band and his big chair to sit on in battle, you're mistaken, sir." Bemrose reached for the wooden splints. "But I should keep my mouth shut on all but medical matters. I'll be as happy as you the day I no longer have to strap these splints back on, Colonel."

Lewis sat up. "How long, Bemrose? Can you tell me any more today? I'm already so indebted to the Setons for caring for my children I dread to face them." His voice began to shake with anger and helplessness. "If only I could be of—some help around here! or if only I had—just one book to read!"

Gathering his bandages and medicines, the aide said, "I'm

not stalling, sir. I just don't know when you can leave. Surely, not more than two more months."

Lewis stared up at him, his face grim.

"If the woods between here and a waterway to Fernandina weren't still so full of creeping Seminoles, I'd find a way for you to go now," Bemrose explained. "I know you need the loving care of those closer than I. But you can't ride a horse. You dare not try to put any weight on that leg yet. That's all I can say. I'm sorry, sir."

To pass the empty days and to tease his own heart, Lewis wrote as often as there was paper at hand, to the children, to his mother, to Louisa and to his friend Charles Seton. At least twice a week, since there were so many of them to write, he received a letter from Fernandina. "We are all well," George wrote in April. "Old L.I. is growing up some and turning into a very good rider. This week, he will be back from a visit to Grandmother Fleming in Jacksonville and I will tell you more about how he is then. I hope he pulls no pranks on Grandmother, but, being our grandmother, I'm sure she'll know about handling L.I. Mrs. Seton is most kind to us, but somewhat distant. It is Mr. Seton and Miss Margaret who deserve and get our devotion."

The letter both heartened and worried Lewis. His sons were growing up away from him. Not really among strangers and yet the monotonous hours spent lying on his pallet or sitting in the one straight chair or outside against his favorite tree, strung his mind with outlandish thoughts. Thoughts he tried to control. The worst, he told himself, had already happened to his children. Their home was gone, their mother was gone. Except that he still lived, they could not have lost more. Still, at times, not too happily he reminded himself that all three actually seemed quite content, enthusiastic in fact, with their life at Fernandina. "The only thing that bothers L.I. and me now that we know you're on the mend," George wrote, "is one day leaving Miss Margaret. I'll bet you'll be surprised at how much she's taught us. Once we were settled here, she hasn't missed one day of lessons. For a woman, she surely is smart."

Of course, Lewis's gratitude knew no bounds. Or did it? What about the times he had been forced to admit to himself that he resented Margaret Seton? Not the generous young lady herself, but the fact that it was she and not he teaching his children. It *would* be hard for them to leave her when at last he could take them back. Back where? To one of the cramped primitive outbuildings still standing at Hibernia?

Every time he faced the fact that there was no place to take his children, the still lingering weakness brought despised hot tears. On those days, both his sons appeared to him to be stronger than their father.

Then, one May afternoon Bemrose brought him another letter from Charles Seton—and wonder of wonders—two books. A thin, well-worn Thomas Aquinas and Milton's two long poems *Paradise Lost* and *Paradise Regained*. Propped against the thick ancient trunk of the magnolia he had picked out as his own, he sat holding the books for a long time, the letter unopened. The two volumes from his friend's library were to Lewis dearer than gold. Both had long been favorites. Seton had chosen well. Hours could be filled—days, weeks—if he read slowly. At last, he opened the letter. Seton had such a level head, was a man of such taste and sensitivity, each letter from him had been like a soothing balm to Lewis's soul, raw as it was from so much time spent in crude, brutally primitive surroundings. He felt a surge of hope. Always, in a letter from Seton there was something to which he could hold.

> 1 May 1836
> Calle Amelia, Fernandina
>
> My dear Fleming,
>
> Only my daughter, I suspect, is aware that I am as unwell as I feel, and in view of this, I have thought to write frankly to you today. I do not feel I am in danger of leaving this earth, but that date no man knows. My wife's father, Mr. Charles Sibbald, and Mrs. Sibbald were with us yesterday and he and I spoke at length of you. The tragedy which you have suffered at Hibernia must be faced. There seems to be a way which could solve your problem for the present and that of my father-in-law as well. You will remember that during my last visit to New Switzerland at Christmas now over a year ago, I mentioned Sibbald's need for a competent manager for his Panama Mills operation. He wants you, Fleming. You and your children would be supplied with a good house and the salary is excellent. From it, in a matter of a few years, with his cost price to you of lumber and bricks, you could rebuild your home at Hibernia.

I confess to feeling too poorly today to set down more details. It is simply my fond hope that this bit of news will give you renewed faith in your future. My wife, Matilda, joins me in hoping you will agree to manage her father's mills. Your youngest son, L.I., has had an enormous adventure about which, due to my frail condition, I have asked my daughter, Margaret, to write as an amendment to this letter. Her words giving account of the extreme bravery and skill of your son follow.

Lewis hurried to the next page, written in a fine, slanted hand:

It is my joy to be able to tell you, sir, of your son L.I.'s act of courage. While visiting his grandmother in Jacksonville recently, he volunteered in the presence of Florida's new governor, General Richard Keith Call, to make a fast, hard ride through the woods to Fort Heilman at Middleburg with important messages needed more swiftly than our erring winds could be counted on to make the journey by sailing boat— some twenty miles away. Of course, neither my parents nor Louisa nor I would have agreed had we known. The boy was evidently on his own that day and wanted to please your friend, Governor Call. You have been our hero up until now. But it is my duty to inform you that since our own Louis Isador did this magnificent thing at the tender age of twelve years and with complete and total success, you have, of necessity, been forced to share honors with him. May I be so bold as to add one personal word? While I still cringe at every thought of his making that dangerous ride alone through Indian territory, I am now proud, proud, proud. He not only succeeded, he is not one bit boastful of what he has done. Nor is George one bit jealous. Both boys have seemed to mature from it—L.I., in that he feels a man now, and George, who seems quite willing to accept the fact that a daring and rugged adventure of this nature would be far out of his means to accomplish. What I hope to convey is that, watching them both daily, as I so enjoy doing, I see two very different but very worthy young men developing like wildfire and in good balance about themselves. My father will sign this letter, but I must send the deep and growing love of your children and the warmest love from Sophia and Louisa, who are so proud that you are now *Colonel* Fleming. My mother wants to be remembered to you, too, as do I.

Lewis refolded the letter and slammed it down on the ground beside him. Tears burned his eyes again, but these were angry tears. A surprising anger seemed suddenly to be filling his being like acid poured into an empty jug. He boiled with resentment. Resentment that seemed aimed more at Margaret Seton than at anyone else. *Why wasn't Louisa teaching the children?* Why hadn't *Louisa* been the one to write him of his son's new maturity? At least Louisa was family. Families went the second mile for one another and usually without incurring the outsized amount of indebtedness he felt toward the Setons. Of course, he would have to find a way to earn some money now that his home lay in a charred shambles and, of course, he'd always liked and respected Charles Seton. But it did seem strange that Seton's father-in-law couldn't have made the offer himself. Nothing lined up. The whole matter seemed off kilter.

Unable to sit still a minute longer, he reached for the heavy wooden crutches and, bracing himself against the tree, managed to get to his feet and begin the awkward labor of hobbling in the direction of his hut. The exertion helped. One more moment of sitting like a helpless lump and he would have broken apart with—with what? Obviously, Margaret Seton considers herself benevolent in the extreme, he thought, teaching my children, reporting their achievements to me, and the worst part is that anyone else on the face of the earth would consider her kind, too. Well, I don't! At this minute, *I don't consider Miss Seton anything but an intruder in my life*.

He swung his still-weakened body across the weed-grown yard and up to the doorway of his hut. The effort winded him. The effort and the anger. He leaned against the doorframe and stood looking out across the forlorn, crumbling, filthy spectacle of General Clinch's Auld Lang Syne plantation. How he loathed it. He must drag himself into the miserable hut and rest, but for another minute or so he just leaned there, his eyes closed. "My children don't need her," he said aloud into the spring afternoon in a voice that held no resemblance to his own. "They need their mother!"

"How'd do, Mister," a young woman's voice said brightly. "You talkin' to me?"

Startled, he opened his eyes to see a girl of perhaps sixteen smiling at him, twisting back and forth on one heel, looking straight into his face with luminous eyes, her smile exposing a row of yellow-green stained teeth. Her brown skirt was in tatters and the soiled, ragged military shirt she wore was so much too large for here, the neckline hung low enough so that no one—certainly no man—could avoid seeing the rounded, full breasts.

"I was jist takin' a walk," she said. "Kin I do somepin' fer ya, Mister? You been hurt bad, I hear."

"Yes, I was wounded some time ago," Lewis answered stiffly. "You're—refugeeing here, I suppose?"

She laughed and tossed her tangled brown hair. "You s'pose right. We're from over past Micanopy. Indians burnt our place."

"I see. They burned my home, too."

"You want some comp'ny?"

"Why, no, thank you. I'm fine." Revulsion and pity pushed away some of his senseless anger. "I—have a lot on my mind."

"Betcha I could relieve ya of most of it with some lovin'. Even if you are crippled, I'm not."

She was smiling at him with an almost childlike expression. It was plain to Lewis that the offer she'd just made was, to her, nothing out of the ordinary. He both loathed and pitied her and found himself staring against his will at her breasts and her blue shameless eyes. Fort Drane had always had its share of loose women. So far, Lewis had been too ill to be annoyed by them.

"I ain't never slep' with no real gentleman in my whole life," she said simply. "It's plain you be a gentleman. You got children, ain't you? I heard you say they needed their mother. Your wife leave you fer another man?"

A wave of weakness—near nausea—swept over him. Not anger. Not even disdain. He slumped against the doorframe.

"My—wife is dead."

The girl took a step toward him, her smile gone. "I be turrible sorry. I'd like to help."

He found himself looking again at her breasts. The young skin over them was dirty. Her face was dirty. *She* was dirty. But her sympathy rang true. Except for her kind and the older women who had come and gone from the shelter of Fort Drane, Lewis had not seen a woman since he left St. Augustine.

"We could manage with your bad leg, Mister. Course, you

do look kinda weak an' sick. I reckon I oughtn't to bother you. You sure I can't fetch you nothin'?"

"Yes. Yes, I'm quite sure. I'd be ever so grateful if you'd go, please."

The open smile returned. "All right. But effen you need—*anything*, just tell somebody to go git Fanny. My name's Fanny."

"I see. Well, thank you, Miss Fanny."

"Whoo-ee!" Abruptly, Fanny upended in a cartwheel. As she came back upright, she laughed. "Ain't nobody ever called me *Miss* Fanny before!"

With equal abruptness, she turned and hurried off, whirling once more to wave.

For a long moment, Lewis slumped heavily over his crutches. Then, he began to smile, his anger and resentment drained away. How much of it, he wondered, had really been resentment? Perhaps it was all jealousy that Margaret Seton was with his children and he was not.

Back inside the hut, he sank onto the straight chair by the rickety table and laid the crutches on the dirt floor. He had believed that brazen, unkempt girl! Had believed that she was truly sorry about Augustina and that she had freely offered to help him in the only way she knew.

For perhaps an hour or more, he sat brooding. The camp was full of younger men. Why had she singled him out? That didn't matter either. She would probably be gone by tomorrow. The refugees came and went like rabbits scurrying here and there hunting safe shelter.

He looked down at what remained of his once handsome uniform—the shirt patched and repatched, once laughingly by General Clinch himself. The trousers, one leg cut off, the other hanging tattered and limp, washed in the pond now and then, but never really clean. How long had it been since he'd seen his own reflection in a looking glass? How did he appear to that soiled child who had offered to make love to him? How, for that matter, would he appear to his loved ones if ever the day came when he could leave this filthy hole? He examined his hands. They were bony, the skin thin, though tanned by time sitting in the sun. He felt his hair. Still thick. Evidently, little had fallen out during the fevers when his leg had been gangrenous. Last week, as best he could, hanging his head over a bucket of water strong with lye soap, he had washed his hair. Bemrose had poured a fresh bucket of water over the suds and then vowed that the combing job he, Bemrose, had done, was in the latest style.

A wry, bitter smile came. Fanny had both attracted and repulsed him. I am thirty-seven years old, he thought. No longer young, but neither am I old. Not old enough to be cut off forever from—so much of what a man's life should hold.

Tina had been an infant in his arms the day they buried— so much of his life. Tina was past four now and, if Louisa's letters were any indication, the child had all but found a new mother. Margaret Seton.

He buried his face in his hands and wept—envying his own little girl, who couldn't, no matter how hard she might try, remember her beautiful, once warm, laughing mother.

After a while, he reached again for the crutches and hobbled almost briskly to the still open door. The resentment against Miss Seton, her family—everyone who had known the joy of his children during the long months—was gone. And at least some of the jealousy which had caused it. A more manageable feeling gripped him: deep, painful gratitude. *One more month*. This very morning, Bemrose had said, "One month *if* you work harder than you've ever worked in your life to learn to walk again without those crutches."

He would work. He was going back. A business opportunity was waiting. Charles Sibbald, who would hire him at Panama Mills, was one of the most influential men in Florida. Managing a large lumbering operation would not be Lewis Fleming's choice as a life's work. But it didn't need to be a life's work. He would, of course, be fair to Sibbald in all ways, but Seton had already indicated in his letter that the money earned at the Mills would help rebuild Hibernia. Sibbald would not expect him to stay permanently.

Feeling far less alone and almost hopeful, Lewis swatted at a deerfly.

The truth was, if he faced it squarely, that Miss Seton had been thoughtful to write as she did of L.I.'s daring ride alone from Jacksonville to Middleburg in the dead of the night. She had *not* intruded at all, she had only tried to help him keep up with his own boy. And Margaret Seton is beautiful, he thought. He was even grateful for that now, since his children had been born to the beauty of Augustina.

14

Margaret and L.I. played a game of hopscotch on the hard-packed dirt at the intersection of Calle San Fernando and Calle Amelia which ran by the large, square Seton house in Fernandina.

"Old George is missin' a lot with his nose stuck in a book on a day like this," L.I. said, hopping on one sturdy leg down three squares and back up the other side. "Do you think he's gonna be a preacher or schoolteacher or something, Miss Margaret?"

"I wouldn't be surprised," Margaret said, also hopping lightly through three squares. Then, on one foot, she asked, "Why?"

"Oh, I dunno. He's so serious about books and stuff, he could grow up to be—most anything."

Margaret laughed. "So could you. It's your turn."

L.I. made his hops, then stopped. "Do you know what George told me? He said he couldn't have made that long twenty-mile ride from Jacksonville to Middleburg like I did. Do you think he could?"

"No, I don't. And that's no reflection on George, either. You have different talents."

The boy stood looking down the street deep in thought. "I wasn't scared a bit, except about getting lost."

"Do you think a lot about that long ride, L.I.? At night, perhaps? When you're not quite asleep?"

"I think about a lot of things then. I don't always conk off to sleep as fast as old George says. Sometimes, a lot of times, I think about my mother."

"I'm sure you do."

He sighed heavily. "But, I guess I worry most about Tina. After all, when George and I were little kids, we had—a mother. You kind of need one then, quite a lot."

"Yes, I know."

"You sure do know a lot about—a lot of problems I have, Miss Margaret. I like to talk to you."

She gave him an open, appreciative smile. "Thank you, sir.

I don't quite know how I got along when I didn't have you—and George and Tina—to be with. Well, now," she said brightly, "I'm bored with hopscotch. Shall we go for a walk? Let's go where we can't see a single house or shop. To the old fort?"

"Wanta race?"

"No, I don't. I want to walk—to breathe spring. To—breathe May! All right with you?"

"Sure."

They strolled along hand in hand for two blocks, then turned west toward the Amelia River and the ruins of old Fort San Carlos. At Calle de la Marina, they crossed a field of grass studded with wild flowers, the crumbling tabby foundations of the old Spanish fort in sight.

"Want me to pick you some flowers?" the boy asked.

"I certainly do—on our way home."

After a while, he said softly, "Your house does seem—like my home now."

She squeezed his hand. "If you thought about it all day, you couldn't say anything that would please me more."

They reached the first big slab of ruins and climbed up the powdery sides to the very top and sat down. For the first few moments, they sat drinking in the blue of sky and water.

Then, in a barely audible, husky voice, L.I. asked, "Do you think my father will ever marry anybody else?"

Margaret took her time answering. "You know him far better than I."

L.I. tossed bits of crumbled tabby down into the marsh below for a time, then he said, "My mother was—beautiful. You saw her, didn't you—sometime or other?"

"Oh, yes. And she was not only beautiful, she was so much fun to be with. Your parents visited us once for several days when you were a baby."

"Here in Fernandina?"

"Right here—same house."

She caught his quick frown. "You never did answer my question," he said.

"About your father remarrying someday?"

L.I. nodded.

"What worries you about it?"

"Well, I think Papa's awful changed. He—well, when I was little, he used to laugh as much as anybody. He really had fun, once you got him started. I'm afraid he's gonna be even more changed when he gets back. George says he's—burdened down with grief over our mother. George says Papa'll never get over—losing her."

Margaret laid a hand on his knee, but said nothing.

The boy sighed. "It's all pretty hard to imagine. I mean, what he'll be like. If we'll ever—have good times anymore." Another heavy sigh came. "I—I guess I'm kind of scared he—might be so lonesome for our mother, he'll marry—somebody that—doesn't like me much."

Margaret pulled him to her. "Listen to me a minute. You have one of the finest, most sensitive fathers on earth. He would be sure to take you and George and Tina into first consideration. I know he would think first about all three of you. Why, he could never be happy with anyone who didn't love and understand you."

Picking at a loose shell in a chunk of tabby, L.I. said, "Yeah, I guess you're right." Then he gave her his direct look. "I think you *do* know my father pretty well, Miss Margaret. And, you really haven't been around him much at all."

She weighed her response as carefully as any she'd ever made. "You're plenty old enough to have learned that some things we just—know, L.I. I simply *know* about your father." She made herself laugh lightly. "The way I knew about you—right off. The way you know about me." On her feet in one light motion, she said, "I think we'd better start home. And don't forget, you promised me wild flowers."

Within two blocks of the Seton home, they recognized George galloping toward them on Charles Seton's handsome brown mare. He waved, urgently. Margaret stopped in her tracks. Her hands—one crammed with blue and white flowers—dropped to her sides.

"You—think somepin' bad's wrong, don't you, Miss Margaret?"

"Yes," she gasped, "I do, L.I. Something—horrible."

Her face drained of color, she stood rooted in the sandy street until George rode up.

"What's the matter, George?" L.I. asked.

"Miss Louisa sent me to find you, Miss Margaret." He reached down for her hand. "Get on behind me. I'll take you right home. It's—your father."

*   *   *

Kneeling beside Charles Seton's high, carved bed, Margaret held out her wilting bouquet. "Papa? L.I. and I brought you—flowers."

He opened his eyes and managed a smile. He was in his sixty-second year, his face lined and waxen, but, for an instant, Margaret saw him as she had always pictured him when they were apart—as he was when she was a little girl. As he had been when the miniature she loved was painted in Paris years ago—his shoulder-length, tawny hair full of light, the large, deep brown eyes like pools of dark river water, the barest hint of a smile that said, "Don't do anything to hurt me. I love you."

At last, as though he'd read her thoughts, he whispered, "You've never done anything to—hurt me in all your life, Margaret. If I've hurt you, forgive me. I love you with—all my heart. Now, don't worry too much about your mother. She's—a very strong woman. Stronger by far than I."

With every ounce of her being, Margaret longed to say something—anything that would help him even a little. No words came. Tears streamed down her cheeks, but no words.

He rested a moment, then said, "My—heart acted up—just after you and Fleming's boy left the house."

"I shouldn't have gone! But you seemed the same as—"

His pale hand lifted slightly to stop her. "You—should be with those boys—all you can." Weakness overcame him so that he lay there a long time scarcely breathing.

Margaret stared at him, the limp flowers still clutched in her hand. "I'll—get Mother!"

Ever so slightly, he shook his head. "Not yet. Not until I—tell you that—no matter how long it—takes Fleming to—find out, I believe he will. Try for patience, Daughter. I'll—be closer to you—than now. And—very, very happy for you—both."

Margaret leaned over to kiss him. "Papa," she whispered. "Papa, I love you so much!"

At the door, she took one long look at his serene face, closed his door and almost bumped into her mother, who stood waiting stoically just outside in the hall.

"He—needs you now, Mama. *Now.*"

Matilda Seton, taller than Margaret and always so strong, allowed herself one shuddering, dry sob. When Margaret touched her, she stiffened, stared for a moment at the closed door, her face like stone. "If he needs me, I'll go," she said as to a stranger. "Today is no time to stop trying—to give him everything he needs."

Louisa, Margaret and the two boys waited for over an hour in the upstairs sitting room across the wide hall, in full view of the still closed door.

"Louisa?"

"Yes, Margaret?"

"Do you—think Papa's gone? Could Mother just—be sitting—with him?"

"I don't know, my dear. And I don't know how to go about finding out. Your mother is so—different from most of us."

Margaret nodded. "She's very strong."

"Maybe—maybe he's—just better," L.I. offered.

They sat without speaking for another time, then L.I. said, "Me and George will—be right with you, Miss Margaret."

"Oh, yes," George said. "Right here with you."

Her eyes bright with tears, Margaret whispered, "I don't know what I'd do without the two of you."

"Honest?" L.I. asked.

"Honest."

Slowly, quietly, the door opened and Matilda Seton walked steadily into the hall. "He's gone," she said. "Your father isn't here—with us any longer."

"Mama!"

"I'm all right, Margaret. I'll be in my room. I don't need a thing. Except that—you'll have to make arrangements. I'll want no supper." Then, "Louisa? I'm glad you're here."

When she had gone, Margaret wept like a child on Louisa's shoulder. Sensing that their adored Miss Margaret needed her grown-up friend now, the boys slipped away.

"I know, Margaret," Louisa comforted. "I know. Believe me—I know." The weeping continued, Louisa holding her. "My dear, I want you to believe also—that I know how much you—need Lewis now."

Margaret lifted her tear-streaked face to look at Louisa. "How—do you—know that? When—Lewis doesn't?"

"Because I loved my father as much as you loved yours. And—I didn't have—Roger when Papa died. I—couldn't even let Roger know. But you can. I'll handle everything here. The boys will help me. And I feel strongly that it will help you—if you sit down just as soon as you're able and write to Lewis. He loved your father very much."

"It—wouldn't be—forward of me?"

"Indeed, it would not. Do it now, please."

15

Margaret's letter reached Fort Drane on May 9. Bemrose brought it when he came that cloudy morning ready for the big event. Today, the heavy wooden splints would be unstrapped and never put back.

Eagerly, Lewis took the letter, examined it, saw that it was from Margaret Seton and tossed it aside.

Bemrose laughed. "Never saw you so casual about a letter before, Colonel. You must really want to be rid of these splints. For once, I have time to wait if you care to read it first."

"No," Lewis answered, his mind entirely on what Bemrose was about to do. "Right now, nothing matters but being free of those splints. Take them off."

The splints removed, Bemrose carefully examined the withered leg, feeling the flabby muscles, urging Lewis to bend his knee back and forth, no matter how much it hurt. "Well, sir," he said finally, "it looks good. If you'll massage the leg well, I'd say by next week we should try to put some weight on it."

Lewis grinned. "Without those clumsy crutches?"

Bemrose nodded. "And as soon as you can walk in reasonable comfort—after you've toughened up the muscles—you'll be released. You can—*go home*."

Lewis's grin faded. "That's just where I'm going first. Back to my old home at Hibernia. To see what's left of it."

Bemrose stood up, his hands on his hips. "I was sure you'd say that, but you won't be up to it. We'll have to work here for at least three weeks and even then, you're going to need help—lots of it. You're going to Fernandina, Colonel. You must have family care."

"Nonsense!"

"You'll see what I mean once you try to walk on that leg. Five months of inactivity is a long time." Bemrose clapped a hand on Lewis's shoulder. "We've had a hard pull of it, sir.

You must do as I say. And don't get too frisky. You can walk—but not this week without those crutches."

"We'll see about that," Lewis joked.

When the young aide had gone, Lewis sat for a long time staring at the shriveled, scarred leg. The only pair of trousers he had left had one leg whacked off to accommodate the splints. Oh, well, he thought. Who cares at this point how I look around here? And, General Scott had promised a new pair for the day he could leave. Louisa had thought to send him a fresh shirt. His old officer's jacket hung on a peg on the wall of the crude hut, but it was already too hot for a jacket. He smiled crookedly. Of course, he meant to look his best when the children saw him for the first time again, but there was no way whatever of knowing what his best might be by now.

He picked up Margaret's letter and reached for the crutches. His injured leg felt naked. It had been bandaged and splinted for nearly half a year. He felt naked, too. Nervous. Vulnerable. Night and day he had dreamed of the moment when he could leave Fort Drane and now that the time was near, he felt as helpless as a child.

The letter crushed in his hand as he gripped the heavy crutches, he swung his tall body along over the rough ground toward his favorite magnolia tree, the wounded leg held, from habit, off the ground. From habit, or from fear of touching it down? He stopped within a few feet of the ancient tree, his breath short from unaccustomed excitement. The unopened letter still crumpled between his hand and the crutch, he took one step barely touching the bad leg to the ground. Then another. And another. It was a dead leg! He tried to laugh. How could a dead leg hurt so much?

At the tree, he tossed the crutches to the ground and, his hands behind him against the gray trunk, eased himself down into the familiar, almost comfortable spot where he had passed so many long hours.

"I'll—have to get a lot stronger than this in—two or three weeks—or I'll prove Bemrose right," he said aloud, still panting. "I'll also have to break this habit of talking to myself once I'm back with the children. They'll think their old father has lost more than the good use of one leg."

Slowly, carefully, he smoothed the creases from Margaret's letter, which he still held. It was thoughtful of her to take the time to report on how the children were doing in their studies. He broke the seal and scanned the first two pages bearing the news of his friend Seton's death. His eyes filled with tears. So many tears, he laid the letter aside unfinished. Uncontrollably, unashamedly, he sobbed, both hands covering his face. His friend Seton would not be there! He would now have two graves to visit: one at Hibernia and one at Bosque Bello Cemetery in Fernandina.

A cart rattled toward him down the road. Quickly he dried his eyes and sat staring at the ground until the cart passed out of sight. Why had the news of Seton's death struck such a hard blow? Seton had warned him of failing health. "I had counted on him," he said hoarsely. "The blow is so hard because—I had counted on the man. Counted on his help when I go to work for Sibbald! Seton knew how strange it would be for me to try to manage sawmills."

His hands trembling, he picked up the letter, tears coursing again down his cheeks. This time, for shame. Not for the tears, for his own selfishness. He was thinking only of how much *he* needed Seton.

Without doubt, his children were suffering, too. Charles Seton was the kind of man one came quickly to love, revere, depend upon. And poor Louisa, taking complete charge, he was sure, of still another funeral—still another death to scar her gentle life. His thoughts went to Matilda Seton, with whom he'd never felt well acquainted. Did she have the inner resources she seemed to have? Was she enduring the same shattering disbelief that he had endured when Augustina died? Did strength really have anything to do with the depth of grief?

"I have written this," Margaret's letter went on, "at Louisa's urgent request. I frankly felt hesitant. Not wanting to add to your burdens with my own sharp sorrow."

He let the page fall again. Until she mentioned it herself, he had still not given one thought to Miss Margaret's grief.

A fly bit his naked, tender leg. Too much is happening too fast for me, he thought, wincing from the pain as his hand brushed at the pest.

"I know with my whole being," Margaret Seton wrote, "that this is but a temporary separation. I will see him again, as you will one day see your lovely wife. If I did not have that sure knowledge, I would not want to live any longer on this earth without my father. Forgive me if this seems impertinent, but I find it easier to tell you in a letter, that I have, in a vivid way, lived through your grief, Colonel Fleming. The loss of exceptional beauty may be the keenest loss of all."

Lewis let the pages fall to his lap. What an amazing thing for her to have written! She, along with her parents, had been most kind to have come to Hibernia to help out when Augustina left him, but—he frowned. To see in her own handwriting that Seton's daughter had *experienced* some of his pain seemed almost too strange to believe. He reread that, then went on: "I pray you will accept this understanding of at least a part of your suffering in the spirit in which I send it. The only way I know to express it is that I have wept often over Mrs. Fleming's death. And, in my own way, have tried to support your children during their lonely months without you."

The letter ended rather formally, with the good word that her mother, as they all expected, was bearing up well.

Lewis stared, still frowning, into the green-white late spring air. No definite thoughts formed in his mind. He was trying to think, but the outcome was anything but logical. Bright and dark images seemed to float through his brain like butterflies—weightless, highly colored, testing this imaginary flower and that—never lighting long enough anywhere for him to be sure. Sure of what? Of anything.

He was certain that Miss Seton had written sincerely. There was no nonsense about the young woman. He'd rather taken that for granted during their brief and, to him, almost unnoted meetings. For all the months at Fort Drane, he had felt gratitude—in spite of the jealousy—because she had taken his children into her home.

The idea that she had cared enough to weep for Augustina, was too new, too startling, for him to comprehend.

He closed his eyes and leaned his head against the trunk of the tree. Poor Seton, he thought, as one tends to pity the dead. And then he remembered what Seton's daughter had written: The separation will only be temporary. That he would see his own father again in some future life had not seemed too remote, nor had he dwelled on it. Not once had the reality of Augustina's ongoing life been within his grasp. He missed her laughter too much, the touch of her hands on his face, her warm, soft body beside him at night. Since her death, she had always only been lying out there in the cemetery at Hibernia under the sandy ground—cold. A life-less, pale end to his every thought of ever being whole again.

With a sinking feeling, he remembered how he had counted on Seton's actually going with him for the first interview with Charles Sibbald.

Lewis sat up abruptly, feeling trapped by the necessity of accepting a position for which he would never be fitted! He felt capable of doing it. But Lewis Fleming had always been a planter—the manager and owner of his own land. He would hate being superintendent of a sawmill, even a large, thriving operation such as Charles Sibbald owned in Panama Mills. He would loathe the constant noise and hubbub. Contact with the caliber of men who worked at a mill would do his sons no good. Tina would have to be watched continuously. He could, of course, count on Maum Easter's going with them, but a little girl in such surroundings needed a mother.

He was tired. His back ached. He reached for his crutches and pulled himself painfully to his feet. The two wounded army officers who had shared his cabin had been released late yesterday. He could be alone there. Could think more clearly.

As he adjusted the crutches, he saw Margaret Seton's letter still on the ground. A man on tall, heavy crutches can't bend to pick up anything! If swearing had been a habit, he would have sworn. He would *need* that letter. He would need it to help clarify his confusion.

Slamming the crutches to the ground, he eased himself back down beside the tree and reached for the folded pages. There. "Struggle to your feet again, old man," he mumbled, "and you're ready to go."

Was he? Less so, surely, than before he had read the letter. And yet, stark need consumed him. He felt as though he could not wait to reach the cabin in order to reread every word.

As best he could, across the stubbly ground, he hurried.

Just before dawn the next morning, Lewis dreamed of his late friend Charles Seton. In the dream the slow, gentle, knowing smile came to Seton's living face and he heard his friend's voice plainly: "My daughter, Margaret, is at times, hard to believe. Oh, not that her word isn't good. She's disarmingly honest. It is Margaret herself, who, with all her impetuosity, is hard for a man to take in. For example, can you believe that in no way has the girl ever disappointed me?"

The dream brought Lewis bolt upright on his lumpy straw

pallet. He was wide awake and too captive to the dream to consider even one more attempt at sleep. He lay there until the first dim, gray sign of dawn lightened the one high window. The dream did not fade. Lewis knew only that he had been given an inexplicable *hope* which he did not begin to understand. Bemrose had said that he could try to walk in a few days. Why not now? Alone in the hut, he would need feel no embarrassment if he failed.

He reached for the crutches and pulled himself to a standing position. Slowly, carefully, he tried a little weight on the injured leg. It hurt, but he had grown accustomed to pain. His body jerking sharply, he took one and then two steps, still leaning on the crutches. Suddenly, he tossed them back onto his bed and stood alone on the dirt floor. Out of breath already from the ordeal, so weak he felt the cabin turn around him, he gritted his teeth and tried one step. The leg felt as though it belonged to someone else. He took one and then two more steps. He waited, then tried again. He had taken three steps! Breathing loudly and hoarsely, he stood in the middle of the floor—frighteningly far from the bed where his crutches lay. And he was alone.

Standing very still, he felt the panic begin to fade. He would simply wait for a return of his strength and *walk* back to his bed. In the midst of his struggle, the dream was still there. Seton's voice, urging him on, Seton's face—the dark eyes certain and full of faith.

Still standing, Lewis rubbed his eyes roughly, then his whole face, in an effort to convince himself that he was truly awake. His friend was dead, but somehow, again, he had given to Lewis. This time Seton had given much more than news of the offer of a position from which Lewis could support his children and one day rebuild his home. But what *was* the new gift Seton had made? Lewis could feel his heart pound. The three-step walk back to the bed did not frighten him. He would simply make it. And he did.

At noon, with Bemrose beside him, beaming—he walked again without crutches. This time from the magnolia tree to a camp stool which the young aide had placed a reasonable distance away, where Lewis could rest before retracing his struggling steps.

"You amaze me, Colonel!" Bemrose said warmly. "I—wasn't expecting results like this for—"

"Yes, I know, Bemrose. Not for another week. Well, perhaps I can explain. You see, I'm suddenly in more of a hurry to—get to Fernandina." Lewis smiled sheepishly. "You'll be glad to know that I've weakened. I'm not going to Hibernia first." He could hear some of the old vitality in his voice. It buoyed him. "Bemrose?"

"Yes, sir?"

"Do you believe in dreams?"

"I'm usually too tired to dream, Colonel."

"But do you believe a mere dream—could put a drastically new idea in a man's head?"

"I suppose so."

Still smiling, Lewis said, "Do you want me to tell you something? I *know* it can." He reached for a hand up from the camp stool. "Now, come on. It's time to try it again. Then, this afternoon, I'll write my sons to come for me in— two weeks."

"Three weeks, Colonel. We still have a lot of work to do."

Lewis sighed. "All right. Three weeks. But not a day longer."

"Are your sons old enough to make that trip alone? They can come by water to Jacksonville, but there's still a long ride."

On his feet, Lewis announced: "My youngest son, Louis Isador, will see that his brother, George, makes it just fine. My horse, Cotter, will look after me."

16

For the third time, Margaret took all the snapdragons and yellow roses out of a silver vase in the room that would be Lewis's and rearranged them in a still different way.

Louisa laughed. "They're beautiful, Margaret. Don't touch them again."

Facing her friend, Margaret said solemnly, "Louisa—I'm scared. I've waited so long for this day and now I'm scared."

"Of course, you are. But, I promise it will be all right. The children will have his full attention for a while. You'll have plenty of time to make the—bridge from—"

"—from what I've imagined for so long to—what it might really be like!" Her voice shook.

Louisa's firm, steadying look helped. Her hands trembling, Margaret moved one yellow rose to the other side of the bouquet. Then, she stood to her full five feet four and said, "I'll—still wait, Louisa. No matter how long it takes."

On June 9, astride Cotter, riding proudly but wearily between his two sons, Lewis entered the lane that led to the large, commodious Seton home. On the front porch, he could see Louisa and Sophia and Mrs. Seton. Maum Easter was there, too, restraining Tina in her ample arms. Lewis waved.

The boys, acting very grown-up, slid from their horses to help their father dismount, and Maum Easter let Tina go. Her cries of "Papa, Papa," as she ran to him in the driveway, caused Lewis's heart to swell until he thought it might burst. He was still too weak to pick her up, and so, awkwardly, he bent to embrace her as the child clung first to his arms and then his legs. More than he remembered, she looked like Augustina. How long he hugged and kissed the child, he had no idea. Nor did he care. The others could wait.

It was Tina who grabbed his hand finally and hurried him, as fast as his severe limp would allow, toward the front porch.

"Lewis—oh, Lewis," Louisa exclaimed, her arms outstretched. "Lewis, you look fine! You're thin—but you look just fine."

"But—you are thin as a rail!" Sophia shrilled, weeping.

"I'm all right, Cousins. I'm—all right."

"Papa," Tina cried. "Papa, come here." Over to one side of the big porch, the child was holding Margaret Seton's hand, jumping up and down.

"Just a minute, Tina. Your old father's slowed down considerably." He bowed to Matilda Seton and took her hand in his. "More than gratitude to you, Mrs. Seton—more than my sympathy," he said, "you have my—shared grief in your loss. I thought no more highly of any man than your husband. I already miss him."

"Thank you, Colonel Fleming," Matilda said, her voice steady, but warm. "Your children have been most welcome—as are you, now."

"Papa! Papa, come *here!*" Tina was trying now to drag Margaret forward.

"I'm coming, Tina, but I haven't hugged Maum Easter

yet." He felt the plump, familiar arms encircle him and strength flowed into his entire being. "Thank you, Maum Easter—for all you've done. Is Pompey all right back—home?"

Lewis saw her mouth tremble and hugged her again. "You two should never be apart," he said.

"That's right, Mausa Lewis. The last I hear, he's doin' good as he could—without me."

"*Papa!*"

This time, Tina's voice commanded. Slowly, trying extra hard not to limp quite so much, Lewis made his way to where the child and Margaret stood. He bowed deeply. "How indebted I am to *you*, Miss Seton."

For an instant, he was so stunned by how much her dark, knowing eyes were like her father's, Lewis could think of nothing further to say. Margaret was silent, too. He focused his gaze on the fluff of bright curls above her forehead, then their eyes caught. Even Tina was quiet, standing as were the others—watching.

"Colonel Fleming," Margaret said finally and curtsied, then laid her hand on Tina's dark, thick hair.

She loves Tina, Lewis thought. She loves—my child. My Tina, so like her mother.

"May I—present my best friend, Miss Margaret Seton?" Tina chimed proudly as though she'd just that minute remembered rehearsing her little speech. "Miss Margaret, this is—my papa!"

"Your father and I have met before, darling. But thank you for the beautiful introduction. Welcome to Fernandina, Colonel Fleming." Then, her smile flashed and she said in the confident, cheerful manner that Lewis vaguely remembered. "You walk extremely well, Colonel. You must have practiced faithfully!"

For more than five long, empty months, he had accomplished nothing beyond managing to stay alive and learning to walk again. How did this surprising young lady know that to be complimented on his halting gait would please him more than anything anyone could say? The thought made him feel foolish. He would have to learn how to be with his own kind again. Too much time had been spent alone in that rough, isolated world—and inside his own head—nearly every conscious moment focused on his injured leg.

"You must be very tired," Matilda Seton said somewhere in the little group standing behind him.

"An' hungry!" boomed Easter.

"You know Easter hopes you're hungry," Louisa laughed. "I think we just avoided a battle royal in the kitchen this morning. You did what I suggested, didn't you, Easter?"

Lewis smiled at the familiar pout which seized Easter's normally pleasant mouth.

"Yes'um, I done it. *She* makin' the biscuits *her* way." Easter straightened her shoulders. "But all the rest of Mausa Lewis's first dinner—I do *my* way. Shrimp pilau, collards an' *my* Lady Baltimore Cake!"

The easy laughter all around helped enormously. Lewis was peripherally aware that he had not responded to Margaret Seton's compliment about how well he walked. He bowed to her again, hoping that would suffice. He was tired. More tired than hungry, but if Maum Easter had dinner ready, he'd eat. No one needed to explain that Easter and the Seton's cook did not get along.

Without a word, Easter, mumbling to herself about Lewis having to eat half-Indian biscuits, left the porch. Louisa steered the others into the spacious Seton parlor, then left to see about the tea, taking Sophia along. Lewis sank heavily onto a handsome, ornately carved horsehair sofa, Tina immediately on his lap and, before anyone had to think of something to say, L.I. and George strode proudly into the room.

"Horses all right, boys?" Lewis asked.

"Sure, Papa. I think even George is learning how to handle horses," L.I. grinned and placed himself directly behind his father, a hand on each of Lewis's shoulders.

"Why don't you sit down, son?"

"Oh, I'm not a bit tired. Go on, George. You sit beside Papa."

When his tall, quiet eldest son sat beside him, Lewis communicated with him in the way he'd always done—a hand on George's bony knee.

"Why do you look so pale now that we're here, Papa?" L.I. asked, leaning around to look at him. "You didn't look so bad before—even with all the weight you lost. You sure you feel all right?"

Turning on his lap so quickly to hug him that she hurt his bad leg, Tina began to cry.

"Here, here," Lewis said. "What's wrong with my girl?"

"I think she's just overly excited," Margaret said.

"Miss—Margaret—" Tina choked out the words—"I—don't—want my papa—to die, too!"

Lewis's weary face went whiter still. He looked for help first from Mrs. Seton, then Margaret. Did Tina remember her mother's death after all? Or was it the more recent death of Charles Seton that had so frightened her? He held her very close, not knowing what to say

"You don't have a thing to worry about, Tina," Margaret said. "Your father wouldn't be here if he weren't almost well. Did you forget? He's back with you because he's going to be just fine from now on."

"Yes, yes, I—forgot." Lewis felt Tina disengage her arms from around his neck. She sniffled moistly, eased herself down from his lap and ran to Margaret.

His momentary jealousy vanished into—grateful relief. He could not have explained why at that moment, but it was more than all right with him, it was good that Tina loved the beautiful young lady who sat quite straight in a high-backed chair across the room, firmly holding his little girl's hand.

A week passed pleasantly, Lewis reveling in the care and love he received on every side. Daily, Margaret Seton maneuvered him and Louisa off alone for long talks. He told his cousin all he knew of the opportunity at Panama Mills; he spoke at length—to Louisa only—of his battle experiences, but not until another week had gone by did either mention the almost total damage at Hibernia and New Switzerland.

"Sophia and I will never again be your neighbors across the river, Lewis," Louisa said one showery afternoon, as they sat together on the Seton front porch. "There is some money. Maybe enough to rebuild our house again, but it would be foolish to do it. I have no one to run such a big plantation. I will have to see to future income. Sophia needs me and may always need me." She smiled. "And—you and I aren't as young as we once were."

Lewis studied his cousin's quiet face. In spite of the warm hospitality of the Setons, he could tell that Louisa was tired—inside. And, today was not the first time he had considered how lonely life at New Switzerland must have been for her after most of her family had died.

"You're always welcome to move in with us, Cousin," he said. "Of course, I have no house at the moment." After a big sigh, he added, "I may not have one at Hibernia for years.

But we'll have some kind of shelter at Panama Mills. You and Sophia would be more than welcome."

"I know that, Lewis. But you mustn't saddle yourself with two old maid cousins. Not at this stage of your life. All manner of good and wonderful things may lie ahead for you. It came to me this morning before I was out of bed that right now can be a whole new beginning for Lewis Fleming. You deserve the best."

"So do you."

She smiled. "I'll make it the best, whatever I do. Don't worry. And don't add Sophia and me to your burdens. You have enough. I want to stay here until you're settled at the Mills. I might be able to help you do that. Then, Sophia and I will move to St. Augustine. We have friends left there. We can make new ones. It's the Fatio city, you know. Our families began there—both the Fatios and the Flemings. I love the town. I'm sure we can find rooms or a small house to begin with and, then, I'm going to look around for a way to earn some money. Rent rooms, maybe open a small guest house. I'd like that." She laughed at herself. "I've run a big house for so long, I'd be like a fish out of water, if I couldn't ever again run something." They sat quietly, watching the soft rain fall on the wide front lawn of the Seton house. Then Louisa added, "I'm not worried about us."

"Well, you mustn't worry about the children and me, either. I won't have it. Being a mill superintendent isn't my idea of fulfillment, but every day I work there I'll be moving closer and closer to Hibernia again. A new goal will stiffen my spine. I need that."

Louisa reached for his hand. "Lewis? You're not as—downcast as you expected to be, are you?"

He smiled a little. "Frankly, no. I won't really rest until I'm up to that trip back home to see it all for myself. To—visit Augustina's grave. But no, wise woman, I'm not downcast. I'm not quite sure why, but I'm not."

"Lewis! Don't you have the faintest idea why?"

He turned in his chair to look straight at her. "Yes. I admit it's a very faint idea right now, but, yes—I do." He looked away. "Cousin? I may be a touch crazy from all the months of confinement, but—do you think Miss Margaret might—marry me?"

He was looking directly at her again. Her good, open face

broke into a beautiful smile, but all she said was, "Lewis! Oh, Lewis!"

"Well?"

"How long have you known your feelings about her?"

"I'm not sure I do know them. But—for a reason I can't explain, Miss Margaret is *in* my new belief in myself. I'm still a cripple. I may always be. And during those months at Fort Drane, I felt a complete failure not being able to raise a finger to help the children when they lost their home."

"The children had a minimum of trouble, Lewis. Oh, it was a terrifying experience for them actually watching their home burn with you gone. But once we reached Fernandina, they've been fine. Missing you, but fine. Once we knew you were alive. I see no damage to any of the three. I see growth, in fact. And now, you're back."

"Do you—think she'll have me? The children need her."

He felt Louisa studying him for a long time. At last, she said, "That isn't for me to say. But this is. Don't ask Margaret to marry you only for the children's sake. I'm not related to her, but I care about her as much as I care about you." She paused. "I don't think you should say one more word about it to me. Since you have your confidence back, the next step, without doubt, is a talk with Margaret herself."

"But you know her so well, Louisa. Can't you even give me a clue as to how she might respond to me? My confidence *is* returning, but—I've been shattered for a long time. Ever since Augustina died. I haven't felt really adequate—since she left me, Louisa. Do you understand that?"

"Yes. But I also understand that this is no place for a third party. I could give you a clue as to how to act with Margaret, but I wouldn't do it for a rich farm in Georgia! And don't ask me to talk to her for you, either. I love you both too much."

"But, I never see her alone. The children won't let her out of their sight."

"Well," she said, a small smile playing around her generous mouth. "I might be able to help out there. I'll try."

"Perhaps you could speak to her—the two of you arrange a meeting."

"I'll do no such thing, Lewis. But I will tell you this much. You've slept late since you've been here and most likely don't know that Margaret takes an early morning walk every day it isn't raining—alone. Before breakfast."

"Thank you, Cousin. Tomorrow morning, if this rain stops—

I'll be up and outside long before breakfast. At dawn, in fact. Is that early enough?"

"I expect so."

The rain lasted for three more days and Lewis felt he had struggled no harder back at Fort Drane to learn to walk again, than he struggled through those wet, endless days. The struggle sprang from having to go on acting formally with Margaret Seton when he went on feeling less and less formal. Perhaps *formal* was not the word. Merely—*congenial*. And she seemed not to help at all. He had remembered her as far more outgoing, far more talkative and gay. Ever since he reached Fernandina, she had somewhat puzzled him. Undoubtedly, she was simply being herself, with no idea of what he had in his mind. How could she have an idea? Oh, she was warm and natural and playful with the children, but each time he entered a room, her manner seemed to change. Not impolitely. Far from it. Around him, she simply seemed almost to withdraw. Once he had caught her on the floor with Tina, both on their hands and knees racing on all fours from one end of the long parlor to the other. The instant Lewis had limped into the room, the race ended abruptly—Margaret Seton jumping to her feet and assuming her most proper demeanor. He had met no more charming young woman. He should read nothing into any of it, but he did. And what he read threatened his tiny amount of returning confidence.

On the fourth morning, he did what he had done for the past three rainy mornings. He awoke before dawn, sat for a while on the edge of his bed, flexing his bad leg until he felt able to limp to the window to look out. This morning, the lightening sky was pink, underpinned with streaks of gold. The rain was over.

His heart pounded as he bathed, shaved and dressed as quietly as possible. He meant to try to make his way alone down the stairs and be waiting on the front porch when she came outside. To allow her to get a head start would be folly. He'd never catch up with her.

For the first time, he managed it down the stairs without help and let himself out the wide, paneled front door. Winded from the effort, he perched on the banister—preferring a chair—but wanting to appear perfectly able to take a walk. Perhaps she would think him up to it if he perched and did not collapse, as he longed to do.

A scarlet tanager began to sing loudly somewhere out of sight in the tall gum trees in one corner of the Seton yard. One dove voiced its lonely call.

"My call," he whispered to himself. Then a bright crimson cardinal not six feet away in an oleander bush began to sing his throbbing love song—more and more loudly—until Lewis had to smile a little, in spite of his nervousness.

The front door opened behind him, ever so softly—and Margaret Seton walked onto the porch, such a childlike look of surprise on her lovely face that Lewis wondered if she were even as old as he thought.

"Colonel Fleming!"

Standing, Lewis bowed. "Miss Seton. Good Morning. The rain has finally gone away."

"Yes," she said. Then, "Who helped you down the stairs?"

"No one. I came alone this time. I—felt like taking a walk." He laughed almost shyly. "At least, I felt like trying. Will you do me the honor of going along beside me?"

Slowly, Lewis straining to control his limp, they walked along Calle Amelia, exchanging polite small talk about the weather, Margaret explaining what she knew of the progress being made on the new U.S. fort at Fernandina to be named for his friend, General Duncan Clinch. Lewis was interested, of course, but impatient. He could not go far; there wasn't much time to say what he meant to say to her.

"I feel right at home in Fernandina," he said. "I did a lot of growing up in this area."

"Yes, I know."

"You do?"

She laughed. "I'm afraid I've badgered poor Louisa to tell me everything about—her life back then. I know that your families had to flee the Indians once before. In 1812. That eventually you both ended up in the Fernandina area. I wasn't quite in the world yet when Hibernia burned the first time. Not until the next year, 1813."

"Then you're twenty-three."

"In November of this year."

"I'm thirty-eight," he said.

"Yes, I know. Are we walking too fast, Colonel Fleming?"

"Oh, no. Not at all."

"I loved your home at Hibernia. I was looking out my window at the Fatio house—admiring your roofline across the river when—"

"Louisa told me. Miss Margaret, we can talk about houses and family history anytime. I—I made my way down those stairs this morning purposely to speak alone with you." They turned the corner into Calle White. "You see, I simply had to tell you how deeply I appreciate all you've done for my children. They love you very, very much."

"You've already told me—more than often enough. I love them."

"Y-yes," he stammered, "I know, but there's more. My children do love you. And—I think, so do I."

He stepped on a pine cone and stumbled. She caught his arm. "You—you *love* me?"

"I—need you in every way a man ever needed a woman, Miss Margaret. And—just this minute. I no longer—*think* I love you. I know I do. For yourself. Even if there were no children."

Looking straight up into his eyes, she said, as though they were alone in all the world, "Colonel Fleming, that's a very inviting brick wall over there. Shouldn't we both sit down and collect ourselves?"

Side by side on the low, moss-covered wall, they sat like children, clutching hands until their knuckles turned white. He could hear her quick breathing—and his own.

After a minute or so, Margaret lifted their clasped hands and gave a small, relieved laugh. "Well, sir, it appears that I'm holding your hand as desperately as you're holding mine. You must know I love you, too."

"No man ever loved a woman more than I loved—Augustina," he said earnestly. "I want you to know that."

"I've known it since I was a young girl. You two were always my dream lovers. The most beautiful people I'd ever met."

He stared at her. "Is that—true?"

She nodded. "I have to be as honest as you. I loved you, I knew *how* I loved you—the day of her service in the cemetery at Hibernia. I've been waiting all this time. Ask Louisa. She's known since that day. I hope none of this offends you. I expect you to go right on loving Augustina, too."

"You won't feel shut out sometimes?"

"Oh, I can't promise that. But you and I are alive on this earth."

He grasped both her hands. "Yes. We are."

The sun was moving up the light blue sky, bees doned

nearby among the tiny white curled petals of a large clump of jasmine.

"There is one thing," she said at last.

"What? Anything!"

"A formality." She gave him her melting smile. "You haven't asked me to marry you yet."

"I haven't? Are you sure?" And then he laughed. A good hearty laugh at himself. "Miss Margaret, I can't make it to my knees, but will you marry me?"

"Yes, Colonel Fleming. And for one more big reason aside from loving you and your children. I want you to go on smiling like that—for always."

17

In the paneled, high-ceilinged dining room of the Seton home there was a dinner the very next day in celebration of the upcoming marriage. It was Louisa's idea, but Matilda Seton was, as always, amenable and cooperative. Try as she did, Margaret could not tell the extent of her mother's happiness for her. Matilda smiled during the lavish meal, but said little beyond what was required of her as hostess. She seemed neither pleased nor displeased. Simply present. There was no doubt about any of the others—Louisa, Sophia, Margaret, Lewis—and the children made no effort to contain their joy.

L.I.'s first reaction when Lewis had told him was a loud whoop. Then, his open, boyish face contorted with the poignancy of the thought, he asked with his whole heart: "Papa, don't you wish we could—tell Mama how happy we all are right this minute—about Miss Margaret and all?"

To Lewis, L.I.'s question revealed everything: He had not, would not, forget his mother. But he was happy to the bursting point that they would now have Margaret Seton in their lives every day.

"Miss Margaret won't ever leave us again, will she, Papa?" Tina's dark eyes were full of wonder.

"Not ever, Tina. Not ever."

Finally, after some silent thought, George said, "Will we live at Hibernia again sometime?"

"You bet we will, George. If I keep my health, we'll live at Hibernia again. I've set a goal—five years. No longer."

"Oh, boy," L.I. breathed. "Five years. I'll be seventeen!"

George said, "I'll be nineteen."

"How old will I be, Papa?" Tina wanted to know.

"About ten, honey. You'll be a big girl. But we've a lot of living to do in those five years. And, while it won't be Hibernia, we're all going to look forward to our time at Panama Mills as an adventure. Agreed?"

L.I. gave his father a big smile. "Sure. Miss Margaret'll be there, won't she?"

Her open window showed only the first light of a new day. Margaret was awake, still in bed, but thinking as though it were high noon. Two weeks had passed since Lewis asked her to marry him—two weeks without a private talk with her mother about it all. She was not surprised. Any such personal conversation would have to be instigated by Margaret. She and her mother seldom shared confidences. Oh, there had been long hours spent alone with Matilda Seton while her father was away at his mercantile office and her brother, George, fishing or at school at the North. Their conversation had always been pleasant enough—Matilda Seton had tutored her carefully, had taught her to sew and, of course, they freely discussed their Fernandina neighbors—but always with a kind of polite formality. Her childhood heartaches had been poured out to her father and, after his death, to Louisa. Mama's waiting for me to make the first move, she thought, half tenderly, half annoyed. She would never risk appearing nosy. Even with me.

It was still too early to meet Lewis for their now ritual morning walk, but Margaret jumped out of bed and went to the east window to see what the sun was doing to the sky this day. From her earliest memory of herself, she had done this eagerly each morning. Her mother, when Margaret was very small and ill with some childhood disease, had to make a point of arriving at Margaret's room before sunrise in order to keep her in bed "where any sick child belonged." But mornings had always meant one shining thing to Margaret—hope. Hope was still far more than a heart-lifting word. With her, it was a way of life and what the sun had planned for each day was bound inexorably with hope. If clouds covered the color of a sunrise, she needn't mind. The sun was rising anyway. And Margaret loved cloudy days and rain. Even wild coastal storms sent shivers of delight through her. God spoke in the thunder and God loved her. She had that straight because her father had formed her early concept of God as does any father. God, to any child's mind, she believed, was very like the child's earthly father—good and gentle and loving and strong as Charles Seton had been or angry and spiteful and frightening as some other fathers she'd known about.

"What will be in this day?" she whispered to the sun, beginning now to light the earth, its brilliance this morning shut off by such a thick, cloudlike white fog, it set her to thinking again of her mother. Fog. That was it. There was so often a kind of thick fog around her mother. More evident since Papa's death. Mama's protection, she guessed, against showing her broken heart to anyone. All right. Maybe that's the only way she could handle her grief. Margaret had wept and wept for her father, had minded no one seeing her red, swollen eyes. But she was not Matilda Seton, she was Margaret Seton and there was a difference. A difference as wide as the ocean out there.

Thinking of her mother as Matilda Seton helped suddenly. Thinking about one's mother as anyone other than Mother, she supposed, did not come easily. But her mother was—a mere woman, too. A grieving woman, soon to be alone in the big house, which, for her, would still hold memories of the voices and the laughter of her husband—of Margaret's brother, George, now living at the North—of Margaret herself.

Maybe Mama's longing to talk to me, too, she thought. I'll try it once Lewis and the boys have gone to Panama Mills.

She would be vastly relieved when Lewis's position with her grandfather was settled. They were to be married once cautious Lewis had found a suitable house at Panama Mills—"at least half good enough for you," he had said in a firm voice. "I must find our home first and have it refurbished. It won't be like your home here—but we'll be together. I need some time, but we'll be married, my darling," he promised, "no later than spring of next year."

She bathed and dressed in the soft blue cotton Lewis loved. Until she heard him moving about in his room, she would just watch the sun behind its cloud of bright fog and think about tonight when, as every night since they had admitted their love, he would hold her and kiss her in the hallway outside her bedroom door.

* * *

Within a week, Lewis and Grandfather Sibbald had agreed on everything and Lewis and the boys were ready to make the necessary journey. They would go first to Panama Mills to select a house, then into Jacksonville for a visit with Lewis's mother, then—hardest of all for Lewis, she knew—they would make the river trip to Hibernia to see the ruins of his beloved home, to find out how many of his people were still there, and to visit Augustina's grave.

Margaret felt a little embarrassed with everyone except Lewis that the thought of having him out of her sight again so affected her. Waiting now to be his wife seemed even harder.

On the day Lewis and the boys were to leave, her mother, for whatever reason, did not come downstairs for breakfast. Nor did Louisa and Sophia, for a reason Margaret knew well. Louisa wanted her and Lewis to have a little time together. The children, of course, were there and when breakfast was over, all three followed them into the Seton parlor. No one loved the children more than she, but Margetet felt she'd fly apart if the good-bye could not be said alone with Lewis. The tide left so little time. She vowed to say nothing, but when Tina climbed on Lewis's lap and both boys sat down, Lewis came to the rescue.

"All right, you three," he said, his voice kind, but firm. "You'll have to get accustomed to the idea that when two people are in love—they need to be with their children, but they also need to be alone now and then. So scoot."

After a moment, quickly covering her surprise, Tina, tossing her black curls, said, "I don't care. I'll have Miss Margaret with *me* after you're gone!" Smiling knowingly, their little sister between them, George and L.I. went outside.

Margaret rushed into Lewis's arms. "It—will be hard in a—brand new way—to wait for you this time, my dearest."

"I know, but you'll be with me. Every minute."

"Oh, yes! Especially at Hibernia when you—see your people again for the first time, and—when you see the—place where your house stood."

"Thank you. And please don't feel you have to leave me when I visit Augustina's grave. I'll need you most there. Do—I ask too much, Margaret?"

The concern in his voice forced her to give him a quick smile. "Lewis Fleming, I hope to live someday right down a sandy lane from that little cemetery. I wouldn't expect a man to understand this, but Augustina Cortez Fleming and I—are friends. You forget I've had nearly four years to allow her to find her rightful place in my heart. And in my life."

His arms tightened about her. "What can I say? I—couldn't have known my heart any sooner."

"And I wouldn't have believed you if you'd thought you did." She hugged him with all her might. "You must go. The tide won't wait. And please know that all along your journey each thing will work out for the best. Learn this about me now, darling—I'm going to seem foolishly hopeful sometimes. I do believe with all my heart that, after the long waiting time, from now on we have a very real obligation to—hope. If anything discourages you on this trip—remember that. Promise?"

"I promise."

They embraced again and he kissed her deeply.

"You and Tina watch the mails. I'll write a full report every chance I have. I love you, Margaret. With all of me, I love you."

On the fourth day after Lewis left, Margaret walked toward the Fernandina wharf with Sophia and Tina, hoping for a letter from Lewis.

"Do you think Papa will mention me in his letter?" Tina asked.

"Of course, he will, you adorable child," Sophia bubbled. "You're nothing but the apple of your papa's eye."

Even Tina seemed to realize that Sophia rattled a lot about nothing at times. She asked Margaret directly.

"You heard Sophia."

"I know I did, but Papa's going to be awfully busy."

"And with very important things, too. His first stop is at Panama Mills, the place we'll all be living soon. He's finding a house for us."

"Will it be like our old one that burned up?"

"Oh, no," Sophia said. "And you mustn't get your hopes up, Tina. In a mill town, there just aren't any houses like Hibernia. Oh, you poor, poor child. Deprived of your childhood at Hibernia beside the St. Johns! I just wouldn't be half the woman I am if I hadn't been able to grow up beside that river."

"Now, Sophia, listen to me," Margaret said firmly. "We're going to be just fine at Panama Mills. Tina will love it there on Trout Creek. We'll have the millpond, too, to take boat rides and swim. The mill commissary will be close by. Why, you can go right into a mill commissary and buy hard candy already made! Your father will find the best possible house and, Tina, you and I will fix it up as pretty as any picture."

Over the child's head, she frowned and shook her head at Sophia.

"Well, of course there will be—all that," Sophia muttered reluctantly. "And at Hibernia, the poor little darling didn't have any children her own age to play with."

Margaret smothered a smile when Tina hit at Sophia and snapped: "Wherever I live, I always have Miss Margaret to play with, so there!"

Word had spread all over Fernandina that Lewis and Margaret were to be married and, of course, everyone knew that Lewis and the boys had taken a trip. It was no surprise and a relief in all ways to Margaret when Mr. Foot, the skinny, loose-limbed Georgian who handled the mail, came toward them waving a letter.

"It's from him, Miss Margaret," he called. "It's from Colonel Fleming. Cap'n Morehead brought it from Panama Mills early this mornin'."

Margaret, in order to quiet Tina, had read most of the letter aloud right there in the sandy street by the waterfront. Now, the noon meal over, she was alone in her room with time to digest every word to her heart's content.

The first page assured her that they were all three fine and that Lewis was not discouraged at the prospect of the problems facing him when he became mill superintendent. "The general calibre of the workers here," he wrote, "is somewhat above average, especially the energetic young man who has been filling in since the old superintendent left. His name is Freddie Bumback—pronounced, I'm sure Tina will be interested to know—just as it's written. Bum back. He lacks experience and is only twenty-five, but then I lack experience, too. He and I rather hit it off, I think."

There was more about the mill itself, but she skipped that now, in order to read and reread the part she found far more to her liking:

There were two possible houses for us and I have chosen the larger. Along with our three, who love you so utterly, I want a child who is yours and mine. More than one if you are will-

ing. The house is a sharply gabled, rather tall two-storied
affair, unpainted, as are all the houses here. There are two
chimneys, four fireplaces—two downstairs and two up. The
detached kitchen looks fairly rundown to me, but Maum Easter will handle that in no uncertain terms. Tell her I'll do
whatever she says to make it usable. The bedrooms are satisfactory for our present family and more, including a room
for Sophia and Louisa should they need to stay with us before
they find a house in St. Augustine. The dining room, I am
sorry to say, is, compared to the Seton's, a cell. Maum Easter
will hate it, but it is there and that is about the way of the
whole house. It is there and it is ours when at last we are
one.

There was more about the poor condition of some of the
mill equipment—bless him, he was confiding everything as
though she understood about sawmills. What she did understand was the love he sent to each one—by name. The letter
ended with "I enclose my heart to you, who in that heart, are
already my wife."

Her mother had seemed pleased that he had mentioned
her, but then she usually acted pleased when it was expected
of her. Suddenly, Margaret's heart began to thump. Lewis
could well be with his own mother this minute in Jacksonville—
having their talk about his future marriage. Why not, as soon
as she heard her own mother stirring after a nap, go right
across the hall and knock on her door? She had procrastinated
for four whole days and there was really no need to fear a talk
now. She was no longer a child.

Looking around the large, airy room where she had slept
since she was much younger than Tina, Margaret felt a small,
sharp pang. From a little girl's room with her old blue rocking horse, her set of blocks and her dolls placed neatly in one
corner, the room had changed to a woman's room. The small
pine child's bed belonged to Tina now. Charles Seton had
given Margaret her very own high, four-postered mahogany
bed for her fifteenth birthday. The next Christmas, her mother
had given her the handsome pier glass which stood now
beside the window where the light was good even on a
cloudy day. She adored the imported flowered carpet that
covered the center of the room, its corners patterned with
blue plumed birds. How she would love to take all the
beloved furniture with her for *their* room at Panama Mills.

Night after night, since she had known of his love, she had tried to imagine Lewis lying beside her in that ample bed. Would Mama be pleased or hurt if I asked to have it? she wondered. There was no way to know. Unless she offered, Margaret meant to say not one word.

She slipped across the room to press her ear against the wall. Her mother was up and moving about. Clearly, Margaret heard the always lonely and somehow always severe-sounding, dry, nervous cough. Then, as though she were about to speak to someone, Matilda Seton cleared her throat firmly. Both sounds were as familiar as her mother's voice.

Before any logical reason to postpone the talk came, she hurried out into the hall and knocked on her mother's door.

"Yes? Who is it?"

"Margaret, Mama. May I come in?"

"Of course."

Softly, she opened the door into the huge, predominantly rose-colored master bedroom where her mother and father had conceived her. It had always struck Margaret as the most spacious room in the house. Without her father, it seemed even larger. The thought that she hadn't been in that room since he died stabbed at her. "I'm not a very good daughter," she blurted.

"Nonsense! Is something wrong, my dear?"

"No. But—I haven't been in this room—since Papa went away."

She looked at her mother, standing slender and straight, her rose crepe de Chine gown falling in delicate folds on the thick Aubusson carpet. She seemed to be holding herself, especially the thin, patrician face, in that becoming posture by enormous effort. But then, she had always seemed to Margaret to be holding herself. For what? Against what? Against the shock of the day when she would at last be alone in the great house?

On impulse, Margaret hugged her. Matilda's body felt stiff, unyielding. She neither returned nor repulsed the embrace. She simply stood there, giving her daughter a genteel smile.

Margaret sat down. Even the small, sturdy love seat was rigid under its green and rose satin upholstery. "Mother? Won't you sit down here beside me?"

"Of course, if that's what you'd like."

"I would."

For a long, stifling moment, they sat side by side, not

touching. At last, hating the distance between them, Margaret laid her hand over Matilda's. "Are you—happy for me, Mama?"

"Of course, Margaret. I'm especially happy to have three new grandchildren. They're remarkably well behaved. Well bred."

"Yes, yes, they are." She smiled. "I—I'm glad you like them."

"Well, did you expect me not to like three motherless children?"

"No. No, of course, I didn't."

"Of course," was Matilda's own well-worn phrase. Margaret cringed every time she heard herself use it. Her mother's use of it had always sounded superior, indicating that she knew everything already—and that anyone should realize that she did.

"I—truly love Lewis, Mama. I've loved him for a very long time."

Matilda Seton sat even straighter. "Of course, I didn't know—during all those years. I'm sure your father did. I'm sure you told *him*."

"He guessed. I didn't tell him."

She watched the thin, sad smile crease her mother's mouth. "Charles was always wiser—about you. Not once since the time you were born did I ever try to break into that private world. Yours and your father's."

"Why, Mother? Why didn't you? We would have welcomed you! Neither of us ever meant to shut you out. We tried."

"Did you, indeed?"

On the defensive with her, as always, Margaret felt the old brief panic. The same panic she'd felt as a child when she and her father returned from a long walk together, laughing at some secret joke or discovery. The panic always vanished, though, because Matilda saw to it. It was always she who changed the subject or covered the moment with a soft, clinging blanket of social amenity. Do it again, Mother! Margaret pleaded inside herself, but what she said was: "Papa and I did have private jokes, I guess. Why, sometimes we'd just look at each other—and I'd giggle and he'd laugh. We really didn't have any secrets from you. I—don't want any now. I mean, I'd like to discuss our house at Panama Mills. I need you to help me decide about so much."

"Have I ever refused you anything, my dear?"

Margaret longed to say: "Yes, you've refused me yourself. You're doing it right now!" What she did say was: "No, Mother. I've been a very lucky girl. Thank you."

"Of course, I'll help in any way I can. And, I feel you've chosen well in Colonel Fleming. He's more than fifteen years older than you. You'll be a widow early, I imagine. As I am. Your father was thirteen years my senior. But, until then, you should have a good life. Not easy having to live at your grandfather's mills. You won't find people there in our class. But you'll have the children. I'm satisfied with you, Margaret."

"Just—satisfied? Is that all?"

"Your father was devoted to Lewis Fleming. He would be overjoyed, could he know. Pleasing your father has been the rule of my life." She glanced briefly at Margaret. "It still is. I fully approve of what you are about to do—because I know he would."

Margaret picked at a loose thread in the seam of her long, cotton print skirt. "Thank you," she said. Nothing else came. In a moment, she stood to go. Her mother remained seated, but smiling.

"You're not to worry about me here—alone in the house," Matilda said. "I'm going to be all right."

Outside her mother's door—closed, as Matilda preferred it—Margaret's thoughts raced to Lewis. How had he fared with his own mother in Jacksonville? Better, she hoped, than she had fared with hers. And yet, she had done her best. True, she had hoped for more. Well, hope itself had not been diminished. She would cling to it for her mother, too.

Still standing there in the wide hall, she smiled at herself because she was hoping right now. Hoping that Tina was awake after her nap. She needed to be with Lewis's little girl.

Jacksonville
15 August 1836

Dearest, dearest Margaret,

I have just spent the afternoon with my mother and I only hope that your private conversation with Mrs. Seton came off as well. Oh, Mother was Mother, but at least she seemed pleased that I am so happy and that I looked almost healthy enough. When you know her better, you'll not be surprised that I got a long lecture on bracing myself toward a greater effort *not* to limp. She spoke at length of my father's graceful stride, of my once agile step. Somehow, this time she did not make me feel guilty. I limp, the doctors say I may always limp, and you find it—romantic, I believe you said. I am laughing as I write. Thanks to you, I am laughing quite a lot again. You appear to have Sophia Fleming's full approval. She approves of your education, your family connections, your beauty.

Early tomorrow the boys and I board a steamer with our horses for Hibernia. That will be hard, but George and L.I. are fine and such a help to me. We have two good sons, my dearest, and they love you almost as much as I love you. They will be with me when I first see the remains of the house, when I visit Augustina's grave. I pray that there, after such a long time, I will be what the boys need me to be. I feel now that I can handle seeing everything at Hibernia and that is so because of our life ahead. Tell Maum Easter that I will give her love to Pompey. I am certain that he misses her as much as she misses him. But, one day—oh, one blessed day, we will all be together again at our beloved Hibernia.

> You still have my heart,
> Lewis Fleming

18

Its reversed paddle wheel churning the gray water of the St. Johns, the steamer slowed and then began to move steadily in from midstream toward the Hibernia dock. At the boat's prow the boys unhitched their horses and stood with their father, who leaned against Cotter as though drawing strength from the faithful animal, watching the familiar shoreline—almost as in a dream. At first glance, Lewis saw none of his people. His eyes moved up the gently rising low bluff, the giant singed oaks standing as before among Augustina's scorched magnolias. Where the high-gabled house had been, there rose only four stark chimneys—lonely watchers through the now empty days and nights that passed over the once sheltering plantation home. The familiar breeze was there, making the cloudy, moist August heat bearable and, in the breeze, a charred piece of cloth blew about the riverbank.

As they rode slowly off the boat onto the dock and began to

walk their horses up the gentle slope, George pointed to the blackened cloth. "I know what that is blowing there, Papa. It's a piece of our dining room curtains. I can see the stripes."

Struggling to keep his voice steady, Lewis said, "I believe you're right, son. But, hasn't Pompey done a good job of cleaning up? I wonder how many of our people are still here—giving him a hand."

"Do we know if any of our furniture—I mean, did everything burn up?" L.I. asked.

"The Seminoles did a thorough job of it," Lewis answered, wheeling Cotter on the pretext of riding over to examine the remains of the parlor chimney and fireplace. He didn't want the boys to see, but the sight of the roomless foundation, lonely and forlorn, had brought tears.

In a moment, from back toward the quarters, they heard and then saw Pompey running toward them waving both arms high above his head, calling them all by name over and over.

Lewis dismounted and stood waiting with his arms out. The two men embraced, pounding each other on the back. "Pompey, it's good to see you! Good to see something—still the same." Turning to his sons, he shouted: "Off those horses, fellows. Come help me let Pompey know how good he looks to us!"

After tears all around and laughter and attempted jokes, Pompey stood to his full height, well under six feet, and announced: "I made 'em give me a minute by ourselves first, Mausa Lewis, but when I whistles, the rest will come arunnin'. They's waitin'." A big grin lighted his thin, bony features, "But they don' dare come till I whistles."

"Hold that whistle just a minute, Pompey," Lewis said. "I need to know how many of our people are still here. There were forty-seven when I left."

The slender black man hung his head, his grin gone. "They be—fourteen of us lef', Mausa Lewis. They kill ten. The rest run off wif the Injuns." His head lifted, proudly. "My chillern ain't gone nowhere. Lil' Jim an' Betty an' Ezra an' Owen an' they kinfolk, Laddie's boys, is all still here."

"What about old Laddie himself?"

"Dead. I know an' he knowed he done wrong, but once the chillern an' Easter went acrost the river to the Fatio's fer Christmas, Laddie, he got one of your guns. He had it—that evenin' the Injuns come hollerin' an' firin' our place. Laddie took aim. They blew his head right off. I—buried him myself when I got back acrost. Laid him in the cemetery to one side of yo' pap, Mausa Lewis, an' Miss Augustina."

"You did the right thing," Lewis said hoarsely. "I hope you put the other—nine—there, too."

"Yes. sir."

"What have you been eating? Surely, they stole our cattle and chickens and hogs."

Pompey nodded. "But two hogs got loose in the woods an' come home. We ain't had Easter to cook, but we eat. We eat. I had me some seeds stashed. Got me a piece of a garden. They forgot a few settin' hens."

Lewis sighed heavily. "It hasn't been quite eight months, Pompey. It seems a lifetime."

"Yes, sir."

"But you've done a lot of work. Considering all the damage they did, you've got—the ruins looking neat and orderly."

"Yeah," L.I. said, trying to sound cheerful. "Looks good."

Pompey twisted a soft, trampled pine cone into the sandy ground with his worn shoe. "I was wishin' ever' day I could be buildin' a new house 'stead of just cleanin' up that mess." He pointed to a huge stack of half-charred boards—siding, heavy beams, parts of blackened windowsills and a few half-burned lengths of the familiar downstairs floor boards. "Knowin' you, Mausa Lewis, I knowed we'd be rebuildin' someday." His grin was hopeful. "We might could find some use for some of that ol' lumber. I clean it up the best I could."

"Papa got wounded in the leg," L.I. said, "but he walks pretty good again now."

Pompey's face saddened, then his grin came back. "You git you a Injun, Mausa Lewis? You get you one before they got you?"

"Sorry to disappoint you," he answered. "They got me first."

A soft, almost melodic peal of thunder sounded from out over the river.

"I think it's time to whistle, Pompey," Lewis said, looking at the darkening sky. "We'll want to say hello to everybody and then the boys and I will visit their mother's grave."

Pompey's whistle brought the remaining people scurrying to welcome Lewis and the boys home again and after the greetings, Little Jim, Pompey and one of old Laddie's sons led away their horses. The others shuffled slowly back to the quarters.

For a long moment the three stood just looking after the straggling line of faithful servants. Finally, Lewis took a deep breath, forced a smile and said softly, "We're lucky to have fourteen of our people left besides Maum Easter in Fernandina. I heard at Fort Drane that some of the plantations burned south of St. Augustine lost all their people. Indians can talk some Negroes into almost anything." He sighed. "I guess that's understandable. In a way, they have a common bond against those of us who happened to be born white."

"How many of our people still here do we own, Papa?"

"Only about four or five, George. I'll want some to stay on here to watch over what's left. Keep out white squatters. The others we'll probably need at Panama Mills."

"If you don't own 'em all, though," L.I. said, "they won't have to go."

"That's right, son. The decision will be up to them."

"I think they'll do exactly what you need them to do," George said. "I know Pompey will. And he's free."

"We can talk that all over with them tomorrow," Lewis said, his mind elsewhere. "It's time we visited your mother's grave now."

Lewis took them each by the hand and they walked in silence across the wide Hibernia lawn under the great trees, then along the sandy lane that led to the little cemetery. Before they reached the grave site, all three knew Maum Easter's daughter, Betty, had been there before them. In Augustina's favorite silver vase—scrubbed, though discolored from the fire—stood a brave bunch of magnolia leaves.

A few feet from the graceful, slender marker, the three stopped. "Betty had no way of knowing exactly when we'd get here," Lewis said in a quiet voice. "Those leaves are fresh and green."

"Maybe Betty's—just lonesome for all of us—since the house burned," L.I. said. "Maybe she keeps the vase filled every day."

Lewis looked at his youngest son and saw that his face was wet with tears. George was merely very pale. Neither boy, he knew, could remember seeing the vase without their mother's magnolia leaves in it. She had kept it filled, fresh and welcoming, for as long as she lived. Lewis had done it himself after she was gone.

"It's kinda—like home, isn't it, Papa?"

"Yes, L.I." He took another deep breath. "Let's go—nearer."

The wind sang in the cemetery trees now. The sky had lowered, thunder rolled, but a towhee chirped, "sweet—sweet," and the sound of the wind off the river was sweet to their ears. Sweet, familiar, painful.

For a long time, they knelt in silence by the grave. Then, L.I. got up and began pulling a stray weed here and there from the now low, settled mound of earth—barely a mound after nearly four changes of the seasons. Beside his father, George still knelt. Lewis studied his sons: L.I. needed to be active at such a difficult time; George, his eyes closed, was more of a mystery. Was the boy praying? Was he trying to make some contact with his mother? The thin, sensitive face told Lewis nothing beyond the irrevocable fact that neither son was a mere boy any longer. They were young men, forced to mature early.

"Pompey or somebody sure has kept the weeds back," L.I. said, almost grumbling. Lewis knew that if L.I. could have pulled an armful of weeds, it would have helped. Instead, the boy brushed and brushed the loose sand over the grave, smoothing, almost caressing it.

Four years, Lewis reminded himself, was a far longer period of time for the boys than for him. Neither would—could ever forget such a beautiful, lighthearted mother, but pain faded, as all things fade, more rapidly for the young. At least, Lewis hoped that was true. For his sons' sake. Not so for him.

Suddenly, his head began to reel. He was dizzingly close to Augustina. He could feel the warm arms around him, could smell her fragrance—feel his lips against the tender spot on her young, smooth neck below her pretty ear. He heard her softest whisper in the always disarming Spanish accent: "*Lu-is . . . Luis . . .*"

Margaret! his heart called.

But aloud, in an almost desperate voice, he cried out to L.I.: "Son! Help me—help me up. I—can't stay here another minute . . ."

George jumped to his feet and both boys lifted their father from his kneeling position.

Trying to laugh at himself, Lewis said hoarsely, "I—got down all right, but—I couldn't make it back up on this—frazzlin' leg. Not—fast enough, anyway."

"We—wish we could help you—more," George said, his dark eyes brimming with the tears which hadn't come until now. "But, Papa—don't forget—we all have Miss Margaret."

"Yeah," L.I. piped. "Yeah. Funny, George, but I was just thinkin' the same thing. The very same thing!"

"Does it—help you to know we have Miss Margaret, Papa?"

Lewis held out his arms and George and L.I. rushed into them as though they were still very small boys. He looked about the little cemetery—the very place where Margaret first realized that she loved him—longing to tell the boys how *much* having her helped now—this minute. He could find no words. Where had she stood? Beside Louisa, she'd told him. But where? Under that big magnolia so near Augustina's grave? Perhaps. That long-ago day held no memories for him beyond his own pain. He hadn't seemed to remember that Margaret Seton was even there. But—the pain of this sharp encounter eased because she had told him she was there. *Here*. Perhaps she and Louisa stood where he and the boys stood at this moment embracing, under the old magnolia.

Crimson pods were forming on the lower branches. Crimson seed pods which Augustina had gathered the way a child collects seashells. Gathered and planted because there could never be enough magnolia trees at Hibernia . . .

The boys loosened their hold on him, stepped back.

"What's so funny about that big old magnolia, Papa?" L.I. asked.

"Nothing's funny about it, son. It's a fine, strong, *memorable* tree."

For a few seconds no one spoke. Then, George said wonderingly, "You—look almost happy, Papa."

"You know, L.I., I think I may *be*—almost happy again. And I think Miss Margaret would be proud of all three of us right now, don't you?"

"I wish she could be standing here with us," L.I. said.

"Son? You may be too young to understand this, but take my word for it, Miss Margaret will never be closer to us than she is—this minute."

After two rainy days of sorting and sifting through the pathetic, soggy remnants which Pompey had so carefully cleaned and saved, Lewis and his boys astride their horses, Pompey beside them on foot, moved slowly down the familiar path to the dock where a few salvaged belongings waited.

The steamer from Picolata would be puffing into sight soon. Today, the air was clear—the rain all gone. A bright, cobalt sky stained the wide St. Johns only a slightly darker hue. Across the river, Lewis could see almost every tree outlined at New Switzerland. They had crossed over to inspect Louisa's disaster, too. It was that—a disaster. Even the quarters had been burned. All of Louisa's people were gone. Undoubtedly, they would never know what happened to Scipio or Polly or anyone else. Certainly, Louisa is right, he thought, not to try to rebuild.

L.I.'s urgent voice broke Lewis's reverie.

"Pompey," he was saying, "you don't know what you're talking about! You're gonna be awful happy working for Miss Margaret, won't he, Papa?"

"That's what I've been trying to tell him, L.I. I don't think he believes me."

"Well, you believe Maum Easter, don't you?" George wanted to know.

Pompey looked up with a half smile. "I jus'—loves Easter. Don' know as I believes her."

"You wait, Pompey, and find out for yourself," Lewis said.

"Yes, sir," Pompey said, looking at the ground. "I wait."

"Now, then," Lewis changed the subject. "Do we have my remaining readable books in that barrel there?"

"Yes, sir. All 'lebben of 'em. I pack 'em myself, right on top of your one good suit the Lord spared from the flames. I put in two skillets an' a little pot, too."

Lewis laughed. "Good work. I'll need that suit to be married in and heaven knows Miss Margaret and Easter will need every pot and skillet possible when we set up housekeeping at the Mills." He shook his head. "Eleven books out of more than five hundred!"

"Mausa Lewis? I reckon you'll say somepin' to—Easter for me?"

"What would you like me to say? That you miss her?"

"Somepin' turrible. An' that I—done good work here in the mess we had."

Lewis leaned down from where he sat Cotter and patted Pompey's lean shoulder. "She'll get a glowing report, don't worry." Then, he added in a confidential voice, deep with concern for the slight black man who had been his friend for so long, "Pompey, it's time I let you and the boys know what I've decided about when we'll all be together again. When I'll be married, when we'll move to Panama Mills, when you'll leave here to join us and so on."

"Oh, boy! Do we know all that now, Papa?"

"Well, L.I., I have come to some decisions on this trip. How they'll all work out, I don't know, but as of now, I figure it will take me until the end of this year to get my hand in at the Mills. The house we'll live in there, Pompey, needs a lot of repair before I can bring my family from Fernandina. Mr. Sibbald's account books at the Mills are in a sorry state. I'll need time for that. I want to get accquainted with the folks there, find out ahead of time who is and who isn't trustworthy. Miss Margaret is a genteel young lady. It's going to be hard enough for her living in a place like that. She's accustomed to city life. To far easier living than we knew right here at Hibernia."

"Aw, you may be going to marry her, Papa, but you sure don't know Miss Margaret the way we do," L.I. scoffed.

Lewis seemed pleased, but he merely smiled and went on talking to Pompey. "My plans go something like this. I'll spend as much time as required at the Mills over the next several months. Maum Easter and the Fatio sisters will be welcome to stay right in Fernandina. Then, say, early in March, we'll change Miss Margaret Seton's name to Fleming. And, soon after that, home will be Panama Mills. I'd like you to join us, Pompey, you and Little Jim, Betty and the others—about mid-March of next year." He frowned. "Pompey, do you have to look so glum?"

"Yes, sir. I reckon so. 'Cause I won't see Easter in all that time."

"The steamer's coming, Papa," George said. "She's already swinging this way."

"All right, son. We're ready. Pompey—I'm sorry. But Miss Margaret will have so much work to do—she'll really need Easter."

"Papa," George said, "just before we left Fernandina, Miss Margaret made me promise something."

"She did? What?"

"That if Pompey had to stay here, L.I. and I would talk you into letting Easter come back to be with Pompey until we can all live together at Panama Mills."

Lewis stared at his son. "Did she really get you to promise that? How does it happen that you've waited until now, with the boat in sight, to tell me about it?"

"You got tired of being asked exactly what your plans were," L.I. said. "Don't you remember how often we've been asking?"

"Well, yes, but—"

"Miss Margaret isn't helpless like you think she is," L.I. argued. "She's strong, and—"

"He's right," George broke in. "And Miss Margaret is so fond of Easter. They're really friends and she hates Easter and Pompey being apart so long. She did, Miss Margaret really did beg us to promise her that."

Lewis, dumbfounded, slumped in the saddle. "Well, I—I believe you, but I believe you simply because I know you wouldn't lie to me."

"No sir, we wouldn't."

"Aw, Papa, you've just got to understand that George and I know Miss Margaret a lot better than you know her. We've been friends an awful long time. She's not a shrinking violet. She can handle all that packing without batting an eye. We think you'll get off on the wrong foot with her, if you don't agree to let Easter come back here to Hibernia until time to move to the Mills."

Pompey, his face shining, reached up to shake Lewis's hand. "Mausa Lewis, right quick, it looks like you marryin' yo'self a fine lady! Yes, sir. The finest in these parts!"

"Hurray, Pompey," L.I. laughed. "Now, you're catching on!"

Gradually, cautiously, Lewis, too, began to smile. Reaching his hand down to Pompey for a good, firm handclasp, he chuckled. "You see, Pompey? Miss Margaret *is* an amazing lady. She's won you over without even being here. It's settled, then. As soon as the boys and I get back to Fernandina, we'll put Easter on the first possible boat coming this way. How does that strike you?"

"Praise the Lord, Mausa Lewis. Thank you, sir. Oh, I does thank you an' thank you, sir!"

"You better not forget to thank Miss Margaret, too," L.I. teased.

"That's right. That's right," Pompey agreed vehemently.

The steamer whistled as if puffed toward the Fleming dock. Lewis felt his heart beat faster. That little boat would take him directly back to Margaret. No more stops. Within minutes, they'd be aboard and on their way. The boys had dismounted and were helping Pompey haul the pitiful barrels of salvaged possessions out onto the dock. Lewis turned once more in the direction of the lonely chimneys, the charred earth, the stacked, blackened lumber, the desolate trees.

"I'm—coming back, Augustina," he whispered to himself. "We're all coming back—someday. To stay."

Part Three

1838–1851

19

On a sunny May morning a year after they had moved into the plain but fairly comfortable house at Panama Mills, Margaret stood in the doorway of Easter's kitchen watching the chunky brown woman. In one series of rhythmic motions, Maum Easter was kneading dough, singing and beating time with her heels on the bare, scrubbed pine floor. Without missing a beat, Easter gave her a preoccupied smile and, Margaret, starting slowly, valiantly tried to duplicate the complex rhythm. When Margaret managed to get the beat of her heels all wrong, they both laughed so hard, the singing stopped.

"Lord, have mercy, Miss Mar'ret, you feelin' good today!"

"I have news for you! News I haven't even told my husband."

Easter threw her a sharp look, but gave her dough a few extra jabs before she turned around. "Now, what you up to? You ain' made another pair of curtains for that parlor!"

Margaret perched on the heavy wooden table which held Easter's doughboard and sat swinging her legs, a sly, merry look in her dark eyes. "No more curtains. I'm satisfied with our house now. Easter—I'm going to have a baby!"

For a long moment, the round brown face registered nothing. Then it broke into pure sunlight with the smile reserved only for times of real joy. "Lord be praised!" she whispered. "Git down from there, so's I kin hug ya! You knows my arms is short an' fat. Git down!"

Still holding her, Easter asked, "When you gonna have the baby?"

"Early next year. January or early February—if everything goes well." Margaret stepped back to look at her friend, the merest hint of anxiety in her eyes. "It will—go well, won't it? I don't know how I'll act—at a time like that, you know."

Easter picked up a damp cloth and scrubbed at a perfectly

140

clean cupboard top. "If they's one thing Easter knows, it's how to birth a baby."

"Oh, Easter, I'm so relieved to hear that!"

"Mausa Lewis don't tell you I birthed the other three?"

"No."

"Well, I did. An' lots of nigger chillern since. I was younger'n you when I birthed Miss Augustina's babies. We got along fine—till Tina." Easter's face saddened. "Course, Tina, she got here all right without no trouble. It was—just that poor, lil' Miss Augustina, with her weak heart, she couldn't get herself well again." The warm smile came back. "You good an' strong, Miss Mar'ret. Now, when you gonna tell poor Mausa Lewis? How long you gonna make him wait?"

"Tonight—if I can catch him alone when he gets home from the mills." A sudden frown came. "He will be glad, won't he? I know he wants children of our own, but—he talks and talks about how he wishes they could grow up at Hibernia— not here. Maum Easter, I don't see how we can find enough money to build a house at Hibernia for—years! Maybe four or five."

Easter picked up her cornhusk broom and began to sweep the immaculate floor with hard, excited strokes. "If you don't think a child four or five years old has got a lot of growin' up left to do, you ain't as smart as I thinks." She stopped sweeping. "We gonna go back to Hibernia, Miss Mar'ret—an' in plenty of time. You mark my word. Not just for this baby comin' to us now, but for more babies, too!"

On a sudden, sharp intake of breath, Margaret said irritably, "Why doesn't my grandfather come back from Philadelphia, see for himself what a splendid job Lewis is doing and double his salary?"

"Things don't go on comin' easy like they always has for you, child."

"I know that, Maum Easter. I don't mean to be ungrateful. But—four or five years is so long for poor Lewis to wait!"

Easter shook her head. "You thinks you already had a *lot* of waitin', don't you? Waitin' for Mausa Lewis all that time. Honey, you just begin to wait. Waitin's a burden the Lord He lay on us all." She smiled slowly. "An' Easter don't think it's Mausa Lewis's waitin' time you worried about. It's your own. You good at lots of things, Miss Mar'et, but you might never be no good at waitin'."

"I thought I'd learned by now." She sighed. "But I don't

care who knows it, I hate—hate having to wait until next year for my baby to come!"

Tina met her father first when he came home that afternoon and Pompey called him to inspect a new rope swing he'd hung in the only half-decent oak in the small, bare yard, but Easter handled things for Margaret. She silenced Pompey with a look and hurried Tina off to the kitchen for a cookie—normally forbidden before dinner. Margaret grabbed Lewis by the arm, propelled him outside across the yard and down the road to the big mill dock on Trout Creek.

Seated beside her on the rough boards, Lewis took her hand. "Now, tell me."

"Tell you what?"

"For the past few minutes, you've been acting like a nervous squirrel scampering to hide a big hickory nut," he laughed. "Something's on your mind, Mrs. Fleming. Out with it."

Margaret turned to look straight into Lewis's amused eyes. "You like to laugh at me, don't you? But that's all right. Just so you're laughing. Dear, handsome, gentle, good, beautiful Lewis." She touched his cheek, smoothed the dark, elegantly formed brows. "I do love you."

"And I you, Mrs. Fleming. Do you tire of my calling you Mrs. Fleming? It makes me feel so *sure*."

In answer, she laid her head on his shoulder.

"What is it, Margaret? What is it you need to tell me?"

"Lewis," she whispered, "—we're going to have a baby."

He seemed to freeze. Not a muscle in his strong arm moved. Then, roughly, more roughly than he had ever embraced her, he grabbed her to him, his whole body trembling. "Margaret—are you sure?"

"Yes. Yes, I am very sure."

Abruptly, he let her go and got to his feet as quickly as his bad leg allowed. For a long moment, he stood there, his face toward the river, his back to Margaret. The river glowed warm gold from the lowering sun.

"Lewis!"

"Give me a minute, Margaret—please!"

Her thoughts in wild disarray, she gripped the splintery edge of the dock, trying with all her might to understand why he was acting so—unlike Lewis. "You—you said you wanted *our* child."

She watched his hands clench and unclench. Slowly, he turned and without moving a step nearer, said, "I know—I know. It's just that—that—" He stood staring down at her, his face contorted with what struck Margaret as stark fear. Suddenly, he pulled her to her feet and held her so hard her shoulders ached.

"What, Lewis? I wish I didn't have to ask, but I—must know."

"Help me, Margaret! I can't face the thought of—losing you, too! I—didn't know I still had this fear inside me. I didn't know it, I swear. Help me! Even the children wouldn't be able to keep me here if I lost you—too!"

He began to sob so hard she wondered if indeed he had ever really cried out his grief for Augustina. A surge of jealousy swept Margaret, then vanished. She and Augustina were friends now. *Friends,* she breathed into the late afternoon silence, broken only by a dog barking down by the mill and the gentle slap of the river below them.

Margaret could not have told anyone how long they stood, Lewis clinging to her, his tall, strong body trembling. If anyone had chanced to walk out onto that dock right now, neither of them could have spoken. Margaret struggled for words, the right words—strong, clean words to comfort him. She failed.

"Margaret," he gasped, "don't—ever leave me! Please—please let me go—first!"

He held her against his shoulder so hard she fought for breath enough to answer. "I promise, Lewis. I'll—never leave you. I don't know how I'll keep that promise—how I'd ever live for one hour—without you, but I do promise."

In time, the madnes of such a request and such an impossible promise broke through to Lewis. He relaxed his grip on her. Tears continued to stream down his tanned cheeks, but slowly his eyes began to soften, almost to smile. "Forgive me," he whispered. "Only God knows when a man or a woman will die. What I asked took me by surprise, too. Can you believe that?"

Near tears herself now, she nodded encouragingly. "Yes. I'm—crazy enough to believe anything you say—and to promise anything you ask."

"How could any two people be so—close, Margaret?"

"I don't know, dearest. How would I know that?"

Sitting side by side again on the dock, they were quiet for a time. The sun, behind a cloud now, no longer cast its gold light. The dock was gray again and the trunks of the skimpy pines brown. Back to normal, Margaret thought. Lewis and I are back to normal. It's past. He will never be so afraid again.

"I feel sure I'll never be so afraid again," he said simply.

Margaret decided not to tell him that in whatever length of time it took for a thought to form—before he spoke those words—her mind had formed them. Instead, she said, "Maum Easter says I'll be fine. That I'm strong and healthy and that I have her."

"Yes. Thank God, yes. We have Easter." Then, "Do you want a boy or a girl?"

Her eyes twinkled. "A son!"

As quickly as the fear had struck, their laughter came. Laughter and a full return of their own special kind of joy. In the gathering dusk, she could almost see Augustina toss her lovely, dark head and laugh, too.

20

On a cold, gray blustery day—February 9, 1839—Maum Easter and Margaret labored together until after suppertime before perfect Charles Seton Fleming came into the world in the boxlike bedroom on the second floor of the plain, frame house at Panama Mills.

"Thank you for wanting to name him for my father," Margaret whispered to Lewis when at last Maum Easter left them alone. The astoundingly beautiful baby—sturdy, with a head of thick, black hair and blue, blue eyes—lay wriggling in Margaret's arms, Lewis sitting beside them on the bed, drinking in the wonder.

"Didn't you hear me, Lewis? I said, 'thank you for wanting to name him for Papa.' "

"Charles Seton was my friend. I hope our son grows up to be half the man he was."

Dark shadows circled Margaret's luminous eyes, but they were smiling mischievously up at Lewis. "Since we already have our George named for your father, I want our next son to be called Francis Philip—for your uncle, Louisa's father. Agreed?"

"Say, not so fast!" Lewis touched the baby's head. "Is he—is Charles Seton Fleming as wondrously beautiful as his old father thinks?"

"Yes! Oh yes! And, Lewis, how can I wait for Louisa to find out that he's here—and that he's—perfect?"

"I promise I'll have a letter ready to hand to the captain of the first boat for St. Augustine tomorrow. Are you sure you're all right, my darling?"

"I'm fine! Oh, Lewis, I want lots more children. Lots more!"

"But, Margaret, it was so hard on you! I've never thought it fair for the woman to have to go through all that—alone."

"Fiddlesticks. Men could never manage it. I now know—it isn't any fun—but when the child is *your* child—it all becomes wonderful. Wonder-filled."

He kissed her long and tenderly.

"Now, bring Tina in first, Lewis. I don't want her to have time to build up one smidgeon of jealousy of Charles Seton."

"Tonight? You need to rest."

"Tonight. Tina first and then L.I. and George. L.I. has such a case on Susan L'Engle's child, Mary Evelyn, I want to show him a real baby."

Lewis chuckled. "Did I tell you what I suggested to Susan's husband the last time L.I. and I were in Jacksonville to visit Mother?"

"No, what?"

"L.I. is so taken with little Mary Evelyn, I thought we might just as well betroth them to each other right now. John L'Engle nearly exploded. Put his foot right down because L.I.'s fifteen years older than Mary Evelyn."

"And did you remind him that you're fifteen years older than I?"

"I did not. I've long ago learned that when John has an opinion, he holds it. I let the matter drop, but stranger things have happened."

She sighed happily. "Yes. Such as the miracle that you found out you loved me—after all that time. Do you know sometimes I feel very superior that I knew about us first?"

He kissed her again. "I'll always be a little behind you, Mrs. Fleming. Now, get some rest."

"Not until Charles Seton and I have seen the children.

Tina first. Then, the boys. Pamper me, Lewis. I've just given you the world's handsomest baby."

When warm spring days began to stir the Florida land after its short winter rest, Margaret and Lewis made plans to take the whole family for a visit to the new infant's grandmothers—Fernandina first, and then Jacksonville.

"Will your mother be offended that we named the baby for my father, Lewis?"

"We already have one George in the family. We couldn't have named him for my father, could we? My hope is that since his name is Charles Seton it might help bridge the gap with your mother." He waited. "Do I imagine that there is one? I didn't offend you, did I?"

"Of course not!" Margaret stamped her foot. "Oh, blooey!"

" 'Blooey?' "

"That was one of Papa's favorite expressions when he felt—trapped. I said, 'Of course not.' That's Mama's expression and I hate it. Did I sound superior? I didn't mean to. No, you didn't offend me. Lewis—if I dared, I'd shake Mama until she put her arms around me and kissed me. I know she loves me. She's always so considerate and courteous—but who wants a mother to be—" She broke off laughing. "Why can't I just leave her alone—as she is? Why do we go on *needing* our mothers to be as happy and as excited as we are when—well, look at me, Lewis. I'm a grown woman with—four children!"

"And a husband."

In his arms, she said with vigor: "And a husband! The most wonderful, the kindest, most understanding husband any woman ever had. Not just most women, Lewis—*any* woman."

Matilda Seton, perfectly groomed and wearing an unadorned wine and gray striped silk dress, its full, long skirt touching the floor, the wide collar accentuating her still trim waist, stood waiting on the front porch of the Seton home when Lewis's hired carriage stopped on Calle Amelia in Fernandina.

"There's Grandmother now," Margaret said cheerfully to the children. To Lewis, she whispered, "Doesn't she look lonely?"

None of the loneliness was in evidence as Matilda greeted the three older children. And when Margaret held out the baby to her, she saw her mother's eyes fill with tears. With her usual steely control, the tears did not spill down her cheeks, but they were there.

Holding Charles Seton, Matilda breathed, "He's the most beautiful baby I've ever seen. Even more beautiful than you were, I believe, Margaret." Then, to Lewis, "Both my children were pretty babies. Especially Margaret, but, Colonel Fleming, your son is—almost beyond belief."

"We had to name him for your late husband," Lewis said simply.

"Yes. Yes, I can understand why you had to do that." Then, "He has your eyes, Colonel Fleming. Perhaps—bluer."

"You noticed, Mother!"

"Of course! Well," she said, still cradling the baby, "come inside. I imagine you'll be glad to spend a few days in a comfortable house again."

"Oh, Mama, our house at Panama Mills is just fine," Margaret insisted. "The handsome old sideboard you gave us looks quite at home in our dining room."

"Not too large for the room?"

Lewis laughed, "Well, not much."

"Besides, Mother, we're not going to live at Panama Mills forever, you know. In fact, we're all going to Hibernia soon."

"Whatever for?" her mother asked.

"To begin to make plans for—a house. Oh, not the fine house we'll be able to build someday, but one we can live in until we can build our permanent home."

"I see. And what about my father—your Grandfather Sibbald? He's not at all well, according to my latest letter from your grandmother. Will you be able to leave the Mills in other hands anytime soon, Colonel Fleming?"

"Mother," Margaret answered for him. "We're only going for a short visit to Hibernia. It will be two or three years before Lewis can safely leave the Mills to Fred Bumback— and certainly we won't have enough money to build even a makeshift house before then!"

Matilda gave her a cool but genteel smile. "Well, there is certainly no need to grow defensive, Margaret, my dear."

Margaret bit back the words she wanted to let fly and Lewis came to her rescue.

"Mr. Sibbald and I have been together more than two years, Mrs. Seton. I'm devoted to him—and to his interests. The last thing I'd do is be unfaithful to the trust he placed in me. I promise you I will never leave—no matter how I long to return to my own home—until the Panama Mills operation is in capable hands. I do have a good man there. I'm training him now to take over someday. Your father understood perfectly that Margaret and I would be there only for as long as it takes me to scrape together enough money to return to my own land."

"Yes," Matilda said. "I also recall having invited you inside minutes ago."

L.I., Tina and George had been standing to one side not knowing how to take part in what had been said among the adults. Finally, George said, "I'll carry little Seton."

"I know all about holding babies," L.I. offered. "I spend a lot of time with the L'Engle's daughter, Mary Evelyn, in Jacksonville."

"I can hold him, too." Tina piped.

With a tiny, absent smile toward all three children, Matilda carefully placed Seton in Lewis's arms. "Perhaps you'll take him, Colonel Fleming," she said. "Margaret looks exhausted."

"I'm not a bit tired, Mother!"

"You and Colonel Fleming and the baby will, of course, have your old room, Margaret. The two back guest rooms are ready for the boys and Tina. I'll be in my room resting until dinner." She smiled graciously. "Welcome to Fernandina— all of you."

Alone in Margeret's spacious old room, the baby asleep, Margaret and Lewis stood in the middle of the floor—Lewis smiling, Margaret looking helpless. She rushed into his arms. "Oh, Lewis—is my mother as cold as she seems to me? Do you think she's going to call you 'Colonel Fleming' forever?"

"Whatever causes your mother to keep her arm up against us, against all of life—you and I can't help. We can only try to understand."

"But I've been trying all my life! Papa, too! Papa tried for forty years! Lewis, does she really think she's—perfect?"

"No, I'm sure she doesn't. She's protecting herself, I'd say."

"Against what? Against me? Her daughter, who only wants to reach her? Who longs for her to be warm and pleasant and welcoming?"

Lewis, still holding her, smoothed her back, his hands, roughened from hard work, making little scratchy sounds against the water blue silk of her dress. "Do you want her to change—to be warm and welcoming for her own sake, Margaret? Or so it will make our visit more pleasant? So we will have one fewer worry?"

"Both, Lewis! I want her to change—for both reasons!"

"I married *you*, Margaret Seton Fleming. For you. Not for any other reason. I didn't marry your mother. Although I think she needs all of us."

"But she almost ignored L.I. and George and Tina. How can she do that?"

"I don't know. I don't know the answer to any of your questions, but I know our children. They have you and they have me. That completes their lives. They'll be fine. And you can count on me to do everything in my power to help with every rough place for the three days we're here."

"Oh, Lewis—I do count on you. I count on you for *everything*. Forgive me for lapsing—just because I'm in this house again. With Mother." She shuddered. "Oh, Lewis, it was providential that I had Louisa and the children and Maum Easter here when—Papa died. I think I might have—perished with confusion otherwise."

He tilted her face up to his. "Not you. Not my girl."

"Yes, your girl!"

"Now, look here, I'm sure little Seton is going to get right into her heart, Margaret. We've got to be hopeful. Isn't that what you told me? That we have an *obligation to hope?*"

She began to smile. "You see? I need you—I even need you to remind me of my own splendid sermons!"

He laughed softly. "But you have me. And I now offer a small sermon to you. A suggestion, at least. Let's not mention again to your mother about how we both long to leave Panama Mills and move back to Hibernia. I think that will help the situation here a lot. I don't know quite why, but I think it will."

Reminding herself of her own sermon on hope, Margaret knocked on her mother's door the day they were to leave for Jacksonville—determined to try once more to move closer to the woman who, for all the years of her life, had given her everything but understanding and affection.

When Margaret opened the door and walked softly in, Matilda turned from her dressing table to greet her with a smile. "You'll have a nice day for travel, my dear."

"Yes," Margaret said. "Just enough wind to fill our sails, but the water should be smooth."

"I'd say your sails are well filled," Matilda said, turning back to the careful arranging of her graying brown hair. "But then, you've always been a happy child."

"You've been so kind to us all since we've been here," Margaret said. "I'm very grateful. So is Lewis."

"Lewis's children are lovely guests," Matilda said. "And Charles Seton is—almost too beautiful to be true. Such a smile! Every baby isn't that handsome, Margaret. Don't expect it. This child is a gift from God."

Watching the older woman's face in the looking glass, Margaret saw tears well again in the eyes which seemed never to approve or to disapprove.

"The baby is well named, of course," her mother went on. "Your father was the most perfectly formed man I ever saw. His face, his hands, his carriage. I've always been thankful that you look like him—not me."

How, Margaret thought, did one go about responding to such a statement? After an awkward moment, she said, "You just wait. Someday I'll have a daughter named for you—who looks exactly like you."

Taking her time, Matilda smoothed the soft loops of hair down over her ears and turned to face Margaret. "There is one thing you must promise me. No matter how much you and Colonel Fleming want to leave Panama Mills—and, heaven knows, I loathe the idea of your living in a mill settlement— you must promise *not* to leave your grandfather in a lurch."

Margaret looked at her for a long time, then she said, "Do you really think Lewis would do a thing like that?"

"No. Except for the well-known fact of the Flemings' love for that land on the St. Johns River. The Fatios were the same about their land at New Switzerland. Love of the land runs in both families."

"Poor Louisa. That's all over for her—forever."

"Louisa is a strong woman. She'll be all right in St. Augustine. Will you promise what I've asked, Margaret?"

"Lewis makes our decisions and he is going to be faithful to his agreement with Grandfather Sibbald. What more can I say?"

A small smile creased Matilda's face. "Colonel Fleming may make the final decisions, but he worships you. Should you show the slightest discontent at Panama Mills—"

"Mother, listen to me," Margaret cut in sharply. "We both want to move to Hibernia just as soon as we can, but for a matter of years, it just isn't possible. Even if Lewis and I were as untrustworthy as you seem to imply, we can't move back yet."

"And you shouldn't. Certainly not into some kind of makeshift shelter there. You'd be no more comfortable than you are at Panama Mills. Wait, Margaret. Wait until it's the right time."

If only her mother would smile, even her cool smile. If only she would hold out her arms. She did neither.

"I—promise, Mother. For Lewis, too."

"Thank you, my dear. You've always been a good daughter."

Margaret felt her body, her whole being, slump. "Have I, Mother? Have I?"

Late that evening, Margaret, carrying the baby, and Lewis and the boys the luggage, the little family walked the short distance from the Jacksonville dock to the two-storied, unpainted frame house where Sophia Fleming lived with Susan and John L'Engle. John L'Engle, as usual, showed little emotion when they first presented the new baby. Attractive, bright-eyed Susan made them more than welcome and praised and praised Charles Seton's beauty.

Then, while they all still stood in the large front hall, Susan said, "Lewis, I'm going to answer before you ask about your mother. She couldn't make it downstairs today. Not even for such an occasion. The poor darling is in enormous pain. Fuming, naturally, since she delights in being part of a welcoming committee."

"She isn't ill, is she?" Lewis asked. "I mean—it's only the rhuematism, isn't it?"

"That's all," John said. "Absolutely all. Bad enough, I have no doubt. But she's fine otherwise. She just eats too much. If she'd lose some of that weight, she'd walk better."

"Grandmother Fleming isn't fat," L.I. put in. "She's just portly."

"I couldn't imagine her thin," Margaret said. "She wouldn't look like herself. Such a dignified lady. We're so sorry. Is there anything to do for her?"

Lewis smiled. "It's always been a little hard to take care of Mother. Frankly, even at my age, it's hard for me to imagine her needing care."

"Well, she does need it now," Susan said. "And she's very grateful for everything that's done. When this horrible pain strikes, she's—almost like a helpless little girl."

Lewis looked genuinely amazed. "Is that so?"

"I'll go sit on her lap," Tina offered. "She always liked me a lot."

Susan hugged the child. "Everyone loves you, Tina. But I doubt that your grandmother could bear your weight on her poor legs now. You're getting to be such a big girl."

"I'll be eight this year."

"I'd like to try to help Grandmother's pain," George said in a quiet, firm voice. "I think I can. I've been reading a medical book I found in the Seton's library. I think I know what might help. She's kind of—scary, but I'd like to try."

Relieved, Lewis said, "Why don't you do that, son? Sounds like a good idea." To the others, he added, "George just might turn out to be a doctor someday. I don't know how many birds—gulls, woodpeckers, blue jays—are flying around Panama Mills right now because he splinted their damaged wings and legs."

"What would you do for her, George?" Margaret asked.

"Hot compresses, if she'll let me."

"Oh, I'm afraid we've tried that," Susan said gently. "Our Dolly does that twice a day."

"Excuse me, Cousin Susan, but that isn't often enough. I'd be glad to keep them up—for hours. It might help."

"Is Mother in too much pain, Susan, for us to visit her now?" Lewis wanted to know.

"Well, I—I think perhaps for all of you at once."

"Papa, maybe I should go up alone first—just take a pan of hot water and some soft cloths with me when I go."

Lewis gave George a grateful smile. "I think that's a splendid idea, son. But, please do explain why I—why we will wait until the two of you have things more in hand."

"Oh, he'll do that," L.I. grinned. "We both know Grandma."

Being the proper hostess was bred into Sophia Fleming's bones, so much so that everyone knew her misery must be great. Too great even to greet Lewis on the night of their arrival, knowing full well that he and his family had to leave the next afternoon. Only George saw her that first night and he stayed in her room applying hot compresses to her pain-wracked legs for hour after hour. The next morning, she felt up to seeing L.I. and Tina, then Margaret and the baby. Finally, Lewis.

"Come in, come in, Lewis," she called. Her voice was remarkably firm, he thought, as he bent to kiss her. "You look like a duchess propped on all those pillows. I like that elegant purple dressing gown."

"The color is called plum. I am better. Sit down."

He flinched a little as he settled his lame leg over the other, then grinned. "Still not quite able to get that leg to cross itself, but otherwise, few problems."

"You are watching your limp, I notice. Good. Half of mastery over all pain is *will*. I know—and I am better. In fact, I could easily have come downstairs for breakfast today, but my doctor refused to allow it."

"George?"

"George. Lewis? The boy wants to become a doctor. We must let nothing stand in his way. He has the touch for it—and the patience, which is more than I can say for any doctor in this vicinity."

"Why do you think I'm working so hard, Mama? I mean to educate both my boys."

"He's seventeen," she said. "There isn't much time. If you don't have all the money required, just let me know. That boy must reach his goal. He's a real Fatio and a real Fleming. No better blood."

"I wouldn't think of letting you help, Mother. I'm doing well."

"Not well enough to send two boys to school and rebuild at Hibernia. You must do both, Lewis. Your father would insist."

"There's time yet for George. A year, at least. I'm planning to sell off some Hibernia timber to Mr. Sibbald. I'll manage."

"You don't have his gorgeous dark red hair, but you're as stubborn as your father. More so, I think. At least, when he was in a stubborn streak, he could still make me laugh. You're not very good at that, are you, Lewis? A fortunate thing, I'd say, that you have a cheerful wife. I like her very much. She needs to mature, of course, but she will. And, of course, that new son of yours is extraordinary. Sturdy, bright, pretty as a picture. I confess I'm a bit disappointed, though, that you didn't name him for a Fleming or a Fatio. Your wife's idea, I imagine."

"No, mine. I was deeply devoted to her father."

"I see. Well, visit me again later in the day, son. Thanks to Doctor George, I'll be up and around in no time."

Lewis got to his feet. "I'm sure you will be. And—don't forget, Mama, I'll be rebuilding some kind of house at Hibernia in a very few years. There will always be a room for you."

She waved her hand airily. "For me, Hibernia left when your father went away. I'm contented here. Susan is superior company. I ignore her husband when the need arises. But he is kind in his heart, I think. Send George to me before he leaves. And—Lewis, you must be a father to Margaret, too. She's still very young." She smiled the sweet smile that always disarmed him. "Young—and very, very beautiful." She reached for his hand. "You're a handsome gentleman, too, Lewis. Keep your hair. It isn't your father's dark red, but it's a fine head of brown hair."

"I'll see you after a while, Mother."

"Yes. Watch that limp, now."

"Mother and I got along rather well, I thought," Lewis said as he climbed into bed beside Margaret that night back at Panama Mills. "Only two admonitions—'keep your hair' and 'watch your limp.'" He took Margaret in his arms. "Do you think your mother will ever visit us here at the Mills?"

"Never, Lewis. I didn't even ask. Don't tell me you invited your mother here."

"No. Even if she were able, that would also be a waste of breath."

Margaret sighed heavily. "I sigh a lot when we talk about mothers, don't I? Why is that? Why do I expect my mother to be different—just because I'm so happy with you?"

"I doubt that you really expect it, dearest. You—want it. You want to share our joy with her. The fact that you do just proves how great your heart really is."

She nestled closer on his shoulder. "Flattery will get you anywhere, Colonel Fleming."

"I'm exactly where I want to be. We're going home again. We're together. What else is there? Our mill hut here isn't fine enough for either of our mothers, but it's what we have right now."

"I'd be happy in a barn with you."

"How about a remodeled warehouse?"

Up on her elbow, she laughed down at him—her face plainly visible in the light from the full sailing moon outside.

"Are you teasing me, Lewis? What are you thinking of?"

"Just what I said—a remodeled warehouse. A little south of where my house stood at Hibernia, oh, two or three acres distant, there's a good, sturdy, two-storied warehouse. Pompey kept our oranges there before the freeze killed back the trees. It would take a lot of work, but your grandfather offered us whatever lumber we ever need at cost. Carpenter Joe is still there. Pompey's good with his hands. I think I could put that old warehouse into livable shape someday."

"Does the warehouse stand on the opposite side of the road from where the big house stood—down around that curve in the lane?"

"That's right."

"Then I know exactly the building you mean. And it's still there? It didn't burn?"

"Nope."

"When can we start?"

Laughing, he pulled her back down on his shoulder. "Not anytime soon. I can't leave the mills yet and I do have two boys to educate. Mother insists she'll help if I send George to medical school, but I mean to do it myself."

"He wants to be a doctor, Lewis."

"He's told you?"

"Yes. Last year. But darling, he confided in me first *only* because he didn't want to put any pressure on you with all the mill problems to handle here."

"I'm delighted he told you first. I love you for the way you have with my children. They're—your children now, Margaret, because I'm yours."

Margaret kissed him long and deeply. Then, whispered, "Show me, Lewis. Show me how much you love me . . ."

"But it's late. You've had a long day. Shouldn't you sleep?"

"Not when I've just learned that—someday I'll be the mistress of—a warehouse castle! How could I sleep, Lewis? How?"

21

By late the following year, 1840, the Flemings had made their third trip to Hibernia and definite plans to begin work on the old warehouse had caught up with their dreams. Lewis felt he had adequately trained young Fred Bumback to replace him at the Mills and as soon as work was completed at Hibernia, they could move.

"I would like for you to stay at the Mills," Charles Sibbald wrote Lewis on the day after Christmas, "but since little Charles Seton is my own great-grandson, I quite agree that Hibernia provides the best environment for his young years. Consequently, nothing detains you at Panama Mills now except the work on your future home at Hibernia. I trust your judgment concerning Fred Bumback to succeed you as superintendent."

The very day he received that letter, Lewis called Bumback into his mill office. "It could be that the new year will hold some changes, Fred. Before it's over, you will undoubtedly be the new mill superintendent," Lewis said, as the stockily built, curly-haired Bumback straddled a chair across from Lewis's paper-strewn desk.

"I'm ready, sir. And I'm most grateful to you."

"I want one thing understood, though," Lewis went on. "I've never taken anything more seriously than my obligation to Mr. Sibbald. He's taking my recommendation that you're the man. You're intelligent, Fred. You're an excellent supply manager. We haven't had but a few late deliveries and they were caused by the usual holiday celebrations among the millhands."

Fred snorted. "That's one thing I'll never tolerate once I'm in charge, sir."

"And that may be your weak point."

Bumback's boyish, round face stared at him. "My—weak point? To expect a man to report on time for work in exchange for his wages?"

"For as long as there have been lumber operations, there has been that problem of drinking. These men get up at dawn, go to their work, quit at dark, eat, sleep and begin it all over again. No recreation except an occasional game of horseshoes, a little fishing—and a bout of drinking. With no education, no church nearby, they have nothing to feed them—inside."

"They stuff their guts and that's all they know about their insides. You mean to tell me you don't blame 'em when they get too drunk to show up at their saws?"

"I try to understand them."

Bumback seemed genuinely dumbfounded. "*Understand* millhands?"

Lewis nodded. "I see a superintendent's job as going further than merely seeing to timber purchases and supplies. Mr. Sibbald's granddaughter, my wife, agrees. She's helped enormously by inviting some of the wives of our most troublesome workers to the house for talks. Once or twice, she's found that the fault lay with the wives."

Fred laughed. Not unpleasantly. He was genuinely puzzled. "I fail to see what business it is of ours whether or not those yokels get along with their wives!"

"Perhaps that word 'yokel' is a clue for you. Is it?"

Fred shook his head. "Colonel Fleming, I—just don't know what you're tryin' to say to me."

"Only that we hire *human beings* to work here. Educated or not, bullheaded or not, pleasant or ugly, they are human beings and they are to be treated that way. Mrs. Fleming is sure her grandfather would be in agreement on this. He just hasn't known or thought about it."

"I'll wager he's thought about the short profits every time a gang of sawyers is too drunk to work." Abruptly, Fred turned red in the face, his voice intense, hard—his eyes, Lewis thought, almost fanatical. "I have to tell you one thing, sir. It ain't my place to say it—you're still my boss—but you're too soft. The way I figure it, they can't have somethin' that's beyond them. Why, there isn't a man out there who would even know what the word *understanding* means! They understand one thing—rough treatment. They understand when they ain't been paid because they've been sousing it up. No, sir. I never have known why a grown man drinks till he loses control of himself and I never will." Measuring his words, he added arrogantly, "Not a drop of liquor has passed my lips in fifteen years!"

Lewis smiled. "Very commendable, but fifteen years ago,

you must have been all of fifteen. You've never had one too
many since then?"

"I haven't even had—one. And I never will." Bumback
jumped up. "You got something against me. I can tell. I've
got to know what you're drivin' at, Colonel."

Lewis frowned. "I'd hoped you'd see for yourself. You're
the man I've picked out—almost from the start. I'm leaving, I
imagine, within the year. But, unless you change your attitude toward the men who need our help, I'll have to warn
Sibbald that you tend to be a self-righteous bully. That's all I
have to say, Fred, except that I want your word that you'll go
back to your cabin and think this over. Not with a locked
mind, either. Take the afternoon off and think. You have
everything else to offer. You'll make a fine superintendent, *if*
you can find a way to—join the human race with our men."

After Lewis finished his noon meal and returned to the
office that day, Margaret sat for a long time beside Seton's
cradle studying the beautiful features, the thick, dark hair,
the sturdy little fists, doubled even in sleep. He's really not
like any of us, she thought. Oh, he has my father's name and
Lewis's eyes, but such black, black hair. Could my first baby
be a throwback to one of Lewis's Irish ancestors? Lewis's
father, George, had left Ireland alone, so of course Lewis had
never seen his Irish ancestors. He knew only that for some
unexplained reason, the young George Fleming had fled his
village of Shane near the hill where Saint Patrick kindled his
paschal fire in full view of pagan King Laoghaire and his
druids. A romantic story, but it told nothing of why George
Fleming left the turbulent land of Ireland for which Hibernia
was named. Trouble, she supposed. Some kind of trouble, or
perhaps merely a daring spirit of adventure.

The baby sighed in his sleep, twisted his well-formed head
back and forth on the pillow as though being a mere infant
had already begun to confine him. There were some men of
action in her own Scottish background, too. Royalty in one's
ancestry had always only amused her, but it was in the Seton
line, which passed through the royal house of Bruce by the
marriage of Sir Christoll Seton with Christina, the sister of
King Robert Bruce. Sir Christoll, knighted by Bruce, had
saved the king at the hands of the English at Methwen. He
had won the king's sister by his act of daring. Of course, poor
Sir Christoll Seton lost his head to the English in the end.

A loud, hammered knock at the front door sent her flying to the upstairs hall. Easter would answer, since Lewis forbade Margaret ever to open their door unless she knew for certain who stood outside.

In a moment, she heard the front door open and Maum Easter's voice boom: "Who you wanta' see, sir?"

A man's voice, husky, hoarse, replied, "Missus Fleming."

"She restin' right now."

The voice rose. "Tell her Mr. Fred Bumback is here and that what I have to say will be of interest to her."

"Do Mausa Lewis know you're here?" There was a silence, then Easter growled, "Don't you dare push in that door! You hear me? You drunk! Now, git!"

Margaret heard what sounded like a scuffle and then the door banged shut. "Maum Easter," she called. "Is he gone?"

"No, ma'am. I'm right here in your front hall," Fred called back. "Mill business, Missus Fleming."

When Margaret reached the bottom of the stair, there Easter stood, arms folded, glaring at the young man in his best suit and tie, weaving unsteadily in the middle of the downstairs hall.

"Won't you come in, Mr. Bumback?"

His silly grin was somehow pathetic, although Margaret could see that he was indeed quite drunk. She led the way in to the small, dark parlor. Bumback stumbled over the rag hall rug as he followed. Easter cleared her throat loudly, so that Margaret would know she was keeping a vigil just outside the parlor door.

"I 'preshiate this, Missus Fleming," Fred said, with a bow which threw him decidedly off balance. Then, he sat down awkwardly on a straight chair. "I was telling your husband this morning—ain't many men that's got a smart wife like you."

"What is it you need to discuss, Mr. Bumback?"

He grinned. "I—just felt like—I couldn't stand it another minute—without feastin' my eyes on a—bee-utiful woman!"

Margaret stood quickly. "Please leave, sir."

"Now, now, now, hold your horses, ma'am. I don't—mean no harm. I know I've had a little drink, but—" he straightened his stocky shoulders. "But—I'm gonna be the superintendent of these mills one day an' I thought—well, I was wonderin' if you had any advice to give me."

Still standing, Margaret said tersely, "None whatever, except that I guarantee you will never be the superintendent of my grandfather's mills if your present disgusting condition is a habit."

He stood, raising his hand in protest. "You don't understand at all, dear lady. I'm dead set *against* hard drinkin'. That's just what your husband's been tryin' his level best to change about me. He's tryin' to say I'm too hard on the rotten millhands that swill booze like pigs swill slops! I'm against it. He's for it. He says you are, too. An'—" His speech grew still more slurred. He seemed about to fall back onto the chair. "An'—I thought you oughta try to make him see the straight of it."

"Neither Colonel Fleming nor I defend drunkenness. In fact, your accusation is so ridiculous, I have nothing more to say to you. Please go at once."

"The only thing Fleming's got against me is that I'm too hard on the white trash an' niggers when they're drunk. He tol' me!" His voice rose. "Says you an' him tries to help 'em instead of lettin' 'em know who's boss." He gave a silly laugh. "Blamin' their wives for their boozin' 'cause you're afraid to face the men, eh? Well, I'm not blamin' ya fer that. They'd never keep their pants on five minutes around you, Missus Fleming."

Easter cleared her throat with a mighty roar.

Margaret, still standing very straight, said, "And—who's going to get hard with you for the exhibition you're putting on now, Mr. Bumback? Will you horsewhip yourself?"

He opened his mouth to speak, but without warning, burst into tears, rushed out into the hall past Easter and slammed the front door behind him.

Margaret sank into a chair as Easter bustled in.

"You all right, Miss Mar'ret?"

"Yes. Yes, I'm fine. Just trying to figure out what that was all about."

Easter snorted. "Don't reckon you wants me to tell ya."

"There's a plausible reason of some kind, I'm sure. That young man has always been a gentleman around me. He's very capable. He's—oh, Easter, he's—our way back to Hibernia!"

"You reckon Mausa Lewis done tol' him how you try to help some of these women? That they come here?"

"Yes. I'm sure he did, but why was Fred Bumback drunk?"

"Too much rum."

"I remember Lewis telling me that this man always flies into a real rage at the millhands when they drink too much. A kind of—helpless rage." She looked at her watch. "Oh, I wish it were time for Lewis to come home!"

"You gonna tell Mausa Lewis 'bout what he said 'bout them white trash an' their—pants?"

Margaret smiled weakly. "Well, maybe not that. But, we have to get to the real reason behind it all. Fred Bumback has worked so hard to earn his promotion. It's terribly important to him—and, oh, Easter, it's terribly important to us. Lewis won't leave if there's any doubt that Mr. Bumback can handle the work!"

Fred Bumback ran, stumbling, down the sandy road from the Fleming house and across the lumberyard to Lewis's office. Without knocking, he burst in.

"I gotta talk to you, Colonel Fleming," he gasped.

Lewis stared at the distraught young man. "Bumback! What's happened?"

"I—I insulted your wife, sir."

"You—what? Where did you see her?"

His head hanging, Fred mumbled, "At—at your house. I started to my cabin to think about what you—told me. But—for some reason, I stopped on the way and got some whiskey." He stretched his hands in a helpless gesture. "I—I don't know what made me do it, sir. I—hadn't had a drink in fifteen years! I didn't think I'd—ever have another one."

"Is my wife all right?"

Fred nodded.

"Then sit down. There's something I want to ask you. Why is it so important to you not to have had a drink in fifteen years when you're not quite thirty years old now? Boys don't drink!"

"I did, sir. I—was a drunk at fifteen."

Lewis took a deep breath. "I see. And you stopped. How?"

"I—killed my mother. That—made me stop."

"You—what?"

"Oh, the same as. She was sick. We lived alone together in St. Mary's. She needed a doctor. I—was drunk. I was scared I stopped off at a tavern instead of—"

"Instead of going for the doctor. And your mother died."

Without looking up, Fred shook his head yes.

Leaning back in his chair, Lewis thought for a long time

"Fred? I think you've just cleared up my puzzle over you. You *were* self-righteous—you did feel superior to those other men who drink too much, didn't you?"

He nodded. "Yes, sir. I didn't know it, but I thought—if a—fifteen-year-old boy could quit—anybody could. I was a hard drinker from the time I was nine. My—father died—drunk. It was always in the house."

"I see."

"Do you, Colonel Fleming? Can you—can you believe I didn't touch a drop—until today?"

"Yes. I have no problem believing that. And I think I have an idea why you did it today."

Fred made the helpless gesture again. "But I—don't! I've worked like a dog to teach myself things—I've read every book I could lay my hands on. I didn't—don't want to be—a yoke. I—"

"That isn't hard to believe either. Your conduct until today and your work prove it. These mills will be here for as long as you live. You can be certain of a good position—if today marks the end of such childish behavior."

"Childish?"

"Childish, Bumback. A mature man has other resources to turn to. Either within himself—or from God. Or both. Do you believe anything about God?"

"Oh, yes, sir. It was a preacher up in Georgia helped me quit drinkin' all those years ago. Sometimes, I wish we had a church here."

"So do I. Fred, do you understand at all why you went for that whiskey today?"

"No, sir. I sure don't."

"I think I do. You were scared."

"Scared?"

"That what I said about your bullying the millhands instead of trying to help them might influence my recommendation to Mr. Sibbald." Fred was listening intently now. "Taking my place here means more to you than anything in the world. You were afraid you might lose that chance—and you obviously had no idea why. By the look on your face this minute, I have hope that you're beginning to see. Are you?"

Fred studied his stubby fingers, then looked at Lewis with the beginnings of a smile. "I—guess I was full of pride, wasn't I? My mama always said pride made a person hard." Lewis waited for him to go further on his own. "Yes, Colonel

Fleming, I think I've—caught on. I don't think you'll have what you called a 'self-righteous bully' on your hands anymore. You'll have to kind of guide me through the rest of this year—until you leave, but I feel sure I've learned my lesson."

Lewis shook his hand. "I believe you. Now, go home and sleep it off. I'll see you in the morning."

"Sometime, can I drop by your house when you're there, so's I can apologize to Mrs. Fleming?"

"I expect you to. But don't worry about it today. She's a sturdy lady."

The redemptive way in which the Bumback incident turned out—an incident which could have been so ugly—seemed to propel Lewis and Margaret more steadily toward their return to Hibernia.

"Mr. Bumback's apology was very convincing," Margaret said as she and Lewis sat together on the old mill dock on a mild night three days after Christmas. "You handled him so well, sir, I think I will begin right now to love you more."

Lewis laughed. "It wasn't all virtue on my part. I want to get away from here. I want to—go home."

She scooted closer to him. "Do you think we can plan on an actual moving date after our visit there next week?"

"Maybe. The new tin roof must be on the old warehouse by now. I know Maum Easter misses him being here, but with Pompey at Hibernia helping Joe, only the weather can hold things up. The men can't spend full time on the remodeling, of course. But with the roof on, the new flooring can begin to go down." He tightened his arm around her reassuringly. "I'm pretty sure we'll have an approximate date after our visit next week."

They sat awhile, listening to the water lap the pilings beneath them. After a time, Margaret said, "Maum Easter misses her daughter, too. I'll be glad for Easter's sake when we're all back home."

"Easter's the one who insisted that Betty go along to cook for Pompey. That man's as spoiled as I am."

"Do you know what that dear Betty said to me just before she and Pompey left Panama Mills? She made an announcement that sounded for all the world like her mother by informing me that you and I were never to worry about our old ages."

"She did?"

"When Maum Easter is too old to look after us, Betty will be right there. She even said proudly that one day we'd call her 'Maum Betty'!"

"They're probably the best friends we have outside of Louisa."

A decision had been made to send George to medical school at the University of Pennsylvania and for some time they spoke of that. He was to spend the first travel night with Matilda Seton at Fernandina, but what touched both Margaret and Lewis was George's request to say good-bye to Hibernia. Their visit next week had been planned to coincide with George's departure.

"I confess his old father is fairly proud to have scraped up two full years' tuition under the circumstances. It won't be easy seeing him go, though." Lewis rubbed his bad leg, stiffening a bit in the evening chill. "George knows, my dear, that without your inheritance to pay for our new Hibernia furniture, I couldn't have sent him to medical school this year."

"Lewis! I didn't want you to tell him that at all!"

"I know," he answered calmly. "But I did. I wanted him to know that you're behind him as much as I. He was very moved by your generosity."

"Fiddlesticks."

"*And* he's flattered utterly that you're trusting him to select most of the furniture himself in Philadelphia."

"Oh, George has beautiful taste! He's a superior, finely tuned human being. He'll make a marvelous doctor. I have only one question. Can he bear the suffering he'll have to see—and cause? Doctors have to hurt people in order to heal them sometimes."

"I wonder," he mused, "if there's another woman in the whole Florida Territory who *thinks* as much and as hard as you."

"That just shows you how little you know about women, Lewis?"

"Hm?"

"Something else important is going to happen while we're at Hibernia next week. And don't try to get me to tell you now, because I'm saving it until the minute George is out of sight downriver toward Jacksonville."

He embraced her. "Mrs. Fleming, how did I ever find you?"

"You didn't, sir. I found you!"

be right there. She even said recently that one
her Maura Betty.
"They're probably the Lord grants we la

22

On his first night away from his family—the fourth of January
1841—George sat facing Matilda Seton in the spacious, formal parlor of the Fernandina house. The weather had turned
cold and a fire crackled in the large tiled fireplace. Two
hand-painted oil lamps cast almost eerie, wavering shadows
across the beamed ceiling. George was desperately homesick
already. In spite of Matilda Seton's urging, he had eaten
almost no supper. Saying goodbye to his father was far harder
than he'd anticipated. With all his heart, he thanked God that
Miss Margaret had told him secretly that her surprise for
Papa—not to be divulged until George was gone—was the
good news of another baby. "But I don't want you to tell my
mother, George," Miss Margaret had cautioned. "She might
be hurt that I sent word—secondhand."

Now that he was with Matilda Seton alone, he surely
understood. She was, as always, handsome, beautifully dressed,
but a hard woman to talk to.

"I'm sure you're tired, George," Mrs. Seton was saying.
"Don't stay up for courtesy's sake. A boat trip is twice as
tiring in cold, windy weather."

"Yes, ma'am," he said, "I'm a little tired, but I guess—I'm
just wondering about everybody—back at Hibernia. They
were all out on the old dock to wave me off. Miss Margaret
even brought little Seton. You have a wonderful daughter,
ma'am. My stepmother." He grinned. "I still call her Miss
Margaret. L.I. and Tina and I got to know her—and love
her—as 'Miss Margaret.' I guess we might always call her
that."

"My daughter is extremely fond of you, too. She especially
remarked to me once about your sensitivity." Matilda cleared
her throat. "Are you too tired to tell me a little more about
her—living conditions—when they move back to Hibernia?
Margaret is simply not accustomed to anything like—a remodeled warehouse."

"Oh, it's going to be very comfortable and, anyway, she
won't be there always. Just until my father educates my

165

brother and me. Miss Margaret and Papa are already talking about the beautiful place they're going to build at Hibernia someday. Near where the old house stood."

"I see. But that could be years away."

"Maybe ten or so. Mrs. Seton, you don't need to worry at all about Miss Margaret. Fine houses are wonderful to own, but the older I get, the more I believe that nothing is as important as love." He paused. "Miss Margaret is really loved."

"I'm sure she is. Now, it's time for you to retire." She coughed dryly. "By the way, if you should happen to be up early enough tomorrow, I'd like you to help me select a few things here which you think Margaret might need—or like— in that remodeled warehouse."

15 September 1841
Panama Mills

My dearest Louisa,

Your latest letter, mentioning your dream of finding a larger house in St. Augustine for paying guests is beside me as I write and I can't believe six weeks have gone by without my answering. Grandfather Sibbald was here in early August and fully approves of Fred Bumback as Lewis's successor. The way is cleared for us to return to Hibernia—except for foolish me! And equally foolish Lewis. You see, I have not been as well carrying this baby as with Seton. I have had stupid dizzy spells, nausea, and general weakness, which does not leave me even after a night's rest. I am thoroughly disgusted with myself because more than anything, Lewis wanted this child born at Hibernia. Of course, so did I. You know how fear haunts Lewis, though, when I am pregnant, because of Augustina. And so, rather than increase his fears, I have agreed (not very gracefully) to remain at Panama Mills near a Jacksonville doctor, should Easter need help with me. Pray for me, Louisa. Pray for Lewis. I am not one bit worried about myself or the baby, but you have a straight line to God and your prayers will bolster me no end. I almost envy you having a church right there in St. Augustine just down the street. A real Episcopal church of your very own! And just as I wrote these words, I think a small dream formed. As you know so well, Hibernia is as isolated as it is beautiful, but why couldn't Lewis and I build a tiny chapel there someday? I'm sure a priest would stop now and then. And I'd have a real church where I could kneel anytime of the day or night and be with God. He is with me now, I know, since no place is too remote for His loving presence. But the dream has been born, Louisa! Pray about that, too. Lewis, of course, was baptized in the Catholic church there in St. Augustine, but his is a simple faith. I'm sure he would want me to have my church. Funny, but he and I seldom mention my being an Episcopalian and he a Catholic. I am married to the most understanding, loving man on the face of this old earth.

We hear often from dear George. He is, as I expected, doing well and misses us. And I was able to place in our Hibernia house all the lovely things he selected, including the cherished pieces from Mother. L.I. misses George, as do we all, but he, too, is looking toward next year when he will leave for Amherst College. He was definitely decided that he will be a lawyer. Lewis, bless him, is at peace about his sons and has managed, in spite of his dreadful losses, to have their expenses in hand. Tina is so grown-up. She is nine and, as she says, going on ten. And such a help to me. My beautiful Seton is full of energy and joy. I marvel, dear Louisa, oh, I marvel, at the miracle of his growth and awakening to everything around him! I have watched him change from a sleeping baby to a true individual with exuberant curiosity—he is now two years and seven months. And every whit as impatient and ready to grab at life as his mother! Whatever problems he ever causes for himself, I will be forced to understand because already I see so much of the rebel part of me in him. He is going to be poor at waiting, as I have always been. For example, when it is time to eat and right while I'm walking across the room with his bowl in my hands, he beats his high chair and shouts his impatience. He is already making complete sentences. He calls himself "Seton"—never "I." "Seton wants Papa." That means he has a sudden notion that Lewis is to dress him after his bath. I don't think he's selfish, though. He gives of that beautiful smile too freely to us all.

Of course, dear Maum Easter is crushed that Lewis will have a doctor on hand when our next baby comes—now, in about two or three weeks. But she, like Seton, worships Lewis, and so, scowling and grumbling, she has agreed. I secretly hope that she and I will fool both my husband and the doctor, so that Lewis will just come home one day from the mills and find a new—son. Don't I want a daughter? Yes, someday. More than one. But L.I. will be leaving us soon and it did give me such joy to be able to tell Lewis after George left that there would be another *boy*. Of course, he knew I stretched the truth a little, but I mean to hope, hope, hope.

Our remodeled warehouse at Hibernia is going to be wonderful. It is ready now. We'd be there except for Lewis's jitters over me. Surely, we will be there by Christmas—with a room for you and Sophia when you can come.

There has been no Indian trouble near here for months, but I pray for the day when Lewis feels sure it is safe for me to visit you in St. Augustine. I am so excited over your new role as hostess to *Northern* guests. Lewis joins me in sending you and Sophia all the love there is. I still miss you.

> Your aff't friend,
> Margaret Seton Fleming.

After a long, hard trip from Jacksonville by boat and horseback, Lewis and Dr. Smith raced into the Panama Mills house in time for the doctor to examine Margaret *and* the new baby. He pronounced them both fit, took his leave, and a red-faced Lewis sat beside her once more, looking down at another son.

"His name is Francis Philip Fleming, Lewis," she said. "I must write to Louisa tomorrow. She'll be so pleased that we've named him for a Fatio. I'm sure I'll feel up to writing, aren't you?"

"No. And I wish I had something to say about it, but I don't." He took her hand. "He isn't as beautiful as Seton, but even with that sparse light brown hair, I predict he'll be—an important man. Thank you, Mrs. Fleming. Thank you."

"I love you, Lewis."

"I love you, Margaret."

When the sun came up beyond the big mill on November 11, 1841, Margaret's eyes flew open. At last, at last, today, *this day*, they were leaving Panama Mills for Hibernia to stay. Lewis lay sleeping quietly beside her, his hand on her thigh in the tender, belonging way she had come to love—to depend on. Already, Easter was bustling downstairs. She is as excited as I am, Margaret thought, about going back to Hiberia to Pompey, to Little Jim, to Owen—to her daughter, Betty.

Margaret longed to jump out of bed—fly to the window to

see what the sun had planned for the day. She lay still. The
moment was too deep. The last waking up time at Panama
Mills. Now that the years there were ending, they seemed
brief. Time enough for Lewis to offer a new life to dependable Fred Bumback, to put her grandfather's mills in order.
Time enough for her to have given Lewis two sons. Her eyes
filled unexpectedly with tears—so many they dripped into
her ears. She dared not sniffle. Lewis might come awake.
This moment would—could never come again. Sweetly, sharply, the moment held. Everything for which she had ever
longed—lay ahead, was already hers, would always be hers
because the warm, dear, sleeping man beside her had given
her his love.

"Good morning, Mrs. Fleming," he murmured, his eyes
still closed, his hand pressing her thigh ever so lightly, still
too sleepy for the brisk pats with which he normally began
their day. "Good morning, Mrs. Fleming," he whispered
again. "I love you."

"I love you, Lewis," she breathed. "Oh, how I—love you!"

He opened one eye. "This is the day, isn't it?"

"Yes, dearest. This is the day."

His arms around her now, he asked, "Then, why do you
suppose we don't—leap out of bed?"

"I don't know," she whispered, "except maybe we both
think it's too good to be true!" She pressed his head down
onto her shoulder. "Can you believe it? Can you really believe
we're going—home at last?"

The steamer reached the Hibernia dock right at noon, but
poor Betty's meal was cold by the time everyone greeted and
hugged everyone else. There was laughter, shouts, the chickens scurried about, every dog at the quarters barked and
L.I., whooping, ran from tree to tree patting each familiar
oak and magnolia and cypress.

Even Maum Easter approved of what had been done in her
absence. She not only praised Pompey for his work on the
remodeled warehouse, after checking the spotlessness of the
floors, furniture and windowsills, the supply of food laid in,
the new linens properly made up on the beds, she took her
daughter Betty aside to say: "Everything's all right. Yes,
child. Everything's all right."

Thanksgiving and Christmas were festive, with nothing but

George's absence to mar the family closeness and joy in one another.

After dark, on New Year's Day, 1842, mounting the steep stairs behind Lewis, who held the candle, Margaret said, "Colonel Fleming, are you ready for a lovely event in this new year of 1842?"

He stopped halfway up the stairs. "Margaret! You're not going to have another baby so soon, are you?"

"No, idiot. But we will have our fifth wedding anniversary this spring! Are you ready?"

He laughed. "Of course, I'm ready—but that isn't till the eighth of March!"

"I know it, but it is this year. I just wanted to be sure you were ready."

In the narrow upstairs hall, he held the candle so it lit her face. "I'm ready for our fifth, our fifteenth—our fiftieth!"

"So am I, oh, so am I. But, Lewis, fifty years seems such a short time to be with you!"

23

When their fifth anniversary rolled around, the Seminoles having retreated at last to the Everglades, it was common knowledge everywhere in north Florida that all danger of an Indian attack was past. Still, because L.I. had been away in school at Amherst only a few weeks, Margaret waited even to mention a visit to Louisa in St. Augustine. She missed L.T., too. His going had robbed Hibernia of so much downright fun and good cheer, but Tina, past ten now, tried hard to compensate. She adored the baby, Frank, and in no time was adept at changing his diapers, bathing and feeding him. By the hour, she and Margaret discussed Frank and Seton.

"Frank is much better behaved than Seton was at his age, don't you think, Miss Margaret?" Tina asked one rainy April day as she tied a small, careful knot in Frank's clean diaper.

"He most certainly is," Margaret agreed. "Won't it be interesting to watch them both grow up—begin to show even more differences? I can see Frank now—a tall, gangly boy—shinnying up a tree faster than the wind. Jumping high in the air, his arms long enough to reach any magnolia pod I might fancy. I think Frank will be the quiet, thoughtful one of the two. Maybe even serious."

"I wish you were my real mother," Tina said, as they stood watching the healthy baby inspect his own feet.

Margaret embraced the girl. "In a very real way, I am. In fact, you're doubly blessed. You've had two mothers."

"I don't remember my own mother at all. Now even what she looked like—the way she walked or laughed or—anything."

"The next time you look in a glass, you'll see her, Tina. Give yourself a few more years and you'll be as strikingly beautiful as she was."

"Will someone ever want to marry me so I can have a baby of my very own?"

Margaret laughed. "I predict that it won't be long until you're the most sought after young lady on the St. John's."

"I don't care about that. I just want one husband to be kind to me, the way Papa is to you."

"You've become a truly modest girl, with a very grown-up mind."

"There's another thing I want to be and that's a good friend to you, Miss Margaret, the way Cousin Louisa is."

"You'll make me cry in a minute!"

"Well, with both George and L.I. gone, I'm the only one here to be your friend. I mean, you and I have to be close, kind of work together to be sure Papa stays happy . . ."

"From this moment on, we'll team up on him. No matter how hard he's having to work to help Pompey bring back our fields, he'll *be* a happy man. You and I will see to it."

Sitting that rainy evening on the tiny porch that Lewis had added to the old warehouse, Margaret told him of her talk with Tina. For a long time, while a spring rain tapped on the tin roof over their heads, Lewis had not spoken. Finally, his voice as gentle as the rain, he said, "I'm the most blessed man on earth. Why, I don't know. But I am. You've made a strong, safe bridge for me. For my children, too. It's time I did something for you. How about a good visit with Louisa— to show off our two young sons?"

"Oh, Lewis, are you sure you won't be too lonely here? Tina wants so much to go with me. To care for Seton and Frank."

"I want you both to go. You've been very patient. Get your

charges ready and I'll put you on the steamer for Picolata anytime you say. I'll be fine here."

"Are you sure? Are you really sure you'll be all right?"

"With Maum Easter patrolling me? You know I will be."

"I don't want to leave you."

"I don't want you to—except you need to be with Louisa. I'm sure she needs you." He stretched, yawned. "I wish I could go, too. It would do me a world of good just to look at Louisa."

"Can't you, darling? Just for a short stay?"

"Pompey and I have too much to do. I'll be with you in my thoughts. I miss the old city at times. I often try to imagine how good it would be just to stroll up St. George Street again—limp or no limp."

"I love your limp. It's still terribly romantic. Oh, thank you, Lewis. Tina and I can be ready by next week. I'll write to Louisa tonight!"

Seton, now three, chattered a lot on the river trip south to St. Augustine. Frank slept all the way and didn't cry until the steamer blew its whistle in sight of the Picolata dock. Tina, proud of her skill, changed his diaper and had him dry and ready by the time the little boat chugged shoreward and bumped the old wooden pier. Even the long, tiring and always rough ride into the city on the mule-drawn train was a happy adventure. Again, Frank slept on Tina's lap and Seton rode the whole way up front with the driver.

Margaret, watching the blue and yellow wild flowers and the myriad spring greens move slowly by, had time to think her own thoughts. To anticipate—not only the sight of the ancient city again for the first time since she was Tina's age—but the good sight of Louisa, too; the secure, kind look of her friend, the sound of her low, melodic voice and Margaret's own joy at being able at last to show Louisa the two children. The weather was perfect. Sunny, but not yet hot. Even the tide served when the mule-drawn train finally reached the San Sebastián River at the western edge of St. Augustine, where they were ferried directly across without having to wait. Louisa, of course, had a carriage there on the city side of the river to bring them to her rented house on St. George Street. A carriage all her own, with plenty of room for their trunk, an odd assortment of valises and the wooden box into which Easter had packed a big, high, Lady Baltimore cake, made as an arrival present for Louisa and Sophia.

The reunion was exuberant and, after all the others were fast asleep that night, Louisa and Margaret still sat in the small, tasteful parlor of the St. George Street house—windows open to catch the breeze off the bay—talking, talking, talking. Margaret told her all about the newly remodeled warehouse, about both George and L.I. at school and, for more than an hour, she spoke of Lewis. Of the depth of their happiness, their almost unbelievable compatability, his kindness to her—her ongoing, deepening love for him.

"We reminded each other before I left," she said, "that these are the wonderful years. The years when everyone is healthy, when there is good work to do, dreams to dream—children to love and watch over—" She laughed a little. "And more children to come."

"If I tried to tell you how all this makes me feel," Louisa said, "I'd fail, so I won't try. Except that I live it—as much as another person can—right along with you."

"If only we weren't so far apart! We want you and Sophia to share our good, stimulating, laughing years. I know your life is here now, but I want you to be there, to see Seton and Frank learn to climb the Hibernia trees, to swim, to—" She sat up. "Louisa, when can you come?"

Louisa laughed. "Well, as a matter of fact, I've been thinking that Sophia and I might just go back with you. Seeing you and those wonderful little ones and that dear, grown-up Tina has done so much for my flagging spirit, I think I might treat myself to a visit with Lewis, too."

Instead of jumping up to embrace her, as Louisa fully expected her to do, Margaret sat motionless—a smile lighting her lovely, even features. Louisa reached to touch her hand. "You surprise me. I've seldom seen you speechless. Margaret? Does it mean that much to you that I visit Hibernia?"

Margaret nodded briskly, still unable to form words.

"Sophia and I just live here in this little house day in and day out," Louisa mused. "We walk to the market, stroll along the seawall. Visit Mrs. Judge Smith on Hospital Street occasionally. And because I am so envious of her fine, big boarding house, we visit with Sarah Anderson, next door to Mrs. Smith. Then we come back home. And eat and sew and read and sit. I'm not very old, you know. I'm forty-five, just a year older than Lewis. Look how busy and happy he is! I need responsibility, Margaret. I'm—restless for the first time in my life because this is the first time I've had nothing to do. I—need to talk to Lewis."

"Your inn! You're still thinking about opening your inn!"

"Yes. People are coming down in larger and larger numbers from the North in their sometimes pathetic faith in our mild climate. Some are quite ill, expecting miracles. Others are seeking what they believe to be the perfect place for a winter holiday. Sophia and I have enough money from father's estate to live. We're not penniless. But, oh, my dear, now that you're here, hoisting my spirits, I'm really dreaming again. Can't you tell?"

After two pleasant weeks in St. Augustine, Louisa and Sophia made the river journey back to Hibernia with Margaret and the children. Louisa seemed so glad to be with Lewis again, she even went out in the sailing boat on fishing trips—one day, just the two cousins. Night after night, so that Louisa and Lewis could be alone, Margaret steered the children and Sophia off to bed and retired early herself. Her own joy blossomed in the cousins' joy at being together again—like old times.

On a mild, soft, early June night, Lewis and Louisa sat together in the homemade swing hung from the ceiling of the tiny front porch overlooking the river.

"I like the creak of a swing, don't you?" he asked.

"You know I do. Lewis, I've made up my mind. I'm going to buy that place farther south on St. George Street and open up a boarding house. Buying it will take every cent I've got in ready cash, but you've given me the courage. If you can do what you've done with an old warehouse here at Hibernia—and still scrape up tuition for two boys at college—I can open my own establishment."

"You can mortgage some of your New Switzerland land, too," he said. "I mortgaged two hundred acres of Hibernia in order to do what I've done."

She stared at him. "You—mortgaged part of Hibernia?"

"Had to. Margaret doesn't know. I'll have it paid off by the end of this year, before George comes home from medical school to open his practice in Jacksonville. Not bad, eh?"

"Lewis, I had no idea."

"Margaret has a fair-sized inheritance from her father, of course. Bless her, she's offered it a hundred times for the boys' education. We did dip into it for furniture, but I want the remainder kept intact for her future. I'm so much older than Margaret. She'll be here a long time yet."

"Yes. Those are things we have to face. But, losing you would make her as wretched as she is happy now."

"Love runs those risks."

"Lewis? This is the happiest place I've known since I was a girl and we were all at home together across the river."

"Sometimes it scares me, I'm so happy. I didn't expect to be. Ever again."

"But you are. Thanks to Margaret." After a pause, she asked, "Will you take me over to—New Switzerland tomorrow if the weather holds?"

He didn't answer at once. "Louisa, be sure you really want to go. It's a desolation over there. Not a living soul. Now and then I go over alone. Just to walk around, sit on the old foundation and try to figure out what must have happened to faithful Scipio, Polly—the rest of your people. Scipio and Polly—dead, I'm sure. It's empty now—stark. About all I've been able to do is try to keep the cemetery cut back. Are you sure you should go?"

"I'm very sure." Without a trace of self-pity, she added, "I've had enough to face in my life, so that I can gauge myself. I *need* to go. Not Sophia. It would destroy her. But I need to see it as it is now. Then, I can close that door forever and—work out my new plans."

"It's very necessary for us all to have the future to look to, isn't it?"

"Yes, Cousin. And I wonder if you really have any idea how thankful I am for yours?"

After her visit to the ruins at New Switzerland, Louisa dragged Sophia away from her games with the children and headed back to St. Augustine to open the house where she meant to begin to fulfill her dream of entertaining selected Northern guests.

Her first year was successful beyond her dreams and by the middle of summer, George had finished his medical studies and had set up his own practice in Jacksonville. When Margaret and Lewis and the children visited him and Sophia Fleming in September of 1844, it was Dr. George who confirmed Margaret's belief that she was going to have another baby.

"Well, at last," she breathed. "At long last!"

Her dark, slender stepson laughed. "At last? I'd say you've done very well by my father already."

"But what Lewis really longs for, George, is to have a son born at Hibernia. This one will be."

Leaning back in his office chair, George was still smiling. "You're always sure it will be a son, aren't you?"

"No. I say so, but I'm never sure. I do love the name Frederic, though, and if your father agrees, even without a Frederic in either of our families, I'm going to pray for *Frederic* Fleming. Doesn't that sound lovely? Frederic Fleming, born at Hibernia on the St. John's!"

All through the months in which Margaret carried the new baby, she—even with her optimistic nature—found it hard to believe that life could be so good, so smooth. That the normal upsets and problems which come with rearing young children could so quickly right themselves. She felt well, was not ill a single day and when, on May 1, 1845, Lewis insisted that Dr. George be on hand for the birth, Margaret and Maum Easter giggled behind his back.

"You didn't need me, Maum Easter," George said later, after Margaret and the baby, Frederic, had dropped off to sleep. "All I did was stand there and watch you."

"What else did you 'spect to do, chile? I done brought more babies into this world than you'll ever see if you doctors till you die!"

Following Easter across the yard and into her detached kitchen at the side of the Hibernia house, George asked, "Maum Easter? Could I talk to you for a while?"

Tying on a fresh apron, she gave him her special smile. "Ain't no time I've ever been too busy for you, Mausa George. Somepin' ticklin' your brain?"

"I'm not sure 'ticklin' ' is the right word for it. More like scratching. Maum Easter, I got along fine in medical school, but now—" He sat down on the old cane-bottomed chair and leaned both elbows on her worktable. "Well, I think I'd be ashamed to tell my father. I could tell Miss Margaret, but she's worn out. I'm going to tell you. I'll—need a lot of prayer and far more courage than I have now—to go on being a doctor."

Easter stood staring at him. "What you talkin' 'bout?"

"I—want to help anyone who's suffering. I really do. That's

the reason I'm a doctor. But, Maum Easter, I—don't think I'll hold up under it!"

George saw her eyes roll heavenward, seeking wisdom before she answered. An action he'd seen a thousand times. Finally, in a low, rich voice, she said, "You—can't stan' it when you—has to—hurt somebody, ain't that it?"

He nodded. "How can I get over that? I've *got* to go on being a doctor. Sometimes doctors have to cause more suffering. My father has worked too hard to educate me—I have to go on practicing. But—how?" He looked away, out the kitchen window across the trees to the river. "I—I had a patient last week who needed an amputation. Needed it desperately. Dr. Smith was assisting me." George covered his face with his hands. "He—had to do it, Maum Easter. I tried. I couldn't— bear the man's cries."

For a time, neither spoke.

"You better not plan to go back to Jacksonville tomorrow, Mausa George," Easter said at last, just above a whisper, but with that good authority which the young man had obeyed all his life. "You best wait till Miss Mar'ret be well enough to talk to you. She be close to God. Partial to you. Miss Mar'ret, she know 'zactly what to say."

His tormented eyes bored into hers. "But you're close to God, too! You tell me what to do!"

"You heard what Easter say. Miss Mar'ret. She be the one."

That evening, George waited for his father to leave Margaret and the new baby, then slipped just inside her open bedroom door and stood watching her as she unselfconsciously adored the new baby in her arms. How George loved Miss Margaret—her tawny gold hair spread on a high stack of pillows, the rounded folds of a soft shell-pink woolen shawl framing her lovely face. A beautiful woman alone with her own special happiness, unmindful that anyone was watching her.

"Is Frederic even more handsome than Seton was at that age?" he asked from the doorway.

"Oh! George . . ." Smiling, she held out her free hand toward him. "Come in, come in. I need to ask *you*—is this baby truly perfect? Warm, brown curls on the most wonderfully shaped head—straight little nose, rosebud mouth. You're a doctor. Was there ever a baby as sweet as Frederic?"

He tried to laugh. "He's a beauty, all right. And healthy as a rabbit in a clover patch. Maum Easter says he's going to be as well behaved as Frank was, too. Does that mean Seton raised a little Cain?"

"Seton still raises a little Cain. I wish I wouldn't compare the three. But, Seton is still so gorgeous. He'll be dashing when he grows up. Frank was always the quiet, thoughtful one. And—oh, George, I predict Frederic will be the truly gracious, elegantly handsome one. Sit down, dear. Are all mothers as peculiar as I?" She took his hand as he sat down on the bed. Then she frowned. "George? Something's wrong. Do you want to tell me? Is that why you're here?"

He told her all he'd told Maum Easter and much more. "You see, laudanum is all we have to deaden pain and I know now it doesn't really do the job. Miss Margaret, I—I'm so miserable, I wish I'd get very, very sick myself. Then, I'd have an—acceptable excuse to—quit!"

Margaret tucked the baby's blanket more securely around him and handed the warm bundle to George. "Here, put Frederic in his cradle, will you please?"

When George returned, she took both his hands. "Your father must be told this at once."

"I can't! I just don't have the nerve to tell him. He'd be ashamed of me. He's sacrificed so much for my education. All those long years at your grandfather's mills. My papa's a gentleman. He should never have had to do that in the first place. He's—"

"Hush!"

Her voice was so stern, he stared in surprise.

"Just hush all that talk. And don't ever let me hear you say again that you wish you'd become too ill to practice!"

"But it's true! Any kind of physical pain would be easier than—the pain I carry around now—every minute. I want to help people. I really do. I've always wanted that, but—"

"I know you want to help, but maybe—we just decided on the wrong way for you to do that."

A flicker of hope lit his dark eyes and then vanished. "How many educations can my father afford? I'm only one son. Now, he has three more!"

"Yes," she said quietly. "Now he has three more sons. But I have a lot of plans, George. Plans that began to form when Cousin Louisa was here. A lot of big plans for our future. None of which I've even mentioned yet to your father. They have to do with our making all the money we need someday."

A puzzled frown creased his forehead. "What kind of plans?"

She smiled a little. "If I haven't told Lewis, I certainly don't intend to tell anyone else. Not even you. I just want you to forget about educating the three younger boys and answer this question. Have you managed to save any money from your practice so far?"

"Yes. Living with the L'Engles and my grandmother in Jacksonville, I've had very little expense. I also saved some of what I earned at school."

"Enough for one year of schooling somewhere else?"

"I—guess so. What are you driving at, Miss Margaret?"

"At getting that dreadful look off your face! Do you think this is the first time anyone may have made a faulty judgment? Now, tell me, what would you really like to be if there's a way—and there will be—to train you for another profession?"

His troubled eyes lighted a little. "Well, there's only one other real way—to help people, I guess. Oh, I don't mean that lawyers like L.I. will be don't help. They do, but I'd never make a good lawyer. I'm too soft."

"You are not 'soft.' You are sensitive."

"If I tell you what I think I'd like to do, will you believe that I haven't just thought of it now that I know I'm a failure as a doctor? Will you believe it's something I thought about— even before you and Papa got married?"

"I'll believe whatever you tell me."

"Well, when Mama died and Papa was so—torn up over it, I thought a lot about how good it would have been if he'd had a—priest or a minister to help him."

Margaret tightened her grip on his hands.

"It—it seemed to sort of help him—way back then—when I'd remind him that God knew all about his broken heart over Mama." He laughed an embarrassed dry laugh. "Does that sound too kid-like? Well, I was just a kid. But I—I still believe that. It—helps me that God knows the mess I've got myself in now."

She waited a long time to answer. At last, she said, "George, can you go back to Jacksonville—and try it awhile longer? Now, wait before you answer that. Can you, knowing that I will explain to your father—knowing that I have plans for the future and enough money left me by my own father to see you through seminary—knowing those two things, could we try it just a little longer to be absolutely sure?"

He was looking straight into her soft, brown eyes, unable to believe what he'd just heard her say about giving him her own money. "You'd do that, wouldn't you? You'd really help me with your own inheritance."

"Of course, I would!" Her easy laughter came. "And I'd never expect it back either because ministers don't make much money!"

"I'd find a way to pay you back. I don't care about a lot of money."

"That's good, because I don't have a lot. But I do have enough, with what you've saved. What do you say? We should be very sure."

"Would trying it for another year be long enough?"

"Oh, my, yes."

He stood up. "And—not tell Papa anything now?"

"Not a word. That isn't being unfair, either. He's just beginning to feel carefree about money again. If we have good weather, he's optimistic about his crops. I think you'll give yourself a fairer chance, too, if only you and Maum Easter and I know for now. Try it one year longer, all the while asking God to show you what He wants you to do with your life. Then, when you're sure, we'll talk again." She held out her arms to him and he hugged her long and gratefully. "Oh, George," she said. "I'd be so happy to have a man of God in the family!"

24

Florida, just that year, 1845, had become the twenty-seventh state in the Union, but the historic fact made scarcely a ripple at Hibernia. For months, on trips to Jacksonville, Lewis had heard all manner of talk about Florida's future prospects now that it had become a full-fledged state. He listened, but Lewis Fleming had always believed in Florida—under the Spanish as well as the Americans. Of course, Louisa Fatio meant to risk her entire future on the influx of Northerners to St. Augustine seeking Florida's temperate climate. Jacksonville had begun to grow by a few stores and houses each time Lewis went there. The population, he figured, must be over three hundred by now. Still, except for marketing crops— seed and feed corn, cotton, garden vegetables in season and a few oranges—Lewis worked and planned for a self-reliant plantation again on the land he loved. Unlike neighboring planters, he and Pompey had managed to bring to fruition an acre or so of new orange trees. Lewis doubted that he would live long enough to harvest oranges at Hibernia as he'd done before the hard freeze a decade ago. But he was working now in order to grow enough for family use and some, at least, for the Jacksonville market. He meant to take every possible advantage of any mometary gain, no matter how small. Along with educating his sons, he would never rest until the Hibernia house had been rebuilt.

"It won't be right until then, Pompey," he said to his friend as they rode slowly, side by side, from the far north field one late summer afternoon of the following year, 1846. "I want Miss Margaret to be the mistress of a house—fine enough for her."

Pompey chuckled. "She be the happiest one lady I ever seen right now livin' in the warehouse. Mausa Lewis? You want some more children?"

"Why—yes. Between you and me. But not at any risk to Miss Margaret's health." At the stable, dismounting, he said, "We have to keep Miss Margaret, Pompey—Miss Margaret and Easter, no matter what."

"Miss Mar'ret be a wiry little lady, sir," Pompey said, still sitting his own horse and grinning down at Lewis. "Hand me Cotter's reins. You go on inside. They's a whole family waitin' for your footsteps."

After the usual wild daily greeting from Seton, now seven, and Frank, almost five, Lewis went with Margaret to look in on Frederic, a year old last spring. For a long time, they stood watching the sleeping child.

"He's looking more like you every single day, Lewis," she said. "He'll have your straight, fine nose, that intelligent high forehead—your thick, wavy brown hair—and, oh, if he'd open those melting blue-gray eyes this minute and look at me, I might swoon. Do you know I feel like swooning lots of times when you look at me? Even after all these years?"

He hugged her. "You know I do have a strong feeling

about—Frederic. It's as though I know he will always look after you."

"Lewis? I've known for nearly three months that—we're going to have another child."

He turned her to face him, the old anxiety sweeping his handsome face—then, the little laugh he'd begun to use to cover it. "You've—known for three months? Why on earth didn't you tell me?"

"Because you get so frightened. And you've been too busy with the crops. Maum Easter knows."

Lewis sank into a chair near Frederic's cradle. "Pompey said Easter never tells him one single thing you confide in her."

"Lewis. I do want this child. Do you?"

"Oh, yes, yes! Hibernia has never had enough children playing under its great trees."

"Do you want another son, sir?"

He chuckled. "I honestly don't care. Boy or girl—the child will be a part of you. For me, that's enough. And we'll have good Dr. George to help out again. Oh, that really bolsters me, knowing our very own George can look after you."

"Lewis, let's go out for a little walk. I need to talk to you about George."

Arm in arm, they strolled along the riverbank, Margaret attempting to keep the mood quiet—to keep Lewis receptive to what would surely be a severe blow to him.

"Listen, darling," she said softly. "Don't you love the late summer sounds? The cicadas rubbing their hind legs in serenade—just for us? Remember just a few weeks ago our evening walks were wild celebrations? All that birdsong? I like this, too, don't you?"

"Yes. But what about George?"

Watching his face, she told him in careful, tender detail of George's uncertainty—his near revulsion at being a doctor. When she'd finished and Lewis had said nothing at all, Margaret stopped, turned him toward her. "He *isn't* quitting, Lewis. I can tell by that closed look on your face, you think he is. George isn't a quitter. He's—he's just different from L.I. Very different. L. I. will go on loving the law more and more up there in Amherst, just because he's there in the midst of it. Because he's L.I."

"I don't see that L.I. has anything to do with his brother's—weakness," he said coldly. "Why don't we leave him out of it?"

"Darling, wait. Let's start again. L.I. is simply the uncomplicated, certain kind of young man who has the happy faculty of being involved in whatever he's doing. He's blessed, actually. But he is not George. Some of us are more complex. George is complex. And very, very sensitive."

"Call it 'sensitive' if you like. I call it weakness."

"Shame on you, Lewis." Her voice was casual, affectionate, almost teasing, but her heart pounded. She and Lewis had never come this close to an argument. They must not argue now. "Does your leg hurt?"

"No more than usual. Why do you ask?"

"No one can think clearly in pain. We must both think clearly about George. Because we love him."

"I love him, but I don't mean to pamper him. He's twenty-four years old, Margaret. A grown man. Or he should be. I forbid you to go on spoiling him. You had no right to sympathize. He had no right to tell you—instead of me."

Margaret waited to respond. She was *not* George's mother. Perhaps he should have told his father first. But he didn't. He chose to tell her. Had even told Maum Easter. George *was* still trying, still practicing medicine in Jacksonville, but on his latest visit to Hibernia a month ago, he was thinner and more withdrawn than ever. With all her heart, Margaret had longed to question him. She had not. George had offered nothing. She could only conclude that he was desperately trying to make it work—and failing. His drawn, troubled face still haunted her. So much so that, suddenly, in a frantic attempt to keep George from pulling more and more into himself, she had told Lewis. And now he was angry.

"Did you hear what I said, Margaret? The boy had no right to tell you—and not me."

"I heard. But I wonder if rights have anything to do with it. His heart is broken over how hard you worked to pay for his medical education. He hated every day you were hired to be superintendent at Panama Mills. George, of all people, is aware of the sacrifice you made for him—"

Lewis's hard laugh stopped her, but only for an instant.

"Even if your leg doesn't hurt, will you sit down beside me on Pompey's new bench over there by the big water oak? *I* think better sitting down."

Slowly, their arms no longer engaged, they moved toward the wooden bench which circled the ancient tree and sat down, not as close together as usual.

"I know this has been a blow," Margaret said. "I've dreaded telling you. But I insisted that George let me handle it." Lewis gave her the only cold look she had ever received from him. "And I don't think I deserve that icy stare, either. I've done all any woman could do to keep the happy memory of your children's mother alive for them. I've also done all a real mother could do for all three of them. Willingly, gladly, gratefully. I love them as much as I love my own children. I loved them before you knew you loved me, don't forget. I simply won't allow you to close me out of this discussion as though George were not my son, too. He is. For some reason, he told me first. I rather think his reason is his business. Not ours. George *is* a man now. And if he sees clearly that he's made a mistake in his profession, he should be free to change. I think he's considering the ministry, but he won't be expecting any more financial help from you. None at all. I'm sure he's living like a pauper, saving every penny."

"It's his total lack of maturity—his weakness—that angers me, Margaret."

"You—are really angry, aren't you?"

"Furious. Humiliated. Surely, in those years at medical school, he found out that he—faints at the sight of blood and pain! Why did he wait so long to—to—"

She moved closer, took his unresponsive hand. "Lewis, didn't you notice his face when he was here last? Didn't you see the torment in his eyes? He tried to be a good doctor—he's still trying, but he didn't even give me a chance to ask him a single question. I don't want George to shut me out. I don't think you do, either."

"He's already done it to me, I'd say. He did that the day he told you about his hankering for an easier profession."

"Being a good minister is not an easier profession!"

Lewis snorted.

"It is not. And—aren't you completely closing your own mind to the fact that God may be calling George into the ministry?"

"Did he say that in so many words?"

"He was too confused, too miserable to—think beyond his guilt over all the money you spent on him."

"A likely story."

"Lewis Fleming, look at me. Don't look at the ground. I

want you to look straight at me. Now, tell me you don't care about George's own fulfillment."

"Of course, I care about that, but I make no sense of him. He should have found a suitable wife by now. He should have given us a grandchild."

"Why? Is there a law about that?"

For a long moment, he said nothing. Then she caught the merest twinkle in his eyes and a slow laugh came. Almost his good, easy laugh.

"What's funny?"

"You, Margaret!"

"All right, I'm funny. I'd like to know why I'm so funny, but—" She caught his arm and held it. "—so long as you're laughing, I won't ask. I guess I don't really care. Oh, Lewis. You scared me terribly!"

Returning her embrace, he asked why.

"Because that was the nearest thing to a quarrel we've ever had! I should have told you long ago. Especially with L.I. loving the law so much he's still working in it at Amherst even though he's graduated. I'm proud of him—an assistant teacher of law! But L.I. is—not George."

Lewis laughed again, softly. "So you've said."

"So I've oversaid, I have no doubt. L.I. is settled for life in his profession. Don't you see how much harder that makes it all for George? Especially being older than his brother? L.I. will be home eventually, and if I know him, he'll find work down here to earn money against the day when he can set up his own practice. In George's mind, he pales beside his younger brother. And do you know why? Because he fears your humiliation that he—heard God's call so late."

"Margaret? Do you really believe God has called George to the ministry?"

She nodded. "But only George can really know that. Lewis, please make it easy for him to talk about it."

Lewis stretched his legs, rubbed the bad one. "I'm going to Jacksonville next week. I'll give him my blessing—if he's sure."

Then abruptly, "When is the new baby coming?"

"Sometime in March of next year."

"I see. I did want George to be on hand to look after you."

She gave him a smile. "With Maum Easter in full charge? With Betty perfectly trained by her mother so she can help?"

"They're not doctors!"

"Our new son and I will do all right. You wait and see. What matters to me right now is—George."

He ignored that. "Mrs. Fleming, did you say—our new son?"

"I did. And I don't know any more than I've ever known. But, well, I just thought how exciting it would be if we had at least one more son so we could name him for Uncle William Seton."

"Ah, yes. The dashing bachelor, merchant marine Captain William Seton. I can guess why," he teased. "If you had a son named for him, he—or you—might inherit the handsome silver Seton bowl given to the gallant captain for fighting off that French privateer."

"Well, shouldn't his namesake have that beautiful bowl? Don't you think even my mother might agree? I know how pleased she'll be that we've named a son for Uncle William."

"And if we have a daughter and name her Wilhelmena, do you think that will work?"

"I'm serious. I want a son. Just one more, Lewis. Then, we'll start on daughters."

She saw the teasing grin fade from his face and in its place, the familiar look of love.

"Margaret . . . George did have a right to tell you—first. I see that now. He didn't mean to burden you. Or to shut me out. He was *giving* to you—of his deepest concern. You are more than his mother. You're his—friend. You're my friend, too. My very closest and best friend." He got stiffly to his feet and reached his hand to help her. "I'll ease George's mind when I go to Jacksonville next week. I promise. He can leave for divinity school right now, if he likes. I—wanted to begin building our new home here in two or three years, but that can wait. If it's all right with you."

"Lewis, I'm so happy in the warehouse, I don't think I could bear—a new home. We're at Hibernia. We're going to have another son born beside the St. Johns. That's really all that matters, isn't it?"

Lewis sat across the small desk in George's office studying his son's thin, almost ascetic face. They had been talking for an hour or more. After a long silence, Lewis, still dumbfounded by what George had told him, finally spoke. "I hope Miss Margaret will be glad when I tell her the surprising news that you now feel you'll give your medical practice still another year. But I can't help wondering how she'll feel about what she believes is a call from God."

"I don't understand myself, frankly, Papa. I—hope I'm not disobeying God. But I'd already made up my mind to go on yet awhile, before your—understanding attitude today."

"That attitude is entirely due to your stepmother, George. I gave her some trouble when she first told me. I admit, I'm overjoyed at your news. We need good doctors. Your own mother might still be with us if—"

"No, Papa. Don't say that or even think it. Dr. Jones did all anyone could have done. She—wasted away from something that caused that fever. And—her heart."

"Still, a young man with your keen mind can learn new things. Make new discoveries. God uses doctors, too, son."

"I know." He changed the subject. "How's Miss Margaret doing? You say the baby's coming in March of next year?"

"She seems fine and, yes, March." He laughed. "Of course, she's already named him."

"Him?"

"You know Miss Margaret. She wants one more son so she can name him for her famous uncle, the sea captain, William Seton."

For the first time, George gave his father the old playful smile. "The Seton silver bowl, eh?"

"I accused her of that." Lewis, steadying his lame leg, stood up. "Come back with me for a visit, son?"

"Sorry, I've got some pretty sick people here, right now. Maybe later." He came from behind the desk and took his father's hand. "Thanks, Papa. I wish with all my heart that I could be a satisfaction to you—as L.I. is. Will he be coming back south soon?"

"His letters are not altogether informative. But the boy's optimistic about finding legal work down here. He's writing various southern companies, inquiring. Then, later, his own practice here in Jacksonville. You'll be together again. Depending, of course, upon where you are by then."

"Right."

On the steamer en route back to Hibernia, Lewis pondered the fact that George seemed neither resentful nor relieved at his own decision to go on yet awhile with his medical practice. At least, the boy *had* come to the decision on his own. And, whatever his feelings, he was determined, showing the courage Lewis had accused him of lacking.

* * *

Embracing Margaret and young Seton on the Hibernia dock where they had run to meet him, Lewis tried to act happier than he really felt when he told Margaret about his talk with George.

"You're not fooling me, Lewis," Margaret said. "I know you want him to go on with his medical practice. Why aren't you more relieved?"

For the moment, forgetting the inquisitive boy, Seton, Lewis said, "Because George didn't seem relieved. He's—well, he's restless. Still withdrawn. He—just doesn't act like himself."

"What's wrong with my brother George?" Seton demanded.

"Nothing, son. Nothing at all. Now, run along and play with Frank and Frederic. Your mother and I need to talk."

"Aw, they don't care anything about guns."

"And you care too much," Margaret said. "Mind your father. We need you to look after the younger boys."

"But I wanta know about George." The boy beamed at them. "I love George."

Both parents relented, as they almost always did when their beguiling son turned his smile on them. "All right, since you're going to be pleasant about it, Seton. George is just fine. He'd thought about entering the ministry and giving up his medical practice and now he's changed his mind."

"Oh," the boy said, disappointed. "Is that all?"

"Why, we think it's a very important decision. Don't you?"

"Naw. Old George is all right, but he never is interested in anything important. Not guns or swimming or even fishing anymore. Not like L.I. L.I.'s coming home sometime, isn't he? I bet he takes me huntin'."

"Don't drop your g's, Seton," Margaret reminded. "The word is *hunting*."

The disarming smile came again. "I didn't drop a single g till I got to huntin'. Me an' L.I. decided it was okay to say *huntin'*. We decided that a long time ago. He's good. L.I.'s good. Ol' George is a sissy."

"Where did you hear a word like that, Seton?" Lewis wanted to know.

"Somewhere."

"Undoubtedly. Now, your mother and I do need to talk and we'd like to talk alone. We'll meet you and your brothers at the house after a while."

Smiling again, the impish, lovable child saluted his father, turned in what he considered a soldierly manner and ran across the big Hibernia yard toward the new sandpile Pompey had unloaded under a big tree.

"I'll get a bucket of water from the well," Seton called back, "and build me a wet sand fort. What Fred and Frank wanta play is dumb—like blocks or rolling hoops."

"We may have a budding military man on our hands," Lewis laughed. "We'll have to watch him. First thing you know, he'll be into my gun collection."

"I guarantee that he won't," Margaret said. "Pompey and I put it under lock and key while you were in Jacksonville." Then, "Lewis, is—George all right in his new decision? Did he tell you how he reached it? I'm dying to know everything."

"He didn't strike me as relieved. But he is determined. I was glad to see that."

"Is he unhappy?"

"Lonely, I'd say. Lost. The boy needs a wife. I asked him pointblank if he'd found anyone. He hasn't. He sleeps and eats under the same roof with my mother and Cousin Susan's family, but lives entirely inside himself." Noticing Margaret's frown, he tried to change the subject. "Now, what's this about putting my gun collection under lock and key? Was Seton into it?"

"Worse than that! He was missing for nearly two hours day before yesterday and Big Owen found him almost a mile away—deep in the woods—hunting squirrels with your gun. All by himself—a little seven-year-old boy moving through those tangles and over fallen logs all alone with a loaded gun!"

"Who loaded it for him?"

"He loaded it himself!"

Lewis mopped his brow. "Well, he and I had better have a talk. In fact, for doing a thing like that when I'm away, he needs a good licking."

Margaret smiled at him. "You sound very impressive, but you're as helpless as I am against that smile. And Lewis, we've got to learn how not to be helpless against it. Seton is a good boy. He's extremely generous with everyone, his impulses are all loving—he's fearless—but he isn't eight yet. We've got to learn how to control him without giving in to that smile."

"It's always at the most unexpected times that he turns it on us, have you noticed? When I try to scold him, instead of pouting or scowling, as the others have always done, he smiles."

"Seton is special, isn't he? He does affect you as he does me, doesn't he?"

"I miss all of you when I'm away, Margaret. But I miss Seton's smile more than anything else—except your kisses. Could I have one more, Mrs. Fleming?"

Margaret kissed him playfully, then, abruptly serious, she held his head hard against hers. "Oh, Lewis, Lewis . . . so many children don't live even as long as our baby, Frederic. Not even to two years! We won't lose—even one of our sons, will we? Will we?"

He held her. "No one but God can know that, dearest. I pray not. Oh, Lord, I pray not!"

Slowly, they walked hand in hand toward the house.

"Did—George say he felt—clear with God about not going to divinity school?"

Lewis sighed. "He didn't exactly say. On the boat coming home, I thought of a dozen questions I should have asked. But he seemed—almost like a polite stranger. I—I'm afraid I found out very little. I'm sure you'd have done far better."

"Oh, no. But—if you think I should, I'll visit him!"

"You'll do no such thing. Not until after the baby's born. Absolutely no trips for you, young lady. And no more for me. I don't intend to have you out of my sight."

25

On March 14, 1847, the new baby came—once more, as Margaret predicted—a son. When Easter had finished with both her charges, around the foot of Margaret's bed stood George, Maum Easter and her daughter, Betty. Sitting beside Margaret, Lewis held the tiny, warm bundle. "You proved your mother right again, little fellow," he said to the infant lying unusually still in the folds of a light blanket. "You don't even seem very excited about it, either. Never saw such a well-behaved boy."

"I'm counting on him to help me keep order," Margaret said, smiling weakly. "Does Frederic know the baby's here?"

Maum Easter slapped her hands together. "Lemme outa here so's I kin go tell that boy he's finally got him a baby in the house! Frederic done pester me half to death 'bout when that baby gettin' here. Come on, Betty. We done our work."

"You did indeed, Easter," George said. "Good idea to tell Frederic. It seems two-year-olds are fascinated with a new baby." When Easter and Betty left, he leaned over Margaret. "Feel all right now?"

"Fine. Just tired. William actually came easier than any of the others. He's going to be a good boy."

"So, his name's William, eh?" George asked.

She nodded. "After my daring uncle William Seton."

"Did you hear that, William?" Lewis still spoke to his new son. "You're named for a famous sea captain and someday, because of you, your mother will inherit a handsome engraved silver bowl."

"Lewis, hush! *Maybe* I will. Who knows about Mother?"

"I'll write to her about William tomorrow," Lewis said. "At least, I can start the ball rolling."

"Stop teasing. I have a serious question for George. When can I go to St. Augustine? I want William to be christened there with Louisa as his godmother. How soon can I go?"

"Exactly when I say and no sooner," Lewis declared.

George smiled. "You heard the master speak, Mrs. Fleming. By the time he's willing to allow you out of his sight, I'm sure it will be all right for you to go. Time for me to get my things together now. My boat's due in about half an hour."

"Oh, don't go back tonight, George! Please stay with us a few more days."

"Your new gentleman guest is safely here now. You don't need me any longer, Miss Margaret."

The quiet of the half-darkened room was shattered by a child's scream of anguish. One scream and then repeated cries which brought Margaret out of her bed to stagger weakly toward the window.

"Lewis! Lewis—it's Frank! He's lying on the ground—screaming!"

George was out of the room and bounding down the stairs before Lewis could lay the new baby in its crib and reach Margaret, slumping at the window—her gaze fixed in horror on her child below.

"Lewis! Frank's hurt!" He all but forced her back into the bed. "Go down, darling—go find out how bad it is."

"George is with him. I'll go—as soon as you lie back so that I can cover you up again. Thank God, Dr. George is here. He'll take care of the boy. Margaret, try to be quiet. I'll send you word—right away. Just as soon as I know."

For an agonizing half hour—which seemed forever—Margaret lay motionless on her bed, her hands clenched together, listening to Frank's screams of agony. Short, sobbing screams, long, wailing, pain-wracked shrieks. Maum Easter sat beside her, failing to soothe, but trying, wincing herself, with each new cry of anguish.

"Mausa George, he be—finished soon, honey," Easter kept saying. "Mausa George know what he's doin'. He be a—doctor now. Doctors, they know how to set broken bones."

Margaret said nothing, her eyes scarcely blinked as she lay staring in her own helpless anguish at the patched bedroom ceiling.

"Ain't nothin' else broke, Mausa Lewis said." Easter went on. "You hold onto that. The little fellow broke his left arm. Nothin' else. Fallin' outa that big oak tree." Easter sobbed softly. "Them cries, they hurts me, too, Miss Mar'ret. Mausa Frank, he be my boy, too."

Margaret nodded, but kept her lips tightly clamped.

"His papa, he hold the boy till Mausa George git the bone just right." Shaking her head, she mumbled, "I don't know how many times I done tol' Mausa Seton to keep Mausa Frank outa dat tree till he got a few more years on him. I done tol' him an' tol' him. You tol' Mausa Seton, too. I hear ya."

Again, Margaret, still tight-lipped and white, only nodded.

Easter's wide brown hand smoothed Margaret's forehead, over and over, praying in the same voice she used to comfort her: "Sweet Jesus, we got need. Down there in the parlor where that little boy gittin' so—hurt. We got need."

In a few minutes, both women realized that the sharp screams had stopped. There was now only sobbing and the low voices of Lewis and George. The soft, caring voice of Tina, who had, unknown to Margaret and Easter, helped Lewis hold Frank while George pulled and twisted and reset the broken bone in the boy's upper arm.

Tears of relief began to pour down Margaret's cheeks. Easter wiped them away. Then they heard Tina start to sing the melody she'd made up to go with the rhyme Frank had always loved. Margaret's tears came faster. Tina, now almost sixteen, was downstairs taking her place.

The clear, light voice reached her:

> Ride a cockhorse Banbury Cross,
> To see a fine lady upon a white horse;
> Rings on her fingers and bells on her toes,
> She shall have music wherever she goes.

"Go down, Maum Easter. I want you to see for yourself how Frank is. And—thank Tina. Tell her I thank her. And George. What would I have done without them both—today?"

Easter had been gone only a few minutes when George literally lunged through Margaret's bedroom door and collapsed in a chair by the window—his face drained of color, his hands trembling so that he was forced to clench them together on his lap.

"George! Is Frank all right?"

He nodded. "Frank's a lot better off than—I am."

Margaret stared at him helplessly. Her stepson seemed about to faint and if he did, what could she do? "Does your father know where you are now?"

He shook his head no. "He's—with Frank."

"George, can you walk over to that basin of cold water on the table across the room? Or, please let me get out of bed so I can—"

"No!" He was breathing hard. "No—no. I'll—get—to it myself."

Holding first to the corner of her clothes press, then the foot of the bed, George reached the small, square table and managed to splash his face with cold water. "There," he gasped. "I think that—will do it." His weak smile tore at Margaret's heart. "You see? You—see what happens to me when—I have to do—what I just—did to Frank?"

"Yes. Yes, George. I do see. But, oh, thank God you were here and knew how to do it!"

Slumped back in the chair by the window, he laughed weakly. "Oh, I know how to do it all. I studied hard." He shuddered. "It's—just that I—I'm too—soft. Nature—caused your pain when the baby came. I—caused Frank's. It's—*that*— I can't endure."

"Did—your father notice how it all affected you?"

"I don't know!"

"Is—the broken bone going to—knit all right?"

"Yes. He'll have to wear Pompey's splints for a while. Stay out of trees. Pompey cut perfect splints." He sighed. "I'm sure—Papa did see the shape I was in. He—he even wiped the sweat off—my forehead a couple of times."

"That sounds just like him."

George got slowly to his feet and came to stand beside her. "Miss Margaret, I know you'll try to make me stay over to—get myself together. But, don't insist. I—I don't want to talk about any of this. My—patient will be fine without me. I've done all any doctor can do. I'll leave a small amount of Laudanum for the pain. He may not need it. I'll be here at least tonight, if he has a bad time. But—let me leave with no urging on the first boat tomorrow."

After promising Margaret that he'd go to his own room and lie down, George left, a moment before Easter returned.

"Little Frank's just fine. He's kinda dozin' now down on the parlor sofa. Dr. George, he say to let him sleep as long as he will. Pore little fellow's all wore out. I done tol' Mausa Lewis to stay right there with him."

"Good. And where are the others?"

"Miss Tina, she right beside her papa and Frank. Frederic, he done slept through it all." Easter stopped. "Now, where that briggledy britches Seton done gone to?"

"He isn't downstairs?"

"I didn't see hide nor hair of him!" Easter bustled across the room to check on the new baby. "Lemme look at this new one an' then I go huntin' Seton." She leaned close, held her face down to the baby's face.

"Easter! Is something wrong with the baby?"

"Don't he stay quiet? He be the onliest non-cryin' baby I done ever seen!"

"Oh, he cried a little—when George first spanked him, remember? Anyway, I doubt if it's easy on any of us—being born. Maybe it's harder on a baby than it is on a mother. Maybe he's—just tired."

After searching the house and the big Hibernia yard, Easter finally spotted Seton high on a branch of the same tree from which Frank had fallen.

"Mausa Seton Flemin'! You git yo'self down outa that tree, you hear me?"

He didn't answer, but she could see the normally merry young face screw itself up into the beginnings of a good cry.

"Mausa Seton! Don' you dare start cryin' till you is on the ground. Lord help us! You listenin' to me, Mausa Seton?"

"It's all—my fault," he wailed.

"No, it ain't, honey. An' for the Lord's sake, don' cry while you still so high off the ground! Ain't none of what's happened your fault, Mausa Seton."

Slowly, he began to climb down, but he was crying bitterly. "Yes—it *is*—my fault."

"Careful now. Watch where you put that foot. Watch!"

"I—don't care—if I—fall—all the way. I wish—I would—and —" the sobs were out of control now, "maybe I'd hurt, too, the way Frank—does."

Her voice grew tender. "Here, now—you kin jump from where you're perched. Easter's right here to hug you good."

Seton jumped to the ground and leapt into Easter's arms, nearly knocking her flat—crying as though his heart would break.

"There, there, cry it out and then straighten up an' tell Easter what all that talk 'bout you wantin' to fall outa the tree's all about." She held him, smoothing his sturdy little back. "Now, then. Can you tell Easter?"

Between sobs, he managed to explain that he had goaded Frank until he climbed up to the topmost branch. "Frank—was awful scared." Seton frowned. "But I don't understand why a boy's *ever* scared, Maum Easter! *I'm* not—scared of *anything!*" The sobs diminished some, as he warmed to his subject. "Frank's gonna be seven years old. If he wasn't such a fraidy cat he wouldn't have fallen. Why is he such a fraidy cat?"

"He ain't no fraidy cat. He's just younger than you, that's all. You kin do lots of things Frank can't do till he gets to be eight like you." He was crying again. "Now, you listen to Easter. It ain't gonna help poor little Frank for you to cry like that."

"But—I—love my brother." Fresh tears flowed down his firm, rosy cheeks faster than Easter could keep them wiped away. "It's—all my—fault, Maum Easter! I—I sinned!"

"Only you an' the good Lord knows about that. But if you did, then you kin ask Jesus to forgive you—an' when he wakes up, you kin ask Frank to forgive you, too."

"I'll—ask Jesus but I don't think I'll ask Frank."

"An' why not?"

Seton gave her his sudden, bright smile. "Aw, Maum Easter, you know why not."

"I kin guess, but I wanta hear you voice it."

"Well, just in case Frank didn't catch on—that it was my fault, I don't believe I'll—worry him with it."

Easter did her level best not to smile back at him. She failed. "With your pore mother in bed after birthin' a new baby—you oughta be ashamed to cause all this ruckus."

"You aren't gonna tell Mama, are you?"

His smile was totally irresistible now. Easter's good chuckle, which began low in her stomach and seemed to climb up to her expressive brown eyes, only served to widen Seton's smile. In self-defense, she turned him around, gave him a good whack across his bottom and promised she'd at least wait to tell until his mother felt lots better.

Seton grabbed her hand to make her dance with him in a circle on the grass, Easter trying to hold him back, trying hard to give him a stern look. Instead, she hugged him to her soft bosom and wondered to herself if the Lord had ever made a boy as purely sweet-natured and full of the devil as Seton.

William's christening was scheduled at Louisa's Episcopal church in St. Augustine for June 3. On a sudden impulse, leaving the three younger boys in the care of Tina and Maum Easter, Lewis went with Margaret and their new son a day early.

Jolting along side by side in the cramped coach of the mule train from the landing at Picolata into the city, the two were like lovers on a holiday. As usual, the infant William slept quietly. Now and then, as the swaying coach inched along in the clearing between the green walls of forest decorated now with wild morning glories and the pale lavender of French mulberry feather-flowers, they looked at each other long and lovingly, Margaret's eyes as luminous as the shafts of sunlight breaking through the dense summer woods. Blessedly, they were alone. For once, no one else bound for St. Augustine got off the little steamer that day.

"I don't wonder that I have so much trouble disciplining our son Seton," Lewis said out of the blue. "He has his mother's charm, her beguiling smile. I'm helpless against that smile. From Seton—or his mother."

Margaret became serious. "I don't pretend to have his charm, but—oh, Lewis, he has inherited a streak of my impetuosity, hasn't he?"

He took her hand. "Whatever he's inherited from you is only a plus for the boy. I love you, Margaret."

"I love you, but don't change the subject. Am I too headstrong?"

"Not for me." His eyes grew mischievous. "Say, are you devising some new scheme, Mrs. Fleming? One I don't yet know about? I suddenly feel wary."

Gazing out the window, she answered in what she hoped was an offhand manner: "Oh, I do have a brilliant idea. And you will hear all about it. But not one word until the christening is over and we're alone with Louisa." Turning quickly to look him straight in the eye, she said, "I don't love Seton any more than I love our other sons, but—I feel almost foolish at times, because I actually depend so on—an eight-year-old boy. I might be spoiling him, but I *do* depend on him."

"Now, who's changing the subject? But I'm glad you said that, because so do I depend on his love—his fidelity. He's—such a noble little fellow."

"That's where he's like you, Lewis." The sun was overheating the low-ceilinged coach. She loosened the cotton cap on the baby's head. "What will William be like when he's eight?" she asked. "Frederic, too, for that matter. We can already tell a lot about Frank. Serious, a touch argumentative, not very daring, but awfully brave. And careful. I can't imagine a boy being as cautious as he's been with that broken arm. I thought George seemed pleased with the way it's healed, didn't you?"

Lewis sighed. "As pleased as poor George ever seems about anything. If he's going to stay so miserable as a doctor, why doesn't he quit? We've both agreed to help him through divinity school. It's as though he's waiting for something—but what?"

"I don't know. He seems so terribly lonely. Sometimes I lie in your arms at night when you're asleep and wonder what dear George is—thinking lying in his bed—alone."

"You wonder about a lot of things, don't you? Just when I think I know you so well, you come out with something I'd never think about. George, for example, alone in his bed at night." In spite of the heat, he pulled her to him. "Enough of George now. What is it I'll find out when we're with Louisa?

Does Louisa know what you're up to?" She gave him only the smile again. "Margaret? Just one clue?"

In answer, she pursed her lips, turned them with her fingers in a locking motion, then threw the imaginary key out the train window.

He laughed. "All right. I give up. Look, we're almost at the San Sebastián River. Say, won't it be good to see Louisa again?"

"Oh, yes—yes! Next to you and the children—in all the world—I love Louisa."

"I am not his godmother," Sophia announced dramatically, as she excused herself after dinner the evening following William's afternoon christening at Trinity Church, "but in my *heart*, he can be my—godchild. William and I need no formalities, no signed certificates. Our souls are knit together. I knew from the moment I glimpsed the child that he and I are soul mates."

As Sophia swept from the room to sit with the sleeping William, Margaret, Lewis and Louisa murmured agreement and assurances and then—with Sophia safely out of hearing—they laughed.

"I'm glad we all know—she is not being laughed *at*," Margaret said. "Dear Sophia. I hope she isn't really hurt that we wanted you to be William's godmother, Louisa. We weren't together when the other boys came. I did so want you—this time."

"Nonsense," Lousia said. "Sophia would enjoy the experience—I know I did—but she really likes being a martyr far more."

Grinning behind a cloud of smoke as he puffed on his pipe, Lewis said, "Sophia's a harmless sort of martyr, though. Not the kind who makes trouble. Sure you ladies don't mind my pipe?"

"Not at all, Lewis," Louisa said. "If my dreams come true and I get a larger house, then I will have a smoking room. Tonight after such a lovely christening service, I want William's father to be totally at ease."

On the edge of her chair, Margaret asked eagerly, "Tell us all about it, Louisa. I want to know every single future plan you have for your business here!"

Lewis laughed. "Louisa, did you know I married a remarkable woman who not only does well by every present moment, but lives actively in the future as well?" Before Louisa could respond, he turned directly to Margaret. "M'lady, the christening is over—you and Louisa and I are alone and I intend to wait not one minute more to find out what's up your pretty sleeve."

"What on earth is he talking about, Margaret?"

"Don't encourage him, Louisa. He's rushing me."

"Am I now? I didn't think anyone ever managed that."

"Stop teasing, Lewis. I'm very serious about my—idea. But, I have to approach it my way."

For nearly half an hour, Margaret inquired of Louisa about the number of visitors coming to Florida from the North, what class of people they were, how much extra trouble they caused and what rates Louisa received for her rooms.

Finally, after answering carefully—with absolutely no interruption from Lewis, who sat smoking and listening—Louisa folded her napkin, leaned back in her chair and said, "Margaret Fleming, you not only have a good business head, you aren't very subtle. You mean to consider an inn of your own at Hibernia someday, don't you?"

"Yes, Louisa—yes, Lewis!" She was on her feet suddenly, her eyes shining. "I want to do more than consider it—I want us to do it! Don't you see, my darling, it's the answer to our entire future? The way to educate the boys—to make provisions for our old age, to—"

"To—change the entire fabric of our homelife." Lewis laid down his pipe. "Have you thought of that?"

"Lewis, darling Lewis! You didn't sound at all cross or—husbandlike when you said that! You just sounded—*thoughtful*. You're *not* cross with me, are you? You're really interested!" She dropped to her knees beside his chair. "Look at me. Oh, dearest, I know you had to mortgage some of your precious Hibernia land in order for George and L.I. to get their education. I—"

He glanced at Louisa, whom he had told. "How did you know that, Margaret?"

"I guessed. Where would the money have come from otherwise? I know what my grandfather paid you at Panama Mills. I know what it cost to renovate the warehouse. But, Lewis, if we build a large new house with plenty of rooms for guests, our money worries will be over forever!"

"Now, now, I wouldn't be too sure about that," Louisa said with her wise smile. "But, she does have a very workable idea. It *will* change your lives, believe me. But, you do live quite shut apart there in your river paradise. It might be a broadening experience for the children. For the two of you."

A knock interrupted their talk.

"Oh, dear," Louisa said. "Excuse me." She hurried to the door. "Good evening, Mr. Johnson. May I do something for you?"

"Yes, Miss Fatio, I was wondering what time it is. You see, my watch has stopped. I must have neglected to wind it this morning."

"Why, it's half-past eight, Mr. Johnson."

"I see. Nice evening, isn't it?"

"Yes. A good breeze blowing. Is there—something else?"

"No, I guess not. I—may just take a short walk."

"A pleasant evening for a walk," Louisa said, keeping her voice polite, but obviously trying to cut short the interruption.

"Yes. I see you have—guests. I hope I'm not interrupting. I—wonder, sir," he said to Lewis, "if you'd like to join me for a short stroll?"

"Thank you, Mr. Johnson," Lewis replied. "I have a bad leg and the damp night air doesn't help it much."

"Sorry to hear that."

Louisa, then, was forced to make introductions and in so doing, there was no alternative but to invite the lonely man into the parlor. He declined to sit down, though, and after a few moments went for his solitary walk.

When they were alone again, Lewis said quietly, "Well, Margaret, that's just a small sample of how much our life would be changed with strangers in the house. Especially strangers paying their money to be there."

Margaret looked to Louisa for help.

"He's right," Louisa said. "Still, you two would be building a new house with the idea of guests from the start. This is really a modest family house serving as an inn. Your private quarters could be planned ahead of time, since you'll be designing the house with all this in mind."

Margaret, standing now, looked from Louisa to Lewis.

"You agree with her, don't you, Cousin?" Lewis asked. "You think it's worth considering for us." He took a deep breath. "But I'm afraid any such idea would be far in the future. I've just paid back that mortgage. Now, if George decides to go to divinity school . . ." Lewis trailed off.

"I have money, Lewis," Margaret said, her eyes shining

again. "I have more than George will need. In a very real way, George is my son. I know building a new house is maybe several years in the future, Lewis, but—"

"This is 1847. I'd say it would be at least eight or nine years before we can do more than—plan."

"Oh, that's all right. Planning is what's so much fun! And darling, you know what a glorious piece of designing and remodeling you did on our warehouse. That's a genius of yours, Lewis. You could have been a world-famous architect!"

Lewis and Louisa laughed, but Margaret plunged ahead.

"Laugh if you like. I know what I'm talking about. And Louisa's got exactly the right idea about protecting our privacy—you can design our private quarters and—"

"That will only help some," Louisa interrupted. "Guests come first—always, my dear. You'd have to accept that at the outset."

"Well, I'd think that some of them at least, would be fascinating people to know. Lewis, you might meet world-famous scientists and inventors and writers and professors and—"

"—and fuddy-duddy lonely men like Mr. Johnson who will bore you to tears," Louisa said, "and crotchety elderly ladies whose demands indicate that they're convinced the entire state of Florida was created for them."

"But, we do have our wonderful children to help us. I can just see Tina now, being the perfect hostess."

"Tina will be married, I have no doubt, long before we can afford a house large enough to make your business profitable," Lewis said.

"Oh, I know that's what she's longing for, darling, but shut away as she is now, how can she possibly meet an eligible young man? If we had lovely visitors coming steadily from the North—"

Lewis's laughter stopped her. "All right, Mrs. Fleming. You've made your point. I make no promises, but I will give it a lot of thought. No doubt I could get ample mortgage money if we were building a house for commercial reasons."

"There, you see, Lewis? I hadn't even thought of anything so brilliant as that!"

"Margaret Seton Fleming," Louisa chided, "do you expect us to believe that?"

"Yes, I do—sort of. And Grandfather Sibbald will let us have lumber and bricks at cost. I guarantee that."

Lewis reached for her hand. She helped him to his feet. "We've worn poor Louisa out with our talk," he said. "Time we all went to bed. By the way, Cousin, how much is it costing you to entertain us here for this visit? How much are you losing not renting our room?"

Louisa laughed. "That question does not deserve an answer."

"But it's a very encouraging question, Louisa! Don't you see? It means my husband is already thinking like an innkeeper!"

26

Late in July, a tall, imposing young man in his early twenties paced the long, wooden dock at Jacksonville. He appeared impatient, his rather startlingly handsome face intense, as though looking for someone. The boat from New York had unloaded its passengers an hour ago and his valise and small trunk still stood on the dock nearby. A steady wind blew so briskly off the St. Johns that he had given up trying to keep his gray top hat in place and so carried it in one hand, allowing the wind to tousle the thick, dark curls that covered his head and blended into well-cared-for sideburns.

Finally, he hailed a stockily built, light-haired fellow about his own age and hurried toward him, his hand out in friendly greeting. "I say, have you just landed in Jacksonville, too?"

Gesturing toward his one large valise and extending his own hand, the young stranger said, "Yes, I have. From Welaka, south of St. Augustine. My name is Clark Stephens. My family plantation is at Welaka. I'm here on business."

"How do you do, Stephens? I'm Guy Henry, New York City. I wonder if you can help me?"

"Be glad to try."

"I'm looking for a gentleman named Dr. George Fleming. His stepmother and I are first cousins. My mother is Mrs. Margaret Fleming's aunt. Her father's sister. Does Dr. Fleming still practice medicine here?"

"He surely does. I can take you right to his office. In fact, the Flemings and my family have been friends for years. Your first cousin lives twenty miles upriver at Hibernia. She and her young children were out on their dock waving as my boat passed today. Here, I'll give you a hand with that trunk. George's office is quite close by."

A few minutes later, Clark Stephens and Guy Henry sat with George in his office. George appeared pleased with his callers, especially so because Guy Henry was actually related to Miss Margaret. But, as usual, he was reserved; no match at all for the two exuberant young visitors.

"Margaret Fleming and I have never met," Guy said. "I've simply heard of her beauty. Heard all my life what a wonderful father she had, Charles Seton. In fact, to hear my mother speak of her late brother, the man sounded too good to be true—to be even very likable."

"You're wrong on both counts about Mr. Seton," George said quickly. "He was both extraordinarily handsome and likable. I truly loved the man. He took my brother and sister and me into his home during the Indian fighting. Kept us, along with the Fatio ladies, until my father's war injury permitted him to come for us. I was living at the Seton home in Fernandina when Miss Margaret's father died. I—grieved for him."

Clark Stephens, his rosy cheeks rounded in a pleasant grin, said, "He's right about Mr. Seton. And everything you've heard about your cousin's beauty is true, too."

"Now, I really *can't* wait to meet this paragon of womanhood."

"I can have my steamer drop you off at Hibernia when I go back to Welaka tomorrow," Clark Stephens offered.

"Good. I'd like that."

"Does Miss Margaret know you're in the South, Mr. Henry?" George asked.

"Look here, I'm rather your cousin, too, by marriage," Guy Henry laughed. "Must you call me 'Mr. Henry'?"

"All right," George nodded. "Guy. And I'm George."

"Much better. To answer your question, no. Cousin Margaret has no idea I'm down here. You see, I came on the spur of the moment. I'm entering the military early next year. Always wanted to see this part of the country and so I just booked passage. Will Cousin Margaret think me rude? Of course, I've been known to be, but I'd much rather be considered charmingly impulsive."

"You'll be welcomed with open arms," George said. "My father and Miss Margaret are like that."

"Can't you take a few days and go along, George?" Guy asked.

"Sorry. But I hope you can stop off overnight, too, Clark. You know they'll insist."

"Say, I might do that. Just the other day I was thinking about your sister, Augustina. I don't think I've seen her in more than six years, but she was a pretty girl even then. How old is she now?"

"Nearly sixteen."

"And even more beautiful, I'll wager."

"Tina is the picture of my own mother," George said simply.

"Oh, I remember you mother, George. I was only a small boy, but I remember that dark, Spanish beauty."

"Spanish, eh?" Guy Henry asked.

"I'm half Spanish," George said. Then to Clark: "Say, did you know there's another new baby at Hibernia?"

"No, I didn't! Boy or girl?"

"Boy. Miss Margaret vows she's going to start on girls next."

"She sounds delightful," Guy laughed. "I wish we didn't have to wait until tomorrow."

The next day, just about noon, Clark Stephens and Guy Henry were made so welcome at Hibernia, were greeted with such high excitement by Margaret, in particular, that she couldn't concentrate enough to help Maum Easter plan company meals.

"You ain't no help, Miss Mar'ret," Easter fussed. "Have I ever let comp'ny sit down to a lean table? Mausa Lewis, he usin' his head better'n you. He done got me fixin' a picnic so's he an' Mister Clark Stephens an' the chillern can be off outa the way. You need to be with your cousin. Now, git!"

"Grandmother Henry, your great-aunt, is still as pert and bossy and as beautiful as a lady can be," Guy Henry said, settling himself in Lewis's chair in the parlor, shades drawn against the afternoon sun. "It's no wonder that you and I are such handsome people, Margaret," he laughed. "We spring from elite Scottish stock. I wish I'd known your father. Are you like him?"

Margaret laughed with him. "You caught me, Guy. I was

about to say that my father was the most beautiful man I'd ever seen—outside of my husband—but now I can't."

"Why not?"

"Because everyone vows I resemble him. Same hair, same eyes."

"Then he was—magnificent. Looked like a poet, my grandmother always said. You're—like a poem, Cousin."

"And you're absolutely ridiculous!"

"Is your mother well?"

"Yes, thank you. My mother is a very strong woman." Margaret moved to the edge of her chair. "Tell me about New York, Guy. Is it as exciting as the *Godey's Lady's Book* says it is? Do I look terribly old-fashioned? Out of style? I made this dress from a pattern in the Godey book."

"You're gorgeous," he said.

"Be sensible."

"I am. That wide collar affair dropping off your shoulders is right in fashion. That blue stuff is perfect for your golden coloring."

Margaret laughed. "Don't be sensible. I've changed my mind."

"But, what about you, Margaret, here in this isolated spot? God knows it's lovely, but don't you get restless? Lonely for people?"

"With Lewis? With three lively boys and a new baby? And darling Tina? Isn't she pretty?"

"Indeed, yes. Does she know it? She appears so modest, almost unassuming."

"She is truly modest. As for her beauty, she seems only to know that she looks like her own mother. That makes her happy. I'm sure it makes Lewis happy, too."

"And you don't mind?"

"Guy, I love him! Anything that helps keep alive all that was beautiful in his memories of Augustina, I welcome. I keep flowers or fresh leaves on her grave and I have no ulterior motive for doing it. I've come to love her, too."

She felt him studying her. "You're an amazing lady, Cousin. I can't think of a single woman I've ever known who would feel that way."

"Other women are no concern of mine. I simply know it's a comfort to Lewis to have the same dark beauty in his home in Tina."

Guy walked to the window facing the big yard and tilted a

slat in the shade. "One thing I know—my new friend, Clark Stephens, is much interested in that dark beauty. I caught his eye when he first saw Tina again today. They're out there right now playing croquet together."

"Clark and Tina?" Margaret went to look, too. "I'm glad I know what kind of young man he is, or I'd go right out and put a stop to it."

"Why?"

"Because I know Tina. The girl longs to be married, to have a husband—children of her own. All my mother hen feathers rise when I think she might ever become interested in the wrong man."

"But they're only playing a game of croquet before they all go on a picnic!"

"Down here, where we see so few people, things are very different. There just isn't that much meaningless romancing. You're a big-city boy. Take my word, for Tina this could be no laughing matter." She led him back to Lewis's chair. "You haven't told me at all about New York. What is it really like, Guy?"

"Big and growing bigger. Nearly half a million people now. The very, very poor and the very, very rich. The very, very poor are mostly immigrants from Europe—Irish and German in the main. The Irish and the Germans hate each other and the rich take advantage of them both. The rich, who fancy themselves aristocrats just because they're rich, clink glasses and gorge on rich food in lavish hotel dining rooms. They waltz, chatter about every silly new invention, attend the opera and live in mansions with painted ceilings, gilded moldings, splendid mirrors and curtains in the latest Parisian fashion."

Margaret, her eyes wide, thought a moment. "It all sounds—wonderful and ghastly. And crowded."

"It is—all of that. The poor immigrants are bitten even before they arrive by the great American slogan, 'Go Ahead.' They work. Lord, how those people work! Actually, although the rich entertain themselves more than they work, the old Puritan reverence for work still infests them. So much so that they feel such guilt when loafing—they've begun to call their loafing places 'health spas.'" He laughed his infectious laugh. "You see, an invalid can't work. Nothing to feel guilty about if you're at a health spa. So, everyone—no matter how robust, seeks out a fancy health spa in order to handle their guilty conscience for not working."

Margaret was way ahead of him. She was listening, oh, how she was listening, but her mind raced even faster than this Northern cousin spoke. Would she tell him of her plan to build a large, comfortable house someday at Hibernia in order to get the Flemings' share of that Northern wealth? Yes, she would. And for an hour or more—actually, until Lewis and the children came back to announce that Easter's company supper was on the table—they talked.

"To be continued tomorrow," Guy whispered to her as they followed the others into the small square dining room "I'm really quite impressed with all you've said, Cousin. Impressed and touched by your dream. I can picture that big, inviting house out there by the river. Northerners would love it. Colonel Fleming is a fortunate gentleman."

"Guy, please don't tell Lewis I've been talking about our dream." She smiled up at him. "I want him to bring it up himself."

Guy hugged her. "That's the good, logical, smart Seton mind at work, Cousin. Don't worry. I'll listen with both ears when your husband informs me of all these exciting plans for the future."

Lewis lost no time. The next day, out in the family sailboat, he told Guy of their hopes for a large, commodious inn at Hibernia someday. "The only thing that bothers me about it, I confess," he said, when he'd finished, "is that it will vastly change our lives. The family—our closeness—those are my most valued possessions. Margaret and I will just have to see to it that as little changes as possible."

Clark Stephens had not gone sailing with Guy and Lewis. He stayed at the house, more than willingly, to repair Tina's quilting frame.

"Are you good at needle work, Miss Tina?" he asked, as she stood beside him in Joe's carpentry shop. "I'll bet you're good at anything you try."

Tina blushed, but in her usual poised manner, said quietly, "Miss Margaret tells me I'm very good. She also trusts me with the children."

For a moment, neither spoke, while Clark skillfully planed a long, narrow strip of wood to replace one warped side of the frame.

"You're very good, too, Mr. Stephens," she said.

He smiled at her. "My brother, Winston, says I'm quite helpful around the plantation. Are you contented, Miss Tina?"

"Contented? Oh, yes. I mean—for this time in my life."

"And what is 'this time'? You're sixteen, aren't you?"

"Almost." She studied his round, open face. "You're frowning. Is that—bad?"

"Oh, no. Not at all. You seem a bit older. You're quite mature—for fifteen." He laughed nervously. "Would I be welcome if I stayed a few more days, do you think?"

"I'm sure you would be. Yes. You'd be most welcome!"

"Then I think I might do that. Late summer isn't our busy time around the plantation at Welaka. It's a very handsome place, Miss Tina. My family's home for three generations. I'd—like you to visit again sometime, now that you're grown up. Perhaps your stepmother and father would bring you to visit us soon."

A flush spread under her clear, olive skin. "That would be nice, Mr. Stephens. I'd like that."

Clark stayed for three days and as soon as his steamer was out of sight—waved off by the whole family and Guy Henry—Margaret followed Tina to her room, where the girl fled as soon as Clark was gone.

"Isn't it fine that your father wants us to plan a visit to the Stephens' plantation soon, Tina?"

Standing at the window, her back to Margaret, the tight bodice of her new green bouffant cotton dress revealing the slim, well-formed figure, Tina seemed almost remote. Suddenly, the girl was a woman. Sweet and considerate as she would always be, but at this moment, remote.

"Tina? Did you hear what I said? Your father thinks it will be a good idea for us to visit Welaka in the fall and—"

"Yes. I heard. And—I'm scared."

After a moment, Margaret said softly, "I thought you might be."

Tina turned to face her, surprised, frowning. "You thought I'd be scared?"

Margaret nodded.

"Why? Why did you think that?"

"Because I'm a woman, too."

"Do you think of me—as a woman?"

"Right now, yes, I do. It was almost instantaneous."

When Margaret saw tears begin to roll down the lovely young face, she gave Tina her warmest smile. "Those tears are normal, too. Don't fight them. Women cry—at certain, special times."

In the most solemn voice, Tina said, "I—love Clark Stephens. I love him. The way you love Papa. That's—why I'm afraid to visit his family." Her features contorted. "What—if—his family—doesn't like me?"

"If they didn't, then I'm sure they wouldn't be worthy to be your in-laws," Margaret said precisely. "But, what of Clark? Did he mention loving you?"

Margaret watched the young face relax. Tina smiled. A smile of certainty. Not arrogance. Simple certainty. "No. He didn't say so in those words—but, Miss Margaret, I know he does."

"I see."

"You did see it yourself, didn't you? That he—paid me special attention?"

"No one could miss that, Tina." Abruptly, Margaret sighed. "But, my dear, there is—always a certain amount of waiting involved—in love. I loathe it for you. It was so, so hard for me to wait. I wish I could change that for you. I can't. Clark will have to speak first to your father. Evidently he didn't while he was here."

"But, I don't think that means he doesn't love me, do you?"

Margaret embraced her. "Oh, Tina. You have no guile, have you? No tricks. What a blessed man Clark Stephens would be to have you as his wife."

"Should I have tricks?"

"No! No, no, no. It wouldn't be you. But, most young ladies would be too vain—even to tell their mothers—as you've just told me that you're not insulted because he didn't speak to your father."

"That would seem silly if he had. Except when I was a little girl, he hasn't known me but these three days. Do women know more quickly than men when they're in love?"

Margaret laughed a little. "In my case, that was certainly true. I waited for your father nearly six years."

"Oh, I could never wait six years. I'd die."

"No, you wouldn't. You'd think you were dying, but you wouldn't be. And neither will you have to wait that long. Your father had—his grief to handle, you know."

Tina nodded. "I wish I were more like my mother. I know I look like her, but Clark is so entertaining, he laughs a lot. I'd like to be gay and have a merry disposition and have my eyes flash the way everybody says my mother's did. Clark would surely love me then."

"But, Tina! You have the best of both your parents. Your mother's rare beauty—and your father's gentle goodness and honesty. You're very like your father, too, you know. And I still find him the most attractive man on the face of the earth."

Tina did not have to wait even until the Flemings visited the Stephens at Welaka. Within a week of his departure, Clark Stephens wrote to Lewis asking for Tina's hand. In spite of her youth, Lewis agreed and on September 12 of the next year, 1848, in the low-ceilinged parlor of the remodeled warehouse at Hibernia, with Sophia Fatio floating with poetic joy as her maid of honor, Tina became Mrs. Clark Stephens. The wedding was postponed for a year because L.I.'s return from his associate teaching position at Amherst had been delayed. Tina wanted her brother there. Of course, George came, too, and surprised them all by staying until everyone else had gone.

"This is wonderful having you still with us, George," Margaret said, as she walked beside him along the banks of the St. Johns—just the two of them—because George had wanted it that way.

"I need to talk to you," he said. "With all that mob here, I couldn't catch you alone."

"My, you're mysterious, and I thought your father extremely sweet to allow you to inform him that he was not wanted on this walk of ours. But then, your father, is always sweet—except when he gets tangled up in his accounts. He still worries about money for the future."

"I suppose you *had* to bring up money right off, didn't you?" His voice was surprisingly sharp.

Margaret stopped to look at him. "Not intentionally, George. But I can see I've made you angry."

"I'm not angry. I'm—guilty. I—I now know that God is calling me to the ministry and—"

"Oh, my dear boy. You do?"

"Yes. And—of course, Papa has told me of your plans to

build a large house here in order to acquire some of the Yankee tourist money that's around."

"Now, wait a minute." She took his hand and began pulling him toward Pompey's bench around the big oak. "Let's sit down, side by side and clear up a few things." He went with her and when they were seated, Margaret said, "There is no possible way we can build a new place for two or maybe three years. Perhaps even four. Your father has drawn rough plans for a house with thirty rooms—three stories—that will cost money. No point in building a more modest place. It would only cut our future income. But whether you go back to school or not need change nothing. I have my inheritance. It's yours, George. It's still yours. It's waiting for you to decide. For—God to make your call to the ministry absolutely clear."

George took a deep breath, exhaled noisily. "It's clear now. He's done it. I know beyond the shadow of a doubt that He wants me in His service—and I'm miserable."

"Because of money?"

"In part. But am I really *good* enough to stand up in a pulpit and tell other people how to live? I think I've messed up my own life to a fare-you-well."

"Now, you listen to me." Her voice was firm, very firm. "If I know anything at all, I know that no one—*no one*—is good enough to be a minister, or a parent or a doctor or a teacher. No one, without the minute-by-minute grace of God is *good* enough to be—anything! Any other viewpoint is a distortion of God and of human nature. God is *not* a stern deity who demands what none of us can give or be on our own. He knows we're helpless without Him. God understands the human condition. Why else did He send the Savior? No one is ever good enough, George, to be a minister. That isn't the point. You and I—all persons—have only to trust Him to be Himself in us, through us. That way, we manage." After a pause, she laughed softly and hugged him. "I'm preaching, I know. But, did I make my point?"

George shook his head yes. "You'd already taught me that when I was growing up. Just as you taught me that I have an obligation to *hope*." He thought for a moment, then said, "My moodiness, my load of guilt—even thinking I could never be good enough to preach—all that is a direct result of too much time spent thinking about myself. Self-absorption is plain old sin. It cancels hope. I do know that."

Too moved to respond, Margaret said nothing.

"Jesus wasn't dwelling on Himself when He hung on that cross," George went on. "With no thought of Himself, He—hung there with His arms out—to everyone in the world. I know those truths, Miss Margaret. Help me hold onto them. I want to be free—of *me*."

They got up and began to walk slowly, arm in arm, back toward the house.

"It's time now to tell your father that you'll be going to divinity school. You'll find him—relieved, I think. Where will you attend seminary?"

"Princeton. I know I was born Catholic and that you're a dyed-in-the-wool Episcopalian who's won most of us over to your church, including Papa. But," he grinned at her, "somehow I think you'll still love me if I decide to become a Presbyterian."

"You have done some thinking, haven't you? Which church doesn't matter. Only our faith in God matters. How long before you can leave Jacksonville?"

"Six months probably. I hope to enter Princeton early next year. I need to get started. It's taken me long enough to make up my mind."

"But you've done it now—and that's what matters."

27

That evening, when George reached Jacksonville, his cousin Susan met him at the door of the L'Engle home. One look told him something was wrong. "Is it my grandmother?"

"Yes. She's very low. I think she may be—leaving us. We've needed you so desperately. Go to her *now*!"

He dropped his valise in the front hall and hurried toward the stairs. On the second-floor landing, the L'Engle daughter, Mary Evelyn, L.I.'s favorite for all of her nine years, stood with both hands over her mouth, her pretty face stricken.

"George—oh, George," she whispered, "do people—just stare into—space when they're—dying?"

He rushed past the girl and into his grandmother's large front room. She lay on her back, the strong, blue-veined hands motionless on the coverlet—as little Mary Evelyn had said—staring into space.

George knelt beside the bed, laid his hand on her forehead and in as natural a voice as he could manage, spoke softly. "Well, Grandmother, I've come back bringing you love from everyone at Hibernia. L.I. is home again—a big, muscular man now. Tina's wedding was fine. She married well." Then, "How do you feel?"

He had never told anyone—not even Margaret—the extent of his awe of this strong woman, awe approaching fear. With all his heart he admired Sophia Fleming, but he had always feared her disapproval and had never dared speak to her of his own indecision and torment, although he had longed to. In this moment of what was surely her approaching death, he was in awe again—when it was she who needed him.

"How do you feel, Grandmother?" he repeated lamely.

She turned her eyes toward him and in her weakened condition gave an unmistakable snort. "That's—a ridiculous question. A—typical—doctor's question! You know I'm—dying." With a slight jerk of her head, she motioned him closer. "You're a good doctor, George. But I'm beyond that. However—secretive—you've been with me, I know you—love God. I want you to pray for me. *Now*. So—I can—hear you."

George felt his mouth go dry. No words even resembling a prayer formed in his mind. Sophia Fleming closed her eyes, as though waiting. When no prayer came, she opened them and for such faded eyes, so near the end of seeing, managed an almost stern look.

"Your—grandmother is—waiting for you—to pray!"

His head began to throb as though a band were being tightened about it. Desperately, he struggled to bring back the moment of closeness to God, of clarity, which he'd felt with Margaret. The struggle, intensified by his fear that the old woman would challenge him again, seemed the longest he'd ever endured—and the most painful. Then, slowly, gently, the way a Florida dawn eases across the St. Johns, the struggle began to ease. He drew a deep breath and whispered: "Dear—present Lord. Here is—Sophia Fleming, your child. She is in deep need of You now. You have told us that we can be sure, absolutely certain of Your Presence. You said, 'Lo, I am with you always, even unto the end of the world.' Give her this certainty. Make that promise real to—Sophia Fleming, my grandmother, Your child. We all—

love her, dear Lord. But give her a—comforting sense *this minute*—of the height and depth and breadth of Your love. Now, Lord . . . now."

The wrinkled old eyelids fluttered and then he felt, more than saw, through his sudden tears, the look he had always longed to see. A look he could not fear. There was no reason for fear. It was a look of—peace and gratitude and love.

Peace and gratitude and love flowed from George's heart to his grandmother. And to God, who gave him the strength and the quiet and the courage to hold the soft, old hand in both of his until she died.

Sophia's body was brought by steamboat to Hibernia for burial beside Lewis's father, her husband, the first George Fleming. Once more, Margaret stood before an open grave—this time, beside Lewis—their own family and friends around them. Within a few days, there had been a wedding and a burial at Hibernia. Tears of joy and tears of sorrow mingled. But life, happy and sorrowful, was being lived there again—would be lived there through her children and grandchildren after Margaret herself rested in the small, shady cemetery.

She looked about at the gathering of relatives and friends who had come from Jacksonville, St. Augustine, and now that Tina had married into the Stephens family, from Welaka. Louisa smiled at Margaret briefly, giving the kind of warmth and assurance only Louisa knew how to put into a smile. Tina, standing beside Clark Stephens, looked more than ever like Augustina—her black, black hair and dark eyes accentuated by black mourning clothes. Across the open grave, as the priest read the service for the burial of the dead in Latin, Margaret's eyes met George's dark, solemn ones. A corner of his thin mouth curved slightly, the merest hint of a smile which Margaret knew was his way of thanking her for understanding him—exactly as he was. There had been only a few minutes last night, when George arrived, to tell Margaret that God had miraculously given him the freedom to pray for the dying woman who had so awed and frightened him for all the twenty-six years of his life.

Near where George stood, L.I., tall, strong, a man now, but if possible, still more cheerful and lovable, held little Mary Evelyn L'Engle's hand, comforting her in her genuine grief for the dead woman whom she had always adored. A wave of relief flooded Margaret's heart. L.I. would be with them at Hibernia at least off and on until he heard from the men who would form the canal company where he planned to work at Waukeenah, Florida. How she had missed L.I.! But, today, he was there and so obviously giving strength to Lewis just by being there that Margaret's heart poured love toward the young man who sent love flooding back to her with every exchanged glance.

She stole a look at dear Lewis, standing silently beside her, and slipped an arm through his. Lewis, in the silent cemetery again, holding their own baby, William, as he had held little Tina on that other, long-ago day. Lewis, filling her life now with his love, his very being. Her eyes moved then to the ruddy, perfect face of her own firstborn, Seton, nearly ten, and on to Frank, seven years old today, thin and serious. Then, to Frederic—quietly dignified, even at age three and a half.

A life had ended on earth, but unlike the air of stark tragedy which had hung above Augustina's grave all those years ago, peace was here today. Almost quiet joy. The loss of one's mother was always a shock, but she doubted that even Lewis mourned painfully. Sophia Fleming had lived a long, full life—and now, blessedly, she was free of pain. Reunited at last with Lewis's father—the first George Fleming, he of the thick, glorious dark red hair—the one person to whom, according to Louisa, Sophia Fleming had, with abandon, given herself. Margaret had never seen George Fleming, but her heart moved toward him now. It was he who had given them all Hibernia.

She glanced again at her stepson George, who was watching her. Silently, she thanked God for today.

At the end of a week everyone had gone from Hibernia. Even L.I., who went to Jacksonville to visit the L'Engles. Lewis and Margaret and their own four sons were alone again. On the day the last visitors left, Margaret put aside her other planned work and sat with Lewis on the small front porch of their remodeled warehouse. He read or pretended to read. She gave half attention to some mending.

"Good book, darling?"

He sighed. "I'm not sure. For some reason, I can't get into it."

"But it's your new William Makepeace Thackeray novel, isn't it?"

"Yes. I've been waiting four months for it. I'm so fond of the way he writes in his Titmarsh articles. I don't know why I can't keep my mind on his novel."

"What's it called?"

"*Vanity Fair*. The fault's in me, I'm sure."

"You miss everyone," she said. "So do I. Especially L.I. We've seen so little of him for so long, but isn't he fine? Really enthusiastic about that canal company at Waukeenah. I don't understand exactly what his part will be, but—"

"He'll handle the legal work. And if I'm any judge, he'll do it in top-notch form, too. L.I.'s pure joy to his old father. He's simply—all there, out in the open where I can reach him. Unlike poor George." Lewis smiled. "By the way, do you know I think L.I. still holds to the rather touching devotion he's always had for little Mary Evelyn? I've felt he might wait for her to grow up and so help me, I see it happening."

"Do you know, I believe you're right!" She bit off her thread and smoothed Seton's mended shirt over her knee. "Lewis, that marriage would make me the happiest woman on earth!"

"I thought you already were," he teased.

"Now that my husband's the Hibernia postmaster, why shouldn't I be?" she teased back.

He stretched his legs, massaging the bad one as he so often did. "Laugh if you like, but I'm rather looking forward to my new duties with the U.S. Mail. Be nice to see our neighbors a bit more often when they come by for their letters and papers."

"I like the whole idea—and I'm proud of you." Margaret reached to touch his arm. "Lewis, we have everything to hope for—you and I. George will be fine, too. I know he will. Don't frown, darling. Not even that little frown. George will be *all right* now that he's really made up his mind."

"Unless something—unexpected catches up with him."

"What on earth do you mean?"

"Who knows about George?"

"God does. And that's all we need to know right now. Agreed?" In answer, he only patted her hand. "Lewis? I want to hear you say it."

"Yes, Mrs. Fleming. Agreed."

A duet of whoops from the side yard broke the quiet moment, and down past the house, toward the river, raced

Seton and Frank, shouting: "Mail boat! Mail boat's coming! Papa! Mama! The new mail boat's coming!"

Book and mending laid aside, Lewis and Margaret hurried hand in hand after their yelling, excited sons. They had almost reached the Fleming dock when Frederic's sharp crying stopped them.

"Oh, dear," Margaret said. "You go on, Lewis. I know you'll want to talk to Mr. Huston. I suppose Frederic has fallen down again trying to keep up with his big brothers. I'll see to him. Go on. Meet the mail boat. Frederic and I will be along."

Walking as fast as his limp allowed, Lewis headed for the dock, where the boys stood waving as the small white mail boat steamed in from midriver. He, too, waved to George Huston, who signaled back with a short blast of the whistle.

Huston, a successful planter on the adjoining land, had never been a friendly fellow. Had always resented Lewis felt, that the large island—only one thousand acres of which any Fleming had ever owned—had come to be known as Fleming's Island. Now, Lewis supposed, his neighbor would be harder than ever to get along with simply because he, Huston, had been appointed to pilot the mail boat, while Lewis was postmaster.

"Afternoon, Huston," he called. "I see you're carrying out your new responsibilities to the federal government."

"Federal government pays my salary to run this boat and that's all we've got in common," Huston snorted, as he tossed a bundle of mail on the dock. "Don't trust anybody connected with Washington. Liked it better when we were a Territory. They mainly forgot us then."

"But the Mexican War turned out well for us this year. Look at all that new territory we acquired. You don't like the idea of our owning all of Texas outright, plus all of New Mexico and California?"

"Wouldn't mind owning still more, but now they're saying— the federal government—that they'll never stand for slavery in any of the new land ceded by Mexico. Bad business, Fleming. That's bad, bad business. They're out to get us down here, that's what."

Margaret and little Frederic, unhurt, but his cheeks still wet from crying, joined the group on the dock. She greeted Mr. Huston, who bowed as Lewis handed Margaret the mail. "You look through it, dear, for our letters—if any. I don't have my glasses with me. Must have left them on the porch."

Huston gave a half laugh. "I sort all this mail, Fleming, an' you don't see me reaching for spectacles, do you? I'm forty-five years old, too."

Grinning, Lewis replied, "But, I'm forty-nine, Huston. Fifty by the end of the year."

"Hush, you don't look it," Margaret snapped, and shuffled through the letters addressed to them. "Lewis! One from Tina, one from my mother—and already a letter from George! Why, he just left!"

"Saw him this morning at the wharf in Jacksonville," Huston offered. "Ran all the way to be sure I got this letter before I shoved off on my route."

Huston then cast off and after shouted farewells until next week, Margaret and Lewis and the children, with Frank carrying the mail bundle, walked back toward the house.

"What was George's big hurry with that letter, I wonder," Lewis mused.

"We'll soon find out, dear."

"Can I read the letter, too?" Seton asked. "Lemme have one to read, Mama, please!"

"You'll both have your chance later," Lewis said, lifting Frederic up into his arms. "Right now, you have a job to do. While your mother and I read the letters, you and Frank see to your little brother and I mean, this time, keep him close by where you can watch over him. Frank, deposit that mail for our neighbors in my office, please. I'll sort it later."

"Papa," Frank began, in his solemn, thoughtful way, "I think I'm old enough—Seton, too—for us to be able to read the mail when it first comes. If we've learned to read, why are we too young to read letters? I'm seven now!"

"So you are," Margaret said. "And just as soon as a proper mourning period is over, we'll have your party. You were very considerate about your birthday coming on the same day your grandmother was buried, Frank. Your father and I appreciate that. We want you to know."

"Oh, that's all right. I figured out for myself that you appreciated it."

When the boys had gone to play, Margaret and Lewis had a good laugh over Frank.

"Some mind for a seven-year-old, wouldn't you say, Mrs. Fleming?"

"We could easily have another lawyer in the family," she agreed. "That child analyzes everything."

Seated again on the porch, Margaret broke the seal on George's letter first. "I have to see why George was in such a hurry for us to have this. Do you want me to read it to you, Lewis?"

"If you please, my dear. I just hope he hasn't changed his mind again."

"It's very short. Just a note. 'Dear Papa and Miss Margaret, I am writing this in a big rush to catch the mail boat. But, since I know you have been hoping for a wife for me, I had to tell you that I have begun to hope, too. The very day I returned, L.I. and I were invited to dinner by friends of L.I.'s from the North. We dined at the Buffington Hotel, although dining, L.I. tells me, somewhat dignifies the calibre of food served us. I didn't notice. My whole attention was riveted on Miss Mary Bennett, a member of the visiting party. She is, I believe, from Connecticut, with a manner so poised and self-sufficient, an appearance so striking, she captivated me at once. I heard little that was said at the table. But when L.I. and I prepared to leave, I heard myself ask Miss Bennett if I might show her Jacksonville the next day. To my amazement, she not only smiled warmly, she readily agreed. I will keep you posted.'

Lewis, looking out over the river, asked, "Is that all?"

"Yes. But I think that's quite a lot. Oh, Lewis, I hope she's a sensitive young woman. George needs that. How he needs it!"

Lewis sighed. "*I* hope he isn't expecting from her what he's found in you. He'll be disappointed."

"Don't be so grumpy. Mary Bennett may turn out to be just right. I'm delighted. More than that—I'm thankful. He's been so lonely."

"But not in a position now to think of marrying," Lewis said. "He'd never be able to support a wife at Princeton."

"I insist that you do not jump ahead and hunt things to worry about. George's news is marvelous!" She was already breaking the seal on Tina's letter. It was Tina's usual cheery little note, informing them that her in-laws, the Stephens, had such lovely things to say about all the Flemings and that their river journey back to Welaka had been uneventful.

"How like her," Margaret said, "to want us told right away that they're home safely."

"Doesn't seem quite right yet to me for Tina not to be at home here at Hibernia, Margaret."

"You are just plain grumpy and looking for trouble today, Colonel Fleming, and I'm sure there's nothing in my mother's letter to cheer you, so let's go play a game of croquet with the children before Easter calls us to eat."

"Nonsense. Read your mother's letter."

"All right, if you insist."

She scanned the Fernandina news and then exclaimed: "Lewis, listen to this! 'I am grateful for every time you and your family have visited me, but this house is large and my days are lonely at times. Especially with your grandparents in Philadelphia and your brother, George, at the North for good. I make no bones about young Seton being my favorite of your children. So, would you and Lewis consider allowing him to visit me for a few months? That is, if he would like it. There are two nice boys down the block with whom he could play. Children of an excellent family. I shall hope for your willingness to please an old lady who would so enjoy the company of her favorite grandson and who so longs for it.' "

Lewis and Margaret looked at each other in amazement that the woman, who had always declared herself sufficient unto herself, should admit to loneliness.

"My first question," Lewis said, "is, will Seton want to go?"

"If I know him, he'll jump at the chance. Mother was so open about spoiling him—far beyond the others—the last time we visited her. I'm not sure it's good for him, but he'll want to go."

"Of course, there is a doctor there if he hurts himself or becomes ill," Lewis mused. "Nothing so unusual about a boy spending a few weeks with his grandmother, I suppose."

"She didn't say a few weeks—*months*!"

"Margaret, if I'm honest, the whole idea disturbs me. I'll miss the boy too much! Seton is the last one—we can do without, isn't he?" When Margaret didn't answer, Lewis said, "But, I see no possible way to refuse her. I'm sure she is lonely these days. She's been generous with us—furniture, carpets, linens, even pictures for our walls here. We'll have to let the boy go."

Margaret straightened her shoulders. "How like Mother not to leave us a choice."

*   *   *

Early the following month, after Margaret and Easter and Betty spent days readying him for a long visit in the city, Seton, at his own insistence, boarded the steamer *George Washington* alone, under the captain's care, for Fernandina. For the first few weeks, he and his grandmother wrote letters together—Seton adding his own version of the exciting life in Fernandina to enclose with hers. Then early in the next year, 1849, Margaret received this from her mother only:

Fernandina

2 January 1849

My dear Margaret,

It was generous and kind of you and Lewis to allow Seton to stay with me during Christmas. I'm sure you missed him dreadfully at Hibernia and it still seems ridiculous to me that your entire family did not find it convenient to come here for the Holy Season. Our doctor could have cared for puny little William. I am, of course, pleased that you have named him for your uncle, the intrepid captain, but your William does seem a weakly, slow child. My real joy is Seton and daily he lifts my darkness to let in his cheerful light. If I do say so, he seems deeply fond of me. I beg you to let him stay until spring. I have tried to be generous with you and Lewis. Please be generous with me.

Margaret slammed down the letter unfinished—thankful that she had gone to her room in order to read it alone first. Lewis, who adored his son William, would not appreciate such remarks about the child. Of course, it was fine that her mother loved Seton. But the boy was already in danger of being spoiled, although she had to admit he showed few signs. But why did her mother find it necessary to criticize poor William?

Annoyed, upset, Margaret began to walk about the room, moving an object here, another there—brushing off imaginary dust, straightening an already straight doily on her dresser. Her mother could still strip her of all defenses and leave her helpless to do anything but agree—or indeed, to appear selfish.

I wish Mother had given us nothing—not one stick of furniture, not one mirror, not a single picture for even one wall, she thought, her mind blazing. At least, I asked for none of it. She gave to us freely, I *hoped*. Oh, how I hoped.

We need Seton here! His father needs him. His brothers—
I need him. I want him. He's *my son*. Let Mother will
everything she owns to my brother George. All my heart
really cares about anyway is the big silver bowl—but let her
will that to George, too. If she leaves me nothing, I won't be
poor because I have Lewis and— She stopped the ugly
thoughts. Stopped them dead. Stopped pacing about the
room and let her eyes fall on the cherished oil painting of her
father which stood in its ornate gold frame on the bedside
table.

"Poor Mama," she whispered, picking up the picture to
kiss the image of her father's sensitive face. "Oh, Papa, poor
Mama. Poor me, for that matter. She didn't mention one
word about willing me anything in that letter, but she managed to turn my thoughts to—*things*. Help me, Papa. Help
me sort it out. I've watched you try to handle Mother when
she forced you into a corner like this. Sometimes you really
handled her. More often, your gentleness gave in to her."
Margaret stood very straight, still holding the picture to her
heart. "Well, I'm going to *handle* this. Seton is our son and
he will remain our son. I intend to send for him next week!
After all, he's been there for over three months. I want him
back here where I can look at him and enjoy him, too."

Margaret had told no one yet, not even Maum Easter, but
she was all but certain that she was going to have another
child. For one brief moment, her resolve wavered. Was she
being unreasonable because she was nervous until she knew
for sure? Instinctively, as though she were a little girl again,
she looked to her father's face for help. Then, after a long
moment, she placed the portrait back on the table, her eyes
still on the image of Charles Seton's face.

Not in a whisper this time, aloud, her head high, she said,
"*Seton is coming home*, Papa. He's my son and he's coming
home next week. You gave in to Mother, I know, because
you lived in the same house with her. Well, I don't. And
Papa, Seton is coming back to Hibernia where I live—and
where he belongs."

28

During the spring and summer months, after Margaret knew she was carrying another child, she also carried a nagging guilt that she had so flatly ordered her mother to send Seton home. Not enough guilt to spoil the golden, sun-drenched summer at Hibernia, but the September day the baby came—her first daughter—she confessed the guilt to Lewis.

"Would it be all right with you if we named her Matilda—for Mother?" she asked, as Lewis once more sat beside her bed. "I doubt my mother will ever forgive me for bringing Seton home on such short notice earlier this year, but I do love her, Lewis. I'm not good with her, but I love her."

"Matilda is fine," he said. "I'm sure your mother will be more than pleased."

"No one—no one ever knows exactly what is going to please her and you know it!"

"All right, Mrs. Fleming," he said with exaggerated patience. "You mustn't get yourself riled up. Not now. Will you rest if I get out of here?"

"No. I want you with me. I need to talk—about George."

"At a time like this? With such a beautiful new daughter to enjoy?" He touched the child's warm, golden head. "She's just too pretty to be true, Margaret."

"I wanted to give you a daughter this time."

"You always get what you want, don't you?"

"My greatest achievement was—you."

"Very pretty, but you need to rest."

"Pamper me, Lewis. I—want to talk about George. He was right. By now, everyone knows Easter and I don't need any help. But, I wonder if that's really why he didn't come." When Lewis had no answer, she said, "I'm as worried about him now as you are. You know that, don't you?"

"Yes. But you're not disgusted with him and I am."

"No. If he loves Mary Bennett as he seems to love her, I dare not be disgusted. You mustn't be either. We both know too much about loving to—"

"I think he's letting her crush him!" Lewis interrupted.

"She's stopped his going to divinity school already. If he hates medicine as he claims, and still goes on with it to placate her, he'll have double trouble. I wish she'd go back to the North and leave our family alone! No matter how beautiful he claims she is—she's danger. She thinks poor George as a *doctor* is a good catch." He turned away. "He's anything but!"

"Look at me, Lewis. God can handle George. Give the boy time to get his bearings again."

Lewis jerked himself up off the bed and limped to the window. "All we've done for months—years, is to give George time! I'm—ashamed of him. He's so—frazzlin' wishy-washy!"

"Lewis? Lewis Fleming, come away from that window and sit back down here with Matilda and me."

After a moment, she watched him return slowly, perhaps a little ashamed of himself. Margaret waited.

In a moment, he touched the baby's head again with the back of his hand. "Matilda . . . I'll call her Tissie," he said.

"Darling?"

"I'm listening. If—you have the strength to help me where George is concerned, Margaret, I'm listening."

"George is *not* wishy-washy. And I want you to promise never to say that again. He's troubled. He's caught up in emotions impossible for either of us to understand. But we *have* to trust him to God. If George makes a poor judgment, we must support him." She put her fingers over Lewis's mouth. "Don't say it. You know I don't mean that we are to support what may be a bad decision. But we must—we must always support George himself."

Except for the occasional preachment from his neighbor Huston, when he brought the Hibernia mail, Lewis had not spoken much with anyone about the talk of the South's growing antagonism against the North. Huston had nothing against Lewis personally beyond his rancor over the name Fleming Island and Lewis's seeming tolerance of "the rotten federal government." Lewis knew this, so time after time he listened as Huston raged. The man was entitled to his opinion—except that the Fleming boys overheard and this bothered Lewis. Seton and Frank and even Frederic, almost five, counted the hours each Friday until they saw the tiny white steamer chug toward the Hibernia dock.

"What concerns me most," Lewis told Margaret one cold

winter morning in early 1850, "is that Seton slips down to meet Huston alone when possible. I know he's keen on proving he's faster than his brothers, but he seems too taken by Huston. I don't want his young mind warped."

"Oh, do you really think Mr. Huston would talk politics with an eleven-year-old boy? Anyway, we do have to take some chances with the children. Why, look at the chance we take when one of them gets the croup. I was up half of last night giving poor little William fiddler crab tea. I even had to dislodge that dreadful sheet of phlegm from his throat with my finger! I think he might have choked to death otherwise. I really do."

Lewis gave her a worried look. "Did you have to do that with the others? Frank, Frederic? I know Seton didn't have croup."

"No. And—" Margaret frowned. "Lewis, sometimes, I worry a lot about William. He just doesn't seem to be doing—what he should be doing at—nearly three years. He's never been like the others. I know you don't agree with me and I know we want William to be William, but, as a baby he grasped our fingers too weakly, he didn't turn himself over until he was past six months—he didn't say one word until this past Christmas. He was so long returning a smile—even discovering his toes. He's slept so much more than the others. He can barely walk now!"

"Margaret, that's enough!" His eyes blazed. "I won't have you say one more word against William! Do you hear me?"

"Oh, darling, I'm *not* saying anything against him. I love him too much. I'm—I'm—" She caught herself, forced a smile. "I'm—just a fussbudget mother and you must pay me no mind."

"Indeed I won't. All our children are fine, healthy, normal youngsters. And that's the end of it. Tomorrow's mail day. Maybe we'll hear from L.I. Maybe I can even keep Huston's mind off the federal government by telling him about L.I.'s new canal at Waukeenah. Might even ask him what he thinks of the idea. Frankly, there's something about that Wacissa and Aucilla Navigation Company L.I. works for that bothers me. Huston's a smart businessman. I'd really like his opinion."

"But you always trusted L.I.'s judgment."

"That's why I'm eager to hear from him. It's a gigantic job to try to deepen the Aucilla and the Wacissa rivers for steamers. But, as you say—we can trust L.I. to know what's what. And to be honest with us."

"They've even made him secretary of the company, haven't they? He wouldn't have taken that position if he didn't feel sure."

Lewis nodded. "He wrote that he thought the work was awfully slow, the cost becoming prohibitive." He sighed. "It may be just fine. He'll come right out and tell us if it isn't."

Huston brought them a letter, but not from L.I. From George. To Lewis, George's letter contained the worst possible news. He and Mary Bennett had been married for a month—and he would go on practicing medicine for her sake.

Limping back toward the house with Margaret, his face a mask of disappointment, he said coldly, "He lacked nerve to come here to tell *me*. If he'd seen you, he'd have told you everything." Immediately, he sensed her hurt. "I'm sorry," he said. "I didn't mean that the way it sounded. I wanted him to remain a doctor. But not to please a selfish woman. Don't you see the trouble ahead, Margaret?"

"Yes. But has God ever promised anyone a life free from trouble?"

"Don't quote Scripture!"

"That wasn't Scripture. But I am going to *hope*. I'm just sorry for them both."

"I'm not sure I am."

L.I.'s letter came a few days later and, as Lewis feared, the new navigation company had folded. The digging had been entirely stopped because of impenetrable limestone ridges. But, L.I., in his usual manner, had ridden out the disappointment and had already signed on as headmaster at the new Waukeenah Academy in Jefferson County. Further, he was insisting that they allow Seton to join him soon to attend school with his big brother as teacher.

"So, someone else wants Seton," Lewis said heavily. "I'm grateful to L.I., but—can we part with Seton?"

"Yes, we can. I don't want to any more than you do, but what a marvelous opportunity for him! We can let him go, darling, and we must."

In spite of the chill in the air, they'd read L.I.'s letter standing on the riverbank. Lewis turned without a word and limped toward Pompey's bench under the old oak. He sat down wearily. "Oh, Margaret, I feel eighty-one instead of fifty-one." He glanced at her with a sad smile. "I do. I'm not teasing. Even our children are getting old. L.I., a teacher. Seton, eleven. Frank, eight. George—married—"

"William isn't quite three, Matilda is only a year and a half," she said calmly. "And there will be other babies, Lewis. You'll see."

"I wonder if we'll be able to cope with more."

"You don't really mean that."

"Some days, yes. Some days, no. Today—yes."

Still standing, Margaret reached both hands to him. "L.I. is fine, there's nothing we need to decide today about Seton and school, there's not one thing we can do this minute for George, so let's go inside out of the cold and you draw house plans for me. I think I know exactly what I want to do with that front stairway for our new place. "Lewis?"

He smiled halfheartedly. "You just *don't* stop clinging to hope, do you?"

Margaret pulled him to his feet. "Hope is *not* something we cling to. It isn't just a word that covers up or pushes ugly things out of our minds. Hope isn't a pipe dream. Hope is *real*. It comes straight from God. He has a right to expect us to use it." She hugged him with all her might. "Now, we'll go inside and you will put that new stairway on paper for me. I need to look at it to be sure my idea is right."

29

Seton, with Tina and Clark Stephens to look after him, left in March for Waukeenah. Tina's letters, written during their month's visit with L.I. in the tight little cottage furnished the Waukeenah Academy headmaster, put Margaret's mind at ease. As much as her mind could ever be at ease with Seton so far away. Seton's buoyancy and excitement at being able to live right with L.I. never wavered. But as autumn began to color the sweet gum and tupelo trees, Margaret had to exert every effort to keep herself and Lewis from dreading Christmas without Seton. The boy had, next to the sun itself, come to be the light at Hibernia. Christmas without him would not seem like Christmas, but for the other children's sake she determined not to show her own sorrow.

While Lewis and the older children were in the woods the week before Christmas cutting greenery to decorate the house, she did what she'd done through all the years of her adult life when she needed help for her own heart. Seated in her room at the desk her mother had given her, she wrote to Louisa.

18 December 1850
Hibernia

Beloved Louisa,

I am writing this letter for my sake. I need to pour out my heart and because my goal in life is Lewis's happiness, I dare not tell him much of what, thank God, I can tell you. We are all well and except for the gnawing emptiness with Seton away, life here goes along as usual. I ache for Seton's smile at times until I feel I will die of the pain. Of course, I won't. And I have already, during these eight months he has been gone, burdened you far too heavily with my loneliness for him.

There is so much for which to be thankful. Mother does seem pleased that Tissie was named for her and Tissie is daily more beautiful. Her golden hair curls and her blue eyes laugh. Of course, she cries from cutting her teeth—she has three now— but I do believe her father suffers more than she. Someone in Jacksonville told Lewis to rub whiskey on her gums and then drink the remainder himself! He hasn't tried it. Tissie is already walking far better than dear William, who is now almost four. Oh, Louisa, my heart aches for William! *I can admit this to no one but you*. Satisfied so long as he is not challenged to more than he can handle, he appears mostly contented. Then, that pathetic, wary look comes into his pale eyes. My heart aches also for Lewis, who still cannot admit that William is just not normal, but goes right on contending that the boy is simply a bit slow to develop. You know how I have prayed for Lewis to be right. He is wrong. I have cried and cried— during my rare times alone. It is a special stab in the heart for a mother to have given birth to a child even slightly ill-equipped for life.

We hear only good news from Seton and L.I. Seton is learning like lightning and writes excellent letters. In fact, he, and not L.I., wrote to tell us the marvelous news I have for you now: L.I. is going to wait for little Mary Evelyn L'Engle to add a few more years and then they plan to marry. Of course, this does not surprise dear Lewis, who has contended it would happen since Mary E. was one year old! She is, I believe, almost twelve now and it will all work out fine, since L.I. means to return to Jacksonville when he has saved enough money and open his own law practice there.

Frank and Frederic are fine and mostly behaving—and now I come to George, who is as big a heartache to me in his way as is my own child William. According to a recent letter from Susan L'Engle (we almost never hear anymore from George, who has always been so faithful), his life is a Hell on earth with that woman. She seems not only possessive, but so outspoken as to scold George—even in public—for a thing so harmless as the fact that he, by nature, is not a fluent conversationalist. "He keeps reminding me that he gave up the ministry for me," Mary is said to declare, "and at times the man's actually tongue-tied! How on earth could he ever preach?" Oh, Louisa, that this should happen to sensitive, tender George! My heart bleeds for him night and day and I try with all my might not to judge Mary on hearsay. Lewis is still crushed by it all and reminds me that George was not forced at gunpoint to marry her. I am sure George is not easy to get along with these days. No man could be when he is daily disobeying a call from God. The boy must be, of all people, most wretched. How he withstands the tremendous pressures on all sides, I do not know.

Now, I have worn you out with this long letter. We wish you were free to join us for Christmas, but realize that is a busy time for you and Sophia in St. Augustine. I am so happy for your success and can scarcely wait for the day when our inn can become a reality.

Here is one more item, dear Louisa—a secret, please, until I know for certain. But I believe I am going to have another baby! If I'm right, it will be born late next summer. I'm hopeful and I'll let you know soon.

I still hear often from my dashing cousin, Guy Henry, in New York. Our visit from him now over three years ago is still so fresh in my mind. I think how exciting it must be to live up there in his social whirl and with all those conveniences. But I would not change my span of days by the river with my beloved Lewis for any other life on earth. Guy marvels that I remain content—happy in the makeshift confusion of our remodeled warehouse and our rapidly growing family. But I am content, happy, and when Lewis and I are at last real innkeepers, it will all be too fulfilling for words.

There is so little a woman can do beyond motherhood to fulfill herself. Sometimes I think I just can't wait.

We wish for you and dear Sophia a merry and joy-filled
Christmas season. I send you all my deepest affection.

                                        Margaret Seton Fleming

"If your father and stepmother are so eager to meet me,"
Mary said, watching George's face closely as she spoke, "why,
since you have refused for more than a year to take me to
Hibernia, don't they come here?"

Slowly, George looked up from the book he was reading in
a sunny corner of the small rented house where they lived.
"Mary, do we have to quarrel again? You know what it does
to me. Why do we quarrel? *Why?*"

"Because everything is so unnatural! You say you're proud
of me—I know I'm proud of you—as a doctor."

At that, he sighed sharply.

"You sigh more than you converse, George, did you know
that?" She crossed the room, took the book from his hands
and tossed it on the floor. Then, she sat down in his lap. "Dr.
Fleming, I do love you. How can two people love as we
do—and still not be happy? What can I do? Isn't it normal for
you to want to take me to meet your family? Of course, it's
normal. In fact, it's outrageous that we haven't gone! Your
stepmother writes us warm, courteous letters, confiding in
me, too, about the baby she expects this year. I don't think
she's convinced, as the L'Engles are, that I'm a Northern
ogre." She held his head hard against her shoulder. "George,
it's your father, isn't it? You're downright afraid of your father."

His arms were around her. "No, no, I'm not."

"Then, if you're not—why don't you write more often?
Why don't you want him to meet me?"

"I do! I do, Mary. It's—just that, well, I've always been
able to talk more freely with Miss Margaret."

"All right! Who's stopping you—except you? Darling, I've
told you now at least a dozen times that if you really can't
bear being a doctor—if you just have to climb into a pulpit on
Sundays—I'll agree to go to Princeton with you." She got up
from his lap. "What else can I do? I'll hate it. I won't be
proud of you as I am now—but, I'll go. I love you, George
Fleming. I—I'll even love you if you're—the *Reverend* George
Fleming. I'll hate being a preacher's wife, but I'll go on
loving the preacher. What else can I say?"

George picked up the book from the floor, marked his place and laid it quietly on the marble-topped table beside his chair. "Get ready, Mary. We're going to Hibernia tomorrow."

"Oh, shouldn't we give them some warning?"

"No. They don't need any. They're not like that."

Margaret and Lewis and the older children were out on the Hibernia dock waiting for the mail boat when Mr. Huston maneuvered it toward the riverbank the next day just before noon. The fog was so dense, not only was it impossible to see the far shore at deserted New Switzerland, but the tiny white boat was almost at the dock before they realized that George and his wife were standing on deck. George waved. And then, so did Mary.

"She's with him," Lewis said.

"Yes! And it's wonderful. Be glad. Oh, please, please be glad. Lewis, please—for George's sake—smile! I'm counting on you, dearest. I'm counting on you . . ."

Margaret was certain that she had never loved Lewis more than she loved him that day during the hastily prepared company meal. His smile of welcome had undoubtedly been forced at first. But, watching him from her end of the table, she thought, he's trying so hard now.

"I just have to repeat how glad we are you're finally here, son," Lewis said as Easter and Betty listening, slowly removed dinner plates. "We've missed you," Lewis went on. Then, quite deliberately, he turned to Mary with one of his best smiles. "And—of course, we've wanted so much to meet our new daughter, Mary."

Involuntarily, Margaret relaxed a little against the back of her chair. She heard Easter sigh in relief.

"I could only think," Mary said pleasantly, "that George must be ashamed of me." And then, her musical laughter. "I can't imagine why. He found me attractive enough to marry. But," she went on, "I'm trying to understand your son, Colonel Fleming. I love him, but I don't understand him at all sometimes."

Margaret was watching George now. His eyes were fixed on his napkin as he folded and creased it, unfolded it and began folding it again. He said nothing.

After the awkward silence which Margaret found no way to

fill, Lewis said, "You know, Mary, what I think George needs right now?"

"What, Colonel Fleming?" She smiled easily. "I welcome any help I can get."

"He needs to be alone with Miss Margaret. You might as well understand that those two are soul mates. Your husband's far more comfortable with my wife than with his own father."

George's humiliated grin tugged at Margaret's heart. She was humiliated for him, but his father had not meant to speak as though George were not painfully present. As though George were a mere child whose peculiarities needed explaining.

Lewis went on addressing Mary. "I'd like it very much if you'd agree to a walk with me. The fog is still heavy, but it isn't cold out. I can show you our place. I've always felt sheltered here at Hibernia on a foggy day. Makes a man believe he lives in the only safe spot on earth."

Without a glance at George, Mary replied, "Oh, I'd love to walk, Colonel Fleming. How kind of you."

"George and I can take the walk, Lewis," Margaret said carefully. "A damp day like this is bad for your leg."

"Nonsense." Lewis was on his feet, pulling back Mary's chair.

George was assisting Margaret when Easter appeared in the doorway bearing a hastily baked berry pie.

"You ain't gonna have no dessert, Miss Mar'ret?"

She gave Easter an affirming nod. "Not right now. My husband and Miss Mary are going for a walk. George and I will be in the parlor. But keep the pie warm. We'll have it at teatime."

George seated himself near Margaret in the small, boxlike parlor. "I heard the door bang. They've gone outside." He gave her a weak smile. "Hello, Miss Margaret."

"Oh, hello, dear George! You can't know how happy I am to be with you again." After an uncomfortable pause, she said, "Your father is—trying very hard. Please be understanding. He—he seems quite taken with your Mary. He's—trying."

George made a sound somewhere between a snort and a laugh. "Yes. She'll captivate him completely."

"But, isn't that better than—the long, strained silence? There were times when I thought my own heart would break if I didn't see you—or hear from you."

George reached for her hand. "I'm sorry. I'm truly sorry. I—love her so blindly. I've lost my bearing. Mary can make a man do that. I don't know where I am. I feel sorry for my patients."

"You're handling them well, aren't you?"

He nodded. "I've told you, I learned medicine. I still hate it, but I know what there is to be known. I—I guess I love her more than I hate being a doctor." He dropped Margaret's hand and began to twist his own. "Miss Margaret—do I love her more than I love—God?"

"Oh, George, that isn't even a correct question! We don't love another human being more or less than God." His perplexed frown kept her trying to explain. "The love you have for Mary is different from the love you have for God. I've tried and tried to convince our neighbor, Mrs. Huston, of this."

"Mrs. Huston?" he asked, surprised. "Hard to imagine she even thinks about how she loves old cantankerous Huston."

"But she does love him. She—adores the man. He refuses to make the trip to Jacksonville to church with her even once a month and because she's now given up her church, she's guilty for—as she distorts it—loving George Huston more than she loves God."

He grinned. "I thought only a mother could love old George."

"Don't get off the subject. She does love him, but it's with an entirely different kind of love. The love we have for any human being and the love we have for God—amount to a total difference in *kind*. It isn't a matter of degree—of loving Mary more than God—it's a difference in *kind*."

George reached for her hand. "Where did you learn all this, Miss Margaret? Never mind. You know it. And I need to hear it."

"Susan L'Engle wrote to us that Mary doesn't want to be a minister's wife." She sat up straight. "And, I confess I've written some critical things about that to Louisa. But, I've never lost hope that you'll work it out. I'm still hoping."

"Now that you've met her, do you like her at all?"

"I'm not sure. She's beautiful! I've never seen such deep green eyes, such glistening, auburn hair—an overwhelming personality."

"She's overwhelming Papa right now, I'll bet."

"But maybe he can convince her about Princeton. He's

most agreeable to it now and he can be most convincing
when he sets his mind to something, you know."

"Oh, she'll go to Princeton with me."

"She *will*?"

"Yes. But she makes no bones about how she'll hate being
a minister's wife."

"I see."

"You do see—everything about me, don't you?"

Ignoring that, Margaret said, "My money is still yours."

"Money's no longer a problem. I've saved quite a lot and
her family's wealthy."

"Could you take money from them?"

"If it means keeping her, yes, I'll take their money. We've
come too close to—separating lately." After a pause, he said
simply, "I—can't live without her, Miss Margaret."

"Will you be easier to live with if you're finally obeying
God's call?"

"I would suppose so. I know I haven't been easy."

"Then we have to hope all the harder! Maybe you'll be
God's key to—Mary's heart!"

A smile came slowly to George's thin, pale face. "Do you
know I'd give almost anything if I could—hope the way you
do? I feel guilty, not ever being hopeful. L.I. stays that way.
Why, *why*, is it so hard for me?"

After he showed her old Cotter, his four new horses and
the new calves born last week, Lewis and Mary strolled
slowly toward the river. "Well, how do you like Hibernia?"
he asked.

"Certainly, it's breathtakingly beautiful. I love your big
trees, the spaciousness of the yard—the river!"

He chuckled. "Wait until we build our new house. I mean
to build one that will look as though it belongs to the trees,
the river, the woods."

"You know, Colonel Fleming, I really believe you do like
all this—solitude."

"It isn't lonely solitude. Not to me. Not with the children.
And surely not in the future when our Northern guests are
here."

"Don't ask me why, but I've decided to go—*willingly*—to
Princeton with George. Not kicking and screaming."

"Is that so?"

"I expected a far more enthusiastic response."

"Well, I've been slow to understand George, too. My wife had to help me understand why he just *must* become a minister. I was downright angry with the boy when he grew restless as a doctor."

"But you're not—now?"

"No. Perhaps still a bit disappointed. I worked hard to make him a doctor. For a long time, I thought he was merely weak. My wife does understand him. She always has." He took a deep breath. "You'll have a tormented man on your hands if he doesn't follow his call from God."

Without a trace of antagonism—quite honestly, she asked, "Just how can anyone know about so nebulous a thing as a call from God? Do you understand that?"

"Not really, I guess. But I don't need to. George has the call."

"Colonel Fleming, would you believe me if I tell you I'm really a rather nice person? And that I love your son? I'll be a dreadful minister's wife—but I do love him. I truly don't understand any of what he's bent on doing, but—could I promise you that I'll try?"

"And—we'll try, too, Mary. You're a very honest young lady. I like that. I like you."

"And can you influence Mrs. Fleming?"

"My wife will be entirely fair. She's impetuous at times, very protective of George. But her heart is open to you, my dear. And I stake my claim on her fairness—always."

She held out her hand. "Then, as my father the attorney says, we have a deal? I'll be with George at seminary. I'll even try to be at least an unbelligerent minister's wife. But you must always try to understand me—as Miss Margaret understands George."

Lewis took her hand. "Sounds all right. None of us can do more than give a thing a good try."

30

When Huston arrived the next week bringing an emergency call for George from a patient in Jacksonville, he and Mary packed quickly and took the mail boat home.

"He went so willingly," Lewis said as he and Margaret and

the children waved them off. "What a strange son I have. He hates being a doctor, but he didn't blink an eye when he had to cut short their visit. What do you make of him, Margaret?"

"The same as always. He does well whatever he tries. Besides, he isn't fighting life any longer. I haven't faced the thought of how I'll miss seeing him while he's at the North, but I'm as relieved as George is that the decision is finally made."

"What decision?" Frank asked, lagging back with his parents. "What's George going to do, Mama?"

"He's giving up his medical practice—turning it over to Dr. Jones and he and Mary will move North to a place called Princeton, New Jersey. George is going to school to become a minister."

"And before you ask your usual 'why?' Frank," Lewis smiled, mussing the hair of his nine-year-old son, "George is doing it because God has called him."

"How does he know God has called him?" Frank asked.

"He just—knows."

"That doesn't tell me much," Frank said, frowning.

"If I were a betting man, I'd bet you'll be a lawyer, Frank," Lewis said. "Like L.I."

"That'll be fine with me. If L.I. likes it, then I'll like it." He looked from one parent to the other. "Don't you want to know why I said that?"

Margaret gave Lewis a small wink. "Why, yes, if you want to tell us. But you're the inquisitive one."

"It's because I like L.I. better. He's more of a man than George."

"That's unkind, son," Lewis's voice was stern, "and you'll have a hard time in life if you don't learn to make room for those you might not cotton to so much as you do L.I. Even for those who will disagree with you."

Frank kicked a pine cone. "I know what I think about things an' I'll stick to it."

Later, with supper over and after Margaret and Lewis had heard the two older boys' prayers and kissed them good night, they stood together in the adjoining room where Tissie and William were already sleeping. They marveled, as they always did, at Tissie's radiant beauty and wondered how such an active, tumbling little tomboy could have such an ethereal face. Then, hand in hand, they crossed the room to where William slept, his mouth open, his hands lying straight at his sides.

"I thought William had a fairly good time of it while George and Mary were here, didn't you, Lewis?"

"I did. Mary showed him special attention. I liked her for that."

"I'm sure Mary has many good qualities," Margaret's voice was tight. "I just so want her to be—kind to George. One thing I know—George will never have to wonder what she's thinking."

In the parlor in their favorite chairs a few minutes later, Lewis looked at Margaret for a long time, admiring the flying fingers working a piece of needlepoint for a handsome chair she dreamed of for the big house, admiring the deftness of her work when he knew full well her mind was not on it at all. "A dollar for your thoughts, Mrs. Fleming."

She looked up, giving him a smile. "A whole dollar? All right, I was thinking very hard about Seton. How good it's going to be to have him home in another year. Wishing L.I. were coming home to stay, too. Wishing George and Tina still lived here with us by—the river. Being thankful for Frank and Frederic and Tissie and William—eager for our new child to make herself known to us." She patted her stomach. "I'll be losing my figure again soon, Lewis." Ignoring the needlepoint in her lap, she looked up at him. "I'm so eager for this child! Sometimes I think I can't wait for August. Don't laugh. I mean it. I'm thirty-seven. This could be our last. And—there are times when I think I can't bear that."

"Oh, Margaret, Margaret," he said wonderingly. "Don't even think of still another child! It's beyond me right now, with the brood we have, how you'll manage once our house is built and full of guests."

"I'll have you, won't I?"

He smiled. "You will indeed, but the charm of the guesthouse, Hibernia, will be its hostess. And she happens to be the mother of all these children. You already work so hard!"

"Not one more thought like that. I forbid it."

He was chuckling now. "Yes, ma'am."

"Anyway, I have Maum Easter and Betty. They and our other servants are as excited as I am that Hibernia is going to teem with life and laughter and good times—and lots of people!"

"Aren't you idealizing a bit? How long will Maum Easter be able to get around on that bad foot? George says she's losing circulation in it."

"I know it pains her terribly at times and I try to keep her off her feet. But, by the time the big house is open to the public, Easter won't have to do anything she doesn't feel like doing. Betty's a grown married woman now and so like Easter. Her little Rina is Tissie's age. She'll grow up right in the business. There's Pompey and Betty's husband, July, Little Jim, Big Owen—the others to work the fields and groves and tend the yard. Oh, I do all my work now envisioning how our guest house is going to be managed. With dignity, ease, charm. So that every guest will have a home away from home."

He shook his head. "I don't know about the ease, but with you in charge, there will be dignity and, oh, there will be charm. But, I hope—after August, no more children."

"God decides that, Lewis."

The subject, he knew, had been firmly closed. He reached for the Savannah paper which Huston had brought. "I wonder if there's any news in here about that cross-country railroad they're talking about. If President Fillmore doesn't see to it by some means that the tracks swing across the South, I predict George Huston will go right up to the White House and take him down to size."

Margaret was back at her needlepoint. "Is there anything in the paper about it?"

"Not much. Just that some land will have to be purchased from Mexico for a right-of-way west of Texas. That could be a long way off." He laid aside the paper and looked out into the darkness that lay over the river, filling it.

"What do you see, Lewis? It's pitch black out there."

"I know, but the St. Johns is there just the same. All my life, I've depended on that. Even on the blackest nights."

"I know."

"You do, don't you?"

"Yes," she answered softly. "Sometimes I almost forget what it was like living away from it. We're blessed."

After a long silence, he said, "I forget for long stretches of time now, how lonely I once was—even with the river there. Before you—brought me back to life. I was the loneliest man on earth beside that river for more than four years. You may find out—someday, my dear. I'm a lot older than you. Many men have died at fifty-two."

For the merest moment, she stopped working, then went back to it—faster than ever—and said cheerfully, "I never

heard such ridiculous talk! This time year after next, we'll be
building our new house. Why, there's so much life up ahead
for us, Lewis, I'm not only bursting with hope—sometimes I
think I—can't wait!"

Named Margaret Seton Fleming at Lewis's insistence, the
new baby, another girl, was born August 15, 1851, the same
day George and Mary left for the North. With Betty's good
help, Maum Easter, her face distorted from her own pain,
took care of Margaret through it all. Little Maggie was a
healthy, normal baby, grasping her mother's fingers even
before her gray eyes were open. It was plain that she was not
as pretty as Tissie—her dark, straight hair and indefinite baby
features told little of how she would look later on, but even
before Lewis saw her, Margaret knew a special thing about
Maggie. While Easter was still bustling over her, straightening the bed, only minutes after Betty had placed the warm
bundle beside her, Margaret heard herself say: "This child
will truly—be my friend. I can't explain it. I can't even tell
you, Maum Easter—Betty, what it is that I know. Except
that—she will be my friend—for all the days of my life."

Part Four

•

1853–1858

31

Two years later, by 1853, despite the acquisition of additional Southern territory, many planters were more than rankled because the North still encompassed more new states than did the South. Of course, George Huston complained hotly to Lewis, not only because of the uneven distribution of territory, but because it meant that the South had fewer senators and representatives to uphold Southern demands in Washington. Huston's fury rose when a fugitive slave law was passed. "I tell you, Colonel Fleming," he said on the hottest July day Lewis could remember, "that law's an outrage. Nobody up North is going to hunt down and return our niggers when they run off up there. The fugitive slave law accomplishes exactly nothing—except to create more Abolitionists!"

President Franklin Pierce, who seemed sympathetic enough to the South, quieted some of the Southern furor by favoring the area in proposed railroad plans. Pierce had sent James Gadsden to Mexico expressly to purchase, for ten million dollars, a piece of land large enough for the needed right-of-way, thus assuring that the long discussed cross-country line would follow a southerly route. "Nevertheless," Huston muttered on a late October stop at Hibernia, "this is not a Congress I trust. They're after us, Fleming. Those Yankees are out to destroy us down here—and nothing you can say about it doing them no good to ruin a part of their own country convinces me. You need to get your dander up, Colonel. There's a whole evil world outside your snug acreage here."

Just before Christmas, with Seton's term at Waukeenah Academy finished, L. I. felt it was time for him to come back, too, and open his law practice in Jacksonville. When he and Seton reached Hibernia about mid-December, the old remodeled warehouse by the St. Johns was so filled with love and laughter and pranks and merriment that Lewis gave even less than his customary moderate thought to political events. Northern tourists were responding in large numbers to the flood of newspaper advertisements and pamphlets, especially from Florida. The future looked bright for the Flemings—the often ugly machinations of national government remote.

"Patience has never been one of my virtues," Margaret announced to L.I. and Seton the second evening after they reached Hibernia. "And I don't intend to wait a minute longer to unveil your father's surprise! The children are asleep—the time is right."

When she hurried toward the big cupboard where Lewis's rolls of house plans were kept, L.I. and Seton, standing side by side before the fire, winked and exchanged knowing looks. From the corner of her eye, Margaret saw and enjoyed the exchange. The two had grown still closer in the years at Waukeenah. L.I. was nearly thirty, Seton, almost fourteen— but they were closer than brothers, they were friends who had chosen each other.

"Here, let me help you, Mama," Seton was at Margaret's side in a whisk, taking the enormous roll of papers from her, his piercing blue eyes laughing over the armful of house plans, which he held out as though he'd just made a happy discovery. Seton was so full of cheer and laughter and light— his mother marveled. How had she endured the long years without the sight of this son who would always hold her heart in both his strong, brown hands?

"Papa! You've really been working," L.I. laughed, as he scurried about moving chairs and tables back out of the way so that Seton could deposit his load of house plans in the center of the floor. Everyone but Lewis would want to get right down and look. "How's this for a spot for you, Papa?" L.I. asked as he twirled a straight balloon-backed chair smack to the center of the group. "After all, they're your plans. You'll need to do a lot of explaining to Seton and me." Winking at Seton again, he joked, "We're highly educated men, but not architecturally. All right, Seton. Unroll!" With a flourish, Seton spread out the plans, and as he and L.I. sat back on their heels staring at their father's meticulous drawing of the elevations showing the exterior of the big house, both sons made low, awestruck whistling noises.

"What do you think?" Margaret asked eagerly. "Isn't your father a genius?"

"Yes, ma'am!" Seton was unnaturally speechless.

"He's a genius all right," L.I. said, "but this isn't a house—it's a hotel!"

"Of course it is," Margaret laughed. "But it will be our house, too—our home for always and always."

"We'd be foolish to build any less than a thirty-roomed house, boys," Lewis said proudly. "After all, there must always be a place for both of you—for George and his wife—for Tina and her family. *And*, if our estimates are correct, more guests from the North than anyone now imagines."

"Oh, once they find out about Hibernia," Margaret said, "they'll flock to our door!"

L.I. whistled again. "Thirty rooms!"

The boys began to examine one large sheet after another, Margaret in her excitement breaking in when Lewis's explanations moved a bit slowly—her dark eyes shining with joy. Lewis, of course, gave the details—they would build with ten-inch, handhewn live oak beams, the clapboard siding of cypress, the floors of heart pine. There would be three stories and a garret—the family quarters, front and back parlors and dining room on the first floor, insuring their privacy. Easter's separate kitchen would be to the rear on the side, nearest the large dining room. After all, with all those visitors living there, enormous amounts of food would have to be carried into the main house as quickly as possible, since Maum Easter and Betty were already boasting that Hibernia would serve the most delectable food on the St. Johns.

At last, Lewis asked, "What do you think, boys?"

"I'm still flabbergasted," L.I. said. "It's magnificent. And with the two of you as host and hostess, I predict you'll have more people wanting to come than you can handle. The exterior is perfect, Papa. Just about perfect. I love those wide piazzas running the length of two sides of the house. They'll catch every breeze off the river. A lot of people who come down are sick folk, I understand. Anybody could get well in this house!"

"I like the square white pillars," Seton exclaimed. "Looks like a rich man's house!"

Lewis laughed, "By the time it's built, I guarantee you it *won't* be a rich man's house, son. Of course, in her dreams, your mother has us richer than the Flemings ever were."

Still studying the interior elevations, L.I. said, "That's a good size for the wide downstairs front hall. I like the angle of the stairway to the second floor." He turned to the next big page. "And upstairs, very good. Another hall with rooms on either side of it. Everyone gets good ventilation."

"What color will it be, Mama?"

"White, Seton. White, with dark green shutters. And—oh, it's going to look so homelike standing under our great trees beside the river. Our guests can fish, the men can hunt, we'll enlarge the croquet area, people can take long walks or if they're elderly or simply proper ladies, they can dress up and promenade along the riverbank. Your father and I have so many plans for outside."

Lewis laughed. "You mean you have, my dear. Go on, tell the boy."

"I don't really have it all thought out, but one thing I do want is a long, double lane of crepe myrtle trees leading from the front entrance all the way to the river promenade. I can see it now—I can feel myself walking down that lane of trees toward the new, longer dock to welcome arrivals from the North."

"But if you build it on the old foundation, there won't be room for a long lane of myrtles, Miss Margaret," L.I. teased.

"Oh, we're not building it there. This house just has to be set far back from the riverbank. Everything about it must sweep—!"

Seton giggled. " 'Sweep'?"

"Of course, Seton! The lane of myrtles must sweep up to the entrance—the lawn itself must sweep from the house out under the big oaks and magnolias toward the river."

"And the hostess must have lots of sweeping space, too," L.I. laughed. "I can see you now, Miss Margaret—looking like a princess, *sweeping* out and down that long lane of crepe myrtles, each tree lifting its cloud of pink in welcome of every crotchety old rheumatic lucky enough to have endured the trip down from New York or Connecticut. You'll be magnificent!"

"Hush, L.I.," she laughed. "I'm not through explaining. Out back, there'll be a matching lane of water oaks leading out to the barns and outbuildings and quarters. Symmetry! Restful, restorative beauty and symmetry. A home—a real home. For them—and for us."

"And, I should think, a lot of hard work," L.I. mused.

"Life is nothing without work," she answered.

"Of course, that lane of crepe myrtles will be a lane of bare

trees most of the time your paying guests are here, Mama,"
Seton said slyly. "Not many people come down in the summer when crepe myrtles bloom and have leaves."

"Hush, Seton. I won't allow you to spoil my vision. And,
anyway, there's just nothing more striking than the silvery
gray bark of tall, graceful crepe myrtle branches. My lane will
be perfect—summer, fall, winter and spring." Margaret sat in
the floor looking from L.I. to Seton. "You *will*—both—like
calling it your home, won't you?"

"I will, Mama!" a young, quiet voice called.

Surprised, they all turned toward the steep stairs which led
to the second-floor sleeping rooms.

"Frederic!" Margaret jumped to her feet and ran to him.
"Oh, Frederic, my dear, you shouldn't have been sent off to
bed with the younger children. Frank should be here with
us, too. Come on down, son. Get Frank, if he's awake. I'm so
sorry!"

Frederic, seated on the top step of the straight stairs, gave
them all his warm smile.

"Don't worry, Mama. I've been listening for quite awhile.
And Frank and I've both seen Papa's plans. Anyway, I liked
watching all of you. You looked so—happy." That smile came
again, touching them all with the gentleness that was Frederic.

"Come on down, son," Lewis called.

"I kind of like it here, if it's all right. But I hope you go on
talking a long time about our new house."

"You do?"

"Yes." Frederic pushed back his tousled brown curls. "I
like anything that has to do with the new house. I dream
about it at night sometimes." The smile faded. "Seton?"

"Yeah?"

"Will you like it well enough—not to go away again?"

Seton bounded up the steps and sat down beside him, an
arm around Frederic's slender shoulders. "Say, how come
you got off on that subject?" Seton asked.

"Well, I—missed you, I guess. Frank's fine, but he's always
trying to figure things out instead of just having—fun."

Lewis and Margaret exchanged looks. Their children loved
one another. And good, gentle Frederic, especially, was so
open about his love for everyone. A small smile flashed
between them. They had both glanced toward the house plans
still spread on the floor and each knew the other's thoughts.
They would make money—surely they would do well finan-

cially with the house at Hibernia, but it would, it must go right on being a home to their children. Nothing must change that.

"Is old Frank asleep?" Seton asked.

Frederic nodded. "But I can go wake him up."

"You'd better let him sleep, son," Lewis said. "It's nearly bedtime for all of us."

"L.I.?"

"What's on your mind, Seton?"

"You're—not leaving anytime soon, are you?"

"Afraid so. Next week. You've been with me during all these last months of planning. You know how much work I have to do yet in Jacksonville before I open my office."

Seton struggled to keep back the tears. To help himself, he grinned a little. "Sure, I know. But, if Frederic's missed me anything like I'm gonna miss you, he's been bad off."

A few days later, Margaret had just begun a letter to Louisa, when L.I. knocked on her door.

"I know I'm interrupting," he said. "But I feel like talking."

She held out both hands to him. "Dear boy, when is a visit from you ever an interruption?"

He kissed her fair curly hair and stretched himself out on the bed. "I know I'm interrupting or you wouldn't have had your door closed. Letter to Cousin Louisa, I'll bet."

"If I were half as faithful writing to other people, I'd have a lot more friends. Of course, I do quite well with Tina. I still miss her so much."

"Well, let's begin with my sister," he said, settling against the headboard. "I know Cousin Louisa and Sophia are fine. Papa caught me up on them soon after I got home. Looking around for a still bigger house, he says, business is so good. But—what about Tina? I've been gone so long, I simply can't get hold of the fact that my baby sister is a married woman."

"And a happily married woman," Margaret said. "She's blooming! You know how quiet and obedient and—well, kind of submissive she always was—well, now, she's actually getting quite perky. She's found herself. Says she keeps Clark laughing from morning till night."

"Our mother always made us laugh," he said. "What about George? What's the real story about my brother? I know the facts. Know he's married and in divinity school at Princeton—

what about George himself? Papa seems to like his wife well enough now."

"George is head over heels in love with her."

"Infatuation? Or love? The kind of love I have for Mary L'Engle can never be—mere infatuation. I've loved that little girl since she was a baby."

"And now that love has grown into—real man and woman love."

"The best. I guess she's loved me, too. We're going to be married next year, just as soon as I'm finally a practicing lawyer."

"I'm so proud of you, L.I. And I know—so is your own mother. You already know about your father's pride." She sighed. "I only wish George—"

"You only wish George—what, Miss Margaret? He's doing what he thinks God wants him to do now. He loves this woman. Isn't he all right—at last?"

She smiled reassuringly. "I'm sure he will be. Once he's finished divinity school and has his own church. He's just— been unhappy for so long, even I may find any kind of real happiness for him hard to believe."

"That doesn't sound much like you. You've always been our—hope lady."

She straightened her shoulders. "And I still am." She looked down at the floor. "I—need to be, L.I., so much of the time—especially with dear William."

"He seems healthy enough."

"He is, thank heaven. He's shedding his teeth normally, hasn't been ill too much more often than the others. But, L.I., he's past six. And he acts like a three- or four-year-old. He stays alone most of the time with his little dog. He's only now talking well enough to be understood, making sentences— complete sentences—for the first time. He's a pleasant little boy. So easy-going and kind. No tantrums. But it's normal for a three- or four-year-old to brag on himself when he does something. To love praise. Poor William has just begun to show signs of that. Up to now, he's just looked at us when we praise him. He adores Tissie. So far, he's her favorite, but you can see already what a bright, busy tomboy she's going to be. I can't imagine how they might change with each other in a year or so when Tissie can—do more than William. He just stands and stares when Frank or Frederic challenge him."

"He's very obedient, though. I looked around the table at

dinner during grace yesterday and every other young Fleming was peeping but William. His head was not only bowed, his eyes were closed. His lips were moving. I think he was really praying."

"He does pray! He disarms me completely. Your father was out of sorts with him the other day, wanted William to bring him something or other. William just stood there with that wary look in his eyes. He didn't move a muscle. Your father spoke to him crossly. William had brought the wrong thing. Lewis spanked him." Tears brimmed in Margaret's eyes. "That night, right before Lewis—William prayed so tenderly for him, asking God not to let Papa get mad 'when I'm bad.' "

She saw the frown on L.I.'s face. "Being cross doesn't sound like Papa. William just hadn't understood. He certainly wasn't bad."

"No. But, L.I., he *is*—slow. William is far, far behind the other children—in his mind." She took a deep breath. "Your father simply won't admit it."

"Oh-h, I see."

"I'm glad you do. Perhaps you might speak to your father before you leave? Try to get him to face the truth about William."

"Well—I'll try." In one graceful motion, he was off the bed and facing Margaret. "Try not to worry." He grinned. "I learned from teaching, that children are so different. Look at George and me. He takes everything too seriously. I've only begun to take even the right things seriously. Keep hoping, Miss Margaret. I'll talk to Seton about understanding William, too. Seton's quite a boy. He's got the best of all of us in him. Hey, I'd better let you write that letter."

"No! Pull a chair over and sit down where I can pat you when I want to. I need to know all about my wonderful son—Seton. You know him better than I by now."

He straddled a straight chair backwards and leaned his chin on folded hands against the chair back. "There," he said. "That better?"

"Much. You're so grown-up, L.I., but you really haven't changed. Not the part of you I've always loved so. The part of you that's always been—ready for the next thing."

"I think I inherited that from you, Miss Margaret," he teased. "I'm so proud of the way you've got Papa involved in the new house. All the big plans." He laughed. "The man won't have a chance to grow old with you around."

"Seton. I want to know about Seton."

L.I. shook his head in wonder. "He may be the most remarkable youngster around."

"I'm not looking for flattery for the boy. I want to know about Seton, himself—down inside."

"Down inside, I would suggest he is solid gold. No alloy. Gold. He's really bright. I had to study constantly in order to teach him. He made the other pupils look like morons. And they weren't. I had pretty good boys in my school. I really did. But Seton? The boy can learn anything he sets his mind to. The only limitation I see is that he is interested in only one thing."

"What? What?"

"Becoming an officer in the army. He lives and breathes the military."

"Oh, no! I mean—of course, I want him to follow whatever profession he loves, but—war is so horrible, L.I. So horrible. I—don't think I could bear it if Seton—were ever—wounded. Even slightly."

L.I. grinned. "Wait a minute! We're not at war. The boy just wants to go to military school more than anything on earth."

"But he's still so young!"

"You know perfectly well that boys younger than Seton are sent all the time. I've spoken to Papa about this. The family has some funds—income from both the Fleming and the Fatio estates. But, Miss Margaret, building a thirty-roomed house costs money."

She studied L.I.'s even features for a long time, frowning. "L.I., am I—is the new house—putting too much of a burden on your father?"

"No, no, not at all. It's keeping him young and interested. And I think Seton's first lesson in obedience will have to be to help out around here until there is money for military school. Seton is already an expert marksman, fisherman—his troops would never go hungry if he bivouacked them by a stream, and he can ride with the best. He's fearless. Absolutely fearless. Almost too fearless. Already I can see, by the way he led his classmates, that he'd handle men better than most. He can charm the paper off a wall. He's headstrong, but he controls it when diplomacy is indicated. In Seton, you simply have for yourself as a son, one of the most outstanding boys God ever created. But, we all have to learn obedience."

Margaret was thinking hard. "L.I., is he—stubborn?"

"Yes, he is."

"He's always shown signs of it." She patted his hand. "You're very sweet for telling me all this. Don't worry about Seton. He will just have to wait, as you say, and help us here. Then, when there's money, I promise you he can go to military school—*if* he still insists."

"Getting him to wait may be the problem. He knows money is in short supply for a time. He's already talking about a job."

"Why, he isn't quite fourteen!"

"He's a lot older in mind, though. He could find work somewhere in a couple of years. Want me to warn Papa about that, too?"

She sighed. "Not now. I'm sure Seton will make it known soon enough. I've dumped so much onto your fine, broad shoulders. But, what I really hope you can do is—explain William to Seton. There isn't a shred of daredevil in poor William. Maybe, if Seton feels responsible for his brother, he won't challenge William beyond what he can manage. I do feel Seton will listen to you more quickly on that subject."

"I'll do my best. And say, little Margaret Seton Fleming is a nice baby. She's lovely."

Margaret looked away out over the wide river. "Maybe not really lovely, L.I. Although she could turn out to be. But, in a way I haven't yet been able to explain even to your father, my Maggie and I are already—close, *close*. Outsiders would undoubtedly feel Seton is my favorite. I don't have one. Each child has his or her own place. But, I simply *know*—almost as though it comes from God—that through whatever happens from now to my dying day, *I will have Maggie as my friend*. Does that sound a silly thing to say about a baby not yet two years old? Don't answer that, L.I." She laughed softly at herself. "It just happens to be true."

32

16 May 1854
Hibernia

My dearest Louisa,

I've been so busy here with the children, my regular duties, plus making sheets and towels for our new guesthouse, that I can't believe a whole month has passed since L.I.'s beautiful wedding to Mary Evelyn. I know I've described it all in earlier letters, but I must repeat that you and Sophia were sorely missed. Managing a guesthouse *does* tie one down, I see. Your plan to buy that larger place on Hospital Street makes me want to hop on a boat and visit you right now. And to think it is Mrs. Anderson's fine boardinghouse—all furnished for guests!

L.I. is proud as a peacock sitting behind his new desk in his own law office. Lewis and I are strutting around because of him, too. How I wish I could believe dear George to be even half as happy and settled as L.I. George writes often. He is doing well in his theological studies, but knowing him as I do, I'm never sure he tells me everything. He hates to worry us. Of course, his Mary is totally outspoken. In a way I'm glad. Here is a portion of her latest letter: "We may spat—my fault usually—because this husband of mine shuts me out while he pores over those tomes of his, but if he's truthful, he will tell you that after the lamp is finally out for the night, he receives only the warmest reception from me. We are still madly in love." After the lamp is out *is* an important time, Louisa, although most ladies don't admit it, but is it enough to hold a marriage firm? George will finish his studies in two years and he says he will come back South to locate a church. He wrote one homesick letter about how he misses the St. Johns, saying that he understands more and more why the Indians called it Welaka—"the tidal river with a way of its own."

I'm so glad you'll be able to see a stretch of Matanzas Bay from your own quarters on the second floor of the new Hospital Street house. I'm sure you're laughing that Betty and I are already hard at work on the unbleached muslin you suggested for sheets and pillowcases for our guesthouse, when the house itself has not yet been begun. But we are progressing. My dear grandfather Sibbald, before his death, went so far as to leave orders in his will that Lewis be permitted to buy materials for our house at cost, and so my wonderful husband ordered bricks from Scotland through the Sibbald firm last week. He wants a certain quality for our seven fine chimneys and I shall love knowing the Hibernia bricks came from my ancestors' bonnie Scotland. It still seems unreal that Grandfather is dead and that Grandmother will never come South again.

I should stop and get to my work, but please keep praying for dear William. At age seven, he is still not able to dress himself properly. My heart fairly ached the other morning when he appeared at the breakfast table, his thin little face so hopeful of Lewis's approval because he had dressed himself. But, Louisa, William's shoes were on the wrong feet, his pantalets on backwards! I kicked Lewis under the table while praising William for all I was worth, but Lewis could only stare at the child, shake his head and leave the room. Help me, Louisa! Help me find a way to get Lewis to accept that his son William is *not like the other children*. L.I. tried to convince him, but failed. Dear, dear William is my special joy and my special pain. Enough.

Now, I have an announcement to make: Heat or no heat, I'm coming to visit you later this summer while your guests are still safely in the North and I can have you to myself. I must bring my perfect Maggie, who can dress herself at not quite three years and who walks with grace. Tissie is a wild, beautiful colt of a child. All the boys and Lewis are fine and I am always loving you.

Margaret Seton Fleming

The day before Margaret's departure for St. Augustine, Seton, his muscular back even more erect, strutted proudly into her room, carrying the steamer trunk.

"Seton, how on earth did you manage that turn in those steep steps all alone?"

"Easy," he beamed, lowering the trunk to the floor. "I guess after a fellow's been strong enough to swim all the way across the St. Johns, he can handle a measly empty trunk."

"Just don't remind me of what you did yesterday! My heart stops."

"L.I. swam it when he was sixteen."

"But you're not sixteen yet and besides your father went along with L.I. in a rowboat."

His smile shone, proud and shy. "But, Mama, don't you see? Now, I can lord it over old L.I."

She sighed helplessly. "Seton, sit down a minute. I want to talk to you."

"I haven't finished cleaning the toolshed."

"The toolshed will be there fifteen minutes from now, I'm sure." They sat together on the bed. "You know how I long to visit Cousin Louisa, but I also long to be absolutely certain that while I'm gone, you—*you*, Seton, are in full charge of William. When he isn't sitting on the dock alone with Tricksie, he's mostly around the house with me." She paused. "I understand why. Do you?"

"I'm not sure. When I was his age, I hated being inside. Or—by myself." His clear, steel-blue eyes looked directly at his mother. "Papa doesn't believe there's anything—wrong with William, does he?"

"No, he doesn't. At least, he won't admit it."

"But, it's so plain to see. William's a good little boy, but, he's—so scared of everything. Do you know, Mama, I tried just to get him to wade in a pond up to his ankles the other day—with me holding on to him—and he screamed and cried and turned stiff as a board!"

"Oh, Seton, don't ever try to make him do a thing like that!" She saw the quick, perplexed look on her son's face and swiftly put her arm around the sturdy shoulders. "I'm sorry. I didn't mean to sound cross, but—William is deathly afraid of the water. Maybe someday he'll outgrow that fear and maybe not. But we have to give him—time. Plenty of time. Courage and daring—the kind you have, Seton, are splendid in their rightful place. But we're all different. William may have more of another kind of courage in his little heart than all of us put together, but it just doesn't show itself in the usual ways."

The boy took his mother's hand in both of his. "Don't worry, Mama. I promise on my word of honor that I'll do everything I can to see that William is fine while you're away." The irresistible smile came. "I'll even get tough with Papa if he tries to take him fishing. That scares William, too."

Through the open windows they heard far-off cries for help. Seton rushed to look, Margaret after him.

"It's Frederic!" Seton cried and like a shot he was out of the room and down the stairs. Margaret, frozen with fear at the window, saw Seton take the big yard in quick, deerlike leaps. At the far end of the dock, he jerked off his shoes and plunged into the swirling, gray waters of the St. Johns. As he swam, cutting his way swiftly, Margaret saw Frederic gasp and choke; then, his arms flailing, he disappeared, reappeared in silence—no longer able to shout.

By the time Seton had dragged his brother's limp body back to the dock, Margaret, Lewis, Pompey and Frank were all there to help.

"Lord, have mercy," Pompey moaned, as he and Lewis pulled Frederic safely up onto the wide, rough boards.

Stretched on his back, coughing water, Frederic opened his eyes and looked helplessly up at them.

"Why on earth would you try such a thing, son?" Lewis asked, kneeling in spite of his lame leg.

"Yeah," Frank piped. "Just because Seton did it yesterday—sure doesn't mean you can do it. You're only nine years old!"

Margaret looked at Seton, still breathless, water streaming from his thick, dark hair, his shirt and trousers soaked. He looked steadily back at her and shook his head up and down. "I guess—I showed off—once too often, huh, Mama?"

Margaret, without a word, fell to her knees and took Frederic in her arms.

Lewis reached a hand to Seton, who helped him to his feet. "There will be no more exhibition swimming at any time, by anyone, without supervision," he said in a stern voice. Then, he shook Seton's hand. "Thank you, son, for saving your brother's life. I should punish you for what you did yesterday, but—maybe a heartfelt thank you for what you've just had to do will serve better to remind you for the future. Your brothers—all three of them—look to you. For now, at least, you're their—hero. That's a big responsibility."

Seton rubbed his wet forehead with a dripping forearm. "Yes, sir."

"Are you all right now, Frederic?" Margaret asked, smoothing his curly, water-soaked hair.

Frederic smiled a sheepish little smile and nodded yes. Then, abruptly, he struggled to sit up. "Where's William?"

The question struck them all.

Margaret jumped to her feet. "Lewis! Where *is* William?"

"He—was right here on the—dock with Tricksie," Frederic gasped, "when I—first—started gettin' those—cramps. I—I yelled to him. I yelled—'William! William—help!' " Frederic's terrified eyes searched Margaret's face. "Mother! William was right here—now he's gone! Where is he? *Where's William?*"

For over four hours, until the hazy summer sun began to tint the deep woods behind the cemetery, Frank, Seton, Pompey, Little Jim, Big Owen and Lewis hunted for William. Hunted and called.

"Don't sound full of panic," Margaret ordered. "William can't have gone far. I'm sure he's just afraid. Call to him cheerfully, do you hear me? All of you!"

Margaret and Betty hunted, too, in all the plantation outbuildings—the carpentry shop, the blacksmith shop, the orange warehouse which Joe had just about completed. Margaret even climbed the steep ladder to the barn loft and crawled over every inch of stored hay. Finally, when the search party met just before dark outside the last cabin in the quarters, Margaret agreed to obey Lewis and go with Betty back to the house.

"They be moonlight when the dark comes, Miss Mar'ret," Betty said softly, as they hurried along. "It be a wastin' moon, but more'n half there yet tonight—won't be pitch dark. They can see."

Margaret walked faster for no reason except that it gave her something to do. "Hush, Betty! They'll find him—long before dark. Long before!"

Tissie and Maggie had been asleep for an hour—an hour after darkness had come. Margaret, Betty beside her, sat tensely in a straight chair by a window that faced the woods where the search was still going on. She could see lantern flares, eerie among trees, tangled depths of grapevines and brush. Eight lanterns—eight desperate searchers—Frank, Frederic, Seton, Pompey, Little Jim, Big Owen, July and Lewis.

"You'd better go to Maum Easter, Betty," Margaret said after a while. "I'm all right. You know your mother is wretched or she wouldn't have taken to her bed last week."

"My Rina, she be with her."

"But Rina's only Tissie's age—what can a five-year-old do if one of those ghastly attacks of leg pain come on Easter?"

"She can run over here. I'm stayin' with you, ma'am."

Margaret sighed deeply. "You're very like your mother."

"I hope so, Miss Mar'ret."

Suddenly, Margaret jumped to her feet. "Tricksie! Frederic said William's dog, Tricksie, was with him on the dock! Betty—where's Tricksie? Did he come in for his supper?"

"No, ma'am. I ain't see him all evenin'."

"Why don't we call Tricksie? He's exactly wherever William is!"

Margaret ran from the house without stopping for a lantern, Betty right behind her. In as normal a voice as she could manage, she began calling the little dog. She called and then stopped to listen. Cicadas in the trees thrummed and buzzed so loudly Margaret thought she'd scream. Now, of all times, she had to be able to hear the softest whine. Periodically, the insects fell silent and she called again—hoping to sound playful.

Trembling, she called and listened again, and, from under the porch steps, not twenty feet from where she and Betty stood, there came a whine. Soft and urgent as though the small dog could no longer endure restraint.

"Betty," she whispered. "Did you hear that?"

"I sho' did. It's Tricksie, all right."

"Walk very slowly, quietly now—don't act nervous. We'll just stroll normally over to the porch. I'm sure William is under the steps!"

A few feet away, she and Betty stopped. "Tricksie? Tricksie? Are you and William under there?"

The whines, closer to happy yaps now, were unmistakable. And then, the dog ran to her, jumping in glee, as though to show his joy that he and William were free again.

Petting the dog, her voice cheerful, Margaret said, "Oh, Tricksie, I'm so glad to see you! You and William have had a long game of hide and seek, haven't you?"

"Jesus!" Betty breathed.

"Sh! None of that. Be cheerful." Then, almost casually, Margaret called, "William? I won this game of hide and seek. I found you, darling. It's just fine for you to come out now. You'll win next time."

For what seemed an eternity, there was silence, then she heard the first sound of movement from under the steps—the welcome, glorious sound of his shoes scraping the bare ground as slowly, hesitantly, the little boy crawled out of his hiding place.

"*Thank* you, Jesus!" Betty whispered, sounding for all the world like Easter.

"Well, hello there, William! Come and let Mother hug you. After all, I'm the winner of this game, don't I deserve a hug?"

The skinny, shadowy form moved toward her in the pale moonlight and bony arms encircled her neck. "You—found me, Mama," he said near tears.

"Thanks to Tricksie. My, what a smart dog you have! Betty, don't you think it would be nice if you told William's father that I won this game of hide and seek? That, thanks to William's Tricksie, we found this fine hiding place?"

When Betty had gone, Margaret led William by the hand up the steps and into the parlor, lighted by one lamp. "Hungry?"

He nodded.

"Well, I should think you are. It's bedtime. Betty will fix you something good just as soon as she comes back."

William, standing in the middle of the floor, began to twist his fingers. "I—caused—trouble."

"Oh, it's just that we all love you so much, dear, and miss you when we're not quite sure where you are." She knew Lewis and the boys would be there any minute. This was her only chance to reach William with just the right words. But what were they? "Were you—playing a game, William?"

His smudged face contorted with the effort, he gasped: "Frederic—was—going to drown! He—needed me. I—ran away! It—was—deep!"

"Of course it was deep and Frederic had no business doing what he did! Frederic was wrong to be trying to swim the river." She held the boy to her. "But, do you know what Mother has just decided? It's something good. Something you're really going to like a lot."

He didn't answer.

"You know I'm planning to take little Maggie to St. Augustine to visit Cousin Louisa—and I've just this minute decided that I don't want to take that boat trip without you! I need you to go along to help me out with—oh, just everything. Now, will you like that?"

After a long pause, he said, "Yes, ma'am. I'm not afraid of the river in a—big steamer."

"Of course, you're not. And Cousin Louisa and Cousin Sophia are going to be so pleasantly surprised to have you visit them, too. Cousin Louisa is buying a new house. We can even inspect that—all of us together. After all, she's your godmother and that makes you a very special person to her."

On their first night in St. Augustine, William proudly spread out the heavy roll of Hibernia house plans, while Margaret explained every feature to Louisa and Sophia.

"You'll not only make a sizable fortune renting all those rooms in that lovely spot on the river," Louisa predicted, "but William is going to be so much help to you."

Margaret watched the gentle, proud smile light her son's face. "Oh, we're really counting on William's help. And just think of all the fun he's going to have while the house is being built. Our carpenter, Joe, says William's very good with his hands. There'll be all sorts of fine lumber scraps to make lots of boats and tops, William."

The boy's smile widened. "I'll do that," he said. "I'll do that."

After Sophia and William had gone upstairs in Louisa's St. George Street house so that Sophia could tell him a story and check on Maggie in her crib, Louisa said, "He's a dear boy, Margaret. A very dear and obedient and pleasant little boy."

A frown creased Margaret's forehead. "And so happy here. William isn't content like this at home. You see, he isn't challenged here beyond what he can do. He adores his brothers and will sit for hours watching over Tissie and Maggie asleep in their beds, but—Louisa, he just can't keep up with Frank and Seton and Frederic! Seton's learning how to be with William. He really is, but at night, after Lewis is asleep, I'm haunted by William's troubled, helpless face when Seton forgets and urges him to—climb a tree he can't climb. To—gallop even old Bess. He likes to ride horses, but—slowly. Anything fast is—too much for him."

"Let him stay with us!"

"Oh, no—not when you're moving into a new house. You don't need William to think about now of all times, Louisa."

"But I do. Sophia adores the boy. He can help us move. I can think of a lot of things he could do to help out. After all, the new place is only a block away and we'll need to make endless trips with boxes and bundles. I'll be very careful not to overtax him. Let him stay. Give him the chance to take part in something none of the other children have done."

"I'd have to ask Lewis."

"There's plenty of time to do that. You'll be here at least a month. Write to Lewis about William's staying with Sophia and me until after Christmas. He'll love the Minorcan celebration. He'll be a part of things—all on his own. We plan to move before the holidays. Mrs. Anderson and her family have already vacated the house—gone to Tallahassee to live. I think it's a perfect time for us to have William. He can help put up the first Christmas tree in the new house!"

"Well, maybe you're right. But we mustn't say a word to him until I have his father's approval. Oh, Louisa, what would I do without you? What *would* I do?"

The deed was not yet in Louisa's name. In fact, it would be next year before all the slow-moving legal matters were finally handled, but she did have the key to the large, handsome, three-storied white-plastered coquina house on Hospital Street, and while Sophia kept Maggie the next day, Louisa, Margaret and the boy went to inspect it.

"You don't have a yard," he said, as Louisa tried the key in the street door.

"Not a front yard, William, but wait until you see the nice, big backyard. St. Augustine houses almost all have walls and enclosed yards. In fact," she spoke to Margaret, too, now, "the house is built in a huge L with balconies all around upstairs overlooking the yard." The key stuck and William offered to help.

"There, you did it, William," Louisa said, as she led the way into the big, square front hall of her new home on the valuable lot at the corner of Hospital Street and Green Lane.

"Oh my," Margaret exclaimed. "It's—beautiful! And so—large and airy and roomy!"

Louisa laughed. "Nothing like as large and airy as yours will be, my dear. Now, to the left, of course, is the dining room."

"You've got furniture," William exclaimed. "A big table and all those chairs! I thought new houses were empty."

Louisa hugged him. "I'm lucky, William. You see, Mrs. Anderson, the lady who owned this house, rented rooms, too—as I'll do. Basically, the house is ready. Oh, I plan to paint it, buy some new matting for the floors. Those curtains look old and limp and uninviting. I'll get new ones. White Nankeen."

"Is this house old?" William wanted to know.

"The same age as your father," Louisa explained. "It was built in 1798—the year he was born—by a wealthy Spanish merchant named Ximenez, but it wasn't this large. We think he had a store on the ground floor and lived upstairs. But, when the visitors from the North began to come down to St. Augustine way back in the 1820s and 1830s, a lady named Margaret Cook bought and enlarged it as a boarding-house."

"My mother's name is Margaret," William said, proudly. "And L.I. and George are part Spanish."

"That's right, dear," Margaret said. "Now, don't you want to see the rest of this big, wonderful place?"

Upstairs, as Louisa led them from room to room, William, Margaret noticed, seemed to be giving his full attention. When they stopped on the long, upstairs balcony for Louisa to point out needed repairs in the ceiling and cracks along the coquina back wall, Margaret—her heart so happy over William's alertness, had a bright idea. "Why not paint this house wall a soft, cheerful pink, Louisa?"

"Pink, my dear?"

"Salmon pink. You know your guests are going to love sitting out here. Wouldn't it be cheerful to have a pink wall?"

"I like pink," William offered.

"You do, dear? I never knew that."

"I'd like to live in this house."

Louisa hugged him. "Well, you're having a nice, long visit with Cousin Sophia and me now, William."

"I'll stay, Mama."

"But what would Mother do without you?"

He shrugged.

That evening, instead of sitting down for another long talk with Louisa, Margaret went right to her room and wrote to Lewis: "William is like a different child here. He seems so at home and at ease with Louisa and Sophia and, oh, Lewis, you should hear how he joins in a conversation. He fell in love on sight with Louisa's new place on Hospital Street and now she wants him to stay in St. Augustine and help her move. With your permission, I'll gladly agree, since it might help him meet the challenge of his older brothers if he has this experience all on his own. Louisa and Sophia adore Maggie, of

course, and Louisa and I talk for hours on end about the
wonders (financial!) and problems of operating a boarding-
house. Even here in her smaller St. George Street place, she
already has quite a reputation among invalids and travelers.
She has never advertised once. In fact, she receives no one
unless that person comes with the highest recommendation.
Do let me hear by return post that you agree for William to
remain with Louisa over Christmas and through her move
into the grand, new house. The child has his heart set on
staying."

Lewis agreed, but in his prompt reply to Margaret, he told
her nothing of the shock that waited her return in early
September. Seton would be leaving Hibernia again. This
time for Chicago, where, through a connection of Lewis's,
the boy would go to work for Ward, Dogget and Company, a
shoe and boot house.

"He talked me into it," Lewis explained, after they had
gone to bed on her first night home. "Some things have to be
discussed man to man, you know." When she didn't answer,
he went on, "After all, he knew how loudly you'd howl, my
dear. And it is something he evidently has to do." There was
still silence. "Margaret?"

"Give me a minute, Lewis! A job at his age? He hasn't
even been to college!"

"Military school is all he cares about. I'm going to try to
help him get into West Point. Political influence is not my
forte, but even though I'm not hopeful, I promised to try.
Until he's old enough for that—if I manage it—he's determined to work, to earn some money, to be independent." He
waited. "Margaret? Are you—crying?"

"Yes. Mothers—do, you know." She clung to him, his arms
tightly about her, until the sobs subsided. "All right," she
said. "I'm—through now. But Seton doesn't need to earn
money. The acreage you just sold will more than cover the
cost of the new house with what we already have. Why,
Lewis? Why, when he loves us all so much, when his roots
are here at Hibernia, does Seton have to be—independent
when he's so young?"

"It's his nature. My dear, it isn't a bad thing he's doing."

"But he won't be sixteen until next year!"

Lewis sighed heavily. "The only way I know to explain it is

that the boy must have been born—knowing his destiny. Does that sound crazy?"

"Yes, sort of. No. No, I guess it doesn't."

"He wanted me to let him tell you himself."

"Why didn't you?"

"I didn't want you saying anything to him you'd be sorry about later."

Abruptly, she sat up in bed, drying her eyes on the sheet. "All right, Colonel Fleming. Since you've given me a jolt on my first night home—I have one for you. Are you ready?"

He turned on his back to look up at her in the dim light of the one lamp burning in the upstairs hall. "Yes, ma'am. I'm ready."

"While I was with Louisa, I realized that—that we're going to have another baby!"

"Margaret—are you certain?"

"Quite certain."

"I—don't know what to say. I meant us not to—have another child. Not with the new business—the new house. Margaret, I—"

"Sh! I'm just disappointed that the baby can't be born in our new home at Hibernia. She can't wait that long!"

He pulled her to him. "*She*, Margaret? Is that—all decided, too—*again*?"

"Well, I hope the baby's another girl. I want to name her Isabel."

"Why?"

"Only because I like the name. I hope you do, too, Lewis. Do you?"

He nodded briefly, then looked at her with a smile.

"You, Mrs. Fleming, are incorrigible. I suppose Louisa knows. Knew before I did."

"Of course." Margaret lay back on his arm now. "Oh, darling, Louisa's so good with William. You can't imagine how different he is down there."

Lewis stiffened. "William is just fine—anywhere he happens to be. He's a sweet-natured little boy."

After a long wait, Margaret asked, "Wouldn't it be—the right time—*now*, for you to accept William exactly as he is? For William's sake? For your own dear sake? And Lewis, for mine."

He said nothing.

"You know William is *not* quite—like other people. It just

isn't fair for you, his father, to go on treating him as though
he is. You force him to be what he can't be. Heaven knows
he tries. He loves you so terribly. But, Lewis—he does the
best he can. And, William's best—while it may well be more
golden in God's sight—is not the same as the others'—he's
not like his brothers and sisters. *Lewis, that's a fact.*" She
could hear his labored breathing, feel his struggle. She changed
the subject. "When will Seton leave?"

"Right after his sixteenth birthday in February of next year."

"I see. Lewis, is our son Seton a glorious, rosy-cheeked,
bright stranger to you? At least, sometimes?"

His answer came slowly. "Yes. Perhaps God reckons one
remarkable lad like Seton to be enough for any family. Perhaps a Seton doesn't come along—even that often." He took a
deep breath. "I hate having him out of my sight, too. I'm
strangely proud of the boy. Sometimes almost in awe of him."

"That relieves me. I don't love him more than any of the
others, Lewis. God knows I don't. But—somehow he is—so
necessary to my life."

"Margaret?"

"Hm?"

"You're right about more than Seton. You're right about—
William, too. I've—put off this moment—too long. I know
William is—hopelessly behind. Slow. But, no more, please. I
can't discuss William any more right now. Maybe never."

33

Just before Seton's sixteenth birthday party in February 1855,
Margaret and Lewis sent him to St. Augustine to bring William home. Everyone tried hard to make the celebration a
happy one, but, except for three-and-a-half-year-old Maggie,
who didn't yet realize that the birthday itself meant that
Seton would be leaving, the day was a hard one. Seton would
be gone for a long, long time—at least two or three years, if
his work in Chicago was satisfactory to his employer, and no
one doubted that.

"I'll be eight years old by the time you get back, maybe,"
Tissie said thoughtfully.

"I might be seven," Maggie lisped, "or twelve, but—" giving her mother a serious look, the child added, "I stay here—wif' you, Mama." She spread her chubby arms wide. "Forever and forever—Amen!"

Whisking his baby sister up in his arms, Seton said, "I promise not to stay any longer than your sixth birthday, little Maggie." Then he laughed. "But where did you get that—'forever and ever, Amen,' talk anyway?"

"Mama," Maggie said, pointing to Margaret.

"She misses nothing," Margaret said. "Maggie misses nothing."

Her face screwed up to cry, Tissie fairly shouted: "I'm gonna miss Seton!" And before anyone could respond, she turned three somersaults across the parlor floor. As she came upright, her hand struck a thin glass bowl filled with rose geraniums and sent it flying across the room—in pieces.

"Now, look what you did, Tissie," Frank scolded.

"Mama told you not to turn somersaults in the house," Frederic said, already picking up the broken glass.

Maggie laughed, Tissie cried, Lewis shook his head.

"Shame on us all," Margaret said, her voice too near tears to be as firm as she intended. "This is Seton's birthday and we're all making a mess of it. All—except Maggie. Look at that smile!"

"She's smiling only because she's too much of a baby yet," Frank analyzed, "to know that there's nothing very happy about Seton's birthday because it means he's—old enough to—leave again!"

The days came and went, filled with chores and games and attempted jokes. Then the dreaded day—and Seton was gone. Frederic made no effort to hide his heartbreak as they waved the little steamer out of sight. When Maggie, clinging to Margaret, saw Tissie cry, she cried, too. Even Frank, who boasted that tears did no good, had them. Only William, his face stricken, was dry-eyed.

"Seton will be all right," Lewis announced, as the family made its way slowly back along the dock and up the wide stretch of sun-streaked brown winter lawn. "Seton will be all right," he repeated.

"Sure," Frank said, "but how does that keep us from missing him every day?"

"That, Frank," Margaret said, "is just another of your unanswerable questions. But, look up there at those piles of lumber and brick. There's going to be so much activity going on here—we'll all manage." Not very cheerfully, she added, "And—don't forget, there's a new baby coming in May."

Still sobbing, Tissie turned some somersaults and then climbed a big oak to cope with her sorrow alone. Frederic and Frank headed suddenly for the barn, to clean the harness, they said, for once, without being told. William, after a long, troubled look at both parents, sat down on the ground at the foot of a magnolia and began to break a dry twig into tiny pieces.

Margaret, Lewis, and Maggie—clinging to her mother's hand—trudged toward the house in silence. Finally, the child, looking up into Margaret's face said, "I—here, Mama. I—here."

Large with the baby, Margaret stooped as best she could and hugged her tiny friend. "Oh, yes, Maggie. You and Papa and I are together." Blinking back tears, she smiled into the little girl's earnest face. "Mama just couldn't manage at all—without you and Papa!"

As a treat to help them move past their sorrow over Seton's going, Lewis gave the older children a vacation from their daily lessons until after the exciting day, May 1, when, with help from Joe, the Hibernia carpenter, Lewis staked out the shape of their long-planned new home and stretched string between each stake.

"Boy," Frederic gasped when they'd finished. "It's big!"

"Yeah, dummy," Frank scoffed. "Did you think a house with thirty rooms would be little?"

"Where will my room be, Mama?" Tissie piped. "Where?"

"Oh, on the first floor in the rear, next to ours, dear. You and Maggie will have a nice room together."

"I want a room by myself so I can practice turning cartwheels!"

Before Margaret could explain their need to double up in order to have ample rooms to rent, Tissie, as usual, had run off to jump rope, not listening.

"Frederic and I don't mind sleeping in the same room," Frank said. "Nothing new about that. Besides, I'm a pretty good influence on my brother, I think."

Lewis winked at Frederic, who only smiled.

"Oh, darling," Margaret said, taking Lewis's arm. "I can see the house already! Ample and handsome, rising high into the branches of the big oaks. Thank you, oh, thank you!"

William had said nothing throughout the excitement and chatter. Now, he came slowly up to his parents. "I want to be in a room by myself—till Seton comes home," he said.

"You won't be too lonesome?" Lewis asked.

"No, I'll be waitin' for Seton to come back."

"Well, I doubt that you'll have much time in your own room. It's going to take at least two years to finish a big house like this. Seton could be back—even before we move in."

Appearing satisfied, William walked away, whistling for Tricksie.

When Frank and Frederic went to help Joe tighten two of the long strings sagging a little between the stakes that marked out the shape of their dream, Lewis turned to Margaret. "Feeling all right this morning, darling?"

She took a deep breath, laughed a little. "I've felt better. Boy or girl, this one's really trying to push me—out of the way. But, I'm all right. When will the workmen get here from Jacksonville? When can it all—really begin?"

"Pompey and his crew start to dig the foundation today. I expect the men from Jacksonville on the mail boat tomorrow. Betty tells me those three empty cabins are all ready for them. How's Maum Easter? I miss her being here with us today."

Margaret's frown told him everything. "I—almost can't bear to hear myself say this, but I don't think our beloved Easter will be here to see the new house."

In two weeks, Margaret faced the ordeal of her first child to be born without Maum Easter, who lay bedfast in her old cabin with Rina standing guard.

"Let Colonel Fleming stay with your mother, Betty," Margaret urged, fighting back the agony of more frequent labor pains. "Please—let him. Rina—couldn't help her."

"Rina kin run for help," Betty said firmly, massaging Margaret's distended belly with oil of almonds. "You stop your frettin', an' tend to what we's got to do here."

Having a harder time of it than ever before, Margaret tried to laugh. "You sound exactly like—Easter," she whispered. And then a sea of pain swept over her and she clutched the old sheets Betty had tied to the foot of the bed in the struggle to free her body of the child who had made her excessively nervous for months.

In the midst of her pain, the baby very nearly ready to

come, Margaret saw Betty shoot a cross glance toward the hall.

"Mama! Mama, Mama—" Rina called from just outside the door.

"Git outa here, Rina!" This from Betty without another look toward her six-year-old child.

"But, Mama," Rina wailed, "Gran's—dead!"

"*Now*, Miss Mar'ret," Betty ordered. "One more push— *now!*"

"She's—just—layin' there—all still an'—she can't hear me!"

"Now, Miss Mar'ret! *Now!*"

Margaret screamed—the first time ever at the birth of any of her children. And the fiery, red-haired infant girl fought her way into the world.

Margaret's scream had brought Lewis hurrying up the steep stairs as fast as his limp would allow. "Betty, what's wrong?" he demanded. "What is it?"

"Git out, Mausa Lewis! Git out—an' take Rina wif you!"

Sobbing wildly now, Rina shouted, "Me an' Tissie—was jus' jumpin' some rope—an' when I—went back to look at Gran—she was dead! *Dead!* Mausa Lewis—Mausa Lewis!"

"Out! Both of ya!" Tears streaming down her round brown cheeks, Betty stood to her full five feet. "*Out*—till me an' Miss Mar'ret gits done!"

The next day, too weak to leave her bed, Margaret lay and listened as the people sang their sad songs beside Maum Easter's grave in the family plot up the lane. Tears of weakness and grief washed Margaret's pale cheeks. And she prayed. Everyone at Hibernia would need God now more than ever without Easter.

But God and Easter had given them Betty, who yesterday, when the baby was being born, had proven herself for always with Margaret. From now on, she decided, as the low, rich sound of Lewis's voice reached her, reading from the Episcopal Service for the Burial of the Dead, Betty would be known in the Fleming family as Maum Betty.

In September, Margaret felt a strong need to visit her mother in Fernandina. Leaving the new house, its thick-beamed foundations already laid, was even harder than she'd expected. But Lewis promised, in spite of his heavy load in the fields and with the workmen at the house site, to write every day, to enclose every letter from Seton, who, for a sixteen-year-old, had been remarkably faithful in writing page after page about his new work in Chicago. It would be pleasant to share Seton's letters with her mother in person instead of mailing them on.

Matilda Seton was now sixty-six and, Margaret thought, the day she, Maggie, William and the new baby, Isabel, arrived, growing frail. So much more frail than when Margaret had seen her only a few months earlier. Her mother's eyes had grown dim, she moved more slowly, but held her slender body as erect as ever and dressed each day as though she were expecting company. Not only had her eyes grown dim, but Margaret sensed a new, anxious tone in her more voluble talk.

"Your grandfather Sibbald lived to be a spry eighty-five," she said. "But I was never much like either parent. Quite like my grandmother Sibbald, in fact. She died at sixty-seven. That would give me another year, my dear."

"Nonsense, Mother. Lewis and I expect you for many long visits with us in our new home." Margaret tried for a light touch. "But, you know, I have been truly contented in our funny, remodeled warehouse!"

"So far as I know, my dear," Matilda snapped, "you have never been contented! You've always—been reaching."

Not wanting to disagree, Margaret merely smiled.

"I'm sure you know I don't understand at all about my beloved Seton being shipped off to Chicago to work as a common laborer in a—boot factory!"

"Mother, Seton insisted. And he's not a common laborer. He's already a clerk," she sighed. "His real dream is still military school. That's all the boy thinks about."

"Never! You must not permit that! Any of your sons but Seton. He's the extraordinary, valuable type of man who— would be among the first killed, should there be a war."

"Mother!"

"He is. Your poor, slow-witted William could fight through three wars and come out without a scratch. But—the fates would conspire against Seton."

In spite of her efforts not to let it happen, Margaret felt her face flush with anger. She struggled to keep herself from flying at her mother—refuting what she'd said about poor William. Instead, she sat quite still, biting her lower lip until she'd decided clearly what should be said next. "Mama, you'll—learn to love dear William—in a few more days."

"Are you implying that I'm the kind of woman who does not love all her grandchildren? I even rather like your new, noisy carrot-topped baby. Of course, I love Maggie. And I love William well enough. But I don't really feel it's safe for the boy—in his condition of mind—to roam the city all alone as you allow him to do here."

"I'm sure William's having a marvelous time right now. And he doesn't lack judgment. He's just quite—slow." Margaret took a beat, then said, more coldly than she intended: "I brought William because I wanted him with me. As I wanted Maggie."

"I see."

"Oh, Mama, I wish you did! William needs your love. A tiny bit of appreciation goes so far with the little fellow. And no matter who he runs into on your streets here, you don't need to worry. He'll never—humiliate you. He'll just be sweet and kind."

"I can't help wondering, since you're determined to go into the boardinghouse business—a genteel enough profession for a lady, I suppose—what some of your guests will think of William. Some of your—better guests. Have you thought at all about how the lad might embarrass you and Lewis?"

"No!"

"Don't bite my head off, dear. The boy *is*—quite odd."

A small sound from the high doorway leading into the front hall caused Margaret to turn quickly. There stood William, clutching a handful of wild asters. If he had heard her mother, he evidently, blessedly, had not under understood, because, smiling shyly, he marched across the parlor floor and handed the flowers to his grandmother.

"Oh," Matilda said, almost, but not quite recoiling. "Thank you, William. They're very pretty."

He turned to Margaret, who smiled her approval, then, without a word, threw himself in his grandmother's lap and hugged her until she relented, laid aside the flowers and slipped both slim, silk-encased arms around William's skinny body.

The very first letter from Lewis enclosed one from Seton. Margaret felt a little hopeful that her mother might be softening toward William, but to be safe, she went alone to her room to read. Undoubtedly, an especially charming letter from Seton would once more put William out of Matilda's thoughts.

As always, Margaret broke the seal on Lewis's letter with a sense of anticipation: "My dearest wife," she read, "Just a few lines before the mail boat arrives so that I may assure you of our well-being and of the well-being of our foundation. I fear too little has been done beyond the foundation, but it is still a thing of beauty. I also enclose a letter from Seton, who is doing very well and quickly coming by rather strong political biases. Obviously, there is hot feeling against us old plantation owners in Chicago. Our son is so irked by it, we might indeed have to pen him up or he'll never permit a Yankee (as he is now calling Northerners) to set foot on our dock—no matter how much good Yankee money the guest might be inclined to hand us. I miss you terribly and pray often as I work these long hours for you and William, Maggie, and our little screamer, Belle. I do hope Belle is not annoying your mother."

She scanned his last few lines, then quickly unfolded the letter from Seton: "Guess what?" he wrote. "I have been given another raise in salary. I am now a second clerk and will receive an added three dollars per week. Papa, should you need a quick loan for the new house, just inform your prospering son. Laugh. There is much good here, a busy, thriving railroad, the Chicago and Galena Union; there is the Illinois and Michigan Canal and factories galore. Chicago's population must now be more than thirty thousand people. But, I am daily galled by the loose, ugly talk against slave owners. It does no good whatever to insist that my father does not even own all his people, that half of them are Free Persons of Color. I am not believed. I work at an adjoining desk with a rabid young Abolitionist who excites me to fury at least nineteen times a day. His name is Jake Lamm and he is a fool, who refuses to believe that we do not beat Maum Betty and July and Pompey at least every Wednesday. When I declare that Pompey came to Hibernia as a free man—free to leave or stay—he laughs and grows so red and puffy in the face as to burst his freckled skin. Deliberately, I made him accompany me on a walk through Chicago's slums and tried to describe our quarters' cabins—built of good cypress set on live oak foundations with no leaking roofs. The filth and poverty in this city's slums turned my stomach. All Jake

Lamm could say was that those slum dwellers, hungry, ragged and hopeless, were at least free."

Margaret sat for a long time looking out the window of her old room onto the wide lawn, slashed by yellow, early autumn sunlight, the magnolia leaves bright in the motionless air. The tide will change soon, she thought irrelevantly, and with it a wind will rise so that the still, still foliage on each familiar tree will begin to twist and bend under its restless impact. Seton was twisting, but not bending, under the impact of his first hard experience with the slavery-hating North.

Margaret frowned. The truth was, she had not thought much about such things. Oh, from Guy Henry she knew about the underground railway; she had heard, of course, about the radical John Brown and his sons. But until now, it had all seemed remote. She and Lewis had listened to George Huston, but had both considered him a hothead. Extreme. Her frown deepened. Seton sounded like a hothead, too! Well, he had to be wrong about Yankee hatred. Nothing serious must ever happen to discourage Northerners from continuing to travel in large numbers to Florida. The Flemings' entire future depended upon it.

Smoothing Seton's letter over her knee, she scanned a long paragraph in which he bemoaned the fact that President Pierce and Congress repudiated something called the Ostend Manifesto, in which Cuba should have—according to Seton—been taken by force by the United States and added to the South's territory, making possible two more slave states. "Of course, they rejoiced up here," Seton went on, "and their bigoted joy has been heightened—more fires of hatred have been lit—by a lying novel published in 1852 by a rabid Abolitionist named Harriet Beecher Stowe and called *Uncle Tom's Cabin*. I borrowed the book and it was all I could do to prevent myself from ripping out its pages! It is packed with lies. I am sending you a copy. Mother has taught Betty to read—let her read it and she will tell you it is a pack of lies."

Seton ended his letter with love for them all and a promise to write to his grandmother soon. Margaret could have spanked him! Who knew how her mother would react to what he had written? This was one letter which, had she received it at Hibernia, would not have been sent on. Well, she thought, as she changed for dinner, Mother will learn from Seton's next letter to her how upset he is. I might just as well let her read this one.

After checking on Belle, who looked willful even when sound asleep, Margaret went straight to her mother's room and handed her Seton's letter.

When she had finished reading, Matilda Seton smiled—genuinely pleased. "The boy's a true son of the South."

"I found it a bit extreme."

"I didn't. It so happens that the few people still with me are not slaves—but that Stowe woman's book *is* incendiary."

"*Uncle Tom's Cabin?* You've read it, too?"

"Yes. I borrowed a copy and read it through. Seton's dead right. It's a pack of lies from beginning to end."

"I'm certainly going to read it for myself."

"You'll see. That woman's a rabble-rouser. And from such a good family, too. Married to an outstanding scientist, I believe. The sister of a superb preacher." Matilda handed back Seton's letter. "Your son is filled with totally *righteous* indignation! Mrs. Stowe and all those other Abolitionist people despise Seton's people. Why wouldn't he be angry? They despise you, Margaret. And Lewis. Your splendid, high-principled husband is a slave owner. But, as with all our other well-bred friends—he's a slave owner without a whip. Oh, perhaps in Virginia or the Carolinas—even Georgia—there is some harsh treatment. But those do-gooders at the North simply don't understand about Florida. Why, think how many Free Persons of Color we have here because the Spaniards refused to return them to their owners! Use your head, Margaret. Seton's certainly using his."

34

Margaret thought Lewis had never looked so well as the day he welcomed them home after their month's visit in Fernandina. And he had good things to show and tell her. The cypress skeleton of the new house was actually taking shape, Lewis seemed merely quietly amused at Seton's sudden hatred for Northerners and—best of all, George and Mary were coming south again. George had accepted a call to the Presbyterian church in St. Mary's, Georgia, near enough for visits. Even George's wife seemed reconciled. "I have *not* been called to the ministry," Mary wrote at the end of George's letter, "but I *am* called to the minister. I won't be with George in his work, but I will be with George."

Early in the new year, 1856, Margaret reminded Lewis for the third or fourth time that she wanted a chapel of their very own someday. By now, he had begun to take her seriously.

"I know you've just been letting me rattle on about my chapel," she said, as they were waking up on the morning of William's ninth birthday in March. "Pampering me—even teasing me, Lewis, because I dream so much. But, I'm absolutely sure our future guests will favor Hibernia if we have a chapel. Where else on the St. Johns can they find a church right on the premises?"

Taking her in his arms, he kissed her tenderly. "I am taking you seriously, my darling. And just as soon as we can afford it, we'll begin building your chapel." He smiled down at her. "Sometimes I think my one overriding goal in life is for you to have—whatever you want."

"But don't you want it, too? Don't you think I'm right about our guests appreciating a chapel?"

"Dead right. You won't mind, though, will you—if I prefer to build it—just for you?"

"No, Colonel Fleming. I won't mind at all." She sat up. "You can provide the entertainment at William's birthday party today by drawing your first sketch of the new chapel! That way William will be a part of it. I'll see that he's the one to bring your drawing materials out to the new house. Did I tell you we're having William's party in the parlor of our new home?"

"That'll be a little messy, won't it?"

"Not at all. I've never known anything to mean to William what that house seems to mean! He sits hour after hour on the ground outside—just watching the men work. And if he can feel equally as involved in the new chapel—who knows what it might do for him inside? Joe and Pompey can sweep up the sawdust on the parlor sub-flooring and make a table on sawhorses. Betty and I have already planned the picnic lunch— William's favorite things. We have his red and yellow top and his new clothes. The very latest fashion for boys his age. His first pair of straight midcalf trousers and a jacket. Oh, Lewis, William will be so proud to be finally out of tunics and tucked pantalets."

The party was a splendid success. William's eyes shone at

the sight of his new top and, without a word, when he opened the package containing his fashionable trousers and jacket, he ran abruptly back to the remodeled warehouse to change into them. Wonder of wonders, when he returned, everything was on exactly right, so that everyone could praise him for it. After the picnic luncheon, though, he seemed to forget his presents, Lewis's sketch of the little chapel—even his birthday itself. He took no part in anything but sat, until the party was over at chore time, just gazing around at the still-exposed beams and supports of the new house itself. Not a member of the family except Belle, too young to know, thought for long about anything these days except the new house. But, to William, the large superstructure seemed to hold a deep, hidden meaning. A meaning that would undoubtedly remain hidden from them all. He lived and breathed it. And, as the days passed and the roof began to go on—hand-rived cedar shingle after shingle—William scarcely took time for meals. He had, on his own, learned to climb one wide-limbed oak and would sit for hours in its branches as near the top of the tall house as he dared, his pale eyes intent upon every hammer stroke, every newly set shingle.

In the late summer, William received his very first letter—from Grandmother Seton—explaining that indeed she had not forgotten his birthday in March, but had waited for the arrival from Maryland of Margaret's brother, his uncle George Seton, who would be bringing him a new rocking horse.

"I'm absolutely furious with mother," Margaret said to Lewis, as he helped her repot some plants in the barn. "She hasn't even mentioned my brother's visit to me!"

Lewis laid down his trowel. "Can't you—just accept your mother exactly as she is, sweetheart? After all these years? She has been very *good* to us. I'm even the executor of her will now. She evidently feels closer to us all than—she's able to show."

"But why didn't she write a letter to William last March so he wouldn't feel slighted on his birthday?"

He jammed a large ivy plant into a pot and began to scoop soil around it. "Do you really think I can answer that question?"

"No. And we're not even sure that William noticed and was disappointed, I suppose."

"No, we're not. Did she say when your brother George will be here?"

"October. According to her letter—to William."

"Will he visit us?"

"Who knows? George and I were never close. Oh, we're fond enough of each other. He lives his life, I live mine. Who knows whether he'd visit us in a remodeled warehouse? He's like Mother in so many ways. Brother has always been able to talk to her."

"But you're like your father."

"I hope so. Oh, Lewis, I want to be!" She touched his cheek. "You're a magnificent horticulturist, sir. That crooked ivy plant is just as straight as a die in that big old pot. And I dismiss you. You and William must get on your way to Mr. Huston's place. I long for a letter from someone—anyone."

Until the new house could be finished, Lewis had given over his duties as postmaster to George Huston, who had hired a Jacksonville man to run the mail boat. Twice a week, all summer, William had seemed to look forward to making the trip to Huston's adjoining plantation to pick up the Flemings' mail. Lewis felt that his son understood little of Huston's rantings and ravings about the federal government, but they appeared to entertain the boy and so he was never left at home. While Huston gave forth, the amused smile never left William's face. And always, if there was mail for the Flemings, it was William who ran with it to his mother once they reached home again.

On mail day, at the end of the second week in October, the boy ran excitedly across the wide front lawn and into the remodeled warehouse parlor waving a letter from Fernandina.

Addressed to Margaret, the handwriting was not her mother's. Nervously, she broke the seal and began to read: "My dear sister, I have been in Fernandina only two days and it is with deep regret and sorrow that I write that, after seeming to feel fairly well, our mother died in her sleep last night. We will wait until you arrive for the funeral services. I hope that your husband can accompany you, since, as you know, he is the executor of Mother's will. It will be a sad meeting for us as brother and sister after all this time. If I am to get this on the boat for Jacksonville, I must close. Your brother, George Seton."

Two days later, beside the open grave at Bosque Bello Cemetery in Fernandina, Margaret and Lewis stood with her brother George as the familiar Service for the Burial of the Dead was read by the rector of Matilda Seton's church. The service was brief, the air still, the prominent Fernandina friends reserved and well dressed. Margaret was there, but nothing seemed real to her. Now and then, she glanced up at her brother, tall, erect, graying at the temples, patrician of feature. So like their mother and, to Margaret, almost as enigmatic. With quiet dignity, as she would have insisted, Matilda Seton was buried beside her husband, Charles. Even the weather was calm and orderly. Everyone stood dry-eyed, as though in awe of the surprising fact that Fernandina's grand lady, Matilda Seton, had indeed allowed herself to die.

That night Margaret sat alone in the shadowy, quiet Seton parlor for a long time, studying the handsome, handcrafted, silver bowl which she now longed for even more intensely. How its beauty would grace her new home at Hibernia! How near the bowl made her feel to her father, whose brother, William, had been given the splendid trophy for heroism at sea. Her fingers moved over the two magnificently engraved sailing vessels engaged in battle—caught in silver by the famous silversmith, Hugh Wishart, in the year 1799. Margaret had known for years that her mother would leave her a share of the large family land holdings on the Nassau River, but all she really longed to own was the Seton bowl, from whose polished depths, she and her brother had been christened. She had prayed and prayed that if the bowl came to her, it would somehow awaken a new identity in dear William.

For over an hour, Lewis and George had been closeted in the dining room poring over the will. Her eyes filled suddenly with the tears she had not yet been able to shed. "Mama . . . ," she breathed, "will I know any more about the way you loved me when I know—what's in your will? Is there a special, personal something just for me?"

The dining room door opened at last and George emerged alone. "Your tactful husband thought I should tell you the contents of our mother's will without his being present," he said.

"Somehow I wish we didn't have to think about—*things* tonight, don't you?"

He nodded. "But we do. I'll be leaving early tomorrow. You, my dear sister, got *all* of the vast Nassau tract known as the Seton Grant, this house and its furnishings."

"I see."

He laughed dryly, a powdery laugh so like Matilda's. "I got only *that*." George gestured toward the Seton bowl. "And I'll bet you wanted the bowl as much as I wanted that land."

"Will I—be able to see her will?"

"Of course. But I just finished reading it. She left me the bowl, Uncle William's portrait—and oh, yes, the stand on which the bowl rests. Isn't that just like her? You always adored that bowl. You were our father's favorite. The bowl was crafted for his brother, not hers. But Mother, being Mother, was looking out for your financial future with that land, since Lewis is so much older than you." The dry laugh came again. "My future is secure. She was merely being proper, leaving her only son his uncle's trophy."

"I guess—it was what she wanted to do."

"Yes. Don't forget, I'm rather like her. I've always understood her. I'm disappointed, but I understood her."

"I—envy you. I wish I had." She laid her hand on his arm. "George? Please—treasure the Seton bowl. Don't sell it—out of the family. Not ever. Promise me that if you ever decide to sell it, you'll let me buy it from you."

His smile was both sad and a touch bitter. "Mother goes right on exerting her whims on us, doesn't she? Even now. But, I do promise about the bowl. We should carry out her wishes, at least for the present, I feel."

"I wish I'd learned a long time ago how better to carry out her wishes."

"You sound remarkably like my wife, Sister. Are Mother and I so difficult to understand?"

"Yes." She waited in the awkward silence. "But, George? Would I—embarrass you as I always seemed to embarrass Mother if I—hugged you?"

Lewis handled the sale of the Seton home and Margaret worked off her uneasy grief by detailed planning, which meant the making of endless lists of bedsteads, dressers, chests, tables, chairs, linens, lamps, curtains, matting and carpeting which they would have to buy above and beyond her inheritance. She would furnish Hibernia as simply as possible, but its furnishings must befit its handsome dimensions and gracious, country mansion lines. Her mother's furniture would help.

In the spring of the following year, with work progressing steadily on the house, Lewis and Margaret, leaving the children in the capable hands of Maum Betty and her husband,

July, visited Louisa in her new place on Hospital Street.

"We thought we'd better get a firsthand lesson from you, Cousin," Lewis said as they finished dinner, served in Louisa's private parlor on the second floor. "You've got this big house running like clockwork."

Louisa laughed. "I'm glad it appears that way to you. Believe me, it doesn't run itself. Right now, I have only eight guests. There's some financial panic at the North, according to old Mr. Jarvis, who's been coming down for fifteen years. But I do have a full house slated for next winter. Of course, there are always a few cancellations." She pulled the bell cord. A shy, thin Negro girl appeared as though by magic from the upstairs balcony outside the room where they sat. "You may remove the plates now, Pootie. And be careful when you wash them downstairs. Use the dry sink in the dining room just as soon as the guests are finished. Then put the china right away in the cupboard."

The girl made a little dip resembling a curtsy and, without a word, cleared the table.

When she had gone, Margaret asked, "Did you call her *Pootie?*"

"That's her name," Louisa smiled. "Her mother, Mamie's with me, too, and she says that's precisely what she named the child. Pootie's good. I wouldn't want to have to do without either her or Mamie. I had a part-Indian girl, you know, on St. George Street. One day, she simply vanished. Finding Pootie and Mamie was a Godsend." She sighed. "But, how I still long for Scipio and Polly when things get really hectic."

"Never heard anything about what happened to them, did you?" Lewis said sadly.

"Not a word. I grieved. They're dead. Neither of them would ever have deserted me. I've asked over and over for even a trace of what might have happened. Nothing."

"Does Pootie talk?" Margaret asked. "She's so quiet."

"Oh, she talks all right. And little thin, frail Pootie has a remarkably deep voice."

Lewis toyed with his napkin ring. "Are you hopeful there might be another bank here anytime soon?"

"Susan L'Engle wrote last week that there's talk of opening a bank again at St. Augustine, but who knows when. It's certainly taken the state of Florida long enough to settle down financially. I can't see that the new banking legislation has done much good so far. Margaret, you're blessed to have Lewis to handle your finances."

There was a silence and Margaret said, "More blessed than I can tell you. I'd be lost without him. For all reasons."

"A very pretty speech, Mrs. Fleming, but neither you nor Louisa would ever be lost—for long."

A sound like a soft growl came from the open door. Pootie was clearing her throat to get Louisa's attention.

"Oh, come on in, Pootie. My goodness, that pie looks good!"

Standing in the doorway holding a tray with three high, fluffy pieces of lemon meringue pie, was Pootie, doing her best to make her dip while holding the tray level. The girl smiled warmly as she served.

"Thank you," Louisa said. "Did your mother make that beautiful meringue, or did you?"

"I made it," she said in such a low, rich contralto that both Lewis and Margaret smiled with pleasure.

"You really should talk more, Pootie," Margaret said. "You have a lovely voice. Do you sing?"

"Yes, ma'am. I sings in the kitchen and in church."

"I hope you'll sing a lot while we're here—and not just in the kitchen. That's too far from the house."

Pootie snickered. "You don't mean that!"

"Indeed she does," Lewis said. "And so do I."

"Pootie not only sings beautifully," Louisa said, "she can recite Bible verses by the yard! Thank you, Pootie. There's still plenty of hot coffee here in the urn."

The girl dipped again and left.

"Where did you manage to find Pootie and her mother?" Margaret wanted to know.

"They were already working right here. Neither wanted to go with Mrs. Anderson when she left for Tallahassee."

"Sophia must be having a marvelous time having dinner at Mrs. Smith's house," Lewis said, digging into his pie. "If I do say so, they make an odd twosome. Sophia so fey and romantic. Mrs. Smith so—so—"

"Yes," Louisa laughed. "My good neighbor is so elegant and *so* opinionated, and *so* dogmatic and so—brilliant. It's no wonder her son, Edward, is moving up rapidly in the military. His father's a judge, but he gets his brains, I'd say, from his mama. As long as I can keep her off the subject of hating Yankees, we get along fine. Sophia just isn't comfortable with a sensible subject of any variety, so after dinner I'm sure she and Mrs. Smith mostly read poetry aloud to each other. The Smiths have a magnificent library."

"Do you take your meals up here, you and Sophia?"

"Most of the time, Lewis. I do have a lonely clientele, but one's very soul cries out for privacy now and then. In fact, my servants are quite satisfactory. They can handle dinner downstairs when I'm busy. Oh, Willfrid gets a touch imaginative when asked questions about old St. Augustine, but he serves splendidly." She refilled their coffee cups. "One thing you must always remember is that the quality and variety of the food you serve will be your biggest asset. People will stop with you, enjoy your table, and within a matter of days, their friends at the North will have a letter rating your food from A to Z."

"We'll give them plenty of variety. Pompey can hunt to his old heart's content. Now that Maum Easter's gone, he seems to enjoy himself only when he's out in the woods hunting."

"You're lucky to have him, Lewis. I buy a lot of wild turkeys, ducks, turtles every day from the Indians who bring them fresh from the woods and waters."

"Louisa, have you read a book called *Uncle Tom's Cabin*?"

"Yes, Margaret. I've read it. In fact, my Northern guests have brought me a total of six copies."

"What do you make of it?" Lewis asked.

Louisa leaned back in her chair, a half smile on her face. "Well, it rambles quite a lot. I'd say it's rather loosely written."

"Seton calls it a pack of lies."

"You've both read it, I suppose." They nodded. "And what do you call it?"

Margaret frowned. "I—cried through some of it. Such—cruelty, I've just never heard of. I know a novelist fictionizes, but—it's so extreme, Louisa. Did you ever hear of such treatment anywhere—by anyone we know who owns slaves?"

"No, I certainly did not. Of course, maybe in Georgia, perhaps Virginia—"

"But we don't really know that! Do you—own Pootie and Mamie?"

"Yes. I bought them from Mrs. Anderson. I don't own Willfrid though. He's born of free parents. His father owned some land—a hundred acres, I believe, out near Tocoi."

"You can tell us," Margaret said, leaning toward Louisa. "What are your Northern guests saying about the whole slavery issue? Are they—do they speak accusingly to—you?"

"One or two have. Most don't. Most seem only to care about having a good time. They're not here to antagonize me. I'm their hostess. They're lovely—sometimes eccentric—but well-bred folk."

"Why don't we move to a more pleasant subject, Margaret?"

"No, Lewis. I'm worried about Seton. His heart is filling up with hatred toward the people he knows in Chicago—I don't want my beautiful son's heart full of hatred toward anyone. He sent me Mrs. Stowe's book, Louisa. He's waiting now for me to respond to it. I'm sure she meant to be—serving a good cause—but she is very, very biased. Aren't *any* of your guests like Mrs. Stowe?"

"Margaret, you're pinning Louisa down when she doesn't want to be."

"It's all right, Lewis. Yes, there was one gentleman who managed to create chaos nearly every night downstairs in the dining room. I also found him out in the quarters at the back of my lot, preaching his antislavery doctrines to Pootie and Mamie and the others. They just stared at him, saying nothing." She smiled at the memory. "Nothing, that is, until one day Pootie took out after him."

"Pootie did?"

"He called me a name she didn't like."

"What did he call you?"

"Never mind, darling," Lewis broke in. "We all just have to realize that there is probably big trouble brewing over this issue of our owning some of our people. None of us decided to become slave owners. We grew up in the system. I could wish our field hands were all free. But what would they do with themselves? Mrs. Stowe would say I salve my conscience by insisting that I do compensate them by supplying their food, clothing and shelter. Perhaps I do salve my conscience, but—" he smiled a little. "Tonight, at least, we can't do a thing about any of it."

"Lewis," Margaret said, not smiling. "I'm glad you couldn't get Seton into West Point."

He took a deep breath. "His old father's failure isn't going to stop him from attending military school, though. I wasn't going to tell you until after our time here, Margaret, but I picked up a letter from Seton on my latest trip to Jacksonville. Addressed to me. He's saved enough money to pay for his first year at military school in South Carolina."

"Lewis!"

"Margaret, my dear, don't look so stricken. We've known for a long time that Seton would become a soldier." He reached for her hand. "There's good news, too. He'll be home at least shortly after we open the house to guests. I know you think I should have told you that—but he won't be staying long. I—I guess I thought I'd wait until you and Louisa had enjoyed our visit. Perhaps I made a wrong judgment," he added lamely.

"No. No, Lewis. But, why military school—now? We need him at Hibernia. Seton knows that."

"He thinks there's going to be a war between the North and the South. He wants to be ready."

Margaret sank back in her chair, her face white.

"Mrs. Judge Smith, my neighbor, thinks that, too," Louisa said quietly. "But instead of—feeling as you do, Margaret, she's cheering her son on. My dear, the hatred isn't just on one side. The Abolitionists up North hate us en masse, and the hotheads down here hate *them* en masse."

"Louisa, I—don't—want—Seton to hate at all!"

After a silence, Lewis said, "The boy has a mind of his own, my dear. He's eighteen. What we want might not make any difference now."

Margaret looked from Lewis to Louisa. "You—really think all this means war, don't you?"

"I hope not," Louisa said. "But, who knows? Certainly we women don't know."

"Lewis—will there be war?"

"Not anytime soon, my dear." Lewis spoke with assurance. "Our new president, James Buchanan, has always been a successful negotiator. He's a friend to the South. I refuse to be alarmed. Buchanan is a man of long experience at working out national problems. His cabinet is largely pro-South. You are not to worry, Margaret. Seton is going through a phase. It's certainly nothing new that he wants to go to military school. I admire the boy. He's not even asking us for tuition to the school in South Carolina."

"Which school, Lewis? I don't even know which school in South Carolina!"

"King's Mountain Military School in Yorkville."

There was another silence. Then, Margaret stood up. "All right, I'm not going to get upset. Not only because you're being so reassuring, Lewis. Because I've just this minute chosen—hope."

Lewis stood, too, as did Louisa. "Your favorite word," he said.

"Yes. My favorite word. And, oh, how good that we're here in St. Augustine. Just think. I can actually go to church tomorrow!"

"Do you know that my wife vows she's going to build her own chapel at Hibernia someday, Louisa?" Lewis winked at his cousin.

"Oh, I've known about that for years."

"Tease me if you like, both of you," Margaret declared. "But our beautiful, big house will be finished in just a few more months now. It's simply high time to begin thinking about the next dream."

Lewis put his arm around her. "If I were a betting man, I'd wager you already have that chapel planned down to the last pew!"

"I have. In fact, your head carpenter from Jacksonville assures me that we'll have almost enough heavy timbers left over for its foundation!"

"I hear Sophia downstairs," Lewis said. "She and Louisa will want to discuss her evening with Mrs. Smith. Why don't we turn in for the night? I'm going fishing off the pier tomorrow early."

"Lewis?"

"Yes, Cousin?"

"Remember in the old days how we used to hold hands and say our prayers together at night—when you visited us at New Switzerland?"

"Never forget it."

"Could we do that now? I want to hear Margaret pray."

They joined hands and, after a moment, Margaret prayed: "Thank You, Father, for our beloved Louisa and for the warm welcome here in her home. Thank You for my wonderful Lewis. For all our children. Keep them safely through the night." She waited. Then, with a break in her voice: "And Seton, Lord. Wherever he is, watch over him! Oh, watch over our beautiful Seton. Whatever happens in our country— change his warm, loving heart so that it's *free*—of hatred."

35

Back at Hibernia, Margaret clung for dear life to her deep
conviction that—for all their sakes—she did indeed have an
obligation to hope about Seton. As he wound up his work in
Chicago, his letters went on containing the strange mixture of
vibrance and hatred to which she should have become accustomed by now. Her son was grasping life eagerly, confident-
ly. He had found his place. Seton would learn to be an
excellent soldier and the dream to him was just as vital as her
own dreams were to her. There had been no word of his
exact time of arrival back at Hibernia, but he was coming.
She would have a chance face to face to talk with this boy
who so filled her heart. For now, she would hope and not
burden Lewis and the children with her peculiar fears for
Seton.

By summer of that year, 1857, much of the interior of the
big house had been finished. Finished, at least, to the point
where Margaret could spend long, sunlit evenings dreaming
from room to room—sometimes with the children, often with
Lewis, at times by herself. The gracious, wide stairway was
her pride and joy. To accommodate Lewis's lame leg, she had
insisted upon low, shallow treads. The staircase was perfect.
The children loved running up and down it and so did Margaret. She floated up and then floated down, picturing herself
wearing tasteful new dresses she'd have made in time for the
arrival of their first guest early next year. A Jacksonville
dressmaker was even now working on five new outfits for
her—two of cashmere, one a vivid blue, one a soft green.
And, since even February could bring warm days, she had
also ordered three cottons: one fine calico in stripes, one
sprigged dimity and a white mull. Using her own money, she
had placed an order for Lewis, too. The latest style for men
was, Margaret thought, handsomely subdued. Elegant. They
no longer wore bright blue or bottle green. Rather, with the
waistlines eased, colors for gentlemen were restricted to waistcoat and tie. Lewis would have one outfit in brown and one
in dark gray, and to please him, she included a frock coat,

although cutaways were more popular. He'd agreed to one cutaway. She had ordered two. In fact, also on her own, she had decided that her handsome husband would own at least one of the very latest "ditto" suits—with trousers, waistcoat and coat of the same material. Fortunately, since the Jacksonville tailor had made Lewis's clothes for many years, she did not have to maneuver him for fittings. He wouldn't know of her extravagance until the new garments arrived at their dock.

George and Mary were settled in St. Mary's in a modest cottage supplied by the church. The one visit they'd made to Hibernia right after their return from Princeton had been brief. Brief and, to Margaret, not at all satisfying. The growing antagonism between North and South had invaded George's homelife, too. Mary was a strong Abolitionist. George still seemed worshipful of her and she was, in many ways, a good wife. But no one could have convinced Margaret that Mary would ever be a happy minister's wife. George seemed fairly peaceful, though thinner, older-looking, his dark, thick hair brushed forward to merge with sideburns already turning gray. Far grayer than Lewis's.

Frederic, now twelve, was going to be as handsome, she believed, as Lewis. And, to Margaret, that was as handsome as a man could possibly be. She had also ordered new outfits— both for everyday and for dress-up occasions—for Frederic, Frank and William. Ten-year-old William could dress himself now with some help from Frederic. Frederic was not only growing into a handsome young man, daily he seemed even more courteous, kinder, always attentive to his slow, younger brother. And adored by Tissie, now eight. Tissie, Margaret was sure, would have preferred to be able to dress exactly the way Frederic dressed. The girl not only adored her brother, she behaved more like a boy than the golden, curly-haired, blue-eyed, disarmingly pretty girl she was. Maggie, now six, was the perfect little lady—obedient, tender of heart, sensitive. More and more, her mother knew that she had been right about Maggie. "Why, I can't even frown about something that Maggie doesn't notice—run to me and try to help," she told Lewis. "You just watch as the years go by. Maggie will always be our friend." Belle? Two-year-old Belle. Never called Isabel, simply because Isabel seemed not to suit her. It was far too sedate a name for their carrot-topped obstreperous youngest child, who was already jabbering, who now, at two, not only was fussy about what she ate, tossing it deftly to the floor if it didn't suit her, but romped through the house from early morning to enforced naptime in the afternoon, pulling doilies and lamps from tables and shooting fire from her big brown eyes if anyone attempted to tame her. Unlike their other two daughters at her age, Belle hated to be cuddled and held. Unless, that is, the idea came first to her, then woe be unto whatever available adult happened to be too busy at the time. Frank, almost sixteen, all but worshipped his little sister Tissie, who invariably wanted Frederic's attention instead. This seemed to bother Frank only at first. By some quirk of his always analytical mind, he figured out a way not to notice. Margaret and Lewis did observe, though, that whenever Tissie called for help—when she got stuck too high in a tree, for example—it was Frank who rescued her.

So as to properly impress the first guests, Margaret and Maum Betty were making new clothes for the girls. Small replicas of Margaret's in style—but, made of sturdy calicos and cottons. The Flemings would be ready when the house was, and the Flemings included all the household help. Maum Betty and Rina, whose hopeless job it was to keep Tissie out of trees, and the two new girls, Liz and Euphoria, hired out of Mandarin to be trained to clean guest rooms and help at meals, would all have new clothes, too. Lewis had seen to new outfits for old Pompey and July, who were to handle the trunks and luggage. Pompey was very proud of his new clothes, except that he hoped for some red somewhere. Lewis promised a red tie the next time he went to Jacksonville or St. Augustine on business.

The new house would be painted white throughout inside as well as out. Margaret's dream went far beyond the money they would earn from entertaining paying guests in their home. True, light, cheerful, comfortable surroundings would increase that income, but with all her heart, she wanted the time spent at her house to be a time of genuine rest and rejuvenation for the people who paid their money. After all, some of them would be invalids, their spirits needing to be lifted as much as their ailing bodies needed the clean, warm, bright Florida air.

Margaret and Little Jim, who still talked and talked about his mother, Easter, every time he could be alone with his mistress, spent hours laying out the carefully planned paths and walkways where guests could take full advantage of the mild winter days. The double rows of crepe myrtles that would one day provide a graceful canopy over visitors as they first entered Hibernia had long ago been planted and were flourishing—every one of them. As was the double row of water oaks leading from the back of the house to the quarters. The croquet courts were enlarged and ready. And there was high excitement the day the new games—three backgammon sets, four checkerboards, and several decks of playing cards arrived from Savannah.

A new punkah, a large framed cloth rectangle edged with fringe, was already suspended by strong hinges from the ceiling in the enormous guest dining room on the first floor of the new house. Its rope—which would one day be pulled steadily throughout meals by Rina, to keep the table fanned of flies, hung limply now in the middle of the newly carpeted floor. Anytime, boats plying the St. Johns from Jacksonville to Hibernia would begin bringing the new furniture, including the all important, long dining table.

Thanks to Louisa, three people—a couple and their niece—had already made reservations for early January of 1858. Louisa's St. Augustine house had been fully reserved for months. Every new request she received was sent directly to Margaret, who wrote promptly, welcoming the strangers to Hibernia. Even the first year could be a profitable one. And after that? She harbored not one single doubt. She meant to see to it that the Fleming place at Hibernia became one of the most favored stops on the St. Johns River.

They should be moved in, provided the new furniture arrived in time, by the end of September, when the riverbank and woods would be cloud-studded with the feathery white blossoms of the salt bush. To Margaret, late September and October were soft months. That would help. Moving, at best, even if most of what would be placed in the new house could be carried straight there off the boats, was not an easy experience. The air, clear, green-white still in August, would by then be yielding to the yellow-gold for which Margaret waited each autumn. Barring squalls or a hurricane, the river ran deep and glassy through most of the fall weeks.

In a day or so, Lewis's crew of workmen would begin building scaffolding and the first coat of white paint would go on the exterior of the house. White, with a dark green trim. Nothing, she thought, could be more welcoming, more homelike. And love would be there. Each guest, sensitive to it or not, would move about the great house, up and down the wide, gracious staircase, along the halls, in and out of sleeping and dining rooms, in an invisible, but pure atmosphere of love. Oh, they would never forget Cousin Louisa's warning that no innkeeper succeeds without a finely honed sense of humor, and when things went wrong, the Flemings would laugh—but lovingly, and their guests would somehow sense it.

Especially since Easter's death, Margaret and Betty had escaped often into a private world of good laughs. Betty was her mother made over, with even more salt to her humor—a good thing. Betty would be responsible for the quality of the food served and, along with Margaret and Lewis, would be helping to train and manage the other servants. Training, with Maggie, Tissie, Frederic, Frank and William posing as "house guests from the North," had already begun. Liz and Euphoria, in their early twenties, were learning fast. Liz, full of fun, could laugh at herself when she got mixed up and served Frederic from the wrong side at table. Euphoria, her name notwithstanding, tended to run off to the kitchen and cry if she made a mistake. The guest bedrooms and the second and third floors stood empty of furnishings yet, but both Euphoria and Liz had memorized the room numbers for which they would be daily responsible.

Margaret had one day overheard Euphoria laboriously rehearsing her duties: "I'm odd—I'm odd. Odd is 3, 5, 7, 9, like that. First, pick up the slop jar—"

"Thunder mug," Liz corrected her.

"Ain't it the same thing? Be quiet, so's I can think: I'm odd. 3, 5, 7, 9—pick up an' empty, then wash out the slop jars first in 3, 5, 7, 9—*odd*. Then, I make the beds, changin' the linens every three days. Monday, Thursday, Sunday? Do I change linens on a Sunday?"

"If you're told to," Liz snapped. "If they's folks here—sleepin' in the beds, makin' thunder in the mugs, we change. They don't like dirty beds an' smelly mugs just cause it's Sunday!"

Margaret was fond of the two new girls. They would do just fine. They would all do just fine—in time. Fervently, she hoped that the great house would compensate for their shortcomings until everyone got the hang of it. The tall, sheltering trees, slashing the Florida sunlight as it poured toward the ground, would help, too. Some guests would be annoyed, she supposed, but most would enjoy the sound of children's voices in the house, or out in the vast, light-dappled yard. If a guest disliked children, Margaret could do without that guest. By some means, she and Lewis were going to keep Hibernia *their* home, too. With all her heart, she wanted Hibernia to mean peace, a backwater of peace like a quiet cove of the St. Johns, where water lilies and ferns grew undisturbed and still. She longed for her guests to enjoy themselves, to laugh, to join in the group singing around her new piano at night, but most of all, she longed for them to take away with them some of the peace that was Hibernia.

Her stepson George wrote once a week. L.I., only once a month, but always cheerfully. At times, George's letters had the sound of duty letters. In some, he wrote mostly details—as though he copied the minutes of the latest Session Meeting, always with only The Reverend George Fleming and Elder James Steward present. He told his parents who had been presented for membership, who had been received, who rejected. He said he and Mary were well, and that they sent their love.

"Perhaps," Lewis would say almost every time they shared one of George's strangely formal letters, "the church will give him some time off one of these days after we're moved. I feel so sure, Margaret, that a week or two here at Hibernia will heal—whatever it is that disturbs him. The boy's been away from the river so long."

Margaret prayed every day that Lewis was right. In her secret heart, she also prayed, although George had said not one word about his health, that he was not ill in body. St. Mary's was not that far north of Hibernia. George and Mary could have visited them often. They would have visited St. Mary's, but they had not been invited. All things were good in Margaret's own life beside the river. She could ask God for no more than she already had. But, beneath her joy ran persistently the hidden stream of worry over Seton—and over George, who, so far as she could tell, had again closed himself inside himself—even from her.

New furniture, linens, ingrained carpeting and grass mattings for the floors, silver for the tables, china, glassware, new kettles and pots and skillets for Maum Betty's kitchen, the new dresses and trousers and coats, kept arriving throughout the month of September and into October, weeks after the family had begun to sleep in the new house. The older children pitched in to help. William, especially, seemed to enjoy the main duty assigned to him—that of using his father's heavy claw hammer to open crate after crate and stack up the splintered wood for use as kindling in the big house's many fireplaces that winter.

In spite of the full, busy days, a festive mood carried into each evening and there were more quarters parties, when everyone—black and white—played blindman's buff and danced breakdowns between wild, laughter-filled round games called Monkey Motions. Pompey would be there always with his fiddle and his toothless smile, playing patting music accompanied by that good, familiar clapping and stomping with which they'd all grown up. The quarters play moved into the big yard sometimes, especially the night Margaret wanted to try out her strings of new Japanese lanterns, which tossed their mobile shadows easily among the long strands of Spanish moss.

"Can we do this every night when the people start to come, Mama?"

"No, Tissie." Margaret laughed, dancing by herself in and out of the moving lantern light. "Not quite every night. But we're celebrating now. Come on, dance with Mother. That's right. Dance! Throw your arms wide like this—see? We're celebrating, Tissie." Then, "Look, Lewis—we're celebrating! Aren't we all beautiful?"

36

Christmas at Hibernia in 1857 was filled with nostalgia. Surely, it would be the last Christmas with only the family present. In future years, at least some early arrivals from the North would be there, too.

"I cooks enough for a army anyhow, with only the family here," Maum Betty laughed. "Might just as well have comp'ny."

"Comp'ny," from that day on, was Betty's name for guests. And on January 10, 1858, right on schedule, with the guest rooms in perfect readiness, Lewis and Margaret walked arm in arm down to the dock when the children began to shout that the steamer bearing their first "comp'ny" was puffing into sight from Jacksonville.

Careful plans had been made for this moment: The children could watch for the boat, but they were to observe the actual arrival from a ways down the riverbank—out of sight. Lewis and Margaret fully intended to greet their first guests with dignity. Then, on a signal from Lewis, Pompey and Little Jim were to appear in their new white coats and dark trousers to carry the trunks and boxes up the path to the big house and place them in the assigned rooms. The expected couple would be in Room 1 at the head of the stairs on the second floor—"odd" for Euphoria. The niece would be across the hall in Room 2—"even" for Liz.

As she and Lewis reached the dock, Margaret glimpsed Tissie's yellow curls as the curious girl peeped over the low stand of palmetto behind which the children were hidden out of sight until their parents had properly introduced themselves. Tissie peeped, but she did stay hidden and Margaret and Lewis smiled their pleasure at their offsprings' restraint as they watched the little steamer move in from midstream and head for the newly repaired six-hundred-foot Hibernia dock.

Abruptly, Margaret grabbed Lewis's arm. "Oh, Lewis! I wonder what they'll be like! Do you realize these people will be coming right into our house?"

He laughed his good, easy laugh. "Don't worry. They'll be nice folks. And if they weren't coming right into our house to stay awhile, you'd be, of all people, most miserable."

She gave him a brave smile. "I know. But—just this minute—it all seems so sudden!"

"Mama! Papa!" The steamer came nearer and a young man standing in the prow of the boat was yelling at the top of his voice, waving both arms above his head.

"Seton! Lewis, it's—Seton! Seton's on that boat, too."

"Don't have my spectacles. Our Seton?"

Running out on the dock, Margaret began waving and shouting, too, her dignity momentarily forgotten. "Seton! Seton, darling!"

Doing his best to catch up, Lewis called and waved, and when Seton yelled: "Where is everybody?" that was all that was needed for the six hidden children to come plunging out of their hiding place.

"Frank," Margaret called. "Watch out for Belle. She'll fall running over that rough ground!"

At that, Belle set up a yowl from flat on her face, where she lay screaming her red head off. The pull of Seton was too strong. For once, Frank ignored his baby sister and was out on the dock in time to catch the boat's rope tossed to him by Seton. By the time Frederic had picked Belle up, Frank was aboard the steamer hugging his brother. Then, as Seton, on the dock, tried to tie down the boat for the captain, all of the children were there. Hampered by hugs and laughing, his face even more beautiful than his mother remembered, Seton tossed the rope to his father, who finished the job.

Only William hung back, but not for long. Seton gave him the biggest hug of all and then turned to his parents. "This is quite a reception, Mama—Papa, for the prodigal no one knew was coming." He embraced Margaret and Belle, whom Frederic had dumped into his mother's arms—kissed them both, causing Belle to forget her tears. Then, he went to Lewis. "Papa!" They started to shake hands, but neither could resist a bear hug. "Say, everybody—can you believe I'm really home?"

Tears of pure joy were still streaming down Margaret's face when Seton saved the day by remembering the Northern visitors who had been doing the only thing they could have done—wait on the dock until the noisy welcome subsided.

"Mother and Father, may I present my new friends who were already warned that we'd all make a lot of racket when I appeared—Mr. and Mrs. Jerome Bonham of Massachusetts and their niece, Miss Lucy Malloy. My parents, Colonel and Mrs. Lewis Fleming."

Introductions were warmly acknowledged. Margaret still had wet cheeks as she presented her children.

"We'd planned a quiet, dignified first meeting," she said, laughing. "But, welcome to Hibernia. Oh, you are—all three so welcome to Hibernia!"

Mr. Bonham, thick of waist, wearing a bowler hat and a merry, rather vacant expression on his round, shapeless face, bowed. "Say, this is a beautiful spot, Mrs. Fleming—Colonel. I declare—this is a truly beautiful spot. And—right on the river!" His enthusiasm grew the more he looked around and it grew to the point where he felt the need for someone to agree. Turning to his skinny, well-dressed, but travel-mussed wife, he asked, "Don't you agree, my dear? This is a truly beautiful spot! *Right on the river.*"

"Indeed it is beautiful, Jerome," said Mrs. Bonham, smoothing her long skirt. "And, of course, it's right on the river."

"And you, Lucy. Did you ever see a more beautiful spot?"

Lucy Malloy, whose boredom with her travel companions already showed on her haughty, rather handsome face, snapped. "What did you expect, Uncle? A tumbledown shack in a treeless bottom?"

"Heh. Heh, heh," Bonham laughed lamely. "Of course not." He whacked Lewis on the back. "Not at these prices, eh, Colonel?"

The children stood around Seton, their eyes glued on the strange arrivals, in abnormal and absolute silence.

Finally, Margaret whispered to Lewis, "Did you signal Pompey and Little Jim?"

"Stupid of me," Lewis said. "I guess I'm just too excited—seeing Seton like this—and having our first house guests." He bowed to the ladies, then turned to wave toward where Pompey and Little Jim were waiting behind the new summer house not a hundred feet away.

They appeared at once, picked up the two trunks and, with Frank and Seton bringing hatboxes and valises, the whole Fleming family escorted their first three guests along the dock and up the wide yard to begin the promenade through Margaret's head-high double row of crepe myrtles to the wide, welcoming front door of Hibernia.

Seton, his brothers and sisters following him as though he were the Pied Piper, took them all fishing until after the first big meal was served and the new guests made absolutely comfortable.

"So far, so good," Margaret whispered to Lewis in the downstairs hall after they had personally shown the Bonhams and their niece to rooms 1 and 2 upstairs. "I thought Mrs. Bonham sniffed a bit at the size of our rooms—" she giggled, "but she doesn't know how many, many Northerners are going to want to come. We'll need even more rooms someday."

"Your big dream has begun, Margaret. Pompey and Little Jim even got the trunks and boxes in the right rooms. Shall we dine with them, since they're our only guests for right now?"

"Maybe we should. I don't want to make a practice of it, though. This is still going to be the Fleming family home."

"Well, Seton and the children won't be back to eat. Betty sent them with a loaded lunch basket. Why don't we sit down with these people today anyway? Seems a bit cold to seat just the three of them in that enormous dining room at that long, long table."

Margaret frowned. "Having guests has already changed things—hasn't it? Why couldn't Seton have come home—yesterday? We haven't seen him at all. We don't even know how long he's staying with us yet."

"Now, none of that. There'll be plenty of time alone with Seton. Anyway, we'll have dinner with our guests. I'd like to hear a Northern businessman's opinion of things."

"Hm. Do you think poor, dull Mr. Bonham really has any interesting opinions, Lewis?"

"Maybe not very well thought out, but he certainly has the perspicacity to see that we have a beautiful spot here."

They both laughed as Margaret added, "'—*right on the river*'!"

Liz and Euphoria did well serving Maum Betty's delicious dinner of honey-glazed ham, chicken, fluffy rice and red beans, squash and onions, and to top it all off—her mother's Lady Baltimore cake. The Bonhams and their niece ate and ate and Liz sailed about the table with grace and ease, as though she'd been serving in a fine dining room all her life. Euphoria didn't sail and she had little grace, but she managed.

"*Dee*licious food," Bonham said for about the fifth time, as he jammed his large linen napkin into its ivory ring and leaned back in one of Margaret's new dark green, balloon-backed, stenciled chairs. She had chosen wisely in those chairs! Her own taste ran to delicate spindles, but that strong center splat could withstand even Mr. Bonham's gusto. "Don't you consider that delicious food, Mrs. Bonham?" he pressed his wife.

"Indeed I do," she said. "Miss Fatio guaranteed us good food here."

"Louisa Fatio certainly should know our cook. Miss Fatio is my husband's first cousin and my best friend," Margaret said. "We hope you'll be happy here with us—all three of you. You won't have a city to explore, but St. Augustine is only a few miles upriver by boat."

"The ladies can go if they like," Bonham declared. "I'm staying right here in this—beautiful spot! Right on the river. Personally, I've had my fill of noisy cities and factories and traffic. This is just what the doctor ordered for me."

"Oh, have you not been well, Mr. Bonham?" Lewis asked.

"Fit as a fiddle. Just an expression."

"I see."

"Yes, sir and yes, ma'am, the silence in this place is right up my alley. You sit in an office next to a garment factory from morning till night and you eat up a beautiful spot like this."

"Right on the river," Lucy Malloy said sarcastically.

"You own a garment factory, I take it," Lewis offered. "Is business good? Are things booming in the Northern cities as we're led to believe in our papers?"

"Booming and burgeoning," Bonham boasted. "They're even talking about a transatlantic cable. And railroads, railroads, that's our secret. Railroads. And for me, the sewing machine and the laboring class hordes pouring into our fair land from Europe. Why, I work 'em twelve hours a day, six days a week. Cheap labor. Hard-working people. Come here to make their fortunes." He gave a belly-shaking chuckle. "Gonna be Vanderbilts—all of 'em."

Lucy Malloy got up from the table. "Uncle, I've heard all the business talk I can bear now, *and* all the political talk I care to hear from you and young Mr. Fleming on the boat. I'm going for a walk outside. Join me, Auntie?"

Margaret rose, too. "I'd be delighted to take a walk with you ladies. Show you our place. Let the gentlemen talk business—and if they must—" she gave Lewis a warning look—"politics."

"Ah-h, glad to be rid of them, Fleming," Bonham said after the ladies had excused themselves. "Until I met up with your son on the boat from Charleston, I felt as though I was drowning in—women!" He laughed again, longer than called for, as always.

"My son certainly surprised us. We knew he was coming home from Chicago, but didn't expect him to get here on a boat from Charleston."

"Oh, he took a train across country and then down to Charleston, South Carolina, by boat. After all, he wanted to look over the military school he plans to attend."

"Of course," Lewis struggled briefly with a resentment that this strange Northerner knew more of his son's plans than he. "I guess we Southerners haven't learned yet to reckon with train travel."

"Fine boy you've got. Hotheaded, but smart as a whip, I'd say. I'm a pretty good judge of men. Have to be in my position. Why, your son knows more about the politics in this country than any grown man I've run into in months. How old is he?"

"He'll be nineteen next month."

"Got a head on his shoulders like a man of thirty."

"Thank you."

"Hotheaded, though," Bonham repeated.

"He must have been in a vipers nest of Abolitionists out there in Chicago. He hates 'em."

"I would hope my son hates no one."

"Sorry to dash your hopes, sir, but he does. He hates that writer woman—what's her name?"

"Mrs. Harriet Beecher Stowe."

"That's it. Hates her book about the cruelty to slaves down here. Hates Horace Greeley, the newspaper writer. Why, I didn't know what the boy was talkin' about until he jogged my memory. You remember last year when the Supreme Court overturned the lower courts and ruled that that nigger named Dred Scott wasn't free after all?"

"Yes," Lewis said. "I remember. He'd been taken into a free state. The lower courts ruled that he was indeed free."

"Right. Then the Supreme Court, packed with Southerners, overturned that decision. The nigger *isn't* free, they said." The jiggling belly laugh began again under his talk. "Well, sir, your boy is hot under the collar because Greeley wrote that having those Southerners on the Court gave the decision as much moral weight as it would have had, had it been the judgment of a majority in any Washington barroom!"

Bonham was obviously enjoying what to him was merely a joke. Lewis thought a minute before responding. This man was from Massachusetts, but not interested in politics, and evidently absorbed only with making money in his garment factory. Seton must have exaggerated the Northern antagonism against the South. Bonham was something of a fool, but he wasn't a political firebrand. "My son tells me," Lewis began carefully, "that many of the people living in Northern slums have it far worse than our colored folks down here."

"Now, you're throwing off on my workers," Bonham said pleasantly. "But your son may be right. Conditions differ, you know, in a country as big as this one's getting to be." He leaned toward Lewis. "But all that matters, Fleming, is that businessmen—like you and me—make it big. America gives us that chance!" A wide smile stretched his full face. "Your son had just better keep his radical ideas to himself around the folks up there with enough money to pay your prices here at Hibernia. We businessmen have got to stick together, North *or* South."

"I suppose it will take some doing for me to learn to think of myself as a businessman," Lewis said. "I've been a planter most of my life. Still am."

"Then you've got the best of both worlds. You can sell your crops—don't forget I need your cotton in my factory—and you and the missus may just clean up in this beautiful spot. Yes, sir. Not many places for half-frozen Northerners to go like this one. Right on the river, too." He leaned confidentially toward Lewis again. "Say, do you think I might have another piece of that *dee*licious cake—as long as my wife is outside taking herself a stroll?"

"I don't want to be selfish on your first day here, son," Lewis said as he and Seton visited alone on the wide front porch that evening. "You were generous—as always—taking the children out on the river right off. They needed to be with you. But so does your mother. She's in our room. The door is just under the front stairs, in case you haven't had time to discover it yet."

Seton sat on the porch railing, his eyes roaming the gray evening as it hung above the river, almost as gray as the sky. "I'm not sure you're too happy with the talk we've had, Papa," he said in a quiet voice. "I'm sorry."

"Any talk we have is important. I—I'm probably trying too hard to be a good, firm father."

Seton turned to look at him. "You're the best father a man ever had. We just have such different perspectives on things. You're shut away down here where most people are of the same mind; and I—"

"That's not really the case, you know. We're not of one mind down here in Florida. Look at old Huston. You're a mild firebrand beside him. Just a flickering candle to his red-hot blaze blowing against anything Yankee. I wouldn't want to be like him. Wouldn't want you to be. The man's obsessed."

Seton got to his feet. "I'm not obsessed. You can count on that. With all my heart, I wish Northerners understood—or accepted that we know how to run our lives in the South. I'm a man of peace, Papa. How could I be otherwise, growing up by our river? Still, I hope I have some of my father's nobility, too. You understood why the Seminoles hated white men. You fought them anyway."

"Only to protect our home."

"Well, from what I've heard and read and seen at the North, they will do far worse to us than burn our homes—if we fail to protect ourselves." He was silent a moment. "God is on our side, sir. I know that, but I intend to be ready to do my part. The Southern army will need leadership."

"Southern *army?* We're a united nation, son!"

"On paper, yes. But unless we get more territory, more representation in Congress—*they'll* get us."

Lewis pulled himself to his feet. "Don't alarm your mother, please, I beg you to be careful with her. She's so happy over our new place, our future. Don't upset her. You two—just enjoy each other."

Seton gave his father a quick hug and went inside.

Seated at the bedroom window in an armchair beside Margaret, Seton talked to her for a long time. After first assuring her that he would not even learn of his acceptance to military school until late spring—would be at Hibernia until then—he told her at length how he'd enjoyed watching the energetic city of Chicago grow; how he'd liked his work—how rapidly he'd progressed because his employers saw and rewarded his potential from the start. "In short, Mrs. Fleming," he concluded, "your son was a huge success."

She gave him a warm smile. "And very modest."

"Neither modest nor vain. Factual. A man knows when he's doing a good job. Just as he knows it when he's shirking. Thanks to my mother and my father, I was born with a good brain, a strong body—and integrity. Mother, I'm—not a hothead. I am just equipped to see a lot of things other people don't see—yet." He took her hand. "But, God is on our side."

"Our side? I suppose you mean this bickering between Northern and Southern politicians."

"More than bickering. You'll find out one day And I'll be prepared. I'm going to be an—outstanding soldier."

She made herself laugh, when she wanted to cry "Your humility overwhelms me!"

Seton laughed, too. "Good! I'm glad I overwhelm you. With all my heart I want you and Papa to—be proud of what you've helped me make of myself. Not so much yet But just wait." He was on his feet now, pacing the large room. "I was—born to be a soldier, Mama. I feel it all through me. I'd make a poor businessman. I could never be a successful merchant like Grandfather, for whom you named me. I'd make a poor lawyer. Unlike L.I., I'd be trying only the cases I believed in." He grinned. "I'd have trouble right off following a client's wishes if they went counter to mine. And heaven knows I'd make a bad minister. Did you ever know two men more unlike than George and me?"

No, beloved boy, Margaret thought. I never knew two—men more unlike. George, so cautious, so pulled inside himself. Seton, so sure—dashing, even cocky—and certainly capable of giving all joy. Why, when they are so different, do they both hold such special, deep places in my heart?

"I love George—as he is," she said at last. "And, I always want you—to be you, Seton. The very best *you* possible. Your father and I both want that."

"Poor Papa. I upset him tonight, I think. But I didn't upset you, did I?"

"Did your father tell you not to?"

The young man threw back his dark head and laughed. "You know the old fellow, don't you? You really know him!"

"I should by now. But I *don't* like your calling him—*old*. In fact, I forbid it. You didn't upset me because I didn't let you. I trust you too much. Seton? Are you listening? I—trust you. I trust you to God's care—and I also trust *you*."

He kissed her. "Thank you, Mama." Suddenly, he squared his shoulders. "I'll never disappoint you. I promise. God won't permit me to disappoint you or Papa. Or myself. God is on our side. I intend to be one of His—true warriors."

Margaret studied her son, not willing to risk a response to what to her was a contradictory statement. A warrior for God? God needs lovers! Watching his light, steel-blue eyes— eyes that seemed to be seeing far off into some infinity which a mere mother could never see—she felt awe. Seton's youth and verve and manly energy charged the very air in the room. But how could God be on either side? The God who hung on His cross with His arms outstretched toward the whole world could not possibly care more about Southerners than Northerners!

She reached for his hand. "I'm so proud of you. I wish I *really* understood you. But, oh, you *are*—very deep in my heart."

37

By the end of an unusually warm January, fifteen guests had arrived to winter at Hibernia. The Flemings were lyrical—convinced that they would, by next year, have the house filled. Their first vacationers, the dull, but friendly Bonhams, seemed to enjoy themselves more with the passing of each day. Bonham, especially, had made himself an official greeter.

"We shouldn't feel annoyed that Mr. Bonham insists upon meeting every new arrival," Margaret said one afternoon when the family had escaped onto the river in Lewis's roomy sloop for a little sail alone. "But did you see the expression on Professor Cotner's face yesterday when Mr. Bonham nearly pumped his hand off the minute he stepped onto our dock?"

"Professor Cotner is la-de-da academe, Mother," Seton laughed. "He lives so much inside his own bookish head, old Bonham may do him good. Why, the Professor has no idea whatever about the trouble brewing in the country. I found that out right away. And even if he did know that the country's in turmoil, he wouldn't care."

"Son," Lewis said, "I wish you wouldn't start right in on politics the minute our guests arrive. They're here to rest—to enjoy themselves."

"But, Papa," Frank said from his place at the tiller, "Seton sees the truth of things. Somebody's got to wake people up. We're tired being stepped on by those Yankee Abolitionists."

"I don't think we have a single Abolitionist staying at our house, Frank," Margaret said, a bit more sharply than usual. "You're being influenced by Seton."

"Can you think of a better person?"

"Well, it's just that your father and I still don't understand what kind of Northerners Seton met in Chicago."

"Just what does it mean to be a 'Northerner'?" Tissie asked. "Doesn't it just mean you live in the North?"

"Yes, Tissie," Lewis said. "That's exactly what it means."

Seton gave his parents his sunny smile. "Let's change the subject. Didn't we Flemings maneuver this time alone to have some fun?"

"Sure," Tissie chimed. "Let's have some fun! I think I'll take off my dress and jump in the water!"

"You'll do no such thing. That river's cold," Seton scolded playfully. "Besides, this is family time. We're all going to do the same thing and have the same kind of fun together. After all, didn't we do our chores fast and early so we could all come out here on the river?"

"I did what you told me to do in the parlor, Mama," Maggie said, patting Margaret's hand and scrunching closer to her on the wooden seat. "I'll be seven in August. I can dust chairs now."

Margaret hugged the quiet child. "And you do it so well, Maggie."

"I'm too young to work," Belle shouted, leaning over to splash in the gray water.

"Yes, you are," Lewis said, pulling the child back. "You're also too young to lean so far over the side of the boat."

Belle hit her father. "I'll thmack you," she lisped.

"You already did," Frederic laughed.

"I can thmack Papa if I want to!"

"No, you cannot and that's final." Margaret reached across Maggie to give her youngest a shake. Then, she turned to William sitting quietly on the deck. "Are you having a good time, William?"

He nodded and smiled—lost or happy in his own thoughts; no one knew for sure.

They skimmed the glistening river downstream toward the mouth of Doctor's Lake, a wide bayou off the St. Johns which ran some lily-choked nine miles around the north end of Fleming's Island. Their goal—and these days the Flemings always had a goal—was to buy some shad from the shad-fisherman usually at the mouth of Doctor's Lake at this time of day. The new guests from the North, one family of five from Rhode Island, the Professor, his wife and two children from Connecticut and three spinster sisters from Long Island, would, Margaret knew, relish shad for the big meal tomorrow.

"They'd better all get to the table at once," Frederic laughed. "I never saw a man eat the way Mr. Bonham does."

"You're very quiet, Seton," Lewis said. "Anxious about that letter from Major Jenkins at the school in Yorkville?"

"Not really, Papa. I'm pretty sure they've already made up their minds to accept me. I'd just like to know—when I have to go." He stretched his arms wide in the mild winter sunshine. "Some days I can't wait to get to military school. Other days—like this—when I think how far I'll be from the river and all of you, I'm not so sure."

"You could wait," Margaret said quickly. "We need you here. As hard as you've been working, you know how much there is to do."

"Don't tempt me, Mama. I have to go. It's my calling."

A few moments passed, with only the creak of rigging and slap of the water as the boat's prow sliced the river. Then, Lewis said, "You know, I've been thinking. I seem to stay far busier than I'd expected with our guests. I wonder if I shouldn't try to find someone to oversee the fields, the place in general, tend the kitchen garden. Do what you've been doing, Seton, after you're gone."

"I'm sixteen. I'm plenty old enough to oversee," Frank said. "I've been doing it with Seton."

"Of course, you're old enough, son," Margaret agreed. "But it won't be long until you'll be leaving, too—to read law with L.I. in Jacksonville. No more than a year anyway. I wish you would get someone, Lewis."

"I could do it," Tissie piped. "I'd like to ride a horse all day! I'm eight years old." They all laughed but Tissie, who grumbled, "I might have known. Girls can't do this and girls can't do that." Then, abruptly, Tissie's way of doing everything, she shot Margaret a cheery smile. "I just thought I'd try, Mama."

"I know what you thought, Tissie. I always know what my tomboy's thinking."

"Don't be too sure. Sometimes I think surprising thoughts."

"We all do," Lewis laughed. "But I still believe your mother knows—even our surprising thoughts."

"You make me sound most peculiar," Margaret said.

"Come on, Mama, you love being the smartest one in the family," Seton teased. "Stay that way."

Only half smiling, Margaret took a deep breath of moist, river air and let her gaze move slowly from one to another of the eight people—the children and Lewis—who made up her world. She did *not* know everything they thought. She wouldn't want to, except that knowing might help her love them more creatively. And—knowing Seton, as she so longed to know him—would in a way she couldn't explain, help her own heart.

She smiled at them all and hugged her little friend Maggie.

* * *

Sitting in her nightdress on the side of their bed after
Lewis had already tucked in, Margaret said, "Darling, I feel
uneasy about George. How long has it been since we last
heard from him?"

"Oh, not quite a month. But we both thought he sounded
happier. Busy with his parishioners. As much in love with
Mary as ever. Why?"

"I guess I'm just a mother hen."

"You're not a mother hen, but you do get uneasy feelings
about George so often it makes me wonder. You've always
been so close to L.I. and Tina—still they don't prey on your
mind the way George does."

"I think so often about—your Augustina, too." He pulled
her down in the bed beside him. "I do," she went on. "She's
still very real to me. Because she is, I—I feel some sort of
added responsibility for George."

"She always did, too."

"You never told me that."

"I guess the occasion just didn't come up. Augustina was a
happy-hearted girl. But, she worried about George's moodiness. Even then."

"It doesn't hurt quite so much to talk about her now, does it?"

"No. She's—well, it's as though she were a part of *our*
early days together. I'm healed, Margaret, thanks to you."

Snuggled now under the covers beside him, she lay patting
his chest for a time. Then she said pertly, "We have another
guest coming tomorrow and he's coming because he saw my
advertisement in the Philadelphia paper. Isn't that exciting?
One lone man. Mr. George Causey of Pennsylvania. I wonder what he'll be like?"

"Who knows? At least, he recognized a good thing when he
saw it in the paper."

Her mind already off Mr. Causey, Margaret sighed. "I miss
Louisa. I miss L.I. I miss Tina. But, oh, Lewis, sometimes I
miss George so much it hurts. I hope he's all right."

He held her head close against his shoulder. "I'm sure he's
fine. And, I'm also sure it's time for a hard-working someone
I know—and love—to go to sleep. Right now."

Along with their Pennsylvania guest, rail-thin, graying Mr.
George Causey, the steamboat captain brought three letters
for the Flemings. When Seton had taken Mr. Causey to his
room, Margaret and Lewis turned their attention to the mail:

One letter was from L.I., one was from St. Mary's, Georgia, in neither George's nor Mary's handwriting, and the third was for Seton from Major Micah Jenkins, principal of King's Mountain Military School in South Carolina.

Standing in the winter sun just below Margaret's double row of myrtles, they looked at each other, dread in both their faces.

"Well," Margaret said, forcing a smile. "Seton will want to open it himself. It's his mail, after all. His—acceptance, I don't doubt."

Lewis took a deep breath. "Yes. And another hard good-bye for us."

"Who could be writing to us from St. Mary's?" Margaret wondered, her voice as cheerful as she could make it. "While we wait for Seton to settle Mr. Causey, let's open L.I.'s letter. We always know what will lift our spirits."

"I don't have my spectacles, my dear. You'll have to do it."

"It's short, as usual."

She broke the seal. " 'Dear Miss Margaret and Papa, I am shy on time, but with much good news. I have just been appointed state's attorney and, although I will write details later, I wanted you to know. Your loving son, L.I.' "

"Well, well, well!" Lewis said, his face glowing.

"Just think of it—our L.I., the attorney for the whole state of Florida! Oh, there comes Seton now. Seton! Seton! Hurry. There's great, good news!"

Out of breath from lugging Mr. Causey's trunk, Seton raced up calling, "What? What's the good news?"

"L.I. is the new state's attorney!" Lewis exclaimed.

"Hurrah for old L.I.! Now, we can all get into all the trouble we like and he'll get us out. What else came in the mail?"

"Your letter, son," Margaret said, handing it to him. "The one you've been waiting for."

Seton's smile vanished and his hands trembled as he broke open the letter and began to scan it in silence. Then, the smile returned, brighter than ever as he picked up his mother and whirled her off the ground. "I'm in! They've accepted me. I leave in time for the summer term no later than May 15. Papa, congratulate me!"

Lewis shook his hand, then hugged him. "I do, son. I'm proud—not only because they accepted you. I expected that. I'm proud because you've earned your own tuition. You're a big, big help to your old father."

"Lewis, you're not old!"

He laughed. "I certainly don't feel old today after so much good news."

"What's the other letter?" Seton wanted to know.

"Oh, it's from someone in St. Mary's. I don't even recognize the name on the outside. A Mr. James Steward." She frowned. "Do you suppose someone from St. Mary's wants to rent a room with us?"

"Read it, Margaret."

As she was opening the letter, Lewis suddenly snapped his fingers. "I know who James Steward is. He's an Elder at George's church. Don't you recall that George mentioned his name so often when he used to write all about those dull Session Meetings?"

Abruptly, frowning, Margaret handed the letter to Seton. "You read it. I'm—suddenly afraid!"

Grinning his teasing grin, Seton took the letter. "All right, I'll read it. 'Dear Colonel and Mrs. Fleming, It is my sorrowful duty to inform you—that—our pastor—your son, Reverend George Fleming, died—' "

"No!" Margaret grabbed the letter, her face ashen. "It's not true, Lewis! There's been a terrible mistake . . ."

"Please read the letter, Seton." Lewis's voice was clipped, almost sharp. Supporting Margaret, he waited. "Seton?"

Tears overflowed Seton's eyes as he read: " 'Reverend George Fleming died—suddenly, as he was dressing preparatory—to visiting—a sick member of our congregation.' "

"Suddenly . . ." Lewis whispered.

"Yes, Papa. 'He did not suffer and the doctor believes it was his heart.' "

"His beautiful, sensitive—troubled heart," Margaret said, sounding far away.

" 'We of the church extend to you and yours our deepest sympathy and the promise of our prayers in your hour of grief. Your—fine—son is in the Presence of the Lord he loved. Mrs. Mary Fleming, his widow, will be—bringing his body to Hibernia—two days from the date of this letter.' That's—about all," Seton said brokenly. "And—that's—tomorrow, Mama, Papa. Mary will be—bringing George—home tomorrow."

In the late afternoon of the day they buried George near his mother, Augustina, in the Hibernia cemetery, Margaret knocked softly on his widow's door.

"It's Margaret Fleming," she called. "May I come in?"

When Mary opened the door, Margaret embraced her. Mary did not return the embrace.

"Is there anything I can do for *you*, Mary?"

In answer, Mary turned and walked to the window overlooking the river. Standing ramrod straight, her black silk mourning dress caused her to look smaller, even more unapproachable.

"I loved him so much, too," Margaret said. "I loved George—so dearly. And I'm—here. If you need me."

Slowly, Mary turned around, her eyes red-rimmed, swollen. "I'll—be going back to St. Mary's tomorrow," she said. "I need only one thing from you, Mrs. Fleming. I need to know that you are sure—how terribly I loved George. How—he loved me." A bitter smile jerked at the corners of her almost perfect mouth. "Why he—chose to leave me—just when we were beginning to be—even closer—I'll never know."

"Mary, we don't choose. God does."

Mary lifted her hand. "None of that, please."

"George is with God now. Doesn't that make you want to—come a little closer to Him yourself?"

"I know you mean well, Mrs. Fleming, but tonight I am angry at God—if He exists. No two people were ever so close as George and I—just three nights ago. If God chose this for us, He is a cruel God."

For the next several days after Mary Fleming had gone back to St. Mary's and then to her family at the North for an indefinite stay, Margaret alternated between near anger and relief that there were strangers in the house. Mary had insisted upon such a quick burial that Louisa, Tina, L.I.—no one had time to get there. And so, day after day, letters of comfort poured in. The boarders varied in their reactions. It was, of course, awkward—hard, to grieve before strange eyes. Difficult for the guests, too, Margaret knew, to be exposed on holiday to the kind of sorrow that hung over Hibernia. Certain guests tried to help. One stood out—Mr. George Causey.

More than once since Causey's unobtrusive arrival on the same boat which brought the news of George's death, Lewis had mentioned the bean-pole skinny man to Margaret. "He doesn't say much. Nods, usually, when I happen to see him walking the verandas or the yard. But Causey's nod and friendly smile say more than most of these poor folk when they take ten minutes to extend their sympathy. As soon as I have the chance, I'm going to get better acquainted with him."

A small chance to know George Causey better came suddenly and at the moment of still another tragedy. One month after George died, old Pompey died alone in the tight, tidy little cabin where he'd lived for most of his life with Maum Easter. Rina, Betty's daughter, had been the one to find the dead body of her grandfather as she had found Easter. Right after Lewis had comforted the child and sent her to fetch her mother, along the path between Margaret's double row of water oaks near the quarters, ambled George Causey—straw hat on his head as straight as a die.

"Couldn't help hearing what the little girl said about old Pompey, Colonel Fleming," he said in his thin, reedy voice, extending his hand. "You've had a peck of sorrow lately. Hope you'll call on me if there's anything I can do. Time's no good on a man's hands. You're welcome, sir, to my time and my hands."

The early May morning when Seton said good-bye to the whole Fleming family, everyone managed a smile. There was much joking and teasing and crying and hugging and kissing and then the boat came and he was gone.

As always, when Seton went away, some of the Hibernia light dimmed for Margaret. But, so soon after losing George, Lewis more than ever needed her capacity to hope. And hope, she would manage.

"Seton left us his joy," she said, holding tightly to Lewis's arm as they walked slowly along the path from the dock that led to her crepe myrtle lane—rosy now, with new spring foliage. "I, for one, am going to make use of the boy's joy. Can you, dear Lewis? So much has happened to hurt you. Can you, even when we don't feel joyful—help me practice Seton's joy?"

"I'll try, my dear. I'll try."

"I've thought so much about—understanding him. And, do you know, I've decided that I don't for a minute believe that he really—hates. He couldn't. He's too happy-natured."

"Perhaps it isn't hatred. I'd rather call it loyalty, devotion, pride in his Southern roots. But, one thing I know—when a man fights, when he's expected to kill another human being, a kind of hatred *has* to spring momentarily to his heart. It's a form of self-defense. If a man's a soldier, he will, in wartime, be expected to kill. Even a good man *has* to have at least the momentary help of—hatred."

Margaret stopped walking and made him look at her. "Never, never speak that way again, do you hear me? Lewis—do you hear me? You may be right. You're a man and I'm a woman. Seton's a man. But God is God and—" She began to sob helplessly and Lewis, before one of the few remaining winter guests or the children came running to see what was wrong, led her swiftly up the front steps, across the veranda and back to their room where they could do their weeping alone.

By the end of May, when there was sure to be spring weather at the North, all their guests were gone but one. George Causey remained and because they had grown so fond of the gentle, caring, courteous man, everyone had been cautioned not to ask when he planned to leave.

At dinner one night early in June, after the children had excused themselves from the table, Causey broached the subject himself. "Don't think I don't notice and appreciate that all of you nice Flemings have taken to eating your dinner down here in the guest dining room to keep me from eating alone," Causey said.

"Oh, we enjoy it, Mr. Causey," Margaret said.

"My wife is right, sir."

Causey toyed with a spoon for a moment, made the imprint of a few triangles on the tablecloth with the handle, then said slowly, "Well, I've been meaning to ask—if there's any particular time you folks want all boarders off the place."

"Why, no," Lewis laughed. "Naturally, most of our tourists are here in the winter, but Hibernia is open all year round. You're more than welcome. In fact, I'll hate to see you go, Causey."

"Oh, I wasn't planning to go anytime soon. That is, if you're sure you and your family don't want to be by your-selves after all the strangers you've had for so many—difficult months."

"These have been difficult times for us," Margaret said, "but I honestly think we've all been better off having our people. And, you, sir, have been most welcome. Colonel Fleming has told me often how fond he's grown of you."

Causey smiled, his paper-thin face crinkling. "Now, is that a fact! Well, I'll tell you what I've been turning over in my mind. I'm alone. Got no family at all. My wife's dead. My only son's been dead since he was in his late twenties." He nodded. "That's one reason I could feel so for you folks when your son George passed. Nobody's expecting me to go back to Pennsylvania at any time. Nobody needs me—anywhere—for anything. I'm not a man of means. I saved for this trip. Saved all the last year I worked and now I'm on a small pension from the ironworks where I kept books. I like this place. It's—come to be home to me. I like all you people. Sincerely. I like to garden. I'm sixty-six years old. Skinny as a fishing pole, but strong as an ox. Right good with my hands. Pompey's gone. Seton's away now. I'd help out all I could if you'd feel you need me. What I'm saying is, I'd like to stay and work for my keep. Nothing extra. Just my keep."

Margaret's face held such a look of delight, relief and hope that Lewis felt completely free to reach for George Causey's dry, warm hand. "That will be splendid, Mr. Causey!"

"Oh yes!" she agreed.

"In fact, I'd already told my wife I thought I'd better look around for someone to help us out."

Causey nodded. "Well, I hope it will be fine for you folks. I know it will be for me. I'm greatly obliged. And, by the way, I don't usually talk so much as I have tonight."

"I like to talk to you, Causey," Lewis said. "In fact, one of these evenings when our work is done, there are several things I'd like to hear your opinion on."

"Troubles you some that your boy Seton wants to rid the world of Yankees, doesn't it?"

"Frankly, yes. It does," Margaret said. "And yet, he's been so kind to all of you—from the North here with us."

"That's entirely different for him, I'd say." His dry chuckle came. "They've been some peculiar folks here, but not one of 'em took out after Southerners. They paid their money to be among you. Just as I did. A lot of Seton's fever is due to his brain being young, noble and brighter than most, I'd say."

Margaret laughed a little. "Why, you've helped me already, Mr. Causey. You have. I—I'm afraid I don't always understand our son. Maybe he's so—radical only because he's young. Maybe in a few years—"

"If we make it for a few years, Mrs. Fleming."

"Do you want to elaborate on that, sir?" Lewis asked. "My wife is one woman who can discuss any subject. She and I talk everything over. On an equal basis. Some don't understand that, but it's our way."

"Be glad to elaborate. Fact is, it won't take long at all. Strikes me as simple. This country, since the death of Daniel Webster and Henry Clay hasn't had any real leadership.

Everybody's out for himself. Back in Revolutionary times, we had a coastal north and a coastal south. But this was about all we had. Both small. Small enough so they banded together to help the country grow after the fighting with England ended. Different now. Sectionalism. No leadership for the nation. Everybody's out to better himself. Southerners want more representation in Washington. Need more territory to have it. You know how they even tried to get Cuba and Mexico, to make 'em slave states. Up north, Abolitionists yelling against Southerners. Everybody fighting, fuming, to protect his own interest. I'm an American. Born in Pennsylvania, but if I stay here, Florida'll be my state because the United States is my country." He cleared his throat. "That's just about the size of it, I reckon. Don't usually talk that much."

"We welcome your opinion," Lewis said. "We're Southerners. Both born Spanish subjects, in fact. Spain owned East Florida when we came along. Then we lived in an American territory. Now the state of Florida. The United States is our country too."

"My husband fought in the final trouble with the Seminoles, but only to protect his home. Only to protect Hibernia. We're *not*—war-minded." She shuddered. "If there's anything I truly hate—it's war."

"There's a difference, my dear," Lewis said gently, "between hating something—everyone hates the idea of war—and being fired with the desire to protect that which you hold dear."

She sighed. "I know. I get too excited. Too stirred up. Mr. Causey is going to think I'm foolish—just another foolish woman. But—"

"Never!" Causey said with the nearest thing to passion he'd shown to date. "I've watched you too closely during these trying times, Mrs. Fleming. Nope. You're strong. But the truth as I see it is we've only got sectional spokesmen now. Seward, Summer and Chase in the North. Toombs and Jeff Davis down here. Sectional spokesmen, not leaders. Now, maybe I'm tromping on toes when I say that about Jefferson Davis, but he is sectional. Every man for his own good. North and South, East and West. That kind of thing tears apart—we need mending. This country needs a good piece of mending."

"I take it you don't think President Buchanan is up to that kind of job," Lewis said.

"Don't think he is—or he'd be doing it. He's a Northern

man. But very amenable to the South here and there. Maybe weak, maybe just trying a compromise when it's too late for one."

"Too late?"

"Too late without a real leader." Causey stood up, as did Lewis and Margaret. "I've worn you out," he said. "Only one more thing. You'll need my room on the second floor. I enjoy fixing up a place. With your permission, I'll repair and paint Pompey's cabin."

"Oh, you wouldn't be required to live in the quarters, sir."

"I know it. But I don't hold a thing against the colored folks. Specially not the type you've got here. I've looked at the cabin. Stout. Roof's good. Floor's good. No use letting it go to waste." He grinned his thin, pleasant grin. "I'd sleep better tonight than any night since I've been here if I knew tomorrow I could light into fixin' up that cabin."

Part Five

1859–1865

38

Not quite all the guests who stopped at Hibernia, or with
Louisa in St. Augustine, were Northerners. By 1859, both
houses were receiving a few well-to-do people from Georgia
and South Carolina. In fact, Florida's permanent population
was growing by leaps and bounds and most of the new
settlers came from those two states. Lewis believed that the
trend of Florida politics and economics—the very thinking of
many Floridians—had begun to be strongly swayed by the
viewpoints of the Georgians and South Carolinians who visited or settled there. Of course, they brought along their
deeply rooted Southern traditions and states'-rights philosophy. Some of that philosophy, the more insular part, was new
to Margaret and Lewis. Native Floridians of their generation
had, after all, been born Spanish subjects. Even residing in a
state instead of a territory was comparatively new to them.
And to Louisa Fatio. Sophia, being Sophia, gave politics and
economics little or no thought whatever. As always, she dwelt
on needlework, flowers, poetry and cousins.

In letters exchanged during the period since Seton had
begun to espouse his rigid states'-rights beliefs, the senior
Flemings and Louisa agreed to move slowly, to weigh matters carefully, to wait until their own opinions had time to
form. States' rights endorsed the absolute right of a man to
his property and, by law, slaves were the property of plantation owners. Lewis was a plantation owner who owned some
of his people. But, at Hibernia there were also free Negroes.
Men and women who willingly worked for their keep, as did
George Causey, a white man from the North.

"Lewis and I are thinking more deeply than ever and we
are praying for God's guidance," Margaret wrote to Louisa
late in the year. "Seton, so sincerely convinced of the right-
ness of the influential South Carolina faction now in Florida,
grows more adamant with each letter from military school in

Yorkville. I'm proud of him, though. He is doing brilliantly in his studies and has been appointed orderly sergeant of his company, the highest rank attainable by any cadet. He finishes in a few weeks and I am overjoyed that he will be home for Christmas—I pray not too restless to settle down for a time here at Hibernia before temporarily entering L.I.'s law office in Jacksonville, where Frank is doing so well. I pray, too, that Seton's rigid political views will not prevent his handling the work L.I. has for him. One thing I know, Seton *does* influence both Frank and Frederic. They idolize him. I am blessed that my three oldest sons are young men of courage and patriotism. I merely hope for cool heads."

When Seton came home, Lewis listened to him attentively, but still urged caution. His son, he had no doubt, once he entered his brother's law practice in Jacksonville, would affiliate with the growing radical wing of the Democratic party—the rabid state's-righters. Carefully, Lewis pleaded with him to wait, to get his bearings in the city, to become acquainted with its people.

"You're wasting your time, Papa," Seton said, only half teasing, "by reading those Northern newspapers. Subscribe to them for your Yankee guests. That's fine. But you and I, as true Southerners, need only our own patriotic papers. The Whig party's a thing of the past now. You might just as well jump into my wing of the Democrats." Seton's words were inflammatory, but the sunny smile kept Lewis off guard. "We're on the winning side. God's side. You're my father and I respect you, but I hate to see you poison your mind with even a news item about that wild man John Brown and his madness at Harpers Ferry, Virginia. Honest, I'm just trying to look after you."

Lewis returned the smile. "I'm thinking, Seton. Your mother and I are of the generation that ponders a long time before we jump—either way."

"You're right. There *are* only two ways. Oh, we've got several parties—splinter groups. But the line is drawn between those black Republicans of the North—Lincoln's people—and true Southern Democrats. You really have no choice, now, have you? If that man Lincoln is elected president next year, Papa, there'll be a war between North and South just as sure as my name's Fleming!"

"Say what you like to me," Lewis spoke firmly. "But I

forbid you to speak that way before your mother. Is that understood?"

"Yes, sir. I hear you."

"But, do you understand me?"

The young man thought a moment. "No, I'm not sure that I do. Mama is perfectly able to face facts." The smile flashed again. "I may not understand you, but I love you, Papa. No son ever loved his parents more than I love you and Mama. Whatever happens, I truly hope you both might have cause to be proud of me."

"We are proud of you. Now, tell me—and let me break the news to your mother. When will you be leaving us for Jacksonville?"

"In one more week. You see, I'm keeping a promise to William. I'm eager to be off, but he has my word that I'll stay until I finish the new cart I'm building for him."

"That's like you." Lewis sighed heavily. "Well, we *should* be accustomed to saying good-bye to you by now, son. The truth is, we'll never be."

The first two newspapers to reach Hibernia after Abraham Lincoln of Illinois was elected president in November 1860, were the *St. Augustine Examiner* and the *Fernandina East Floridian*. Both papers called for the secession of Florida and predicted that Lincoln would be burned in effigy in many parts of the state.

"A secession flag is already flying here," Louisa wrote from St. Augustine, "and many of our citizens are wearing blue cockades. It all seems too quick and too impetuous. There is even talk of forming vigilance committees to keep watch over our Northern visitors and, of course, our Negroes. I am deeply disturbed and, like the two of you, only want to be allowed to mind my own business. But how long will our guests from the North stay with us? Hibernia's guests longer than mine, I have no doubt, because of your blessed isolation. Already some of my choice people are planning early departures."

Margaret read that portion of Louisa's letter aloud at dinner. Maum Betty was listening openly at the dining room door, and because Lewis enjoyed his terse, sensible conversation, George Causey was still taking his meals with them. When Margaret finished reading, there was a heavy silence.

"What's everybody so still about?" five-year-old Belle demanded.

"I guess nobody knows what to say," Frederic offered. Unwilling ever to leave his brother William out of things, Frederic added, "How about you, William? What do you think of Cousin Louisa's news?"

William gave them all his wan smile. "I—wasn't—listening."

"Well, I was," Tissie said sharply. "Even at age eleven, a person knows there's going to be some kind of trouble in St. Augustine. I think Cousin Louisa and Cousin Sophia should shut up that big house and move in with us. We don't have enough people coming from the North to fill our rooms anyway!"

Margaret looked at Lewis. "I wonder if our people who've already made reservations—will cancel?"

"Only fifteen are coming anyway," Tissie exclaimed. "We'll be bankrupt!"

Lewis chuckled. "Where did you learn that word?"

"Seton taught it to me."

"We won't be bankrupt, honey, but we need the cash. No two ways about that."

"What are they mad about? Why are they watching Yankee guests and colored folks in St. Augustine?"

Maum Betty had contained herself as long as she could. "I tell you why, Miss Tissie. Everybody's lost hold of their senses, that's what."

"But, Maum Betty—*why*?" the girl persisted.

"Ain't nobody got thankful hearts no more, that's why. 'Cept us here at Hibernia. An' we gonna keep our thankful hearts or I'm gonna take a big switch to ever' single one of us!"

In a little over a week, because of the new telegraph line with a branch to Jacksonville, the Flemings received cancellations from every expected guest. No one was coming. Not from the North, not from Georgia or South Carolina.

Five days before Christmas, South Carolina seceded from the Union, followed early in the new year, 1861, by Georgia and five Gulf states: Mississippi, Alabama, Louisiana, Texas—and Florida. On a cold, gray day in February, delegates met at Montgomery, Alabama, and established the Confederate States of America, drafted a constitution and named Mississippi's Jefferson Davis president. The cry went up: "No power on earth dare make war on us. Cotton is King!"

In his inaugural address in March, Abraham Lincoln answered the South: "The government will not assail you. You can have no conflict without being yourselves the aggressors."

On April 12, General Beauregard of South Carolina fired upon the United States at Fort Sumter. Union Major Robert Anderson, in command of the fort, refused to evacuate. War had begun.

Almost at once, the still wavering states, Maryland, Delaware, Kentucky and Missouri chose the Union. Virginia, North Carolina, Tennessee and Arkansas joined the Confederacy.

Seton's prediction had unbelievably come to pass.

The news reached Hibernia at the end of April on the kind of soft, light-filled, pale green spring day which had always made Margaret believe most deeply in her obligation to hope. This day, she and Lewis sat by the river on Pompey's tree bench, the newspaper still in Lewis's hands—and stared, without seeing, out over the blue, sun-sprinkled water.

Finally, Lewis said, "I keep remembering what my old friend and commanding officer, Richard Keith Call, wrote to the people of Florida back when all this secession talk began. He not only called any thought of secession outright *treason* against Constitutional government, he didn't believe for a minute that Lincoln's election was the cause of it." He glanced again at the secession headline, then let the paper fall to the ground. "I wonder if secession didn't really come because of the long-cherished hatred of the federal government by our Southern politicians."

"There's that ugly word again," Margaret gasped. " 'Hatred.' I—can't bear our sons to hate—how can I bear for them to—go to war? Lewis—you know Seton will be one of the first to go!"

On July 10, the dreaded letter came from Jacksonville, signed by both Seton and Frank: "With all our hearts, we wish we had time to visit you at Hibernia before we leave. But we have both already enlisted and are mustered into the St. Augustine Rifles, Company H of the Second Florida Infantry. This was accomplished right here in Jacksonville and we depart for Virginia on 13 July. We are sure of victory. There is no means by which the brave spirit of the Confederacy can be dimmed. In fact, we see only the light of the glorious day ahead when God has honored us with His just triumph over the Yankee oppressors. Our cherished way of life *will go on*. And, undoubtedly, due to the certainty of our cause and our superior fighting abilities, we will be home with you even sooner than if we were staying here with our bossy brother, L.I., in his stuffy law office. If you can manage an immediate trip to Jacksonville, Papa, we will be happy. If not, we know we are followed by the prayers and love of both our adored parents. Without fail, we will do our best to keep the letters coming from the victorious fields of battle. Your loving sons, Frank and Seton."

Margaret longed to bury her face in Lewis's shoulder and cry out her pain. Instead, she made herself smile. "Seton wrote that letter. They've both signed it, but that's Seton in every line." She drew in a long, sob-shaken breath. "Frank will fight every bit as bravely, but—that analytical mind of his won't be as cocksure of—victory." Then, "Oh, Lewis—our sons!"

When he put his arms around her, she gave into her pain and for a long time they held each other and wept.

Finally, Lewis said, "Well, now. We must—think of something to do for them. I—I really am not up to making the trip, but—"

Margaret studied his tortured face. "Don't you feel well?"

"I'm not sick. Just sensible. This heat would get me before I reached Jacksonville, so why chance it?" He sighed heavily. "Maybe—letters are the best means of—saying good-bye anyway. I'll make up a small bundle for the boys and write to them this afternoon. Plenty of time to catch the evening boat on its way back to Jacksonville."

10 July 1861
Hibernia

My dear Seton and Frank,

I long to see you before you leave for Virginia, but the heat has made me feel a little feverish and unwell. Your mother and I wish you could both come here, if only for a day, but we know all you have to accomplish before departing. I am sending a bundle of woolen socks. You will find them most comfortable in damp weather on long marches. Let your old father give you a little of his experience in campaigning. On a march, in the morning eat but a light meal; never drink anything stronger than coffee, and water is best. When you eat but little, you will not suffer from thirst.

At night, make your best meal and wash your feet in cold water and put on dry socks. You will find tea very refreshing and easy to prepare. Morning and night retire to yourselves and offer up a prayer to your Heavenly Father for His protection and grace to do His will and guard you in the hour of danger. Do your duty to God and your country and all will be well.

> Your mother joins me in much love to you,
> Your affectionate father,
> Lewis Fleming

"Do you want to add anything, my dear?" Lewis asked when he had read his letter aloud to Margaret after their noon meal.

Words stuck in her throat. She shook her head no and patted his hand. Then, at the window, watching him limp down through the avenue of crepe myrtles toward the dock, his letter and the bundle of socks in his hand, she gave way to still more tears. That dear bundle of socks had done it. She cried so hard and so openly, Maum Betty came bustling from the back of the house to comfort her. Not with words. There were none. The loving, well-padded arms simply encircled and held her, the strong hand smoothing her back in firm, circular motions. For this dark moment, Maum Betty's special way of giving solace to the children, belonged solely to Margaret.

Margaret was waiting, her dependable little friend Maggie beside her, when Lewis came slowly back toward the Hibernia veranda.

"Is Papa sick?" Maggie asked.

"A little, darling. Like me, he's sick at heart."

"I'm sick at heart, too, Mama. I'm sad most of the time. And, it makes me even sadder when Frederic keeps fussing because he's too young to go to war." The child returned Margaret's hug. "We need Frederic here with us, don't we?"

"Of course, we need him. And—he's only sixteen. I'm sure the—war will be over before he's old enough to enlist."

"I hope so," Maggie said softly. "Mama?"

"Yes, dear?"

"I'm doing what you always tell us to do."

"What's that, Maggie?" Margaret answered absently, her mind on Lewis's tall, stooped figure limping toward them.

"I'm—really, truly—*hoping*," Maggie said in a firm voice.

Margaret looked at the child. The open, serious little face released something in her. Something she had buried without realizing it. "Maggie," she whispered. "Oh, Maggie, thank you! I do thank you. You've helped Mother more than you'll ever know."

"I have?"

"Yes. I dare not—*we* dare not—stop hoping!"

The girl gave her a shy smile. "I guessed that you had—kind of stopped, Mama."

Margaret embraced her little daughter. "How like you," she breathed. "Dear Maggie, you know—so much more than you—understand."

"Well, the socks are on their way," Lewis said, puffing up the front steps. "How are my two girls? Where are the others?"

"Tissie's washing Belle's hair," Maggie offered. "William's helping Frederic out at the barn."

"I—guess I should have—pushed myself and gone to say good-bye."

"You did exactly what you were supposed to do," Margaret scolded. "With both Frank and Seton away, all three of our men—you, William and Frederic—have to take good care of yourselves."

"Is Virginia a long way off, Papa?"

"Yes, Maggie." He sank into a porch chair. "Something like a thousand miles, I'd say. Depends on where our boys will go in Virginia." Abruptly, he took a letter from his jacket pocket and handed it to Margaret. "I'm sorry, my dear. My mind's on too many things today. It's from Louisa. Sit down on the steps with us, Maggie, while Mama reads what Cousin Louisa has to say about St. Augustine these ugly days."

"I guess," said Maggie thoughtfully, obeying her father, "that days can be ugly and beautiful at the same time, can't they?"

"Yes, darling," Margaret answered, opening the letter. "I'm glad you found that out so early in your life. Well, this is what our beloved Louisa has to say: 'First, I must let you know that Sophia and I are well and keeping our own peace.

The last, in spite of having our ears bent by frequent tirades from our good neighbor across the backyard, the Rebel Incarnate, Mrs. Judge Smith. Bless her, she rises in the mornings, I sometimes think, for one reason: To find yet another way to blame the Yankees for everything that's wrong in the world. Daily, I caution Sophia simply not to answer her. Mrs. Smith doesn't notice anyway. Her mind is ever on what she calls "the just Confederate Cause" and it would not surprise me to learn that she helps out that cause in more ways than meet the eye.' "

"I wonder what Cousin Louisa means by that?" Lewis interrupted.

"Hard to tell," Margaret shrugged. "Mrs. Judge Smith has high connections through her son, Major Kirby-Smith. Now, where was I? Oh, yes, Louisa's house is empty, of course, as is ours. And, she goes on: 'Sometimes I feel I might scream in this vacant, vacant house. I won't scream. I'd scare myself if I did, but my mind is cluttered with all manner of confusion typical of the city itself. Mr. Lincoln's blockade of our supply centers, Charleston and Savannah, and the total loss of cash money—gone with the desertion of our Northern visitors— keep us confused as to where the next meal may come from.' "

"Margaret!" Lewis interrupted. "Louisa and Sophia had better come here, as Tissie says, while they can still get away from the city. Why don't we insist that they come to us right now? I can't tolerate the thought that they're doing without because of that blockade."

"You know I'm always longing for them to come, but is it safe on the river?"

"Oh, yes. Our river's safe enough and they'll certainly be better off here. If you get a letter written tonight, I can get it on the morning boat."

"What else does Cousin Louisa say, Mama?"

"That's about all, Maggie. Except that—they sincerely hope—that Seton and Frank are still—with L.I. in Jacksonville." Margaret let her eyes wander out over the river. "Seems strange that Louisa doesn't know yet about Seton and Frank. I will write to her—this minute, Lewis." On her feet, she gave Maggie a knowing smile. "And—I'm really going to *hope* they'll come!"

Maggie returned the smile. "I'm proud of you, Mama."

"Thank you, little friend."

Inside the front door in the wide entrance hall, Margaret heard Maggie say, "Mama calls me her little friend an awful lot these days, Papa."

Lewis's reply: "I want you to promise me that you'll always, always be Mama's friend."

"Oh, yes, sir," Maggie said quickly, naturally. "I wouldn't know how to be anything else with Mama. I love her so much."

39

Throughout the late, muggy summer weeks, Lewis did his best to convince Margaret and Louisa, who, with Sophia, had arrived by mid-August, that there was no particular need to worry because Frank and Seton had written only once. Almost daily, as much, perhaps, to convince himself as to calm the ladies, he explained in detail about training camps—the war games—the long, exhausting marches. Over and over he repeated how sure he was that letter writing at the end of such days was all but impossible.

"You can be certain our boys had a head start on some of the city boys," he said resuming his efforts to ease Margaret's anxiety one early September morning before they were out of bed. "Growing up here on this island by the river, they're good swimmers, they can shoot, they're at home in the woods. But none of that means military training isn't hard on them." When Margaret only lay silent beside him, he plunged on. "Don't forget they'd both been cooped up in L.I.'s office for months. I'll wager all they think about at the end of one of those grueling days is sleep."

For a long moment, there was only the sound of William's Tricksie barking at a squirrel and the low, murmuring voices of Sophia and Louisa from the front veranda. Then, Margaret asked, "Lewis, how do we know they're still in training camp?"

"Because they haven't told us otherwise. Our sons will make every effort to keep us informed. They've never caused unnecessary worry, have they?"

"No." She nestled her head on his shoulder. "I know we

must get up, but, oh, your shoulder helps me far more than your earnest, dear words. I didn't sleep. My imagination goes wild once we put out the lamp at night. Nights are—much worse, aren't they?"

"Yes, my dear. Nights are the worst of all." He sighed wearily, more wearily than usual. "I do believe I could stay happily in this bed all day."

Sitting up for a better look at his face, Margaret asked nervously, "Are you—not feeling well again, darling?"

"Well enough, I guess." He smiled weakly. "Just very tired for some reason."

"Let me see your hands!"

"What's the matter with my hands for goodness' sake?"

"They're swollen! Give me the other one. Lewis, your fingers are—swollen. Puffy at the knuckles. Look."

"I'd rather look at you."

"Are you sure you're all right?"

He swung his legs out onto the floor. "There. How often do you see me able to swing that game leg so easily? Proves I'm fine, doesn't it? On your feet, Mrs. Fleming. Louisa and Sophia will be starving for breakfast and, after all, we brought them here to feed them."

Margaret and Sophia took the children on a picnic later that morning and Lewis and Louisa welcomed the chance to speak frankly alone.

"I keep nothing from Margaret," Lewis said, as they settled on the far end of the veranda in the shade of the thick jasmine vine, "except what I fear may worry her unduly."

"I'm the same way with her." Louisa arranged the long, full skirt of her gray cotton daydress and leaned her head against the high back of the rocking chair. "She's very brave. And, I'm happy to see, still deeply loved by my favorite cousin."

"She's my life," he said simply.

"You're hers. You and the children. Still, there are seven of them—and only one of you. She's loved you well, hasn't she?"

"Too well, perhaps. I'm sure I'm spoiled."

"Nonsense. But I'm not prepared to say Belle isn't—just a little."

Lewis laughed. "A little? My tiny carrot-top is spoiled

rotten. I hate to think how she'll lead some young man around by the nose one day."

"If—we have any young men left," Louisa said sadly. "Am I being an old maid pessimist, Lewis? I'd never say that to Margaret, but how long can the Confederate armies fight on only spirit and courage and patriotism?"

"Do you have a particular reason for that viewpoint, Cousin? You know our Southern papers and I haven't seen a Northern newspaper in months."

"I know only what I hear in St. Augustine. And—" she laughed a little, "my sources are not, to say the least, all rooting for the same side in this nasty war. My neighbor, Mrs. Judge Smith, is, of course, absolutely convinced—especially now that her son is Brigadier General Kirby-Smith, that it is only a matter of weeks before the Confederacy will have subdued every last Union soldier. But, as I said, all my connections there are not Confederate sympathizers."

"That brings to mind my longtime friend A. M. Reed. He's from the North. Settled years ago on a plantation downriver at Black Point. Used to come by every week or so. I'm sure his sympathies are with the North. I wish he'd visit me. I don't suppose he will."

"You could visit him. I often drop by the house of another St. Augustine friend who is anything but a Confederate. In a strange way, it helps me to talk with her. Like me, she's made close, abiding friendships up there. Lewis, we just can't suddenly begin to hate our friends because they don't hate the North!"

"That word 'hate' haunts Margaret. Me, too," he said thoughtfully. "I honestly did not hate the Seminoles. Why is—hatred necessary—except at the moment that trigger is pulled?"

"Oh, it has to do with wanting to be proven right. I suppose we feel superior if we find things to hate in those who disagree with us. If heads North and South had stayed level, no one would be pulling a trigger now. But, more to the point in a practical sense, Lewis, is that St. Augustine could any day fall right smack into the hands of the Unionists without a shot being fired!"

"Defenses that bad, eh?"

"There simply are none. I'm not the only one who wonders why the Yankees don't just land and take us over! We don't have any Confederate troops there to defend us. Most of the guns have been moved away from Fort Marion. Of course, Mrs. Smith won't admit it, but from odds and ends I've been able to piece together, I don't think the Confederacy could defend a foot of the Florida coast! The Yankees could land anywhere they pleased—Fernandina, Jacksonville, St. Augustine—they'd have a free hand. I wonder, frankly, what's stopping them?"

"They're not prepared for war either, I guess," Lewis answered. "And, my other neighbor, George Huston—a redhot Confederate who's hated Washington for years—rants and raves now every time he comes by here, because Florida's Governor Milton isn't doing more. I don't know what the governor can do. Heaven knows Florida doesn't have that kind of tax money to spend on munitions and supplies. Huston's in a rage because Milton has done nothing beyond plead with President Jeff Davis for help. Huston also swears that Lee has warned that he can protect only Charleston, Savannah and Brunswick. Where that leaves us—especially those of us who once earned our living from Northern guests—I'm sure I don't know." He rubbed his face with both hands. "Of course, I pray—I pray every night for victory wherever Seton and Frank may have to fight. If I never earn another penny from a Northerner on holiday, I pray for my sons' success." He shook his head. "It's all so crazy, Louisa. Really insane. Maybe not for the folks in Georgia, the Carolinas, Virginia—but it's insane for Florida. Tourists were our mainstay."

After a silence, Louisa asked, "Are you feeling quite well, Lewis?"

"Hm? Yes. Oh, I tire more easily if I try to work too long at a time. My bum leg aches a bit more. After all, I'll be sixty-three before this year is out."

She laughed. "Don't forget, I'm already sixty-three. But—your hands seem to look a bit puffy. Do they pain you? Rheumatism, maybe?"

"No. That's one ailment I still don't have, thank goodness." He examined his hands, made a fist, then extended his fingers. "My wife mentioned that today. Maybe they are a bit swollen. But if that were all I had on my mind, I'd be a still young sixty-three. I'm all right, Cousin. There'll never be a restful moment for either Margaret or me until our boys are home again—but otherwise, I'm fit as a fiddle."

* * *

The long-awaited letter, signed by both Seton and Frank, came just before Christmas. They were well. As yet, their company had seen no fighting. The news helped. At least, the brothers were still together.

Louisa, too, had received a letter from her Northern friend in St. Augustine, urging her to come home. So far as her friend could tell, St. Augustine would fall soon to the North. But the sisters stayed through Christmas—a quiet, subdued holiday without any plum pudding or Lady Baltimore cake because the blockade had begun now to affect Hibernia's supplies, too. There was almost no wheat flour left and no sugar except what Lewis was able to get from his Rebel neighbor, Huston. That was precious little, since almost all of Huston's slaves had been stolen or had fled to what they believed to be a Yankee haven. Northern forces had just captured Hilton Head Island in South Carolina and had made it their base for the South Atlantic Squadron under Flag Officer Samuel F. DuPont. Other Yankee onslaughts could well be only days away.

"DuPont needn't expect much resistance anywhere else," Louisa said, as she and Sophia waited with Lewis and Margaret for their boat. "A woman isn't supposed to know these things, but I'd wager DuPont can take both Fernandina and Jacksonville as easily as he will undoubtedly take St. Augustine." She smiled bravely. "That's why Sophia and I must get home. My property is valuable. I have to be there when the change of government takes place."

"You really don't think there will be any resistance?"

"No, Lewis. None. For a long time, it hasn't been *if* the Yankees will take St. Augustine. It's been—*when*."

Louisa was correct on all counts. Major General George B. McClellan, the North's ranking general in the East, before undertaking the difficult business of capturing Charleston, took Fernandina on March 3, 1862, with only a few shells lobbed after a fleeing train carrying the last evacuees from the city and Fort Clinch. Jacksonville fell next with even less trouble. On March 12, DuPont's warships were actually welcomed at the docks by a throng of relieved pro-Union Jacksonvillians who had been frightened half out of their wits during the night by a band of Confederate sympathizers who had burned sawmills and killed several people.

Lewis and Margaret, watching from their dock, could see the flames of the Jacksonville fires, and when heavy rains

drove them inside, neither slept. They were thankful that
L.I. had moved to Lake City and that before he left had seen
George's widow, Mary, on a boat for the North.

"I do hope the L'Engles are safe," Margaret said, as they
lay in bed wide-awake. "And, oh, Lewis, we must keep
praying for Louisa and Sophia! St. Augustine is bound to be
next. There are plenty of Confederate hotheads there to set
fire to the old city, too. Just to punish their Union neighbors.
I hope, oh, I hope they at least *think* Louisa and Sophia
are—Rebels."

Lewis sighed. "Our cousins are exactly where we are, my
dear—neither Unionists nor Rebels. They just want peace
enough to earn an honest living."

They waited two weeks for word from Louisa. Two weeks
of tense, anxious waiting and wondering. And then, her letter
came. The city of Augustine had begun to panic the day the
Yankee warship *Keystone State* was spotted off the bar at
sundown on March 8; and the next morning, when its commander sent a small boat to inspect the difficult channel and
the town more closely, communicants at Mass in the cathe-
dral ran shouting and weeping into the streets. But the panic
was premature. The *Keystone State*'s longboat returned to
the warship and in no time, mysteriously to some, the ship
left the harbor. Those who thought at all knew the Union
sailors were only testing the difficult St. Augustine bar for the
future takeover. "Then," Louisa wrote, "sure enough, early
on the morning of March 11, another Union warship, the
U.S.S. Wabash, appeared in our harbor. Sophia and I stood
at the waterfront with the others and watched its longboat
move in toward the city. As the small landing party rowed
past Fort Marion, the white flag of truce was acknowledged
from the old fort. There, another white flag was hoisted
above the ramparts—this one of surrender. Sophia and I
understood that the white surrender flag had been stitched
by Rebel Lizzie Smith's Union aunts, while poor Lizzie
seethed. My neighbor, Mrs. Judge Smith, was on hand, and,
of course, was also seething. When acting mayor, Christobal
Bravo, met the Yankee landing party at the wharf, ready to
surrender the city, dignified Mrs. Smith shouted: 'Look at
old Bravo, the low, ignorant Minorcan—shaking in his boots
and [making up] already to the cursed Yankees!' Then, Mrs.
Smith vanished from the crowd, along with Lizzie Smith and
Sally Hardy and a handful of other known Secessionist women

in town. The next morning, when the Union forces attempted to raise the Stars and Stripes in our Square, they found the flagpole chopped off at the ground! These ladies, armed with a sharp axe, in the dead of night, had gained for themselves, at least, the satisfaction that the hated Stars and Stripes would not fly above the Square until a new pole could be erected. They had knocked on our door hoping Sophia and I might accompany them on their mission. Needless to say, we did not. We are still simply doing what has to be done and watching, as much as possible, from the sidelines."

Almost overnight, after the surrender of the three key coastal cities, Lewis saw the tone of Secessionist editorials change from cocky certainty that their side would triumph in no time at all to solemn warnings of the long, hard struggle ahead. The government of the Confederacy simply no longer operated along the coastlands.

In April, Louisa wrote that although the change of government, certainly nothing new to St. Augustine, had gone rather smoothly, there had been trouble among the people themselves. Lines were drawn and positions reversed. Unionists among the town's residents, who had stayed inside and kept their mouths shut before the surrender, now felt free to express their sentiments and as Confederate supporter Hannah Jenckes said of St. Augustine's women, with some irony, "We are beginning the game of 'rise ladies and change places' and between two stools your humble servant is coming to the ground!" Even Mrs. Judge Smith had been warned by her illustrious son, Confederate General Kirby-Smith, to behave herself and to obey the Federal authorities so long as they were in charge. His words, Louisa thought, would run off Frances Smith's back like water. They did. The Episcopal rector of Trinity, the church Louisa attended, in spite of his Rebel sympathies, was ordered and agreed to pray for President Abraham Lincoln and the Army of the United States. As he spoke the opening words of the first enforced prayer, Mrs. Judge Smith marched up the aisle and out of the church declaring she'd never attend services where prayers were offered for "Old Abe." She kept her word. In fact, she split the church's loyalties and agitated until the rector left town.

"We are divided horribly," Louisa wrote, "but what makes it bearable is that in some cases, even with my neighbor, friendship holds. We will exchange visits in spite of her frustration at not knowing where I stand. Mrs. Smith is, above all, a lady and that helps. Especially does it help Sophia, who just tries not to think of which side is in charge of the city or anything else. Bless her, she permits as little change in her daily life as possible. For the rest of us, there is no choice but to obey whatever authorities are here. I find the Union soldiers and officers most courteous and, although they are cracking down on anything that resembles treason against the Union, we have no real trouble. To my knowledge, our mail is not censored, but how I long to see you. Travel, because of the threat to the Union of spies in the area, is, of course, out of the question. But the Unionists have supplied us well with food. No one is hungry any longer in St. Augustine. And many were."

40

During the spring of 1862, Seton and Frank fought side by side in Virginia through the Battle of Peach Orchard and into Williamsburg. Their letters had been few and so brief, about all Lewis and Margaret knew for certain was that they were all right and still in the same company. Then, no letters came until Frank's long one to L.I. dated May 10, written from "near Richmond." Having heard that the St. Johns River was now in control of the enemy, Frank had sent the letter to Lake City, where L.I. was serving as judge advocate of the Confederacy with the rank of major, asking him to forward it by some means to Hibernia. The letter reached them on a mild, bright morning in late May at the hand of their longtime neighbor to the north, A. M. Reed of Mulberry Grove at Black Point.

"Glad to see you appear pleased to have a visit from a Union sympathizer like me, Colonel," Reed called good-naturedly to Lewis, who had been waiting on the Hibernia dock since his first glimpse of Reed's fine sailing boat. "I knew you'd want this letter from Frank at the earliest possible moment." Reed tossed a rope to Lewis and leaped onto the dock to shake hands.

"And why wouldn't I be glad to see you?" Lewis said, pumping his old friend's hand. "Things get a bit lonely around here. My wife and I feel pretty cut off most of the time. She'll welcome this letter. We're most anxious about our boys. But I find out so little—can you tell me how things are in Jacksonville under Union occupation? We haven't seen a paper in days."

"You are behind. Jacksonville is back under the Confederacy."

"You can't mean that!"

"I certainly do mean it. The river is still Union—I'm sure you and Mrs. Fleming see their gunboats patrolling up and down. I'm free, as a Union sympathizer, to make my way by water from my place to St. Augustine—also still Union. But the Federal troops just up and left Jacksonville the first part of last month. I had to send some of my people to close my house there. Moved everything to Mulberry Grove, where it's safe."

"Did you lose your city house?"

"I don't know. I attended a bank meeting in Lake City a few days ago, but nothing was known about Jacksonville property yet. By the way, that's where you son, L.I., gave me the letter for you. L.I. says the news in that letter is as good as can be expected."

"I'm ever so grateful. Is my son all right?"

"Looked fine. Sends his best to all of you here. And—Fleming, it makes a man feel good to know old friendships like ours still hold. I wish I could go up to the house and pay my respects to Mrs. Fleming, but"—his smile faded—"everyone on the river except me—is suspect. Anyway, I'm en route to St. Augustine."

Lewis smiled sadly. "I know I don't dare leave my dock anymore. Having two sons in the Confederate forces, I don't feel it's safe—or sane—for me to be at any place but right here."

"It probably isn't," Reed said, shaking his head. "They've changed our good, neighborly lives, haven't they?"

"Maybe more than you and Mrs. Reed realize. If you see my cousin, Miss Louisa Fatio, in St. Augustine, take our love, please."

After Reed's boat had moved away from the dock, Lewis hurried to the house with Frank's letter.

To avoid the children's questions, he and Margaret took chairs on the veranda. Her hands shaking, Margaret unfolded the closely written pages. She scanned the first page and

Lewis saw the horror on her face before she'd read one line aloud.

"What, Margaret? What?"

" 'We are in retreat from the battle of Yorktown and Williamsburg,' " she read in a tight voice, " 'in which Seton was—severely—wounded—and is now—in the hands of—the Yankees . . .' "

As though to escape the ugly truth, she jumped up and began to hurry aimlessly about the porch. Lewis caught her as she swayed too near the front steps and led her back to the rocker. "Please, Margaret—sit down. I have my spectacles—I'll read the rest of it."

Staring at nothing, she nodded.

Nervously, Lewis settled his spectacles in place and, seated beside her again, began to read: " 'I must tell you right off, though, that Seton's wound is not mortal and that is the word of the two surgeons who examined him. The ball entered to the left of the backbone—and—came out—just above Seton's right hip. It did not break a bone and so far as could be ascertained, did not injure the intestines. Our general would not allow me to remain with him as I longed to do, but I left him at the house of a kind lady in Williamsburg, who I have no doubt will take good care of him. But, now, to tell you about the fight. We left Yorktown last Saturday and marched—' "

"No! No, Frank," Margaret cried. "Don't—write—about—the fighting!" She broke into uncontrollable sobs. "Tell—us—about *Seton!*"

Handling the pages as best he could with one hand, while steadying Margaret with the other, Lewis hurried through Frank's account of the Battle of Williamsburg—the long, hard march in nearly knee-deep mud and rain along the York Road at 2 A.M.—the soldiers forced by lack of time to double-step. Lewis's hand trembled so that he dropped a page to the floor, and leaning out of the rocker to pick it up, he actually felt the pain in his sons' legs on that march, the ache in their backs, the sandy burning in their sleepless eyes. At the end of Frank's battle account—Seton had been hit while trying to retrieve the body of his fallen commanding officer—Lewis turned to Margaret. She was sitting motionless, her eyes riveted, unseeing, on the bright water of the St. Johns.

"My dear, I've come to more about Seton."

Woodenly, she turned to look at Lewis.

"It seems that Seton and three of his comrades risked their

lives to bring back the dead body of Colonel Ward, their commanding officer. They were almost back to their own lines when Seton was struck. The three left him behind, believed him dead. Frank would not accept that. He ran to where Seton lay and found him alive and conscious."

"Thank God," she breathed. "And—thank you, dear Frank."

"Do you want to hear the rest of it now? Or later?"

"*Now*, Lewis!"

"Frank writes: 'I got some men and a litter and took him to a house near Williamsburg at dawn, where I remained with him until quite late that night, waiting for an ambulance to take him to the hospital. It did not come. We carried Seton on a litter to another private home in the dead of night. That is where the two surgeons examined him. The lady of the house was as kind as any lady could be. I left in search of a conveyance, since I wanted him in a hospital, but I failed to find one and while on my way back to Seton, General Stewart met me and ordered me on with the army. I begged to return to my brother. The general explained that the Yankees were fast advancing on the town and that Seton, being wounded, would be cared for, but I, if found, would become a Yankee prisoner. I did not see Seton again. It was the hardest thing I've ever had to do to leave him. But, I am trusting God and that kind, kind lady. Seton was so cheerful and made so little complaint that my hopes of his speedy recovery are great. His only regret was that he had been wounded after having done so little fighting for the Confederacy. I have now learned that Seton would have been elected major had he not been wounded and left behind.' "

Lewis stopped reading to look at Margaret. She was more herself now, cheeks wet with tears, but on her face, a quiet expression of pride. "It—would be just like Seton, wouldn't it, Lewis—to be cheerful, to make no—complaint . . ."

"Yes. Just like him. And how tragic that he missed being promoted to major."

She stood up. "I don't care if he's ever—a major! He's *alive*. A kind lady is caring for him and—if I know Seton, she already adores the ground he walks on." A sob caught in her voice. "If—he can—walk."

"I'm sure he can by now. He's young. With care, he'll heal quickly. Of course, he is in Yankee hands."

"No!" Her chin went up. "He's in God's hands, Lewis."

* * *

June and nearly all of July passed with no direct word of Seton. Frank wrote three times—at least three letters reached them. He had heard no more of Seton, but Frank was well and, for the time being, in the Quartermaster's Corps under their relative by marriage, Captain Edward L'Engle. Margaret cried no more tears and for the children's sake, she and Lewis seldom mentioned Seton, except when they were alone.

Throughout that anxious spring and summer, they had watched and wondered, as at least three times a week, black-hulled Federal gunboats patrolled up and down in front of Hibernia—the square-riggers *Ottawa*, *Pembina*, and *Seneca* sailed silently, eerily past, and at other times , the quiet, deep waters of the St. Johns were churned by the powerful sidewheels of the armed steamers *Ellen* and *Darlington.* They knew nothing of these boats beyond the fact that they were part of DuPont's South Atlantic Blockading Squadron and that they were on the prowl for Confederate spies and blockade runners trying to bring supplies to Hibernia and neighboring Confederate plantations. George Huston vowed that the Yankees, those aboard each patrolling gunboat had them all under surveillance—Huston, his wife, his people, Lewis, Margaret, Causey and the older children—as Confederate spies. Reed, in his gentlemanly way, had as much as said so, too.

Just after sunrise on August 1, Margaret was on her knees by the bedroom window, praying for strength and courage to hail the sun again. Pleading with God for the will to hope through one more anxious day. Begging for deliverance from the fear which twisted within her—even as she prayed. Struggling to *feel* thankful that she still had her girls, William, Frederic—and Lewis. And—her home at Hibernia.

Her prayer ended, she waited, as her custom had always been, for God to give her His assurance that He had heard. She was still on her knees when the shots rang out. Distant, repeated—splitting the quiet morning. She jumped to her feet. Silence. Then, Frederic called to his father, who had gone to the barn early, and the shots came again—six, seven—ten. Blessedly she heard Lewis answer Frederic. Margaret's body slumped in relief. They were all right. The shots, she should have realized, were too far away to harm her family, but fear gnawed constantly at the edges of her mind. She had been terrified and was now weak with relief.

At the window, she called to Lewis. "Where were those shots?"

"Sounded as though they came from Huston's place," he called back.

She reached the big yard in time to hear Lewis forbid Frederic to ride to the plantation to find out. And for one of the few times in his entire life, she saw her son Frederic angry. He obeyed his father, but for the remainder of the day, he sulked. When at the noon meal they spoke of the gunfire, Frederic left the table.

"Why, Lewis? Why did Frederic do that? He's always so—strong and—in control of himself."

"I know why, Mama," Maggie said.

"You do, Maggie?" Lewis asked gently.

"I'm pretty sure I do. Frederic is very unhappy because he isn't fighting the war with Seton and Frank. He told me he was really angry. He feels old enough. When you wouldn't let him ride to Mr. Huston's place, I guess it just made him madder than ever"

Lewis took a deep breath and let it go slowly, wearily. "Maggie, I think you're right. In fact, I know you are. Frederic is seventeen now and it's time we all faced up to the fact that he won't be here with us much longer."

Margaret gasped.

"Frederic will be enlisting soon. We've all known he would the minute he was old enough." Lewis reached for her hand. She jerked it back. For the first time, she jerked away from him. "I know how you feel, Margaret. But nothing—not even you, my dear, can keep the boy from going to help his brothers. Frederic's a man now."

"He is not. He's a boy."

"He's working long hours to help Causey finish shoring up the big barn. I expect him to go next month."

"I'll still be here, Mama," Maggie said. "I can do a lot to look after you."

Margaret heard the child, but her eyes were fixed on Lewis's face, anguish distorting her own—her struggle so terrible that he looked away. Maum Betty appeared in the doorway to clear the table, caught the pain in all their faces, turned quietly and left.

"Can't we—do what you always say, Mama?" Maggie whispered. "Can't we—put Frederic in God's hands, too? Like Seton and Frank?"

Margaret glanced at her little friend's earnest face. Then, she turned to Lewis, who was looking at her. Once, twice, her hand moved toward him and drew back. She looked at Maggie again, then reached eagerly for his hand. Lewis smiled. And in a moment, she felt her own smile begin to come— involuntarily. It was not a forced smile to make Lewis feel better, to ease Maggie's mind. The smile came because—by the miracle of relinquishment, she had followed Maggie's advice. Frederic *was* now in God's hand. Dry-eyed until that instant, tears coursed down her face.

"I'm—through being ungrateful," she whispered. "I'm all right, Lewis—Maggie. I've stopped adding to both your burdens. I won't be the only mother with—three sons—in the war. And, after all, I have you, Maggie—and oh, Lewis, I—have *you*."

After ordering Lewis off to read a book and rest, she went straight to the barn and told Frederic that she knew he'd be going and that she was doing her best to understand and accept it.

Then, feeling stronger than she'd felt in months, she headed for the kitchen. By now, Tissie, Maggie, and maybe even lazy little Belle were there hard at work with Betty and Rina peeling all those peaches. Hurrying along the still carefully tended path she'd laid out for her Northern guests, who now seemed part of a once beautiful dream, for no reason, Belle popped back into her mind. Would Belle really be there helping the others? A smile came and Maum Betty's priceless remark about her peculiar youngest: "Miss Belle, she work when she's able, but she ain't hardly ever able!" Margaret vowed to give Belle more attention, more discipline. Of all her children, Belle was the only one who refused pointblank to pay any mind to Margaret's teaching about responsibility and unselfishness. Life seemed never to treat Belle quite fairly, according to Belle, and Margaret meant to change that. Belle was every bit as fey as Cousin Sophia, which was all right, except that unlike Sophia, she was too often bad-tempered. Goodness knows, she reminded herself, we've spoiled and pampered her from the day she came yelling and fussing into the world. But, if she isn't there helping with those peaches, I'll give her a good, tough dose of authoritative love—right on her little sitter.

Margaret walked briskly into the kitchen where Betty and

Maggie and Tissie and Rina were making the peelings fly.

"And where is Belle?" she demanded.

"I think she's in the parlor with Papa," Tissie said, adding another peeled peach to the big brown bowl on the table.

"Sit here by me, Mama," Maggie offered.

"In a minute, dear. I'm going to find Belle first. And I don't intend to be salved by any sweet talk of how much Papa needs her to sit with him when he takes his afternoon nap, either."

She hurried out the door and along the latticed breezeway toward the big house. She had reached the back door and started down the long hall when Belle burst wild-eyed from the parlor.

"Mama! Mama, come quick—something's wrong with Papa! He—can't—get his breath!"

"Run to the barn for your brothers! Run!"

The child stood rooted to the floor. "Is—Papa dying?"

Margaret shook her. "Belle! I need—your brothers!"

Before she reached him, she could hear Lewis gasping for breath. In the doorway, the sight of him slumped forward in his chair, both hands clutching his chest, turned her to stone. Irrelevantly, she remembered poor Belle rooted in her tracks in the hallway. Then, as in a nightmare, she was kneeling beside him rubbing his swollen hands, talking to him in surprisingly soft tones, words undirected by her, pouring out: "All right, my darling . . . it's going to be *all right*. Frederic and William are coming. They'll put you in bed—and I'll be with you, so everything will be all right again. You know, dearest Lewis, when we're—together—how everything always gets to be—all right?"

"Mar—Margaret," he gasped. "Help me! Help—me—" Hard coughing overcame him, his gasps almost growls.

"I am—helping you, beloved. And God is helping you. Try to—rest just a little bit." She held his head between her hands, steadying it, feeling his ghastly struggle in her own chest, her own heart. "Just a small rest time, Lewis," she went on, her voice soothing even to her own ears. Oddly, she seemed to be listening too. "Not a big effort—for a big rest—just a tiny one at first. Slowly, between breaths—a little rest. There. There." His head went limp in her hands, the full weight of it, and for a few seconds, his agony seemed to lessen, so that he was able to draw two or three shallow breaths without such struggle.

Then, both boys were bending over their parents—Margaret still kneeling on the floor, holding their father.

"Hello, Papa," Frederic whispered. "What's going on here?"

William stood like a thin reed, his face white, his eyes—not on his father—on Margaret, questioning her: "Mama?"

"Papa's much better," she said. "He just—had some trouble getting his breath. In a few minutes, I want the two of you to carry him to our room."

"He needs a doctor," Frederic said sharply. "I'm not afraid of Yankees on the river—I'm going to Jacksonville!"

"No, Frederic! Don't say such a thing. You'll only upset Papa." She got to her feet, bent to brush back Lewis's lock of graying brown hair. "He'll be just fine once he's in—our own bed. With lots of pillows behind him. There will be no more talk of—Jacksonville. Your father would forbid it. So do I."

In the doorway, Margaret barely glimpsed her three girls, pale and shaken. Even Belle was still as a mouse, her eyes wide.

After another spasm of coughing, Lewis rested his head against the high back of his chair and was quiet.

"We're all here, dearest," Margaret said, her voice low and reassuring. "Just give us a little sign with your hand—when you feel up to a good ride in the arms of your two sons."

"Better—better—get—July," Lewis managed hoarsely. "They'll—need—July."

"He's in the barn helping Mr. Causey," Frederic said. "I'll go."

"No!" Margaret spoke more harshly than she intended. "No, Maggie will go. Or Tissie. Stay—with us, Frederic. Please."

When Tissie returned with July, Lewis lifted one weak, swollen hand in a sign that he was ready, and his two sons and July lifted him tenderly and carried him down the front hall to the familiar room behind the wide, beautiful staircase. Slowly, gently, Frederic helped undress his father and when Margaret said, "Leave us alone, children—July, please," they left the room in a silent, single file.

She sat down in the armchair beside the bed to wait.

Lewis rested, his eyes closed, his breathing heavy, but blessedly regular, for more than an hour. Margaret scarcely moved a muscle, never took her eyes from the dear face. Prayed. Longed for George, who would know what to do. Now and then, to help clear the shock and confusion from her tortured mind, she rubbed her own forehead. George could not come. George was dead. Out there in the cemetery, under the ground. Slender, sensitive, troubled, compassionate George. But George, the essence of George, his spirit, the part of him which was always with her even after he lived away from Hibernia, she knew, was alive and at this very moment was praying for his father, for her. George, fully aware of what had happened to Lewis, was even now with his mother, Augustina, praying for them both. The certainty helped.

If only Frederic and William dared take out the boat and go for a doctor! Such a thought paralyzed her with a new fear. Yankees as such had never really frightened her until now. They were simply the sons of Northern people. The same people who had once been her congenial, courteous guests. She had not even feared Yankee men shooting at Seton and Frank as she found herself fearing them now—out there in their black-hulled gunboats on the familiar river! *Her sons dare not go for a doctor*. Frederic, straining at the bit to enlist, could not be trusted to keep his head should a patrol stop them. Not trust quiet, dependable, intelligent Frederic? She shuddered. The fear had nothing to do with trusting anyone. It was rooted in the strange remoteness of the ashen, aging, still beautiful face propped against an enormous stack of pillows. Lewis—Lewis is ill. Lewis is very, very ill!

After the sun had gone down, Maum Betty stopped trying to convince Margaret to come to the dining room for a bite to eat. She simply opened the bedroom door softly and brought a tray. Then stood watch to be sure Margaret ate.

"That little halfa' biscuit an' honey all you can manage, Miss Mar'ret?"

She nodded, her hands, cold on such a hot day, cupped around a small, steaming Chinese rice bowl of tea. "I—can't swallow, Betty." Then, "Do you suppose I should try to rouse him? Would a sip of tea be good for him?"

"I'd let him rest. But I'll be back in a little while. You call if you need me."

Darkness began to fall outside and soon the black branches of the oaks and magnolias, visible from where she sat, were blotted out. She could not see the river from their bedroom— that view had been saved for guests. But, the river was there. Her beloved St. Johns, innocent of the enemy gunboats moving on its wide, guileless surface, as kind to enemies as to friends.

How many nights she and Lewis had sat side by side on their dock, watching the river, holding hands, making small wagers as to how far Lewis could count before the bronze moon rose full above the New Switzerland treetops and began to turn platinum in the sky. Small wagers of two kisses, three. Wagers gladly paid—no matter who won or lost. Neither ever lost. There could be no real loss as long as she and Lewis could be—together.

When the scalding tears came, she sat up very straight in her little needlepoint armchair and whispered, "Well, we're still together! What's the matter with me? Where's my faith? Lewis is right here—sleeping. Breathing with only a little effort. He even snores his quiet little snore now and then, just like always."

On one of her later trips to check on them, Maum Betty had lighted a lamp, and assured her all the children were in bed except Frederic, who would be sleeping on a pallet in the hallway right outside the bedroom door.

"That's good," Margaret whispered. "Thank him for me. That helps."

"An I'll be on another pallet," Maum Betty said, her eyes snapping a warning against any objection, "no more'n ten feet away from Frederic."

Alone again, Margaret longed to crawl in bed beside Lewis. Why not? she reasoned. How could that disturb him? It will disturb him far more to awaken and find me—not there. Suddenly, she was hurrying out of her dress, petticoats, slippers and into a nightgown. Then, she eased herself into bed, scarcely breathing, for fear of waking him. Settled, her heart slipped into a strange rest. It had pounded through every moment since Belle's terror-stricken cry that something bad was wrong with Papa. Now, it beat evenly, almost quietly. Off and on, she dozed.

Dawn was forming thin, bright pink streaks around the closed shutters when Lewis, in the old familiar gesture, laid his hand on her thigh. "Just have to make sure my wife is still beside me," he always said in a rich, sleepy voice as they had both come awake into all their mornings.

Tears stung her eyes. "Just making sure your wife is still beside you, darling? Well, she is. Right here, where she'll always be."

Very slowly, a weak smile softening his gray, strained face, he moved his head against the stack of pillows to look at her. Then he nodded, closed his eyes again and sank into another deep sleep.

About midmorning, she let the children in to look at their father to be reassured that he was quiet, breathing satisfactorily and getting a much needed rest.

"I think there's even—a little more color in his face today, don't you, Mama?" Frederic whispered.

"I know so," Tissie said.

Belle and Maggie both nodded yes, that they thought so, too.

As always, being careful to include William, even at a time like this, Margaret especially asked his opinion. Too frightened and confused at the sight of his father to speak, the boy nodded hesitantly at first, then with his thin smile, vigorously. Too vigorously.

"We're just going to go about the business of another day now," Margaret said softly. "That's exactly what Papa wants us to do. But we'll all try to be quieter than usual. Tissie, you have Belle's doll clothes to finish . . ."

"Aw, I hate doll clothes," the tomboy said, a scowl on her exceedingly pretty face.

"I know you do, but today that doesn't matter. Sewing doll clothes is a quiet occupation. You work with them, Maggie, and if I need you, I'll call you."

"July and Little Jim and Mr. Causey are going to do our work today," Frederic said firmly. "William and I are staying right outside in the hall. We've got chairs there."

"Me, too," Tissie insisted.

"Tissie," Margaret snapped, "you will do as I say. You'll make your brothers nervous if you stay with them."

Tissie ground one bare heel into the carpet. "Oh, all right. I just might climb a tree and sit there all day."

With two of their mother's dining room chairs tilted against the wall, Frederic and William sat side by side in the hall outside their parents' room. Now and then, Frederic, at a loss to know exactly how his brother was feeling inside about their father's illness, stole a glance at William's thin, expressionless face. William's head was also leaning back against the wall, his pale eyes looking straight ahead at the carved, heavy spindles in the handsome, wide staircase.

"I don't think you have to worry so much about Papa," Frederic said, "now that he's getting a good, quiet sleep."

"Oh, I know I don't *have* to worry. Nobody's making me."

Frederic sighed a little. So often, when he said something to William or asked a question, his brother would answer sort of—at an angle. The answer wouldn't necessarily be unrelated to what Frederic had said, but usually William left him almost no sensible reply. He tried again, carefully. "What I meant to say, William, is that I believe there's a good chance Papa's over the worst of it, whatever's wrong with him."

William thought a long time, then said, "Mama looks pretty sick too, to me."

"She's sick at heart, as the saying goes. You know our parents really, truly love each other. And it's only natural when one of them is sick—real sick like Papa—the other one is going to have heartache. Mama's almost forty-nine. She's had a lot of people die. But you watch, just as soon as Papa is up and around again, she'll look as pretty and pert as ever."

"Frederic?"

"Hm?"

"I don't want you to die, either."

"Well, thanks, buddy. I don't plan to."

"You could—if you go to war."

Frederic stretched his long, slender legs in front of him. "Oh, sure. Men do fall in battle. Seton did, but he didn't die, did he?"

"We haven't heard from him. We don't know. If you go to war—I'm going, too."

Frederic frowned, but carefully did not look at William. "Don't you know Mama couldn't get along here without at least one of us? Especially now that Papa's kind of old."

"How old is our papa?"

"Sixty-three."

"Grandfather Sibbald lived to be in his eighties."

"Papa might, too." When William went on staring straight ahead, Frederic added, "I don't think Papa's going to die anytime soon or anything like that, William. It's just that you've got to promise me you'll stay right here after I'm gone. Mama needs you."

"Would they let me in the army?"

"Not at your age, no. Why do you ask a question like that?"

"Folks think I'm slow-witted."

Frederic jumped up, took William in his arms in a big bear hug and mussed the thin, stringy, brown hair. "Hey, what kind of talk is that?"

"I know what I can do."

"What?"

"Mr. George Huston knows about a band of local Regulators. They climb trees and snipe at Yankee gunboats on the river. I'm not afraid to climb trees anymore. I'm a crack shot."

The gasping began again from the bedroom. Both boys stood rigid in the hall outside the closed door. When they heard their mother's cry, William turned and ran as hard as he could down the hall and out of the house.

She cried out again. "Lewis! Lewis—*no!*"

Inside the bedroom in three strides, Frederic stood staring at his mother's body thrown helplessly over the dead body of his father.

There was nothing for the boy to do but lay his hands on her jerking shoulders and wait.

Almost—he felt out of place. The love his parents had for each other had never excluded him—but it was *their* love. He was old enough now to know that.

After an anguished stretch of time, he drew his hands back and considered bolting as William had done. But when his mother felt his hands leave her shoulders, she sat up. And as though he were Seton and older and more important to her than Frederic had yet thought of himself, she seemed—without a word—to welcome him into the singular deep agony of her heart.

Her burnished gold curls shone in the August sunshine, slanting in a long, bright streak across the big, four-postered bed.

But it was her eyes that held him. They were almost black now—not a mother's eyes capable of scolding or encouraging or guiding. The eyes of a wounded stranger met his. And for that brief, first moment after his father's death, Frederic was allowed to see in his mother—the very soul of a suffering woman who had just lost part of her own life.

41

The first hard weeping past, dressed in her best black silk, in which Lewis had said she looked like a cameo, Margaret sat at her small bedroom writing desk, her fingers moving swiftly.

3 August 1862
Hibernia

Dearest Louisa,
    If they will allow you to leave the city, please bring a minister and come at once. Lewis is dead. Should this note reach you so that you can catch a boat tomorrow, we will wait for an afternoon service. August precludes our waiting longer. Mr. Causey will read a Scripture if you and a minister have not come and you and I will be together for the minister's service as soon as you can get here. We must have it just right for Lewis. I need you.

Margaret Seton Fleming

Standing between Frederic and William on the veranda of the big house in the heat of high noon—the sun shining as though Lewis weren't dead—Margaret handed the letter to William.

"This is a very important thing I'm asking you to do, William. Cousin Louisa must have this at once."

William looked at her intently, his pale eyes solemn.

"I can handle a sailboat good, Mama," he said. "I'll get it to Cousin Louisa before dark."

"No, William," she said more sharply than she intended. "The river's enemy territory. Now, listen carefully. We will have to bury Papa tomorrow without a minister if Cousin Louisa can't bring one in time. But, I think—and oh, William, I'll pray—that you'll be able to flag down a Yankee gunboat and, by being very gentlemanly, beg someone aboard to deliver this letter to St. Augustine."

"You sure I know how to do all that, Mama?"

"I *know* you do."

"She picked you and not me, didn't she?" Frederic asked.

William nodded and took the letter.

"Now then, did you get your white flag from Mr. Causey?"

"He's bringin' it when he and July get done—diggin' Papa's grave."

Margaret hugged and kissed the boy. "Mother's counting on you. Just be very, very polite—as you always are. Explain why you're asking such an unusual favor and—"

"Did the Yankees hate my father?"

"No! No one hated your father." Her voice broke and both boys could see her struggle. "Go, William. Go now. Thank Mr. Causey for fixing the white flag. Tell him I'll let him know later about—the service."

"You mean whether or not we'll go ahead and bury Papa or wait for Cousin Louisa?"

"Yes, William. You've got it just right. If you can get this letter to Cousin Louisa tonight—we'll be able to wait."

"I want Cousin Louisa to be here," William said simply.

"Oh, so do I, son. So do I!"

The letter in his shirt pocket, his skinny arms hugging his knees, William waited by the river in the shade of a favorite cypress tree for over three hours without once getting up. Mama cried so long we missed that late morning gunboat, he thought. I'll have to wait for the afternoon boat. I guess everything will be all right again when Cousin Louisa gets here.

He reached for a branch of dead pine with one dry cone clinging to its tip. Cracking the dry branch between his hands made a good sound. Something besides the birds chirping, which today made him feel lonely. Things even sounded different since Papa died. Everybody so still. Not as still as Papa, though, lying on the bed where he and Mama always slept, dressed in his cutaway, with a collar and a blue cravat. Mama and Frederic and Maum Betty fixed him so he doesn't look much like Papa, but I'd have known it was Papa. Without any life in him.

He snapped the last tip of dry branch and tossed the cone away. Where did my papa go? Tears began to run down William's cheeks. His eyes burned from all the sobbing he'd done earlier today in this same spot at the foot of the big cypress where he sometimes went to be by himself. Nobody had to tell William his papa was dead. That was why he'd run out of the house so fast. To come here. His eyes burned and he was so hot he almost felt he couldn't breathe, either. Like Papa. And the cicadas were so loud his ears hurt, too. He didn't know why.

The boy stood up to scan the river toward Jacksonville. No boat in sight. He sat down. Mama would be without any of her Fleming men once he, William, had gone to war. Poor Mama. He'd cry, probably, when he told her good-bye, so maybe it would be better if he just slipped away in the night. He knew where he was going. To Mr. Huston's place to find out about the Regulators. Unless those shots they'd heard meant Mr. Huston was dead. William could climb any tree on Fleming's Island and he could shoot any Yankee dead. He'd hate to do it, but they were after Seton and Frank, so that made it all right. After another half hour or so, he stood up again.

The Yankee gunboat—a steamer this time—was stirring the blue water on its way upriver from Mandarin. He reached for his white flag on the ground beside him. A piece of white shirttail, he guessed. Mr. Causey tore up an old shirt of his most likely and tied it to the piece of bamboo. It oughta wave good. By heart, he knew how long it would take the gunboat to come close enough so the Yankees could see him standing on the dock waving Mr. Causey's shirttail. He had plenty of time yet.

Where was Papa? Where did people go when they died? To heaven, he knew. But did he still look and talk and laugh like Papa in heaven?

There was so much to think about, to feel bad about. He thought some more. In fact, just almost exactly as long as he needed to until time for the gunboat to get there.

Slowly, William shuffled out onto the wide, weathered boards and began walking to the far end of the long dock, the shirttail flag hanging limply at his side. The Yankees had to patrol in a steamer today, he thought. They ain't got wind enough to sail today. Guess I couldn't have sailed either. But, I'd have tried.

The patrol boat was close enough now and he began waving his flag back and forth over his head, back and forth, back and forth. At first, he waved it slowly and then when the boat didn't whistle or slow, he waved it fast—hard and fast. His heart pounded. What if they didn't stop for him? What if they were too mean to stop?

His arm ached. He changed the flag to his left hand and

waved again as fast as he could, all the time wondering if Mama and Frederic were watching from the front porch.

And then he heard the whistle and knew the Yankees had seen him. A ripple of pride moved through William's thin body. They had tooted the boat's whistle and he could hear the roar of the water over the big paddle wheel as the black-hulled boat slowed and began to move in. He had forgotten to ask Mama if he needed to keep on waving Mr. Causey's shirttail and so he kept on just in case.

"Ahoy, there! Ahoy!" The Yankee in a blue uniform and officer's cap had a big, coarse voice and it seemed to come in waves toward William across the expanse of river, the distance growing smaller now as the boat rumbled closer. "Something we can do for you, boy?" the man yelled.

"Yes, sir!" William's voice cracked and he cleared his throat and tried again—louder. "Yes, sir! If you please, sir." He took the letter from his pocket and held it up.

The boat was almost alongside now. There was no more reason to yell. At least, no more reason than usual on a river.

"My mama wants to know if you could take this letter to our cousin in St. Augustine?"

The man laughed and so did a handful of sailors gathered now at the rail. William could see the officer plainly. He wasn't nearly as big as his voice and he didn't look especially mean.

"Whata you folks think we run—a mail service? What's the big idea stopping a United States patrol boat to deliver a letter? Tell your mama she's got a nerve!"

"No, sir. I won't tell her that."

The man threw back his head and laughed again. "So, you're a—Rebel, too, eh?"

William had no answer for that. "Will you take the letter to Cousin Louisa, please, sir? It's important. We gotta get it there—today."

"Well, what's so all-fired urgent about a letter to Cousin Louisa?"

"We want her to bring a minister. My papa died early this morning."

"Did you hear that, men? That's a new one. His papa died this morning!"

The roar of their laughter hurt. But, William went on trying.

"Yes, sir. My father's dead and we want him to have a real Christian funeral."

The men didn't laugh, but neither did the officer answer.

"Our Cousin Louisa can bring a minister to give my papa a decent burial." He wasn't doing very well. They still didn't believe him! If only he could think of something else to say. Nothing came. That is, nothing came but tears and he couldn't stop them. He stood very straight and didn't make a sound, but William could feel his whole body shake as his fear of failing Mama piled up and up on top of how scared he already was to go on living without Papa. Suddenly, the man with the big voice turned and began to talk to his crew. They weren't laughing anymore. But William was still sobbing. Finally, the Yankees shook their heads up and down as though they were agreed and the man shouted:

"All right. We can't see any harm in taking the letter. As a matter of fact, a contingent of my men have to go into the city to Fort Marion tonight." He shouted an order and the gunboat inched nearer the Fleming dock. "Hand it out to me, boy. Don't be scared. You're not gonna fall in." The officer examined the letter—broke the seal and read it. Then, he said solemnly, "Tell your mother her cousin will have this tonight. If she's got a Union pass, she can catch a ride with one of our boats or hire a boat first thing tomorrow. I'll even see that she gets from the city to Tocoi. They've moved the dock from Picolata to Tocoi, you know."

A smile broke on William's face. He didn't know, but he wished hard that he could shake the Yankee's hand. "Thank you, sir. Thank you. My mama's gonna be awful—glad."

"Don't mention it, son. And uh—extend our sympathy to your mother, will you do that? Our sympathy to—all of you." He saluted William

For a moment, William just stared back at him, not hating this Yankee at all. Then, he saluted, too.

Maum Betty sat through the night with Margaret, their chairs drawn up close beside the bed where Lewis lay. For Betty's sake, Margaret tried to control her weeping by holding her body stiff until it felt about to break.

"You gonna make yo'self sick, burdenin' back them sobs like that. Go on, let it out. The chillern done hear you cry before."

"I—want them to sleep. Tomorrow will be hard for them, too."

"Ain't but one thing we can do tonight."

Margaret drew an uneven breath. "I know. Be with him. Oh, Betty, I—don't think I've—realized yet that—he won't ever breathe again. Or kiss me. Or—eat. Or laugh."

The little French clock Lewis had given her ticked by what might have been one slow minute, and then Betty began to pray: "Oh, Lord Jesus," she moaned, "we in trouble down here! Dark trouble." Her voice broke, then strengthened to a near command: "Lord, Lord, prop us up in—*all* our leanin' places! We got so many leanin' places tonight. An' prop up Miss Louisa. She gonna need it, too."

"At least, we have hope that Louisa will be able to get here—in time. I'm so grateful to William. He's—very good at what he does, you know."

In a rented sailboat with a crew of two, Louisa and a minister reached Hibernia just before noon the next day.

The Reverend John Cannings, a retired Episcopal rector from the North, who had chosen to remain in St. Augustine for the duration of the war, came with her, gladly, to give Lewis a Christian burial. And by two o'clock, under the big magnolia, near George and beside Augustina, the service over, July and Mr. Causey slowly shoveled back the dirt onto the coffin Carpenter Joe had barely had time to finish. Tissie and Maggie stood in wide-eyed silence. Belle screamed and cried out for her papa. William and Frederic never once let go of their mother, their own grief nearly swallowed in hers.

Across the grave, Louisa watched the little family, her heart broken over Lewis, but more shattered for Margaret. Augustina's grave had settled, an old grave now. To Louisa, it seemed just yesterday that she had stood in almost the same spot beside young Margaret Seton, who quietly vowed to wait for Lewis Fleming and to make him happy. No matter how long it took.

She had done both. Their lives had been almost all joy for over twenty-five years. Today, Louisa felt the anguish of the weight—the leaden weight that lay on the heart of her friend. Two sons in the war, another going soon—Lewis dead. The big house empty of Margaret's shining dream for their future. What would Margaret do in all her tomorrows? Dear God, Louisa breathed, if only they had given me more than a two-day pass! If only I didn't have to leave her so soon.

At that moment, Margaret looked directly across the freshly mounded grave at Louisa. And through exhaustion and grief, she smiled. "Thank you," she said into the quiet afternoon. "Thank you, dear Louisa—for so much. Lewis—will be all right now, won't he?"

Louisa waited until the children were in bed that night to tell Margaret that her Union pass permitted her only forty-eight hours away from St. Augustine. Side by side, they sat in the parlor on the pretty love seat so recently selected for the pleasure of Margaret's vanished guests from the North.

Taking Margaret's hand in hers, Louisa said, "How I wish I could take you and the children back with me."

"I—don't think I can—let you go."

"And right now I have no idea how I'll find the strength to get back into that boat tomorrow morning—without you." She felt Margaret's fingers tighten over hers.

"We're only making things worse, aren't we? You can't take us, dear Louisa. They wouldn't allow it. We're—all suspect—because of Frank and Seton. It's—more than my poor mind can take in, but do you know that Mr. Huston vows—the Yankees suspect us of being—spies?"

Louisa stared at her. "Margaret! Don't you know—about George Huston? Haven't you heard?"

"No. We did hear shots one morning. Lewis thought they came from Huston's place, but—what, Louisa? What!"

"Huston is—dead. Killed by the Yankees—undoubtedly the day you heard those shots. Oh, my dear, you have been shut away! His property adjoins Hibernia—and you didn't even know. Why, L.I. wrote to me about it. He didn't tell you?"

Margaret's voice dropped so low, Louisa had to listen carefully. "We haven't heard—from L.I. Not in months." She got up abruptly and began pacing the floor. "You forgot we're not citizens of a Yankee-held city—not even citizens of a Confederate city. We're—in limbo, Louisa!" Then, "Why did they kill our neighbor? We knew he was a hothead, but—"

"L.I. said they believed Huston to be a spy for the Confederacy. Fifty men came that morning—armed. Huston, it seems, vowed they'd never take him alive. They didn't. Well, at least, he died of his wounds soon after—in a Jacksonville prison."

Margaret shuddered. "What about poor Mrs. Huston?"

"Someone at Yankee headquarters began to pity her—especially since it was known that after they shot her hus-

band, they bayoneted him—in his own house. They brought
Mrs. Huston to Jacksonville, but he was in a coma. He never
knew she was there."

Staring at nothing, Margaret said dully, "I—can't tell Lewis
what—really happened that day we heard those shots—can
I?"

"No, my dear."

Louisa, who had stayed so strong, abruptly began to sob.
In each other's arms, they wept together.

Margaret dried her eyes first. "If only—I had my chapel,"
she whispered. "We could go there now. Lewis could have
been—buried from—a real church. Well, I'm going to build
it. It's the—second part of my dream, you know. Lewis
agreed."

"My dear, you need to rest!"

"I can do that after you're gone. And, Louisa, you mustn't
worry about what I'll be doing—then. I think—this minute—
I've just found out. Yes, I can tell you what I'll be doing for
the remainder of my life. I'll be in—school."

"School?"

"Every day for as long as I live on this earth, I'll be—trying
to learn how—to live without Lewis." She laid her hand on
Louisa's arm. "And Cousin, I promise—I'll work very, very
hard. I'll—really try."

42

25 September 1862
Hibernia

Dearest Louisa,

When this will reach you, I have no idea, but L.I. has
promised it will. He is here. He rode alone through the
woods to be with me for three days. To kneel with me beside
his father's grave. He returns tomorrow to Lake City. Wartime has toughened us all, I think. L.I.'s tender heart could
not otherwise have endured the thought of not being here
for his father's service. His grief is very deep, of course, but
he realizes there was no way to let him know in time.

Nights are hardest. I still cry myself to sleep. But days are

busy and July, Little Jim, Mr. Causey, William and the field
hands are trying harder than ever to help increase our corn
crop. Everyone is so solicitous of me. Even Belle is fairly
well behaved. Tissie climbs a lot of trees, and Maggie, my joy,
reads to me at night. Maum Betty and I are closer than ever.

Oh, Louisa, how can I write what I must say next? Frederic
is gone, too, now. The words on paper horrify me. He
enlisted early this month at Middleburg. Rode off alone on
his beloved horse, Rod. I have only William now and he
seems unusually nervous these days, as though there is something preying on his mind. I ask him what especially agitates
him, but I find out nothing. Now, I must give you my latest
news of Seton and Frank. In all this time, we have known
nothing about Seton's condition. When L.I. got here day before
yesterday, he brought a letter from Seton, written to "Dear
Father and Mother." By now, though, he must have L.I.'s letter with the news that his father has left us. My beautiful
Seton recovered, thank God, and wrote from near Richmond
on 9 August, just six days after Lewis went away. Two letters he said he had written from Williamsburg never arrived.
But, being his thoughtful self, he covered again the period
of his recuperation at the home of the kind, caring lady there.
She cared for him as though he were her own child. If I
had my chapel, I would live in it on my knees giving thanks.
Seton was confined to bed at her house for seven weeks,
suffering more, he said, from fever than from his wound. From
there, he was sent as a Yankee prisoner to Fort Wool—a
ghastly place known as the Rip Raps. An artificial island at the
mouth of Hampton Roads, Virginia—a rock pile really, about
two hundred yards long and a hundred yards wide without a
growing plant on it! He was under constant guard, with little to nourish him. His bed was one blanket. Seton's comment
on this ordeal was typical: "This was no pleasant ordeal, especially fishing for rats to eat as I once fished for trout in the
St. Johns, but such is war and I intend giving the Yankees
another go soon. I'm exchanged with other prisoners now and
our Second Florida is under orders to march tomorrow. I
mean, at least, to pay one Yankee off for what they did to me."
Seton urges us to leave Hibernia. "No one is safe any longer
on the St. Johns River," he declares. Louisa, I *cannot leave.*
I will not. Away from Hibernia, my life would fly to pieces. All that I love is here.

Our love comes daily to you and Sophia. I know you

are always searching for a way to get a letter to me and
how I long for your success.

Your always affectionate cousin,
Margaret Seton Fleming

In early December, William finally persuaded Margaret to
permit him to ride to L.I. in Lake City, hoping for mail from
someone. William was an excellent horseman, she knew,
and—with Christmas coming, the first without Lewis and
Frederic—that some fresh news of the war in general would
help their spirits. Tears brimmed in Margaret's eyes as she
and the three girls and Maum Betty waved fifteen-year-old
William off down the Hibernia road on Margaret's favorite
horse, Pet.

"Will he be back for Christmas, Mama?" Belle wanted to
know.

"Oh, yes. Long before that. After all, it's always William's
job to cut our Christmas tree."

"Will we have a tree this year?" Maggie asked.

"Sure, silly," Tissie called down from an oak branch just
over their heads. "We always have a Christmas tree."

"Yes, Maggie. We're going to have a tree because Papa would
want us to. No plum pudding again, but a tree—for sure."

William was gone until the second week in November, and
about noon on a chill, gray day when the river was turbulent
under a sharp wind, Tissie saw him first, galloping along the
Hibernia road toward the lane that led to the big barn. His
welcome was a hero's welcome and that night he told his
mother all he could remember of what L.I. had instructed
him to tell her. Especially that she should see to her total
neutrality along the river. That, in nothing she said, must she
in any way criticize the Yankees. William also brought a long
letter from Frank, sent to L.I., and from it they learned that
Seton and Frank were once more fighting together. In fact,
on a long march through Maryland, they had met a group of
ladies in a carriage on a main road and one of them was
related to Mr. Tiernan, once a regular guest at Hibernia. The
Tiernans, it seemed, still spoke of "the glorious months spent
at Hibernia and of their love for it." The news gave Margaret
much pleasure. Someday, when the war was finally ended,
she fully expected to be entertaining guests again in her big
house and her spirit lifted because Hibernia had been remembered in such glowing terms.

The only word L.I. had of Frederic was that he had barely been accepted since he wouldn't be eighteen until spring. "L.I. said," William explained proudly, "that old Frederic just hung around until they let him in. That's acting like a man, isn't it?"

Margaret frowned, but answered, "Yes. Yes, it is."

"He's still in training, though, L.I. thinks," William went on, his brow furrowed from trying to remember everything. "I'm also supposed to tell you that the Yankees captured the guns at St. Johns Bluff and uh—Yellow Bluff. They took Jacksonville again, too."

"They did?"

Only for a few days. Nobody was there but old people and children. Yankees didn't even burn the corn on the dock."

"Oh, that's good, William! Some of that corn was ours."

The boy smiled. "Yes, ma'am."

"We made our way with both tears and smiles through the first Christmas without Lewis," Margaret wrote Louisa in January 1863, not knowing how she would find a way to send the letter. "And now winter is over the St. Johns. Of course, we will have some warm days on which the children can be outside, but I must find means of brightening up the daily lessons and concoct new indoor games for the girls. William goes steadily about his work, learning as best he can, but requiring nothing of me beyond confidence and love. I do draw strength watching the river when the time can be found to do it. The St. Johns is always in motion, a living entity to me. Even at night, when everyone else is asleep and my heart aches for Lewis, I seem not to be entirely alone because of my friend, the river. The Yankees think they own it. They don't. I do. And in a very real way, it owns me."

At the end of February, hard, pale green buds had begun to form on the sweet gum trees and even though a cold wind howled often down the seven tall chimneys of the big, empty house, spring was on its way. The first without Lewis. Almost imperceptibly, the air was losing its golden winter cast. Soon, one of the girls would bring her a fistful of the first violets: "The way Papa always did." Margaret steeled herself for it.

L.I. came once that spring, bringing four cherished letters. One from Tina, who, feeling no longer safe on the St. Johns at her husband's home in Welaka, had moved to Lake City.

"Please come live with me," she pleaded. "I know Seton and Frank and Frederic, wherever they are, would feel so much more satisfied knowing you were away from the river." Even Tina didn't understand how she felt about the river. "Anyway," Margaret said to L.I., "why would they harm us here? I've never lived such a neutral, harmless, shut-away life! A woman with one sixteen-year-old son and three little girls can't possibly be of any worry to the government of the United States, can she?"

L.I., too, urged her to return to Lake City with him, but Margaret refused. The other letters were from Louisa, Seton and Frederic. So far, Louisa and Sophia were all right in St. Augustine. Frederic's dear letter, the first she'd received— would go under her pillow. Private Frederic Fleming, Company B, Second Florida Cavalry. He, too, was still safe, although he'd fought through some minor Florida skirmishes. Seton's letter was brief, but he and Frank were still together as of January 9, near Fredericksburg, Virginia, where they had been victorious. "Our gallant old chief, General Robert E. Lee, has once more immortalized his illustrious name," Seton wrote. "Would that we had a Lee in the west!"

When she found a chance to walk alone to the tree-sheltered cemetery, she slipped away to where Lewis lay and spread the treasured letters on the settling grave to share with him. The time spent there no longer depressed her. Somehow, it gave her hope, in spite of the still falling tears. She could not have explained the hope. It was simply there.

Some of her best moments seemed to come now, too, in the big bedroom behind the wide staircase in the fastness of those rare but singular nights when—alone in the big four-postered bed—she felt comfortingly close to Lewis.

The lightning-white truth of what Jesus said to Martha came absolutely clear on one such night: ". . . though he were dead, yet shall he live. He that liveth and believeth in me—shall never die."

Never.

With no struggle that night, Margaret slipped into sleep, picturing the small, graceful chapel Lewis had drawn. The chapel she would, by some means, at some future date, build at Hibernia on the St. Johns. Now, during these busy, isolated, often monotonous and always anxious days, more than ever she needed the dream.

* * *

The summer corn crop was excellent. Now all she had to do was pray and believe that, as with the smaller one of last year, a way would be found to get it to Jacksonville. William and Mr. Causey and July had been able to take last year's corn in a wagon by land. There was too much corn for their old wagon this year, but there would be a way. Her part was to see to it that her hope held.

One special pleasure was to mount her beloved dappled mare, Pet, and ride over the fields with Maggie straddling Pet's bare back behind her. More than ever, Maggie was her particular friend, old enough at twelve, for real friend talk now.

They rode one September afternoon to where the harvested corn was stored in the big, new cribs Mr. Causey had proudly engineered. The sweet grain scent hung on the warm, early fall air. Margaret felt almost peaceful.

Dismounting, they held hands as they walked around the cribs and moved off through a cleared path in the woods—their favorite place to be together during those infrequent moments when the other children didn't need them.

"I don't plan to get married ever," Maggie said. "It's just too good being here with you, Mama. I'm staying always."

Margaret laughed. "That's a dangerous thing to say, honey. As pretty and sweet and sensitive as you are, some young man may have very different ideas for you."

"Would you be terribly disappointed if I didn't ever marry? If I stayed here and helped you when the war is over and we open our house again?"

"Oh, no. That would be my good fortune. But, why all this sudden talk of marriage?"

"Oh, I'm just thinking out loud the way you and I do. I don't think out loud with anyone else but you." Maggie giggled a little. "I guess I'd be embarrassed."

Margaret slipped her arm about the girl's waist and for a time they walked along in silence—just being together. Then, she said, "Maggie, tell me something. Do you ever feel frightened staying here on the river as we are?"

She saw a tiny frown crease the smooth, young brow. "No, Mama. You aren't afraid. Why should I be? What could the Yankees have against us? They don't even seem to look in toward our house when they pass in those gunboats anymore."

"Oh? How do you know that?"

"Sometimes I watch with Papa's long glass. When they first

started coming by, I could see them looking in. They haven't done that for a long time." Maggie thought a moment, then asked, "What does it mean that Seton and Frank and the others lost the battle at that place called Gettysburg? Does that mean the South is losing the war?"

"Oh, child, I don't know! We didn't lose Frank or Seton. I guess we just have to give thanks for that. Beyond the fact that—the last we heard—they were both alive, I don't know anything."

After a while, they mounted Pet again and walked her back through the still, sunny afternoon.

At the stable, Margaret gave the horse a handful of grain, caressed her smooth, silky, high-arched neck and whispered, "I love you, Pet. Did you know that? And I want you to listen to me. William's going to ride you to L. I.'s house again next week. William's the only Fleming man we have now. You must watch over him."

Margaret and Maggie had just come out of the shadowy stable into the sunlight when they saw Tissie racing toward them, her finger over her mouth to shush them—her eyes full of terror.

"Tissie," Margaret whispered, when the girl came up sweating and out of breath. "Tissie, what is it?"

"Sh! Hush, Mama. We can't make a sound. They're out there?"

"*Who's* out there? What are you talking about?" Maggie asked.

"*The Yankees!* They're out there in a big black gunboat and they're stopped—right beside our dock. They're right there— right out there in the river, Mama! William said for you to come quick."

For nearly an hour, Margaret, her children and Maum Betty crouched at the big parlor window and watched, William using the long glass, reporting every movement of the Yankees who seemed to be talking among themselves on the deck of the terrifying black-hulled brig of war.

"One's the officer in charge, I guess," he said. "But, they're just standing there."

"Will—they—kill—us all, Mama?"

"No, Tissie! Don't even think of such a thing! We've done nothing. We've just minded our own business."

"But I—saw something last night," Belle said, keeping her voice low with great effort.

"What, Belle? What did you see?" Tissie demanded.

"I—couldn't sleep cause—I had to wee wee and when I—got up, I looked out the window and—something was burning downriver."

"Where, Belle?" Margaret asked, trying not to sound alarmed. "Far away?"

"I don't know, Mama! I—was too scared. I was even scared to tell you. But it was downriver."

"Probably just a woods fire," Margaret said, shakily. "Yes. I'm sure that was it."

"I decided to think I'd—just had a bad dream."

"And that's probably all it was."

"You just had yo'self a mean ol' nightmare, Belle," Maum Betty said, putting an arm around the child. "I tol' you not to eat all them nuts so late at night."

"Mama!"

"What, William? What do you see?"

"They're comin' in! Look—you don't even need the long glass to see. The man in the officer's cap is first—and about six or seven men right behind him. On our dock now. Comin' this way!"

Belle began to whimper. "Hush!" Maum Betty snapped. "We ain't gonna do none of that!" She held Belle firmly in both arms. "Sh! Yo' Mama, she know 'zactly what to do."

Margaret watched the tall officer, plainly visible now, lead his men along the dock, up the river promenade into her avenue of crepe myrtles—in full bloom, tossing their pink blossoms against the cloudless sky.

Margaret stood up. "Now, these are your orders—all of you. I want you to stay right where you are. Don't get up—stay crouched down right there. And not one word. Is that clear? You'll be able to hear what I'm saying to him. I'll be right outside in the front hall."

"I'm goin' along to look after you, Mama."

"No, William! You're in charge of Maum Betty and your sisters. Now, not a sound."

"I—might have to—sneeze," Belle whined.

"Put your finger under your nose and press."

Her back very straight, Margaret began to walk slowly across the parlor. She stepped cautiously out into the front hall in time to see the officer mount Hibernia's front steps and cross the veranda toward the door, standing wide open as always, to allow the river breeze to pass through the house.

For a long moment, Margaret stared at him down the length of the hall. Just inside, he removed his cap and waited. When she began to walk toward him, the young officer bowed and said, "Miss Margaret. Good afternoon!"

She stopped. The Yankee knew her name! When he stepped inside out of the glare of the sun, Margaret knew the officer's name, too.

"Guy—Guy Henry," she gasped, but did not move a step nearer. It was her Seton first cousin, her father's nephew, with whom she'd spent such happy hours, now so long ago. Guy had amused her and set her imagination winging with his tales of what life was like in New York City. She loved Guy Henry! Dressed now in his Union blue, she dared not rush to embrace him. Could not even welcome him. Her entertaining, warmhearted cousin was now—the enemy.

"Don't you remember me, Miss Margaret? I'm your cousin—"

"Yes! Yes, Guy, I—know."

"I doubt that the best playwright could conjure up a more—dramatic second meeting," he said, his well-remembered charm scarcely concealing his discomfort. "May I inquire after your family? The children? Colonel Fleming?"

"The children—left to me—are well. Three of my sons—are fighting—" her voice faltered "—somewhere." She lifted her chin. "My husband—is dead."

Colonel Guy Henry took an involuntary step toward her. "Margaret," he murmured. "I'm—so sorry."

"Thank you. We're supposed to be enemies now. I don't know quite how—to receive you this time." For a moment, her shoulders drooped. "It's—very strange, isn't it?"

He nodded, looked down, turned his cap round and round in his hands.

"What is it—you want of us, Guy?"

Slowly, he took a paper from his uniform jacket. "First, I have to ask where your son William is. Is—he fighting, too?"

"No! The boy's only sixteen!"

"Are there any other men on the place? Other than your Negroes?"

"One. Mr. George Causey is our caretaker. Like you, he—came to Hibernia for a holiday. Like you, he didn't want to leave. My—husband retained him. Why?"

"Orders." He held out a paper.

She took it, her hands trembling and scanned the short,

terse message: *Clear Fleming's Island of all able-bodied men
and destroy the houses.* Her body stiffened. "Mr. Causey
is—a Northerner. Too old to fight. Past seventy. My son,
William, is, as you well know—not eligible." William was
listening, she knew, but it had to be said. She prayed he
wouldn't understand the word 'eligible.' In case he did, she
added, her voice louder, "William is too young."

"Not to be spying for those troublesome Regulators," Guy
said. "They take anyone, at any age, just so he knows the
woods and the river. Look, I know you're telling me the
truth, Margaret. *I* know it, but—" he broke off, looking at
her with such heartbreak and such caring, she felt her own
eyes sting with tears she had so far managed to hold back.
"Where—would you go?" he asked. "I am an officer in the
Army of the United States—under orders to burn the houses.
But, please tell me, where would—you and the children go?
Your Negroes will not be harmed, but they can't go with you.
Your caretaker *is* too old. He can't go with you, either. What
I have to know for myself is—*where will you go?*"

"Guy Henry," she said, taking a few steps toward him.
"You—wouldn't—burn Hibernia! You—*couldn't* burn Hibernia!" Tears flowed unchecked now. "I beg you, Guy, as one
who—seemed so truly my friend—not just my cousin—my
friend. I've—lost so much! I—can't lose Hibernia! Please
. . . Guy. Please! We're harming no one. I've taken every
care not even to show the inadvertent appearance of—bias in
this ghastly war. I know there's guerilla activity or you wouldn't
be ordered to burn my—beloved house. But, we're not part
of it, Guy! We're not doing anything but—trying to live with
our—losses."

From the parlor, Belle sneezed noisily and Maum Betty
said, "Sh!"

Guy smiled a little. "How I'd love to see them," he said.
"Under the circumstances, I'd better not."

"*Why* are they after us here?"

"Torpedoes. One of our gunboats was blown up—burned
up—in McGirt's Creek. That's getting close to Hibernia.
From our point of view, too close."

"But, Guy, we all stay right here. I've only permitted
William to ride twice to my stepson L.I.'s place in Lake City.
Then, only because I was desperate for word from my sons in
battle. Now and then a mother *has* to know. I know nothing
about any torpedoes. We haven't even heard any go off."

"Don't say that to anyone but me," he advised. "You wouldn't be believed. I do believe you." Once more, he was rereading the order, frowning. He glanced at Margaret, then back at the paper in his hand. "Not very clearly written, is it?"

"I read it all right."

"But, don't you think the order really reads: Destroy the *horses?*"

Her hand flew to her mouth. Pet!

"I do believe I've misread this order," he was saying. "Still, you'd think our forces would need the horses captured safely. Yet, there it is—destroy the *horses!*"

"No, Guy—!"

Without another word, he bowed stiffly, turned and strode out of the house. In a matter of seconds, Margaret heard him give the order to his waiting men.

That night, after the raiding party had gone and the three girls were asleep, Margaret went to William's room. He was sitting—fully dressed—on his bed.

"We missed you at supper," she said, sitting down beside him. "William? It's late. We've had a hard day. Don't you want Mother to turn back your bed so you can crawl in?"

Not once had he looked up since she entered the room. He went on staring at the wall now, in silence.

"I—know how you feel. After all, I—did so love Pet." With effort, she kept her voice even. "I—never had a horse I loved as I loved her. But—Cousin Guy had to carry out his orders. He—*didn't* burn our house, William. We're still going to sleep in our house tonight."

She waited. William hadn't moved a muscle. Now, his skinny young body began to strain and jerk.

"Pet—Pet didn't make a sound," he said. "Except—when she—died. She—was tryin' so—hard for—one more breath."

In her efforts to calm the girls, Margaret only now realized that William had slipped out of the parlor when Guy Henry left the front hall. "William! Did you—go out there? Did you see it happen?"

He nodded, his lips white and tight. "Pet—knows I was—with her. I—saw her eyes. They—won't get by with this," he whispered, shaking as though he had a chill. "They—made up my mind—to that."

Margaret attempted to put her arms around him, but, for

the first time in his life, the boy shoved her away. On his feet, he turned on her, red splotches staining his sharp features. "Don't try to stop me, Mama! An' don't beg me. I ain't hearin' you. I'm—goin' tomorrow." Tears poured from his swollen red-rimmed eyes. In his rage, he hit himself swiping them away. "Don't you—try to stop me." His voice was low and threatening. "I'll—run away if you do."

Still struggling to keep her own voice calm, Margaret asked, "Where are you going, son? You're too young to—enlist."

"You heard *him*. I'm not too young for the Regulators. I already know where to go. I already know their whistle."

"Their—whistle?"

He shook his head yes. "I met 'em out there—both times I rode to Lake City to visit L. I. They—want me. I know the man. I—just been waitin' till—I thought you'd be all right. Not anymore."

"William!"

In his awkward way, he lunged at her, kissed her cheek roughly and ran from the house into the black night.

She waited all night, while July and George Causey and Little Jim and Big Owen and the twelve remaining field hands scoured the woods around Hibernia. There was no sign of William. He had simply vanished.

Daily, sometimes hourly, Margaret prayed that L. I. would sense their need and ride to visit them. She knew L. I.'s days were crammed with difficult cases. Confederate soldiers were deserting by the dozen. She'd known that since L. I.'s last visit and he was the judge advocate who tried each case. He's busy, she kept telling herself. He's just too busy to get away or he'd come. At times, her heart—even her body—crumpled with the growing burden of anxiety. Never before the girls or Maum Betty. Alone in the big empty bed at night. You dare not—give in, she would tell herself over and over again, as she lay there, her hand reaching toward where Lewis always slept. Her hand reaching—toward nothing.

43

A fire burned in the fireplace of the second-floor parlor of Louisa's St. Augustine house. In summer, double doors opened at both sides of this favorite room, affording every possible breeze. The doors were locked now; they were always locked these days, not only against howling winter winds, but against the formless, chronic anxiety with which she and Sophia lived day and night.

"Hard to believe it's actually Christmas Eve," Louisa said, rocking nervously.

"We could have gone to the Christmas Eve services," Sophia answered, winding a fresh skein of green yarn into a ball. "You just aren't yourself, Louisa. I declare, you're downright unsociable."

"I don't feel that way, but burdens get too heavy to talk about with casual acquaintances. These times, everyone had best be considered merely an acquaintance. The less said the better. I want to trust folks, but I dare not." She rocked a moment. "How are your legs tonight, Sister? Pain you any less than this morning?"

Sophia's ball of yarn rolled off her lap and unwound all the way to the doors that led to the back balcony. "Now, look what you made me do, Louisa! I told you I don't want to talk about my old legs! It just calls my attention to the pain. You'll have to get down on the floor and pick up all that yarn for me."

Wearily, Louisa gathered it up and piled it into Sophia's lap. "You know perfectly well why I'm so gloomy," she said, back in her rocker. "Margaret. How *do* you suppose she and the girls are managing through this dark Christmas? I feel Margaret's pain—all the time. Especially now that poor William ran off. And she doesn't have any idea where he is—what he's up to."

Busily rewinding the yarn, Sophia said, in what for her was a firm voice: "I may have a Yankee pass and I may have sworn allegiance to the Union, but I'm now a Rebel at heart. And *I* know what dear William is up to. He's joined those intrepid Regulators. He's probably high in a big tree right now, waiting for daylight so he can snipe at a Yankee gunboat! Bravo, William!"

Louisa smiled a little. "I can see Mrs. Judge Smith has finally cast her spell over you. Not too long ago, you couldn't have cared less about either side."

"Just think, Louisa, beautiful Seton, responsible Frank, handsome Frederic and now, dear, tender William—all defending our honor!"

"But how does Margaret stand it? All four sons in constant danger and the mails the way they are. The last letter I had from her—over a month ago, said L.I. hadn't been there in weeks. I should imagine he's her main source of mail service. Certainly from behind Confederate lines. We'd never hear from her, I suppose, if it weren't for Mr. Reed at Black Point."

"I'll wager Margaret is sitting right now at her lovely pianoforte playing and singing Christmas carols with those adorable girls! I can see them—all with upturned faces singing about the Baby Jesus . . ."

On her knees that night, Louisa prayed: "Thank you, dear Lord, for coming to us that first Christmas. I wish I knew *how* to thank You for—getting into this mess with us. For becoming—one of us as You did. Make it real to Margaret tonight—oh, make it very real—that You are still here. That she is *not alone*."

On the first Sunday in the new year, 1864, Margaret and Maum Betty held a Sunday school class in the big parlor at Hibernia.

"We're going to do this every Sunday afternoon from now on," Margaret vowed, as she and Betty straightened the room after the class, which included the three Fleming girls, Rina and five other children from the quarters. "The young ones need to learn all they can about God right now and—oh, so do I!"

A straight-backed chair in each hand, Maum Betty said, "Miss Mar'ret, you done show me strength—every blessed day!"

Stooping to pick up scraps of paper on which the children had written Bible verses, Margaret said almost grimly: "If I do—it's only because—I don't know anything else to do!"

Three heavy blasts shattered the quiet Sunday afternoon—so heavy they shook the sturdy Hibernia house, and across the yard, shouting and screaming, came the Fleming girls and their quarters playmates.

"Lord have mercy!" Maum Betty breathed. "They shootin' at us, Miss Mar'ret!"

"No, Betty. Those were torpedoes. Our Regulators must have laid the waters around this island with torpedoes. A Yankee gunboat was probably just blown out of the water."

"Good! Maybe our William help lay 'em!"

Margaret sank into a chair. "If only we knew . . . something!"

"What we ever done to them Yankees, anyhow? We never bother 'em none. We just cook for 'em when they used to come here—an treat 'em nice as pie. What this war about, anyhow, Lord?"

On a dark, chill mid-January morning, Margaret ordered the children to stay back while she walked briskly down from the house to meet a small sailing boat which Tissie had spied moving in from the channel.

Huddled in her worn cloak, she waited on the dock, her heart pounding. Mr. Causey had urged her to let him meet the boat. She trusted no one but herself to handle whatever this new threat might be.

When the boat came near enough, a man's voice greeted her. With some relief, she recognized Mr. A. M. Reed, whose plantation, now a haven for Yankees because of Reed's Northern sympathies, was only ten miles downriver from Hibernia. He had been a friend for years, but today, she was on guard.

Leaving the boat to a servant, Reed jumped onto the dock and bowed. "I'm sure you realize that I cannot stay long, Mrs. Fleming," he said, "but I've brought a letter from your son Seton."

"Thank you."

"Perhaps you'd like to know how I came into possession of a letter from behind Confederate lines."

She said nothing.

"Your stepson, L. I., sent it to my place by a messenger who feared to ride all the way here. L. I. asked me to tell you that he is in good health and will visit you as soon as he can."

"I—hope I've thanked you properly, sir."

He bowed again. "You have, indeed. And I must go. Life is—changed for all of us, Mrs. Fleming. Are you and your girls—all right?"

Her chin lifted. "We're doing—fine, Mr. Reed."

With all the dignity she could muster, Margaret walked away from him back to the house, to read Seton's letter alone.

In her bedroom, the door shut, she broke the seal, her hands shaking so that reading was difficult.

> 30 December 1863
> Near Rapidan, Virginia
>
> My dear mother,
>
> In case you have not received some of my letters, let me say that Frank and I are separated in battle. He is now a first lieutenant in the Army of Tennessee somewhere in Georgia. I have heard only that he is well except for a touch of dysentery. I hope your Christmas was a happy one—under the circumstances. I enjoyed a big turkey and no fighting, but I am here to fight for our home and, between the battles, time drags.

She skimmed the long section in which Seton was once more trying to convince her that God is on the side of the Confederacy and only allowed them to lose so miserably at Gettysburg last summer in order to chastise them for boasting about Southern bravery and lack of dependence upon Him. She sighed. The boy did most certainly believe in God. She was grateful for that, but her question remained: Could God be on one side or the other in this hideous war?

> Do not let the few Floridians who croak and deplore the duration of the war make you despondent. We do not depend upon such weak men for assistance and never did. Of course, I am enlisting for another three years. Our fathers fought the British for seven years. We can fight the Yankees longer.
>
> Your loving son,
> C. Seton Fleming

Seton, Seton, *Seton*, she thought, pacing the room, the letter still in her hand. *Your fathers* didn't even fight the British! You've allowed your good mind to be confused by the horror and brutality of the life you now lead. Your fathers, both the Flemings and the Fatios, were loyal British subjects during the American Revolution! On the Seton side, your fathers fled the American Revolutionaries and came to Florida *because* they were loyal to Britain!

Collapsed in her favorite chair by the window, somewhat relieved to know that at least he was alive at the end of last month, she gave a short laugh. Dear, extreme Seton! So like me in so many ways. God knows I've always been impetuous—willing, even driven to believe that the impossible can happen. Has this trait of mine been—distorted in you, Seton, by this ugly war? You're not even thinking straight.

She sat for a long time, only half watching Tissie and Maggie jump rope in the yard. Then, aloud, as though Seton could hear her, she said firmly: "In my next letter to you, son, I certainly intend to correct your mixed-up history about *your* forefathers, but I am proud of you. And I love you, dear Seton. I don't understand your war or your ideas about it, but—I love you in some deep, deep way that only God—can possibly understand."

On the last day of February, when Maum Betty's alarming news that seven of the Fleming fieldhands had either been stolen or had run away in the night, joy came to help soften the blow for Margaret. Right after she learned the terrifying news, as she still stood forlornly in the sandy lane that ran between her double row of water oaks to the nearly empty quarters, L.I. galloped up the main Hibernia road.

The joy came mainly from his strong arms about her as they embraced and went on embracing while July led L.I.'s horse to the stable.

"I thought you'd—never come," she said, weeping, not even trying to stop. "Oh, L.I.—even our—people have begun to leave us! I can't bear that! Somehow—that's—too much! I worry about them. I—*need* them! I'm—so alone."

"I know," he said in his warm, comforting way. "I know, Miss Margaret. But I'm sure they didn't—desert you. I'm sure they were stolen. Why, Yankee soldiers are even stealing slaves from Mr. Reed and he's a strong Union man."

His arm around her, he led her slowly toward the house.

"I've—needed you so," she sobbed. "I need—to talk to you for a—whole day, L.I. But you must be hungry and tired."

"Both," he laughed. "And as soon as I've washed up, we'll eat some of Maum Betty's cooking while I chat with my little sisters. They'll be satisfied then for all afternoon."

"I don't know about that," Margaret said, drying her eyes on the lining of her cloak. She tried to laugh. "They've been watching that road even more than I've had time to do—and that's a lot. But you're here now." She held tightly to his strong arm. "You're here now, L.I. And that's—what matters."

L.I. was his old, joking, laughing self with the girls at dinner and Maum Betty reveled in his hearty appetite. She was really improvising these days with their food supply cut off by the Yankee blockade, but L.I. praised her with almost every bite.

After dinner, Maggie helped convince Tissie and Belle that L.I. did need to be alone with their mother, and for two hours L.I. and Margaret sat together in her room—freely exposing their hearts to each other—as they'd always been able to do. "I've worn you out," she said at last, "but I did need to tell someone who could handle it—how alone and anxious I've been." Then, before he could respond, she went on quickly, firmly: "L.I., I know what you're about to do. Don't. Don't make any effort to convince me that the girls and I should leave Hibernia. Seton and Frank urge me to go in almost every letter. I hear from Frederic more often because he's still fighting in Florida and he hears all sorts of wild rumors. The dear boy begs us to leave. He's so sure the torpedoes and the sniping from the riverbanks put us in danger. But why should it?"

"One reason is because William may be doing some of that sniping. What's more, you must realize that you'd be gone now if any other officer in the entire Union Army but Guy Henry had been ordered here that day."

"But it was Guy—and we are still here. Without a single horse left, but we're still here."

"True. And after Frederic and the others did such a tremendous job of routing the Yankees at Olustee ten days or so ago, you may be safe for a time. On the other hand, frustrations—like Olustee—drive fighting men to do crazy things. Frederic and his comrades licked them. Failure like that often leads to severe retribution. I hate to be so blunt, Miss Margaret, but there's no better way to demoralize a fighting man than to harm his family. You're the mother of four sons in the Confederate Forces, if you include me. And William is almost surely with the Regulators." When she said nothing, L.I., too, fell silent. At last, he smiled at her.

"You can't tell me you're not—scared here, Miss Margaret."

"Of course I'm scared. I've already told you how frightened I am at the sight of even a neighbor's sailboat! But, Hibernia is my home. My life. The river—is my friend. I don't intend to leave either—not ever."

"It wouldn't be forever. Mary Evelyn and I would welcome you and the girls. Did you know the Yankees hold Jacksonville again?"

"No, of course I didn't. I hear—nothing."

"Jacksonville's close by. And it's my firm judgment that everyone on the river—because of those torpedoes and the sniping—is suspect."

"I'm aware of that. And I'm also sure I sound—quite balmy to you, refusing to go. But, L.I.—as long as I'm here, I'm somehow still close to—your father. I simply know how much I can—bear to lose. What I must keep. In order—to go on hoping."

L.I. squeezed her hand. "Don't—ever stop hoping. Why, if you did, we'd all give up. You've drilled hope into us for all our lives."

She nodded. "I drill it into myself these days, believe me. We have no flour or sugar or coffee. I'm wearing patched dresses—but my dreams are here. The house—and the little chapel I mean to build someday. Your father had time to draw just one sketch of it for me. I look at it every day, every night. Oh, L.I., I'm afraid to leave. I'm afraid I'll—lose my house. I live for the day when I can—open it again to Northerners. Someday, they won't be—our enemies any longer. I—have to believe that!"

"You do—still hope, don't you?"

"Yes, I do." She laughed dryly. "Women are a peculiar breed, you know. We don't always see things as black or white, as men seem to do."

L.I. stretched his tired legs. "I don't know about that. According to Cousin Louisa's letters, a lot of St. Augustine women have definite black or white eyesight. Her neighbor, Mrs. Judge Smith, is now being watched like a hawk—she's a suspected Rebel spy."

"Never mind about Mrs. Smith and her friends there. Cousin Louisa and I see eye to eye on—everything. Thank you for bringing her letter, too. How I long to be with her. We see things alike. Even this senseless war."

* * *

Before he rode back to Lake City, L.I. tried once more to convince her to leave Hibernia. He failed. And as day followed day through the winter into early spring, Margaret allowed herself to be lulled into believing that L.I. had been wrong. Feeling that, at least indirectly, she was helping feed Seton and Frank and Frederic—maybe even poor William, she and George Causey planted all the corn they could plant without the help of the seven field hands, who never returned. Causey had become her loyal friend and, next to Betty and July, her most reliable helper. Like Margaret, Causey seemed to be unable to take sides. Like her, he longed only for the return of peace. Maum Betty was in danger of becoming a Rebel hothead, but her husband, July, although he talked less than anyone on the place, let Margaret know that he was with her in her desire only for the killing to stop.

Then, early in March, as Margaret helped July mulch some azalea bushes against the coming heat of summer, a strange, two-masted square-rigged brig of war appeared, plying the channel on the New Switzerland side, slowed and dropped anchor directly out from Hibernia.

Her apron filled with pine straw and fallen oak leaves, Margaret stared across at the black-hulled gunboat. "What now, July? What now?"

Shaking his head, July said, "At least, they be out a ways from our dock."

"Yes, but what are they doing there? I—I don't think it has a thing to do with us here, but—why, July? Why didn't they just—go on upriver, the way the other patrol boats have done for so long?"

There was no answer. The gunboat was simply there.

It was harder than ever to get any work at all out of Belle, as the brig stayed there day after day for a whole week. The child seldom put down Lewis's long glass and sat glued to the front window, watching. Margaret would threaten a spanking, Belle would go reluctantly to help Maggie and Tissie and, in no time, there she was again at the front window, her eye pressed to the long glass. Attempts at disciplining Belle were even less effective than usual, since Margaret had slept almost none at all from the first day the boat appeared. She was too exhausted for discipline. But, as week followed week, a kind of family routine was worked out—around the gloomy presence of the big black boat on the river. George Causey helped the day he decided the brig was there merely standing guard.

"Against what?" Maggie wanted to know.

"Why, against any attempt to lay more torpedoes," he said. "I don't look for any trouble over here. Plainly, that's a boat doing guard duty. No connection at all with us here at Hibernia."

After that, even Belle made fewer trips to the front window with the long glass. Margaret began to sleep some again and work at Hibernia moved along as smoothly as possible under the watchful eye of what Belle had discovered was the *Pompano*. The coming of spring in March restored more normalcy. The girls brought home wild flowers, February buds swelled into leaves on gum and tupelo—bright, soft green to match the pine flowers. Margaret had always loved the soft, powdery pine flowers which stretched into firm, chartreuse candles lit by the spring sun. Sun that would illumine the woods, dance on the river, "trying its best," as Maggie kept reassuring Margaret, "to light our days."

No one pretended to grow accustomed to the ominous gunboat, but when an ear-splitting explosion occurred on April 1, downriver toward Mandarin, George Causey made gallant use of it in further allaying their fears. "What'd I tell you?" he asked. "Just as sure as a gun's iron, that was a Regulator torpedo." He chuckled dryly. "Our *Pompano* crew out there missed seeing the men that laid that one, but that's what they're out there for. Guard duty. Lookouts. Got nothing to do with us."

On June 1, after an almost desperate attempt to follow her custom of making a brand-new start for the new month—of refurbishing her will to hope—Margaret heard Mr. Causey from the front porch. When she joined him, he handed her a letter.

"This was leaning up against my cabin door first thing this morning," he said. "It's from your son Seton, I'd think."

She held the letter against her heart. "But, how did it get there? Who brought it?"

He pointed with his thin finger at the scrawling script on the outside of the letter. "William, I'd say. Could only read his name."

"William?" Breathlessly, she read aloud the almost illegible scrawl. " 'Give this to my mama. Not safe for me to see her. April 1, we blew up *Maple Leaf* and burned. April 16, *Hunter*. May 9, *Harriet B. Weed*, William Fleming. I am well and busy.' "

Causey went to Margaret to steady her. "Better have a seat, Mrs. Fleming." He led her to one of the veranda rockers. "Knew this would be a shock in a lot of ways. First word we've had from William. But the boy's nearby. And he's all right. Sounds as though he's right in his element to me. Feel nervous and torn up, don't you? Wouldn't wonder."

"Yes," she whispered, her eyes on the hated black gunboat. "Yes, I'm more than—nervous these days." She smiled weakly. "You see, I've never been good at—waiting. And, oh, Mr. Causey, there's been so much waiting!"

Causey left her to read Seton's letter alone. As always, Seton gave her too many battle details: The battles of the Wilderness and Spotsylvania Court House. Seton was a captain now with Perry's Brigade near Hanover Junction—still in far-off Virginia. Her heart jumped when she read that he had received two slight wounds, but he made light of them both. "We may fight another great battle any day. I welcome it," he wrote. Her mouth went dry. "The Yankees have fought us more desperately of late. They appear to think that this is the last struggle of the war and that if they are defeated now, all will be lost to them. As it surely will be! Our troops are in high spirits and we are eager for Grant to attack us. God is surely on our side. Continue your prayers that the end will be glorious! I still cannot believe my dear father will no longer be there when at last I come home. But he is with God and God is with us here. And with you there. I am where I want to be. Do not worry about me. God does everything for the best and, by now, I am counting on the fact that good old L.I. has persuaded you to leave Hibernia to be with him in Lake City."

For a long time, she sat looking upriver beyond New Switzerland, avoiding the sight of the loathsome gunboat. Light played across the rippled surface of the water. What would Seton think if he knew she and her girls were still living beside the river, in full view of the hated Yankee boat? She had found no way to mail a letter to him in weeks. Well, we are still living beside the river, son. The St. Johns still rolls steadily past us toward the sea, unlike other rivers— north, instead of south. *Welaka*, the Indians once called it. Lewis had explained long ago, as they sat side by side on the new, sturdy dock watching the tidal river flow by beneath them, that *Welaka* meant: *It hath its own way, is alone. . . .*

Everyone who has his or her own way of thinking, of

seeing, of believing—is alone, she thought. No wonder the river and I are friends.

On this bright, tender June morning, even with the consolation of a letter from Seton, delivered by the hand of dear William, she had never in her fifty years felt so alone.

Three times during the next week they had seen Yankee boats pull alongside the *Pompano*—remain for an hour or so and then leave in the direction of Mandarin. "Supplies," Causey said each of the three times. "The sailors have got to have grub. Three times in one week might seem a little often, Mrs. Fleming, but it's got to be supplies they're bringing. Orders and so on. We'd best not worry. The *Pompano's* been out there over three months now."

A strange, unnatural silence hung over Hibernia in the late afternoon of June 9. Everyone stayed busy at some inside chore, in the big house or the barn, because all day long, a soft, misty rain had fallen, wetting the tree trunks until they stood black in their own shadowless silence across the wide lawn.

In the parlor, where she had moved her work desk so that she could keep a watchful eye on the ever-present gunboat, Margaret mended, read and was now trying to concentrate on her meager account books. The girls, except for Belle, who'd been in a pout all day because suddenly she wanted biscuits, worked steadily on the long dining room table, turning the skirts in their old dresses.

"I don't feel like helping them," Belle had complained. "And I don't think a young girl like me should have to! Nothing goes right for me anymore. I can't see what war has to do with me not having biscuits."

Margaret had given her nine-year-old an exaggerated look of pity: "Poor Belle. To hear poor Belle talk, you'd think everything was just perfect for everyone else in this house! That Maum Betty had flour to make biscuits for everyone but—*poor Belle*."

Remembering the incident now, Margaret had to smile. Especially at what Belle had said next: "Don't talk to me, Mama, as though I'm somebody else! I don't like it when you look right at me and say 'she' and 'her'—as if I'm not even here."

About four-thirty, Margaret took a deep breath, stretched and closed the ledger. Maggie, she was sure, had mended Belle's torn shirtwaist and turned the old flowered skirt for her.

From the habit of three months, her eyes went to the gunboat. In an instant, she was on her feet and at the window peering through the dense fog and misty rain at what she was already certain was movement on their dock. She grasped the window frame to steady herself. Staring into the fog, as thick now as smoke, she could make out a longboat already tied to one of the Hibernia pilings. A dizzying fear gripped her. Her body shook. She caught one breath and held it until she could stop shaking, could regain some measure of control. This is—panic, she thought. This is what panic is like! I must not—*I dare not give into it.*

Plainly now, she could see the Yankees. She should be moving, walking down the long hall toward the front door—to handle whatever crisis they brought. She could not move. Three shadowy figures, the dark blue of their uniforms barely discernible through the fog and the gathering dark, had reached the riverbank now and were striding toward the house. Toward her children! Toward her!

She breathed a prayer for courage, rubbed her forehead roughly to clear her mind, smoothed her long, gray cotton skirt and began to walk slowly toward the front of the house.

At the door, still safely locked, she waited. Heavy boots crossed the veranda and the brutal knock came—on *her* door. The door to *her house.*

Slowly, she unlatched and then opened the handsome door. "Yes?"

"Mrs. Fleming? Captain Clark, U.S. Army. I'm here to evict you." The coarse, heavyset, bearded officer held out a paper. This time, she made no move to take it. "Stubborn, eh? Then, I'll read the order to you." He stepped back onto the veranda to get all available light from the low, cloud-choked sky. In a singsong monotone, as rapidly as he could, he read: " 'Colonel James Shaw, Commanding Post, Jacksonville. Colonel Shaw . . . Information has been received at these headquarters that loads of torpedoes have been sent by the Rebels to Fleming's Island above Doctor's Lake and to the point of land lying between Doctor's Lake, Black Creek and the St. Johns River. These torpedoes have already been placed in the river or will be shortly unless active measures are taken against it. It appears that the residents of that part of the bank of the St. Johns are aroused for the purpose of spying on the positions of our gunboats on the river and the movements of our supply steamers. You are, therefore, directed to send a force of men, not exceeding two hundred, for the purpose of completely vacating the island, except for old men and Negroes; of capturing any Rebel scouts or pickets or torpedo layers and, especially one O'Hern, and you are ordered to cause all the loyal inhabitants to remove to the east side of the St. Johns and all the disloyal to remove west to within the enemy lines. This order to be executed without a moment's delay. Signed, by Order of Brigadier General, William Birney.'"

Margaret felt herself sway dangerously, then, from somewhere, primitive courage began to rise in her.

"You appear to have above-average intelligence, Mrs. Fleming," he said condescendingly, "but I'd be glad to reread any portions of this order pertaining to your immediate departure. And, lady, I mean—immediate."

Her voice hollow, but quiet, she said, "I was wondering if our neighbors downriver, Mr. and Mrs. A. M. Reed, of Black Point, both loyal to the Union, have been forced to remove to the east side of the St. Johns."

He laughed, turned to the two men on the front steps, whose faces Margaret had only then noticed.

"She's a smart one, all right, ain't she? Trying to get our minds off the *dis*loyal inhabitants like herself!" Facing Margaret again, eyes hard, he pulled his revolver. "What the Reeds do is none of your business. At gunpoint—because you are known to be supplying information to the enemy—and because you're known to have a half-witted son active with O'Hern and those Rebel torpedo layers—and because you're known to have three sons and a stepson in the Confederate forces—*you are hereby ordered out of this house within two hours of right now.*"

Standing perfectly erect, she said, "I have never supplied information of any kind to either side in this dreadful war. My sons are fighting, yes. But I'm a lone widow in this place, with only a few servants and three young daughters—fifteen, twelve and nine. What harm could we do to you? Major Guy V. Henry assured me that we would be safe so long as we minded our own affairs. Before God, we've minded no one else's, Captain."

"Lady, it's gonna get dark early on a bad day like this. I'm here for only one purpose. To get you out. My orders plainly said *immediately*. I'm being kind to give you two hours. Out."

"But, I have no horses! Major Henry's men—killed them."

"Lady. This is no easy job I've got. I don't intend to let you make it any harder. I'll send men back to check on you in exactly two hours from now. At seven sharp. If you and your children are not gone by then, you'll be—sorry. Do not take a single servant. Is that clear?"

Margaret, with tears—which she hated—burning her eyes, squared her shoulders, then, let them droop hopelessly. "You—really *would* send a lone woman and three little girls—out into those dark woods—to make their way on foot in the rain, wouldn't you?"

"Yes, ma'am. I sure would. I'm a soldier."

She gave him a weary, not unpleasant look. "A soldier . . ."

"That's right."

"We'll go, Captain."

He coughed, took out his watch, replaced it. "Two hours, lady. Too dark for us to make it to the next plantation tonight. We'll be right out there on the river waiting—till seven sharp. Then, we'll be back to be sure you're gone." At the steps, he turned to her again. "By the way, we know you have an old white man here working for you. He's not to go either. He'll be held here, as a prisoner. The United States Army is now in possession of this entire place and all its working hands."

44

Hour after hour through the longest, darkest night of her life, Margaret lay awake on her damp, pine branch bed, covered over with one of the four thin blankets Maum Betty had insisted they take. Rain still fell, but softly, almost tenderly, onto the half-collapsed roof of old Indian Mary's cabin. July and Little Jim had brought her and the girls that far to spend the first night away from Hibernia. At the cabin, they were at least a mile on their way toward Middleburg, the nearest Confederate town where there was a chance that someone would take them in, until they could find a way to reach L.I. in Lake City.

Her thoughts—if they could be called thoughts—were chaotic. What would they have done without July and Little Jim to guide them through the black, dripping woods? A lone woman and three girls, laden with even the pitifully few belongings they managed, would surely have fallen, been severely injured—perhaps attacked by the Hibernia panther, against which Lewis had warned the boys for as long as she could remember.

Would Captain Clark and his ruffians take over her house tonight? Dear Lord, she prayed, take care of Maum Betty and July and Rina and Mr. Causey and all our people. My friends. Watch over them. Let the Yankees treat them kindly. An involuntary sob wracked her. She buried her face in the folds of her old linen coat—her own weeping echoing. Maum Betty's choking sobs when she had to let them all go and Rina's uncontrolled crying when she said good-bye to her special playmate, Tissie.

Only God knew how far they'd be able to walk tomorrow. What if they met no one on the Middleburg Road? What if—all alone and with only the ham slices and cornbread and roasted sweet potatoes Maum Betty had wrapped up and tucked in Belle's bucket—they had to walk *all the way*? In her state of turmoil on this dark, desolate night, she tried not to dwell on the fact that Lewis had always said it was about twenty miles to Middleburg. Belle, before they'd reached Indian Mary's cabin, had already begun to complain of a blister on her heel.

Margaret dried her eyes on the blanket. Think about something else, she scolded herself. This is tonight. You're not walking down that road yet. Think about—Cherokee Indian Mary. What must she have been like? Old, when Lewis remembered her. Long dead. Murdered by Seminoles because she had loved Lewis's mother and father and had warned them in time for their escape when Seminoles were about to burn the first Hibernia house. Much later, young Lewis had found the remains of Indian Mary's mangled body—decomposed, almost dried out—sprawled across the very doorstep over which Margaret and the girls had stepped, how many hours ago? There was no seeing her watch in the pitch black. She would know, only by the first show of dawn, that it was time for them to eat just a little of Maum Betty's precious food and go.

A half mile lay between Indian Mary's cabin and the road. July had guided them on an angle through the woods so they would come out on to the road at least one mile along their way to Middleburg. Then—two miles to Swimming Pen Creek, where, dear God, let a boat be there, with oars to get us to the other side. To leave boats for emergency travelers had long been a Florida custom, but who could depend on custom with a war on? *What is a soldier, Captain Clark?* A soldier, she answered herself, is Seton and Frank and Frederic and William and L.I.—and Captain Clark and my cousin, Guy Henry. And Lewis. Lewis was a soldier.

Lewis. Tears came again. Helplessly. Lewis would be so worried about them tonight. Or—did he worry now, as she understood worry? "Lewis?" she whispered into her damp, wrinkled coat sleeve. "Lewis? Where are you? I know—you *are*. But, oh, my darling, *where?*" Her taut body went limp. "Will you please talk to God for us, Lewis? Please? I'm—too tired. Too tired . . ."

At last, wide-eyed, she saw first light moving up the sky and quickly called the girls. As usual, only Belle was hard to rouse, and when she did sit up, her blanket twisted under her, she began to sob that they would all surely be killed before the day was over. While Tissie and Margaret shook and folded the blankets and tied them into a bundle, Maggie combed Belle's tangled hair. Then, Belle broke away, grabbed the food bucket and ran outside.

"What's she up to, Mama?" Maggie asked.

"Who knows, darling? Let's just wait a moment and see."

"We oughta start walking," Tissie said, her usual impatience showing. "I'll go get her—I'm hungry."

"Just wait, Tissie. Whatever Belle's doing, it's unpredictable, but it might as easily be something good as something—nerve-wracking."

"Are we going to be—all right, Mama?" Maggie asked.

Margaret hugged her two older girls. "Yes. Yes. God is going to be walking right along with us. I think it's going to be a sunny morning. We'll be just fine."

Belle danced back into the cabin, her beguiling smile radiant, their breakfast all portioned out on Easter's big linen napkin. "I'm not going to be a hindrance today, Mama. I'm helping," she beamed. "Breakfast is served!"

They stared at the food. The cornbread lay in broken, crumbling heaps, the sweet potato was smashed and the ham was literally in shreds.

"Belle! What on earth happened to the food?"

"Ugh. It looks awful," Tissie grumbled.

"Oh, it smells fine," Belle assured them. "And I really think we'd better eat and get to Middleburg. It's a long way."

"Belle?"

"What is it, Mama? Aren't you hungry?"

"What happened to that food? Surely, you didn't manage to tear it up like that just serving it!"

Busying herself handing out portions, Belle said calmly, "I must have, Mama. I'm awfully sorry."

Biding her time until she could learn the truth, Margaret urged them all to eat. Then, they picked up their alloted loads and started cautiously through the sunny, high-lighted woods.

"It's nice the rain's gone," Maggie said as cheerfully as anyone could manage, stepping along in heavy boots—too hot for June.

"I'm doing fine with my blisters, Mama." Belle called buoyantly, walking quite far off to one side.

"That's good, dear. All our boots are too heavy for a warm, humid day like this. But, I have no idea how far we'll have to walk. Maum Betty packed house slippers for us, too, in that bundle Tissie's carrying—we'll need them later at L.I.'s."

For a time, they plodded along, climbing over fallen trees, skirting thick clumps of sharp-tipped palmetto, stumbling now and then over an exposed tree root.

"Mama, are you sure we're going in the direction of the Middleburg road?" Tissie asked, already shifting the heavy clothing bundle from one arm to the other.

"*She* better be sure," Belle said, still from her distance. "*She* better be sure. My blisters might not wait much longer to hurt."

"I don't like to be addressed as *she*, Belle, any more than you do," Margaret said pleasantly.

Belle giggled. "Now, you know how it feels, I guess."

"Yes, darling, and I'll never do it again. But, July gave us very good directions. Don't I see a clearing up ahead now? That must be our road." Suddenly, Margaret stopped. "What is that I hear?"

"What, Mama?" Tissie and Maggie chorused.

"Kittens meowing!"

Belle hurried on ahead. Really hurried, faster than she'd been "able" to hurry since they'd left Indian Mary's cabin.

Margaret called to her. "Isabel Fleming, come back here! You've got some explaining to do."

Belle didn't come back, but she did stop until they caught up with her. The meowing grew louder.

"Let me see that bucket!" Margaret pulled back the cloth cover Maum Betty had tied around the big milk pail. "Oh, Belle!" Abruptly, she threw her arms around her youngest daughter and held her very close.

"I had to—bring them, Mama. I just—had to." Belle began to cry. "They're so—little. I couldn't leave my new kittens with—a bunch of mean—Yankees!"

"Mama, we've got enough trouble without Belle's nasty kittens," Tissie wailed.

Margaret, still holding Belle, said firmly, "Yes, Tissie, we have—more than enough trouble. But she's had to give up so much. Belle may keep her kittens. We'll manage." Swiping at a tear, she tried to laugh. "That's what happened to our food, isn't it, Belle? Kitten claws."

Belle nodded.

For a moment, they stood looking at one another. Tissie began to cry first, and in no time all four, there in the lonely, empty woods, hugged one another and wept. Then, Maggie stopped, dried her eyes without a word and picked up her bundle, which held the few treasures Margaret could not part with—two graceful silver sauceboats which Lewis's father, George Fleming, had brought with him from Ireland so long ago, the fancy French clock Lewis had given her and her wedding day earrings—long pendants of white carnelian set in hand-etched gold.

"I'm ready to start walking again," Maggie said.

"We are, too, darling. Come on, Tissie, Belle. It's still two miles to Swimming Pen Creek once we've reached the road."

At Swimming Pen Creek, at least a quarter of a mile wide, the hoped-for boat was there. It leaked and there was only one oar, but while Margaret paddled as one would paddle a canoe—a stroke on one side and then the other—and while the girls bailed water, they kept their hopes high by singing until the rickety piragua scraped sand safely on the other side.

"Your back must hurt something awful, Mama," Maggie said, when they were out of the boat. "We'll carry your load too. I know our shoes and winter coats are heavy."

Margaret, her worn cotton dress wet with perspiration from the enormous effort of taking them safely across the creek, smiled wearily at Maggie, rubbed her own aching back, flexed her shoulders and said, "All right, honey. But just for a little way. I'll be fine in a few minutes. If I'm correct, we still have five miles to go on this road before we get to Gerry's Ferry. Heaven knows how long we'll have to wait for that."

Belle's kittens, their stomachs full of ham and cornbread, were quiet for a long time. Even when they stopped walking to rest awhile and drink a little of the precious Hibernia well water which Tissie dutifully carried in another covered milk pail, the kittens were quiet. That, Margaret thought, is something to be thankful for. At their next rest stop, they'd give them a drink, too, if a stream could be found. She dared not part with one unnecessary drop of Hibernia water. With every step, she prayed, even while singing songs with her girls to keep their minds occupied, that a wagon, a cart—any kind of conveyance might be moving in their direction from the east on the Middleburg Road. By now, they had covered perhaps two of the five miles from Swimming Pen Creek to Gerry's Ferry. Her whole body ached and although she wouldn't have admitted it for all the tea in China, she, too, had blisters on both feet. The girls, who played outside in winter, were far more accustomed to heavy shoes.

The sun was almost overhead when Margaret heard the blessed sound for which she'd been praying. They stopped, listened—Belle petting the kittens, raging now to escape the milk pail. There was a collective sigh of relief when an old wagon jolted into sight—going their way.

"Mrs. Fleming! What in the world are you an' your girls doin' out here on this lonely old road?"

A slender-faced, sun-browned, middle-aged man looked down at them from the wagon seat, a battered hat on the back of his head. "Don't be skeered," he said softly. "You kin trust me, ma'am. My name's O'Hern. I serve with your boy, William, in the Reg'lators." Abruptly, he jumped to the ground and held out his hand. "Like I said, O'Hern's my name, ma'am. We ain't never met, but I seen you many a time in Jacksonville with your late husband." O'Hern removed his sweat-stained hat. "Fine man, the Colonel. I usta wait tables at the hotel there."

Margaret gave him her hand. His was hard and bony, the

skin as rough as though it had been grated. "You—say you know my son William? Is he—all right? When did you see him, Mr. O'Hern?"

"Yestidy morning." He clicked his tongue admiringly. "William's one of our best shots." He tapped his head once or twice. "Slow, but a good boy. Tough as palmetto." For a moment, he studied the forlorn little group. "What happened, ma'am? They run you off your land?"

Margaret took a deep breath. "Yes, Mr. O'Hern. We were—ordered to leave. And, I think you should know that they're searching for you. Your name was mentioned—only yours—in the military order which evicted us from our home."

O'Hern began to grin, then to laugh. He laughed until he was bending up and down slapping his knees. "Good for me! I say, good for me! That means I'm famous, don't it? But don't worry none about me. Me an' William an' our other fellers is gonna be the ones to send them dad-blasted Yankees scootin' on their—" He coughed nervously and rephrased his sentence. "We're gonna be the ones to send 'em hightailin' it clean outa the state of Florida! We already blowed up four of their gunboats all by ourselves. Your boy William helped, too." Briskly, he began to take their bundles. "Whata's matter with my manners? Here, lemme git this wagon loaded up an' then I'll hep you in. Goin' to Major L.I. in Lake City, eh?"

"Yes," Margaret said cautiously, but so relieved at the prospect of sitting down. "Yes. We're going to Lake City. But, if you could take us as far as Middleburg, I'm sure we'll find other means from there tomorrow."

Jolting along in the rickety wagon, Margaret and Belle on the seat with O'Hern, Tissie and Maggie in back with their belongings, he informed them that they would still have some fifty or fifty-five miles from Middleburg to Lake City. "You wanta take the back way through Kingsley Lake, Raiford, Lake Butler. Might have to ketch a few fresh rides from place to place." He gave Margaret a grin. "But from what William tells me, his ma won't be likely to fail."

A widow put them up that night in Middleburg and Margaret gave thanks with what energy remained before she drifted into desperately needed sleep on a real bed. The bed sagged so that the four of them, stretched crossways, slept with their feet higher than their heads, but it was a bed. Her body ached, her mind was numb, but her last thought was of hope for tomorrow. Tomorrow there would be a way—there would be a way to cover at least some of the fifty-five miles that still separated her from the security and solace of L.I.'s strong arms. Only God knew where Seton and Frank and Frederic and William were, but L.I. would be in Lake City and she meant to get to him.

Late in the afternoon of June 19, L.I., striding along in his gray officer's uniform past the small lake below his square frame house in Lake City, could not keep back the tears. In the breast pocket of his jacket was tucked a short note from Dr. Richard P. Daniel, Surgeon of the Eighth Florida. The hastily scrawled words—even the look of the tall, slanting script—were burned into L.I.'s memory: "I will write at length when the body is recovered, but it is my sad and painful duty to convey to you and, through you, to his mother, Mrs. Margaret Fleming, the tragic news of the death of Captain Seton Fleming."

Tears flowed so freely they wet L.I.'s rusty brown beard. He could imagine anyone else on earth dead—but Seton. For nearly three long years, the strictures and pressures of war had suspended L.I.'s prospering law practice, had cost him his Jacksonville home, had forced him and Mary Evelyn to live in the hardship and confusion of noisy, dusty Lake City, its population of four hundred had swollen to more than two thousand by refugees from Jacksonville. He could accept all that, but he could not accept the fact that his beloved half-brother, Miss Margaret's cherished Seton, would never come home again to the big house at Hibernia. Tears fell because of L.I.'s own grief—but how, *how* could he face telling Miss Margaret?

"I'll wait awhile," he said aloud to himself, nearing his house. "I'll wait to ride to Hibernia at least until I've had time to receive Dr. Daniel's letter giving me details. Miss Margaret will have to know all about everything. How he died, how long he lay wounded, where he's buried." A bit of his load lifted. At least, he would have four or five days in which to begin to learn to handle his own grief.

L.I. picked up a stick and threw it as hard as he could. "Criminals, thieves, wife-beaters, murderers will walk away from this war without a scratch! But, Seton is—dead! Dear God, *Seton is dead.* . . ."

45

For every moment of the time required for his wife, Mary Evelyn, and the aged cart driver to help the exhausted, scratched and bruised girls out of the piled-up cart bed, to unload their dust- and rain-stained belongings, Margaret refused to let go of L.I. The elderly man who had brought them in his oxcart over the last few miles was too feeble, L.I. knew, to do the lifting, but he had no choice. Margaret could almost not speak, but her need, her pain-filled need strained toward him and he held her, comforting her. It had taken nearly ten agonizing days to reach him and so he held her, reassuring her again and again as she clung to him, that they would all be safe now.

Inside, after he'd paid her benefactor with a smoked ham and a warm handshake, L.I. settled Margaret in the parlor on their one sofa while Mary Evelyn took the girls out back to wash and eat. Belle's kittens, free of their bucket at last, were no longer controllable. From a window, as he arranged soft, clean feather pillows around Margaret, he could see the kittens chasing one another like tiny wild beasts round and round the house.

A chair pulled up close to the sofa, L.I. sat with Margaret as though she were a sick child. He sponged her face and tried to let her know how sorry he was that he had failed to convince her to leave Hibernia sooner under more comfortable conditions. She lay with her eyes closed, saying nothing.

"I must stop such talk," he said at last. "You're here now. You're safe. You did well by the girls, too. They're all right."

L.I. watched her as she slowly opened her dark, deeply circled eyes. The pain in those eyes which had once been the merriest he'd ever seen—tore at his heart.

"L.I.," she whispered hoarsely, "I—had to leave—Hibernia. I—had to leave—your father's—grave. This time, I had no choice." Her slender body looked drained of its last ounce of strength, but she struggled to raise herself on one elbow. "Maum Betty, July, the others, will look after it. And—L.I.? One day, I'll go back. One day—I'm going back!"

384

Too full of grief and dread that the exhausted woman would soon have to learn about Seton, L.I. could not speak. Tenderly, he eased her back onto the pillows.

"One day, she went on, this—will all be—behind us. And I can go—home. You'll take care of us here, for a while. But one day, I'll be home again, won't I? Everything will be all right again, won't it?"

He gave her all the love in his heart with his eyes, but for the life of him, L.I. could think of nothing to say that would be—truthful. Except once, long ago, when he had blamed the empty cookie jar on his brother, George, he'd never lied to Miss Margaret. He'd be lying now if he said he believed she might ever go back. Or, that her life could ever be—all right again—with Seton dead.

The deep, shuddering breath she drew and released told him that he was right to wait before he allowed the next blow to fall.

In the gathering dusk, after Maggie had brought her mother tea and good bread and butter, L.I. leaned closer to be sure he wasn't just imagining that Miss Margaret was smiling at him. Yes. Almost imperceptible, but it was a smile.

"Do you remember—all those sermons of mine—about hope?"

L.I. nodded.

"Good," she said on a sigh. "Well, I'm—determined to be hopeful, now. It's—still my obligation to Lewis—and to God." She drew another deep, uneven breath. "Now, L.I., may I sleep right here tonight? I'm—so tired, I don't want to move an inch until morning." She closed her eyes. "This is—pure luxury. Just this once, will you please say good night to the girls for me?"

Later that week, on his way home from his office, L.I. tried to convince himself that Miss Margaret did not suspect a thing. For the past four days, struggling to hide his own grief over Seton, he couldn't be sure. Even when he joked or teased with his half-sisters, Miss Margaret's eyes were on him—not laughing, not joining in. Watching. Quizzical. She was no longer young, but so painfully vulnerable these days that he avoided the wondering dark eyes as much as possible, dreading the moment when he would have to hurt her still more.

The detailed letter from Dr. Daniel had come—yesterday,

June 23. To protect his own troubled mind for closer attention to the difficult desertion cases he'd tried today, L.I. had purposely left the letter at home, carefully hidden under some legal papers on his desk. Seton, he now knew, had died unnecessarily. After his legitimate protest was refused, he had- -as anyone who knew Seton would expect—led his men on a foolish, vainglorious mission ordered by an idiot of a commanding officer. Every man in the mission had been slaughtered—Seton, not thirty yards from his own line. A bullet in his bright, young head. After three days, his body was retrieved and buried for the time being in what Dr. Daniel called "a rather pretty place near where he fell at the Battle of Gaines Farm, Virginia, under a sheltering cedar tree."

L.I. stood for a long time beside the dark water of the small lake, dreading to go home. Dreading the moment for Miss Margaret, but also for himself. Dreading the further pain of watching her suffer. "Captain Fleming, for over a week, had behaved with the sure calm of a man who felt his death was imminent," Daniel had written. "He laughed, he joked, he buoyed our spirits as always, but his eyes sought a far distance at times and they were the eyes of a man who longed to go on living, but who also was not afraid to die."

L.I. turned away from the lake and walked rapidly home. She is suffering now, he thought, not knowing, suspecting. I can put an end to that, at least.

Mary Evelyn met him at the front door and one glimpse of her troubled face set his heart pounding.

"She knows," Mary gasped.

"She—knows about Seton?"

"Belle's kittens. They got loose in the parlor and fought and scratched all over your desk. Papers flew everywhere. Miss Margaret ran to help Tissie pick them up. Tissie—found Dr. Daniel's—long letter! Her eye caught Seton's name. She gave it to her mother." His pretty, sensitive wife laid a steadying hand on L.I.'s shoulder. "Miss Margaret's alone in her room upstairs. She's already had one hard cry. The girls know, too. She comforted them. Miss Margaret is a—magnificent lady, but—she needs *you* now. I told her I'd send you up the moment you got home."

He didn't knock. The door stood ajar.

"L.I.," Margaret said, her voice thick, "come in. I've been waiting for you."

He ran to her, dropped to his knees beside the little rocker where she sat and held her in his arms while they both wept. Then, with an apron, borrowed from Mary Evelyn, Margaret dried L.I.'s eyes first and then her own. She fell back against the chair and looked at him, tears still wet on her pale cheeks. Her beautiful eyes had as much capacity for weeping, he thought, as her beautiful heart for love.

"You've had to shed so many tears, Miss Margaret."

She nodded. "Yes. Yes. L.I.?"

"What can I do for you? Please, give me *something* to do for you!"

"The—only thing—I—want now—is to—run away—from everything. Do—you remember, long ago before I married your father, when your dog, Buster, caught his paw in a crack in the New Switzerland dock?"

"Sure, I remember."

"Well," her breathing was shallow and fast. "Well, I can—still see the little fellow running, running—all over the yard. He was—trying to run away from his pain, L.I."

"I remember what you said to Buster when I finally caught him, too."

"You do? What did I say?"

"That no one can run—from—pain and really escape it."

She made a choking sound, mirthless, dry. "I—was glib—and young then, wasn't I?" She pushed him aside and began to pace the floor. "I was glib and young then, but—I was right!" Trembling, she crossed the room to where L.I. stood and beat her fists against his broad chest. "*I was right!* We can't run away! I can't run away from—the horrible *fact*—that I will never see Seton smile again! Never—kiss him again! Do you have any idea what *never* means?" She slipped her arms around his neck and hung there. "Of course, you—know what—*never* means. You learned as a little boy, didn't you? All those long years ago when we buried your mother under the big magnolia tree in our little Hibernia cemetery. And you learned about *never* again—when your father left us." Her arms dropped to her sides. L.I. led her to the rocker. "Thank you," she said. "Sit down with me a little while, please."

Eagerly, he pulled up a chair and straddled it.

"I—I loved Seton so much," he said simply. "As though he were my own brother."

"Yes. I know. Now, I guess dear Mary Evelyn told you how I—learned about it. Tissie meant well. And I forgive you for not telling me sooner. I've read the whole letter—several times. But, I want you to help me understand one thing." She clenched her hands together. "I know he died—senselessly. I was able to take that in. But, what I need to understand is—Seton's body is buried near where he—fell, now, isn't it?"

"Yes. In a very pretty spot, I believe Dr. Daniel said."

"He did say that, yes. Under a 'sheltering cedar tree.' "

L.I. stared at her, marveling at her determination to reach for every small comfort—even to be comforted by knowing Seton had a familiar kind of shelter. A cedar tree. He had never longed so agonizingly for words. Something, anything to help her. He heard himself say: "I'm—proud of you, Miss Margaret."

"Are you? Oh, that's good, L.I. Thank you for being proud of me. I really need you to be. My life is—in so many pieces right now, I—almost feel a failure. So, please do be—a little proud of me. You see, if I know you are trying to be, it will—help me give you reason."

"I've always been proud of you. But never as much as this minute."

Still wiping fresh-flowing tears from her cheeks, she gave him a small, warm smile. "Now, tell me this, L.I. There was something in that letter about moving Seton's body—to Richmond. When will they do that, do you think?"

L.I. let his head fall onto his arms folded across the back of the chair. "Not for a while, I'm afraid. Our capital is still there, but I'm sure our—dead won't be moved to Richmond until—it's all over."

"It will be one day, won't it?"

"Yes. One day."

She sat quietly for a time, then whispered, "Seton is—with his father. That does help, knowing that. They're together again." Her hand felt for his. "Your beautiful mother and Geroge, too." L.I. could feel her reaching spirit. "Someday, when—this is all over, you know, I'm going to build a lovely little chapel at Hibernia under the trees across from the big house. And when I get my chapel built, we'll have a real service in memory and in honor of your mother and father and George—and Seton." Her shoulders began to jerk ever so slightly, then the iron control snapped and, in L.I.'s arms, she cried unrestrainedly—until she could cry no more.

* * *

Near Pensacola
1 July 1864

My beloved Mother,

Word has just reached me that my idol, Seton, is dead.
But, by God's grace, I learned at the same time that you
are safely in Lake City with L.I., and a day earlier, that Frank
is safe somewhere in north Georgia. What is there to write,
except that never before have I so needed the comfort of your
arms. And, at the same time, I long to comfort you with
mine. I have almost forgotten, but not quite, the joy of being
your little boy, Frederic, at Hibernia, of living my days in
love. The love sustains me in this hard world of today. I do
not complain. That is merely my feeble way of telling you
that, although I can never take Seton's place in your heart—no
one could—I am now a man, aged nineteen, and will devote
the remainder of my life to caring for you. I am tired, but
well and safe at this time. There may or may not be more
fighting here, but I am forced to believe that God, in His goodness, will not allow you to endure further grief. Frank and
I will come home safely—and William. I worry about William,
but can do nothing. As I can do nothing for you except repeat
my promise that, with a heart filled with only gratitude, I will
live the remainder of my days at Hibernia with you. I am
not lively and entertaining as was Seton, nor the conversationalist my father was, but I will be your host when the day
comes that we can once more welcome guests to our big house
by the river. Frank will go back into L.I.'s law office with
him, but my dream is to be your strong right hand at home.
I have thought and planned for hours on end. My first act
when this is all over—even if our noble cause is lost—will be
to take the necessary steps to regain our home. Trust me.
Let your heart rest as much as possible in the midst of your
fresh grief. We will be a team, Mama. Count on me. I am
not writing of the war's progress or lack of it. The tragedy has
gone on too long. I can write only of the day when we are
together again—you, William, the girls and I—planning and
working toward our future. I send you my sympathy, dearest
Mother, and my love.

Frederic Fleming

Margaret read Frederic's letter alone on the front porch of
L.I.'s house. For a long time, she sat watching, but not really

seeing, the carts and wagons jolt and rattle by. Now and then, inattentively, she lifted a hand in greeting to a neighbor walking or riding past, but only her body was there in the tiny, dirty city crowded with other refugees from the war which had torn her dreams to shreds. Her mind, her heart, moved constantly toward Hibernia, toward her three remaining sons, toward Louisa. The life of every person taking shelter in Lake City was so torn, the peopld so distraught and discommoded, shouting and cursing were commonplace. Only at night was there any real quiet. Still, a kind of peace was at this moment—in the midst of the street noise and the shouts and whistles—moving into her heart for the first time since she had been pushed into the wilderness alone with her girls.

Frederic had done it with his letter. Frederic was not Seton, although he was handsome, as Lewis was handsome— tall, quiet, thoughtful, tender. None of her other sons had Seton's strange beauty, his dash, his energy of spirit. But could Seton ever have been contented to live out his life in their backwater of peace and silence along the St. Johns? *Would* he have even tried? She would never know, but Frederic longed to be her partner. And she knew her gentle middle son well enough to know that he would never have written as he did if his heart were not in every word.

Both hands covering the pages of the peace-giving letter, she leaned her head against the wooden back of the porch rocker and closed her eyes. Whatever damage they were doing to her treasured house, her furniture, her lovingly selected carpets and pictures and china and crystal, whatever muddy boots were scarring the wide board floors of which Lewis was so proud, Frederic would help restore.

Slowly, steadily, she got to her feet, tucked the letter into her bodice, called to Mary Evelyn that she was going to visit Tina and left the house, trying to hold her head high.

Yesterday's rain still stood in puddles along the roadside. Wagons rolled and splashed by, their drivers shouting at horses and helpers. Now and then an officer in mud-splattered gray uniform galloped past and, once, she was splashed disgracefully. She glanced down at her splotched black skirt. She was in black again—for Seton. By a miracle, Tina had been able to buy her enough black cambric for an everyday mourning dress. The mud would brush off when it dried. What did mud matter anyway?

Margaret walked the two blocks north to Marion Street and

turned the corner in the direction of Tina's cottage. People jostled one another along the roadsides; a fat lady, her eyes red from weeping, nearly knocked her down, but Margaret scarcely noticed. Her attention was riveted now on one large, rickety wagon moving along Marion Street, its sloping, sagging bed crowded with quiet forms under dirty gray blankets. Suddenly, her visit forgotten, she was running toward the wagon and reached it as its driver slowed and stopped before General Hospital on the other side of the street. L.I. had told her about the military hospital in Lake City, but she had avoided it, dreading the thought that in the chaotic, crowded town boys like Seton and Frank and Frederic and William lay suffering, their bodies being cut and hacked into by exhausted doctors struggling only to save lives. Now, irresistibly, she crossed the muddy street and stood watching as the wounded— some groaning, one sobbing—were carried on stretchers into the big, brick building.

Frederic could be brought here should he be wounded!

Frederic—or William. There were four other Florida hospitals, but today she had no idea where either son was fighting.

She stood rooted at the hospital door, looking after the litter bearers as they brought in the last boy from the wagon. And, without making a conscious decision of any kind, she walked through the open door and inside where the street noises were dimmed by more groans and cries, the rattle of metal instruments and pans and trays. Up and down each long wall, cots stretched all the way to the back of the converted warehouse.

And on each cot lay—Frederic, Frank, Seton, William— *needing her.*

For a moment, she stood unnoticed, her head reeling. Then, she went straight to the first cot and knelt beside the pale young man who was staring at the ceiling. Blood oozed through the thick layers of bandage protecting the stump of his right arm.

"I'd—like to—do something for you," she said. "Can you hear me?"

Slowly, he turned his head and whispered, "Water . . ."

For the remainder of the morning into the afternoon, she stayed, moving from one cot to another, the exhausted doctor addressing her, giving her orders as though she'd been coming for days.

By midafternoon, tired, her back aching from bending over the low cots, her heart torn by the suffering that polluted the very air of the big room, she knew she would be coming every day—if they'd have her.

"You don't know me, Doctor," she said, at the first opportunity, "but I can see you need me. My name is Mrs. Lewis Fleming. I—need to be here. My eldest son has just been killed. I have three more—fighting. I'd like to help."

Frail, stooped, the graying doctor blinked his bloodshot eyes, as though he was seeing her for the first time and said, wearily, "All right, Mrs. Fleming. I'm Dr. Morel. And, yes, I'm—desperate for a matron. Will you commit yourself to—helping me run this place?"

She lifted her chin. "Certainly, Dr. Morel. I'll stay as long as you need me today—and I'll be back first thing tomorrow morning."

L.I. tried to reason with her, fearing for her health, but she missed not one day attending her "boys"—not even Sunday—through the remainder of the summer and into the fall. At night, she wrote letter after letter to their families and, by day, she cared as best she could for their spiritual and bodily pain, easing the pain in her own heart as she worked. Daily, she rushed to look at the face of each wounded boy carried through the high front door of her hospital to be sure it wasn't Frederic or William. And, beyond that, fought back her own grief and anxiety so that she would have love enough for the torn and battered and bleeding boys around her.

On a warm, October evening, her work ended for the day, Margaret trudged wearily home to find L.I. waiting for her on the front porch.

"The sunset was beautiful," she said, giving him a warm smile. "Have you been watching it? I don't think I've seen so much green in an afterglow for years. I've always thought the color green—sings. Have you thought of that, L.I.?"

He embraced her. "No. But it's just like you to think of it."

Margaret stepped back. "Let me look at you, dear boy. Are you all right?"

"I'm fine. Well, I'm not sick, if that's what you mean. Oh, Miss Margaret, I wish I had a lot more wisdom than I have!"

"Fiddlesticks. Dr. Morel was just telling me today that his commanding officer praises your just decisions where those poor deserters are concerned. No man could show more wisdom than you've shown with some of them. Especially the ones who desert so they can go home to plant sweet potatoes for their starving families!"

"I'm not talking about that kind of wisdom. I—just wish I knew better how to—help you. You've had so many hard blows."

She stiffened. "Has something happened to Frank—or Frederic? William?"

"No, no, no. Nothing like that." L.I. reached into his jacket pocket and took out a partly dried sprig of cedar. "This—this is all we'll get—of Seton," he said lamely. "This—cedar from the tree beside his grave."

She shrank from it, then slowly reached to take the prickly, browning branch.

"I wanted so much to find a way to give it to you that isn't so—hard on you, Miss Margaret, but—"

"Sh. You say this is all—I'll have of him? None of Seton's belongings?"

"None. They haven't found anything—anywhere. Dr. Daniel thought, at least, to send the sprig of cedar."

For a long moment, she smoothed the parched needles with her fingers. Then, trying to give L.I. a hopeful look, she whispered: "Well, the cedar—is *green*. At least, it was—when it was picked from Seton's tree, wasn't it?"

"Yes," L.I. said helplessly. "Yes, I'm sure it was green then." Abruptly, almost roughly, he took her in his arms again. "Damn this war! Forgive me, Miss Margaret—but damn this war!"

Part Six

1865–1877

46

Many Floridians didn't believe it was over until almost the middle of May 1865, but the war had been grinding to a close for a year. On April 1, Florida Governor Milton, unable to face defeat, but certain of it, took his own life. And, on April 9, Lee surrendered at Appomattox, firmly telling his troops to "go home and plant corn." To pick up the pieces of their torn lives and go on in the same spirit in which they'd fought so bravely and against such odds.

From all over the South, battle-weary, half-starved Confederate soldiers were making their way home by any possible means. Margaret's son Frederic was among them. Alone, on May 1, his twentieth birthday, astride his faithful horse, Rod, Frederic had covered the long, grueling miles from Tallahassee to Jacksonville after having fought in the thick of what Floridians were calling "the glorious Battle of Natural Bridge." Determination to carry out his promise to his mother kept him moving. The Federal General's office in Jacksonville would, he had learned, be the key to regaining possession of Hibernia. Boy and horse were emaciated, hungry and bone-tired. But he meant to regain possession of Hibernia and devote his life to helping his mother restore it. His head felt light from exhaustion and hunger, but his purpose held. In spite of rumors that the Hibernia house had been burned, he pushed on. And after hours of questioning and waiting, he stood at last face to face with the officer in charge at the Federal General's headquarters in Jacksonville.

"I do not guarantee its condition," the officer said, "but your mother's house has not been destroyed. We've used it as a hospital for sick and wounded horses. A segment of our quartermaster corps still holds it, but show these papers. There should be no trouble regaining possession."

No longer the trusting boy he'd been the day he and Rod galloped out the Hibernia road in such high spirits—now so long ago—Frederic only half believed the officer. But after fording McGirt's Creek at Jacksonville, with only a slab of cold cornbread to eat, he and Rod began the thirty-mile overland ride to Fleming's Island. Thoughts of his mother filled his weary mind. L.I. had written, just before the Second Florida was discharged, that only Cousin Louisa's need of his mother had persuaded her to go first to St. Augustine instead of Hibernia. Cousin Sophia was quite ill. His mother had never refused Cousin Louisa anything. Of course she would go now when she was needed. That is, she would make the trip from Lake City to St. Augustine as soon as the last of her wounded boys at the military hospital had been sent home some time in July. That would give Frederic a chance to clean and at least partially repair whatever damage had been done to their home—if it still stood.

Mama will be safe in St. Augustine and well fed, he thought, as he rode along. The old city had been a Union town for most of the war. Little would change there now that the Yankees had won. It would be the best possible place for Mama—for the time being. Undoubtedly, she needs to pour out her heart to Cousin Louisa over Seton.

Anger rose in him at the thought of what his mother had endured. Not one of Seton's belongings had been sent to her! Nothing but a dried sprig of cedar from a lonely grave in Virginia. Poor Mama. How weary she must be after all those months of nursing the wounded at Lake City. But, how like her not to waste an ounce of her own heart-break in self-pity. She had used her pain—had let God use it to help suffering boys who longed for the touch of a caring hand. Frederic longed this minute—intensely—for his mother's touch. Still, he felt old. Old and lonely and—except for his determination to regain Hibernia—empty of every once cherished security. "Happy twentieth birthday," he said aloud, bitterly. He patted his horse's rough, scarred neck. "Rod? Don't let me be bitter. Just don't let me."

Rod, weary as he was, picked up his sore feet a bit in response. For a short distance, he even frisked a little. "If you want to have a good time, jine the cavalree—" Frederic sang as the horse fell back to his plodding pace. Seton had teased him with that song how many lifetimes ago? Seton, the proud infantry officer, laughing at Frederic's longing for the cavalry because he couldn't face leaving Rod behind. "Good time boys jine the cavalree," Seton had said, laughing. Well, no one Frederic had known had found that "good time."

Frederic saw plainly now, that there had never been anything in his nature that responded to the beat of drums or flying flags or shouts of battle. The truth was, he had simply gone on from day to day doing what he had to do. Oh, he and Rod had galloped out the Hibernia gate in high spirits at the start and for a time he'd tried hard to emulate Seton's daring in battle. It was simply not in him to revel in anything but peace and love and quiet—the kind of life a man could have with his family around him at Hibernia. Frederic had prayed that his mother would agree, as she now had, that he could finish his education from his father's fine library and live out his days by the St. Johns with her, and later, with the wife he might someday be blessed to find. His own family around him, he would be content as host for the visitors who would surely come again.

Would he mistrust Northerners now? He guessed not. More than ever, he understood his parents' once maddening neutrality when the trouble first began. Frederic hated no one. He only wanted to eat good food and sleep in a bed and be clean again—never to feel lice crawling on his body as long as he lived. He longed to see his mother behind the big coffee urn, her beautiful face framed by graying, golden curls, her grace and charm and humor blessing them all. He wanted to smell jasmine—in bloom right now if the house stood—by the side veranda. He wanted to see the river, the sun picking out its little waves, moving, one after another under the kind of brightness that was the essence of his boyhood.

His deep-set brown eyes ached for sleep; his long, thin body drooped over Rod's lean back. Frederic was now six feet two in his socks, but it had been a long time since he'd owned a pair. The memory of that bundle of woolen socks his father had sent to Frank and Seton before they left for Virginia brought pain. Papa. We wept for his father again. Rod offered a soft, understanding whicker.

The quietly dissolving spring day was almost over. If his judgment was correct, he was still more than three hours from Hibernia. In a sheltered pine grove, with a creek nearby, he dismounted. He and Rod would drink a lot of water to fill their emptiness and sleep until morning. It was plain that neither could travel even one more mile.

* * *

The next day when the sun was about midmorning high, Rod skirted a heavy, broad stand of palmetto and scrub pine and cypress and Frederic had his first glimpse of the blue water of good old Doctor's Lake. It was the same as ever—lily- and reed-choked and as blue as the Florida sky. For a long time, he sat on his horse, remembering all the good times he and his father and Seton and Frank had known on Doctor's Lake. A flood of almost forgotten freedom rose in him. He had followed orders for so long he felt almost guilty, but no one was expecting him anywhere today. His hand on Rod's scratched, tick-bitten neck, he allowed himself to look and look to his heart's content—for old time's sake. It felt good.

Then, the precious document that was supposed to give him possession of Hibernia tucked safely in his battered military hat, he and Rod plunged into the water for the long swim across to Fleming's Island.

At the far side at last, Rod was out of the lake first and shaking himself on the shore, as Frederic, almost grotesquely tall and thin, pulled and dragged himself up the slope, dripping water in little dark puddles in the thick, dusty sand.

Only intending to rest for half an hour from the strenuous swim, he found to his horror, when he awoke, that the sun was moving down the sky with several miles still between him and Hibernia.

Rod managed somehow to carry him over the remaining distance—Frederic half dozing in the saddle—wondering during fitful, conscious moments, who, if any of their people might still be there. Negroes were all free now. Where was July, Maum Betty, Rina, Little Jim, Big Owen? Was Carpenter Joe still there? He would surely need him. Had the Yankees permitted Mr. Causey to stay in his remodeled cabin? When might Frank find his way home again? William? No one had heard from William in months. Would anyone be at Hibernia to help him clean up the dear house? For certain, no one could help in his upcoming encounter with whoever still occupied it. Even Rod would have to be hidden in the woods. The possibility that one of the Yankees might shoot or steal Rod was, to Frederic, still very real. They had been his enemies too long.

He slipped again into a half sleep and roused—was jarred awake—when Rod broke abruptly into a canter. It was almost dark, but they were there! His heart nearly bursting, Frederic gasped at the condition of the familiar fields—overgrown with weeds and tangled vines—flourishing as vines had always flourished at Hibernia—up and under and around old pieces of military equipment, a rusty plow, the front wheels and axle of a supply cart.

Dismounting, he led Rod slowly through the big gate by the stable and off into a dense stand of woods where he would be safe. Rod would wait exactly where he left him, but from habit Frederic wrapped the reins around a sapling and began to creep slowly along toward his mother's double row of water oaks that led to the quarters.

Not even a stray dog greeted him. Not one Negro was in sight to say "Howdy, Mausa Frederic." The silence struck a strange terror. He made his way along the overgrown path only because he knew it. And then he could see the house. *It stood*. The big house had not been burned. The Yankee officer in Jacksonville had told the truth. Hibernia stood—its windows broken here and there, shingles missing, paint peeling—but it was there. With not a lamp burning anywhere that he could see from out back. He turned to the left, past the latticed breezeway that connected the house with Maum Betty's kitchen, past the cistern—its clump of white oleanders still beside it. The oleanders were in full bloom, their thick, white clusters almost giving light.

Rounding the corner of the front veranda, he could see a dim glow now from the high parlor windows. The reclamation papers in his hand, fear prickling his skin, he crossed the veranda and peered inside. Four half-dressed Yankee soldiers were playing cards and drinking around an old packing case in the middle of his mother's parlor—empty, except for the makeshift card table. With no idea of what he would say, Frederic knocked on the wide, familiar front door. Peeking again through the curtainless windows, he saw the men's startled faces. One of them cursed and slammed down his card hand. Another, a low-slung, chesty man of about forty, got slowly up from the bare, stained floor and shuffled heavily out of the room. Frederic could hear his boots cross the big hall. Then, the door opened a crack. "Whata ya want?" the man asked.

"My name is Frederic Fleming, sir. My mother owns this house." He showed the paper, still holding it firmly. "I have here an order from the Federal General's office in Jacksonville to reclaim the house in my mother's absence."

" 'Zat so?" The man reached out a thick hand. "Lemme see."

Frederic did not let go. "May I come inside to the light?"

The man opened the door wider. Frederic followed him into the parlor, struggling not to show his horror at what he saw. Wood had been allowed to burn out of the handsome fireplace, to break off burning, so that the once polished floors were charred in dozens of black gashes all around the hearth. Floor boards were missing, the once white walls were stained with soot and tobacco juice. Every stick of furniture was gone.

"Lemme see that paper," the man repeated.

For a moment, fear clouded Frederic's tired mind. In two or three rips with those beefy hands, the Yankee could ruin everything. At last, because there seemed nothing else to do without overly antagonizing the man, he handed over the paper and waited while it was read. Almost carelessly the Yankee handed it back to Frederic.

"When do I get possession of the house?" Frederic asked.

In answer, the man led him firmly by the arm back to the front door, gave him a push onto the veranda, closed the door and locked it. Through the window, Frederic saw him return to the card game and resume play.

Suddenly, weakness, hunger and this new anxiety so overcame him, he staggered to the veranda railing, sank helplessly to his knees, then to the floor and sprawled on his back—unable to manage one clear thought. In his thin clothes, still damp from lake water he slept the night away. The sun was already turning the St. Johns pink when he awoke the next day, stiff and shivering, wrapped only in his own thin arms.

What now? He sat up, rubbing his eyes, trying to think. And then he heard men's voices and the clatter of boxes and harness out back. He eased himself to his feet and peeped around the corner of the veranda. The four men, in worn blue uniforms, were loading an old wagon hitched to one swaybacked horse. They were leaving! Best to stay clear, he decided, and took his and Seton's old secret route to the quarters. From the far end of the house, back of the stables, he crawled, as he'd done numberless times as a boy, on his hands and knees under the low-growing jungle of yellow plum trees, through the green, twilight glooms of the lush branches and came out at the corner of what was always Maum Betty's cabin.

A low whistle reached him and at the cabin window, July was motioning silently for him to come inside.

He wanted to shout for joy. Maum Betty and July were still there! The hugs and pats and handshakes—all in careful, hushed tones, were balm to his battered spirit. Maum Betty fed him hot cornpone, honey and fried fatback.

He was home. With everything still to do—but he was there, back once more with at least two people who loved him dearly.

"I pinch myself each morning when I wake up," he wrote his mother in Lake City at the end of June. "But it's true. I'm home and you never saw people work the way July, Mr. Causey, Carpenter Joe, Maum Betty, Little Jim, Big Owen, Rina and I work from morning till night. Most of our people were stolen or have drifted away but these faithful few remain— Mr. George Causey still in full charge. The old fellow must have conducted himself with true diplomacy these past months—at least Maum Betty says she was the only one who got really angry with the Yankees. We watch the road every day for Frank and William. I could surely use them. But the whole house has been scrubbed. We've replaced the shingles on the roof, and by the courtesy of Mr. Reed, I expect new lumber from Jacksonville to replace the entire dining room floor where they evidently tore up a large section for disposing of slops. I hope I have done right telling you the truth about things here. That you are not too downhearted because all your furniture and other treasures are gone. We will buy more and little by little Hibernia will live again. It seems to me that you could use your time in St. Augustine, if Sophia is not too ill, searching with Cousin Louisa for some good used furniture. We need everything. Every bed is gone, too. Evidently to some Yankee hospital. I dropped off to sleep last night being thankful that Uncle George Seton inherited the treasured silver bowl. It would sure have been lost from the family forever had you gotten it, because you could never have carried it. Give my sisters, L.I. and Mary E. my love, and the same to Cousins Louisa and Sophia when you see them next month."

At General Hospital in Lake City, where she was still caring for six soldiers not yet able to travel, Margaret read and reread Frederic's letter. Along with Maggie, Frederic had become her support. L.I. had heard last week from Frank, who expected to reach Hibernia at the end of July, about the time Margaret would go to visit Louisa and Sophia. William, too, was making his way back to Hibernia, according to one of Margaret's "boys" at the hospital, whose cousin had been with William in the Regulators.

"I will stay with Louisa and Sophia until fall," she promised Frederic. "I know you don't want me to see our house until much more work is done. But, on October 9, I will have been away from Hibernia for more than sixteen months! Ready or not, in October, I'm coming back."

Willfrid, known as Sabre Boy, Louisa's jack of all trades, met Margaret with a carriage on the east side of the San Sebastián River on July 31. She spotted him at once, even before the ferry docked. Sabre Boy, given the nickname by a visiting Northern child before the war, stood out in the crowd. The crowd, if it could be called a crowd that afternoon at the waterfront, was so small, Sabre Boy dominated it: His tall, slender body curved—truly much like a sabre, Margaret thought—as he leaned against the carriage, proud as always to be meeting Miss Louisa's guests.

"Afternoon, Miss Mar'ret." He bowed elaborately and began picking up her boxes and bundles and the valise borrowed from Mary Evelyn for the trip. "I reckon you be plumb tired, comin' all the way from Lake City."

"Yes, I am tired. To the bone. But the hardest part was passing right by my old home without being able to stop. They—didn't even know I was on the boat! But, tell me, how is Miss Sophia?"

His even-featured face fell. "It be hard on Miss Louisa—not havin' time to get word to you, Miss Mar'ret."

"Willfrid! Word about—what?"

"Poor little ol' crippled-up Miss Sophia, she die. Sudden. In her sleep. Miss Louisa, she buried her—four days ago."

For an instant, Margaret covered her face with her hands. "Poor—poor Louisa!"

"Yes, ma'am. But, she actin' just like—Miss Louisa," he said proudly. "Brave, goin' along. She be lonesome in that big house. Ain't nobody sleeps in it now but her. Pootie, she offer to sleep downstairs in one of them empty comp'ny rooms, but—" He shook his head in admiration. "Miss Louisa, she say *no*. That she have to learn how to be by herself sooner or later. She some brave lady!"

Margaret and Louisa had not seen each other in three long years. Not since Lewis died. Their meeting, just inside the door of Louisa's big house on Hospital Street was almost wordless. Each called the other's name, and whatever else their hearts called was communicated in a long, clinging embrace.

After Margaret had settled in and rested a short time in her old room, adjoining Louisa's upstairs parlor, Pootie brought tea and the two women shared all each of them had kept bottled up since their last meeting. More freely, even than with L.I., Margaret poured out her stark grief over Seton, her hourly concern for William and Frank and Frederic—her gratitude to Mary Evelyn and L.I.—and all she could bear to tell, even Louisa, of the time spent caring for her "boys" in the Lake City hospital.

"And now, we're together—sharing another grief. Sophia. I—keep expecting her to pop in with some—fantasy or other. Oh, Louisa, I should have come earlier!"

"You're here when I need you the very most, Margaret. My little sister is—all right now. I buried her here. She thought New Switzerland was too lonely. Her pain was so intense, I honestly wonder how she stood it. She was remarkably brave and uncomplaining. I'm sure death took her quite by surprise. She just went on and on being sure she'd be entirely well—'tomorrow.' Sophia was never—never one to face facts, you know."

"Belle makes me think of her in that way. Not her disposition, goodness knows. Belle, even at age ten, lectures me for—hoping. Nothing is ever quite right for her. Nothing ever quite enough. I know I shouldn't say this—but the child does get on my nerves at times."

Louisa smiled. "Belle would have been in a bad fix if her mother had stopped hoping during that long trek from Hibernia to Lake City. Margaret, how *did* you do it?"

"I don't know now. I—just don't know."

"Tissie is just about sixteen, isn't she? Prettier than ever, I'm sure."

"If I do say so—yes. At times unbelievably pretty. But, unlike Belle, Tissie works hand in glove with my beloved Maggie. Oh, Louisa, I could not have managed at all—without Maggie."

"Are you sure the girls preferred to stay with L.I. instead of coming here?"

"No. They all wanted to come. In fact, I left Maggie in tears. That child has watched over me—as though our roles were reversed. It was much harder for her to let me come alone. But, of course, it was Maggie who helped convince the other two that with—Sophia so ill—as we thought then, four of us would be too much for you. Maggie understood, in spite of her longing to come." Margaret shook her head wonderingly. "She is still more than a mother can believe. In so many ways—an old soul. Wise, wise. Gentle, sensitive to everything that has the least effect on me. I—knew about her, if you remember, when she was still in her cradle. I love each child—now, more than ever, but before God, I couldn't—wouldn't want to live—without Maggie."

After a moment, Louisa asked, "Where do we go from here, Margaret?"

She reached for Louisa's hand. "Where do we go? Ahead. Straight ahead. There's no other place to go. Our guests *will* come back down, won't they? Have you heard any rumors? The surrender was last spring. Has even one Northerner come to St. Augustine since the war? I know they don't like our steaming summers, but have you heard of anyone even wanting to come? Any inquiries at the hotel? Have you had—even one?"

Louisa smiled. "Yes. The only one I didn't particularly want. Talkative Professor Mokes. He wrote a long letter explaining the war to me in his usual monotonous detail, assuring me that he knew I'd remained loyal to the Union and was now grieving over the assassination of President Lincoln and so on and on and on."

"Do you know what I think?" Margaret asked, from habit, in a guarded whisper. "I think this country, torn apart as it still is, would have fared far better under President Lincoln! I—never managed to hate him. Did you?"

"No, frankly, I didn't. Although I'm not sure just how much of my opinion was forced on me by Mrs. Judge Smith's loathing of the man. But he seemed an almost noble soul, who cared about all the states. A sad man, in a way."

"Doesn't it worry you to speak of him in a normal voice?"

"Not at all. Even if Pootie and Willfrid are eavesdropping, they worshipped Lincoln. They're free now, they believe, because of him. Whatever that means." With a small, gentle laugh, she added. "To Willfrid, born free, freedom means using my front door for everything. Why, he even carries in firewood, flour, cornmeal—anything—through the front door. It's all right with me. Just so he sweeps up if he makes a mess doing it."

"Louisa?"

"Yes?"

"You and I still have each other. We have two fine houses— at least, I will have again someday, thanks to Frederic. We *have* a future, haven't we?"

"I'm sure we have. I look every day for mail from the North. We've managed to keep this house up. We could be ready here in less than a month."

The two friends sat quietly for a time, then Margaret said, "When I lost—Lewis, I thought I'd—die, too. I wanted to. I wanted to run after him. When—Seton was killed, I—almost gave up. I didn't. I have managed not to let life knock me all the way down. I'm upright again now. As upright as I'll ever be after all that's happened. Belle never lets me forget that I preach too much about hope. But the fact remains that if we stop hoping, we not only—fail God, in some very real way we cease to exist. To be of any use to those who love us." She stood up. "You're hoping, too, Louisa. Right now—less than a week after you've lost dear Sophia! I can tell. Hope—is a very real way of life, isn't it? The only possible way to—survive."

Louisa smiled up at her. "Yes, Margaret. Yes, it is. And do you know? You look thirty again when you say that!"

From Louisa, Margaret bought some spare furniture and together they scoured St. Augustine for bargains so that in October, when Margaret at last boarded the *John Sylvester* at Tocoi for Hibernia, stowed on the steamer was enough furniture to make ready seven guest rooms. And in February 1866, this advertisement ran in the Florida *Union*:

> Mrs. Lewis Fleming gives notice that she has reopened her house at Hibernia on the St. Johns, twenty-five miles above Jacksonville, and can accommodate a limited number of boarders. The wharf has been repaired so that steamboats can land without difficulty.

* * *

In the same issue, a notice appeared announcing the reopening, after the war, of the law office of L.I. Fleming, in practice with his brother Frank Fleming.

Frank had returned in early August, William a week later. "He just ambled through the gate and down the lane," Frederic told his mother. "William came home as casually and as unconcerned as though he'd been after the cows. Don't ask me where he fought. He acts for all the world as though he's forgotten about the war."

47

To Margaret, her dreams and plans moving faster than the economic and social chaos realistically allowed, everything seemed to progress slowly, too slowly. Actually, during the years between her return to Hibernia and the new year of 1869, a great deal had been accomplished. The yard and river promenades were under control again, the fields were producing, the repaired house gleamed with a fresh coat of white paint and Northerners were gradually drifting back. At every opportunity, Margaret and Maggie took a steamer to Jacksonville or St. Augustine, depending upon where the "pickings" were best, to buy both new and good used furniture, carpets, lamps, tables, beds, chairs and chests—so that now, the entire house was once more furnished. The Hibernia dining room could seat a houseful of guests again. Her chairs didn't match as before, but Margaret no longer minded. In fact, her dining room table, fully set, made her think of Louisa's, surrounded by interesting, rather well-designed chairs, but all unlike. There were spindle backs, balloon backs, splat backs, arrow backs, and three rather handsome used Windsors. Little Jim's seven-year-old son, Friday, was always on hand an hour early to pull the cord that fanned the new rectangular punkah that hung above the long secondhand table purchased in Jacksonville.

A few guests came from the South, but as Louisa predicted, most made the long, arduous journey by water from New York, Connecticut, New Jersey, Massachusetts, Pennsylvania. At the peak of the 1870 season, both Hibernia and "Miss Fatio's" in St. Augustine, were filled to capacity.

When there was time, the two friends wrote "good news" letters to each other: "Except for two top-floor rooms under the roof," Margaret wrote to Louisa in early March, "we've been full all winter. My guests have enjoyed our croquet courts on the lawn, they've taken endless sails in and out of creeks and inlets, they've fished hours upon end. The men hunt with William, who, by the way, is doing fine and seems to be accepted well by most. Big Owen stays busy day after day with his axe and saw and oxcart, so that each room has more than enough firewood for the chilly days and nights. I have worked out a good system of compensation for my people. They are fed and housed and clothed as always and most accept small salaries. Maum Betty and July resolutely turn their backs each time I offer them their pay, but I save the money for them against some future need. I am enjoying being postmistress at the Hibernia branch of the Green Cove Springs post office in the corner of the new veranda room we've added and I receive eighteen dollars a quarter. Neighbors coming for their mail help keep me up on events and gossip and they seem to enjoy talking with our guests.

"Tissie is restless, but she has stopped complaining quite so much about her single state. I still notice, though, that she hurries to the dock each time the plantation bell rings announcing a boat bringing new guests from the North—or anywhere.

"Poor Belle, hair as red and curly as ever, meanders along through her days, avoiding as much work as Maum Betty allows. If I had more free time, I'm sure I'd worry about her. It's always a struggle to get her to attend our weekly Sunday school. What a strange child she is. Since she is now fifteen, I try not to prod her too often for her laziness, her rebellion against authority of any kind or for her odd disinterest in things spiritual. Maggie and Frederic—even William—seem at home with God. As all my children have been since babyhood—except Belle. Well, I give thanks. She isn't a bad girl, has somewhat outgrown that tendency to argue with me no matter what I offer by way of advice. Now, she simply conveniently lets her mind wander or when I demand her attention, looks at me as though I genuinely puzzle her at times.

"Maggie's goal, as she freely admits, is to learn to be the kind of friend to me you have always been, dear Louisa.

What more could a mother ask of a daughter of eighteen? She has handled my accounts for two years—almost perfectly. She doesn't intrude but reads so widely she can converse easily with the most finicky-minded guest. We have our share of finicky ones, as you do. And our share of laughs."

Due to their success, Margaret and Louisa saw less of each other than before the war, but letters went back and forth, some containing names and recommendations for guests who wanted to stop on their way north at Hibernia or see the sights of St. Augustine. Each enjoyed these shared guests, but their closeness grew far beyond the new business exchanges. Louisa, now seventy-two, and Margaret, fifty-six—mature and independent women—still found themselves deeply in need of each other. Louisa wrote: "We remind me sometimes of two youngsters—playing house."

L.I. and Frank's Jacksonville law practice prospered as Florida's economy gradually recovered, and Frederic, as Hibernia's host, reminded Margaret more of Lewis all the time. Maum Betty's food had filled out the skinny body of the young man who had struggled home from war five years before. His cheeks had Lewis's warm glow. His deep-set, expressive brown eyes, the color of Margaret's, but with Lewis's contemplative, gentle expression, more than made up for his quiet manner with the guests. "Your son Frederic made us feel at home the moment he met us at your dock, Mrs. Fleming," a teacher from New Hampshire wrote after a Hibernia visit. "Such a *gentle man*. We've heard for years about the true Southern gentleman, but I confess I thought the stories exaggerated. Now, I know at least one—your handsome, gallant, warmhearted Frederic."

Tissie adored Frederic and did her best to talk him into hunting for a wife. "I will someday," he'd laugh. "Too busy now. Anyway, Tissie, a man can't just—find a wife the way he finds a turkey for Sunday dinner! He has to fall in love first, doesn't he?"

"Falling in love is easy," she retorted. "Finding is the hard part."

Early in 1871, Frank journeyed to Greenville, South Carolina, to marry Lydia Pearson, and at the height of the season, with the house filled, Tissie announced that she was going to visit Cousin Louisa in St. Augustine. No amount of persuasion by Margaret or Frederic budged her. "I'm either going to St. Augustine or—have a nervous breakdown," she informed them. "I'm tired playing nursemaid to all these Yankees!"

Margaret wrote ahead to Louisa, assuring her that Tissie was not on the verge of a breakdown, but begging Louisa to keep an eye on her. "She's after a husband and although that's normal at her age, she does tend to make snap judgments."

They sent Tissie off on the *John Sylvester* in March. At the end of one month, Margaret received two letters in the mail: One from Louisa pleading with Margaret to forgive her for not having had better control over Tissie—the other from Tissie herself, written on board an ocean schooner bound for London as the bride of Mr. Leonard McRae, a wealthy Englishman who had been stopping at Louisa's house in St. Augustine.

Margaret was furious.

"I know it's terribly hard for you, Mama, that none of us got to meet him," Maggie said, as she arranged her mother's gray-gold hair before dinner the night the letter came. "And I'm sure Cousin Louisa feels just awful. But, what can we do to change any of it? Tissie's in London by now. She seems happy. Isn't that what matters?"

"I know you're right," Margaret snapped, "But I'm just not ready to be—generous and sensible about it. We could have given her such a beautiful wedding here at Hibernia! I'm—just so disappointed, I don't know what to say—even to you, Maggie. So, don't push me. How in the world am I going to hide the way I feel—before all those guests in the dining room?"

Maggie smiled at her mother's reflection in the looking glass. "You will simply—be you, Mama. You've played the gracious hostess so long, it will—just happen again."

Margaret inspected her hair with a hand mirror, then slammed the mirror down. "My gracious self is—not very gracious right now." She stood up. "I'm even cross with you—and I don't want to be." Abruptly, she embraced Maggie. "No, I'm not. What would I do without you?"

"That's beside the point, isn't it? You have me, for always. Right now, you need to practice what you preach. You need to—*hope* all will be well for Tissie."

"I'll do that tomorrow. This minute, I want to be angry with Tissie!"

Maggie smiled at her. "Shame on you, Mama. Shame on you."

Margaret gave Maggie a curious look. "Is—the way you make me feel now—the way I make Belle feel when I preach at her?"

"It could be. How do I make you feel?"

"Like throwing something!"

About halfway through dinner, a talkative, younger guest said in a voice heard by everyone around the long table: "I certainly hope it's a sunny day tomorrow. My heart is set on sailing past Mandarin. I've just got to catch at least one glimpse of Mrs. Harriet Beecher Stowe, my favorite author! Is it true, Mrs. Fleming, that she's often seen from the river at her writing on the front porch of her Mandarin home?"

"Yes. But of course, Mrs. Stowe is a very busy lady. She tells me most don't understand how devastating it can be for a writer to be interrupted."

The young lady stared at Margaret in rapt attention. "Have you—really—spoken to her, Mrs. Fleming? Face to face?"

"Oh, yes. We visit each other during the off season. It isn't that she dislikes people. Quite the contrary. But she does work hard."

"Do you mean Harriet Beecher Stowe has actually been in this very house?"

Margaret laughed. "At this very table, my dear."

"And you don't argue over—*slavery?*"

Margaret frowned. "Should we?"

"Well, after what she wrote in *Uncle Tom's Cabin*, I thought—"

"We've never discussed it," Margaret said. "We're simply good neighbors."

The young lady's eyes flew about the table and then back to Margaret. "Well, I declare! Wonders never cease, do they?"

"No, they don't, my dear. In fact, out of the blue last summer, Mrs. Stowe, after listening to my dream of building our own chapel here at Hibernia, gave me a most generous contribution toward it. Like me, she needs a holy place in which to thank God for the—sheer beauty along the St. Johns. Mrs. Stowe has found a whole new life down here— with us."

That night, when the house was quiet and most rooms dark, Maggie, as usual, slipped into her mother's room for their good-night talk. "Mama, you were magnificent at dinner! You were not only *gracious* about Mrs. Stowe, which, of course, I'd expect—you were clever, too. You must have taken up quite a collection for your chapel." Laughing, Maggie asked, "How much did you get?"

"Enough to begin building as soon as Frederic can manage the lumber from Jacksonville." Margaret was not laughing. "That little blabbermouth from the North was right. Wonders never cease. God began the chapel tonight—and I was anything but an obedient servant! I was just plain angry at Tissie when that bit of table talk began. I had to do something to blow off steam. Mentioning Mrs. Stowe's generous contribution was what came to mind." In a moment, she, too, began to laugh. "You're right, as usual, Maggie. It is funny, isn't it? Why have I waited so long to begin my chapel? Our guests will enjoy it. Why shouldn't they help pay for it?"

"Dear dear Louisa," Margaret wrote in the late spring of 1872, "my chapel in the woods is begun! There is only enough money now to lay the very firm foundation and to frame it, but by the time my people return next winter, there it will be—outlined against the tall trees, calling out of its own accord for contributions to finish it. Mr. Causey, in spite of his rheumatism, helps Joe and William all he can. I'm sure, as busy as we all are—and with the price of lumber these days—it may take years. But one day Lewis's little sketch will become a reality to bless my life and the lives of all who spend time at Hibernia. I long for you to see—even the foundation, the bare shape of this dream of mine. But, do take care of yourself. I don't like the sound of those 'occasional slight pains' in your chest. That means you are overdoing."

During the next two busy winters, the church fund grew, but the church itself grew far too slowly to suit Margaret. Joe was no longer young, Mr. Causey was almost incapacitated and William, though willing, was lost without someone to guide him. Months passed when there was no work done at all on the tall, narrow little building, but Margaret believed, the day would come, the day would come.

Another day came first, in 1874, when at the sound of the bell and the Negroes' shouts: "Steamboat! Steamboat!" Frederic and Margaret, at the dock to greet expected guests, greeted a quiet, subdued Tissie among them.

"My marriage is just finished," Tissie told her mother. "I'll be ever so grateful if no one—gets nosy. Leonard McRae isn't with me. He won't be again. He lives in London and I'm here. I'm—home, to stay. It's where I really, really want to be. I—made a mistake."

Tissie cried then, until her tears ran out, unpacked her things and with no more explanation, took up her duties with the paying guests.

"Don't you think she'll ever tell us anything!" Belle demanded.

"I don't know," Margaret said. "Perhaps not. And that's all right. We love Tissie and she's home. We don't need to know."

"Well, I do," Belle fumed. "I need to know all about what it's like to be married, don't I?"

"Not until it's time, dear. Then, I think I can tell you."

"Mama, you make me so mad! You do make me—just plain mad! No matter what happens, no matter how horrible it is, you always act like—in the end, everything's going to come out right! I'd like what you say just fine if it were true. But I don't see all your sermons helping me any. What's there to be so sunshiny about? Nothing good *ever* happens to me!"

"We all—want good things for you, Belle. We truly do. Can you believe—even that much?"

Belle turned away, her face flushed, troubled. "How come Maggie always thinks the world is—so perfect? What's wrong with her?"

"You ask—very difficult questions, darling. Nothing's wrong with Maggie. I don't see that she has anything to do with this."

"Oh, I know I'm the one who's always wrong. I'm the worst of everybody!" Then, "Is Tissie's heart broken?"

"I think maybe it is."

"I'd even welcome a broken heart!"

"Belle, you don't know what you're saying."

"If I don't, who does?" After a moment, she turned her troubled eyes on Margaret—directly. "I think Maggie—is too good for me—to be her sister. Mama, why can't I be—happy and liked the way Maggie is? I—truly love her so much!"

Margaret felt tears burn her eyes, but she knew how Belle hated weeping. "I know you love Maggie. And she loves you. I love you, Belle—you're my baby."

"I'm not a baby anymore," she snapped. Then, her voice

softened. "I know you love me, Mama. I do know that. It's just—that I find—a lot of things so hard to—*believe*. Like—hope. How do you make hope—begin? I know how you've tried to—explain it to me. But—I just find a lot of things—*so hard.*"

On November 10, 1875, on Margaret's sixty-second birthday, she walked arm in arm with Frederic to the end of their dock to find out who was arriving in a small, strange sailing boat moving in from the channel.

"I wonder who that could be?" she asked. "Our first guest isn't due until tomorrow. I've been looking forward to celebrating my birthday with only family."

"Can't imagine," Frederic mused. "It's coming from upriver. Maybe somebody's bringing a letter from Miss Louisa or—it could be that hardware I ordered for the chapel. We'll soon find out."

The light boat sailed steadily toward the dock, and a Negro in a wide-brimmed hat, the only occupant, held the sheet with one hand while waving the other.

"Frederic," Margaret gasped. "It's—Willfrid—Miss Louisa's Sabre Boy! Something's happened."

"Now, wait, wait. Could be good news."

"Miss Mar'ret? It's Sabre Boy—Willfrid. Miss Louisa's Willfrid," the young man called, bringing the boat alongside. Frederic grabbed and secured the tossed rope and Sabre Boy climbed nimbly onto the dock.

"What is it? *What is it*, Willfrid?"

Slowly, solemnly, he removed his hat. "It be Miss Louisa. We—lose Miss Louisa yestidy. Pootie—she find her—dead in the bed."

Frederic caught his mother and held her.

"Pootie and two neighbor ladies, they come in a wagon with the body. We gonna bury Miss Louisa this afternoon—at New Switzerland beside her family, like she wanted. Pootie, she say tell you later, Miss Mar'ret. I said 'no, Pootie, tell her now. Miss Mar'ret, she wanta go—all the way with Miss Louisa.' "

"You did—just right, Willfrid," Margaret said. "Thank you."

"Mama, let me take you back to the house. You need to lie down."

"No, Frederic. I'll—go back, but just long enough to dress." Her chin lifted. "Willfrid? You'll take me across to New Swizerland?"

"Mother, that old Fatio cemetary is completely grown over by now. Papa used to keep it cut back, but you know how busy we've all been. It's wild country over there. I'll go in your place."

"Frederic, you're very kind, but you're also too young to understand yet about—the friendship Louisa Fatio and I have shared for more than *sixty years.* Come to the house and have something to eat and drink, Willfrid. I'll be ready to go in half an hour."

The following week, because she needed a touch with her own family, Margaret wrote to her brother, George, whom she hadn't seen since her mother's death nearly twenty years before. "I always enjoy your Christmas letter, Brother," she wrote, "and hope you received mine. I write these lines now out of my own deep need. No, not financial. Our business will be excellent this year. My need is of the heart. My losses, as you know, have been great. There is still another— my best friend, Louisa Fatio, is dead. I wouldn't expect you, at such a distance, to understand, but somehow losing Louisa has brought back sharp grief for Lewis—and the old days. Louisa and Lewis were so close. She sustained me when he died and since. Enough of my troubles. I will go right to the point of this letter. You, undoubtedly, will think me a senti- mental woman. Well, I am. But, I have never, for a moment, forgotten the silver bowl and, since there is no businesslike, practical way to express this, I will simply state that my heart would be greatly eased, helped, if you would agree to permit me to purchase it. The bowl has always been—is now, even more—a symbol to me of the quality and beauty of life which I have tried so hard to instill in my children. To me, the bowl stands for Uncle William's courage—and I need courage now. I beg of you to accept the five hundred dollars enclosed and ship the bowl to me. Believe me, I will understand if you cannot part with it. Either way, I pray for your understanding."

Early in the new year, on the same boat which brought the freshly cut pine paneling for the interior of her chapel, a large crate arrived from New Market, Maryland. In it was the Seton bowl and a note from George which read: "You should have had it long ago."

Margaret never tired explaining about the magnificent bowl to her paying guests, and over and over, because he kept forgetting, she told William the story of his great-uncle Wil-

liam, whose courage and skill at sea, in battle with a French
privateer, had merited such a superlative reward. Each time
she longed to hear from Louisa—to write to her—Margaret
would slip away to sit by the Seton bowl, touching its soft
patina, looking and looking at the intricacy, the artistry of the
engraving, strangely drawing strength. And after a time, peace.

Sternly, she reminded herself that at her age, one simply
had to expect loved ones to die. When one reaches a certain
time of life—people do begin to die. Death is a part of life.
Hope, its only antidote. Her hope of seeing her loved ones
again had never been mere wishful thinking. That hope was
fact. She had the word of Christ Himself: "Where I am, there
ye shall be also . . . If it were not so, I would have told you."

"Of course, I'm getting old," she said aloud before her
looking glass, touching the age lines on her still vivacious
face. "And getting old isn't all bad. What's bad is that it just
seems to have taken me so many years to live!" She took a
deep breath. "Well, so be it. If, in my sixty-third year, I've
made a start, that's something."

48

The winter of 1877 was one of the best Margaret could
remember. Some chilly days edged between the mild ones,
but even they only seemed to enhance the good times her
people enjoyed that year from early January through March.
Several of Louisa's longtime guests spent this winter at Hibernia, admitting freely that much of their pleasure in the Fatio
house during years past had been because of Louisa herself.
Hibernia was full. Margaret and Frederic were making plans
to build a large, two-storied cottage which would house twenty
more people in the years to come. The hunting was excellent.
More trout and bass and bream were caught in the St. Johns
and at Doctor's Lake than anyone could remember. There
was an abundance of crayfish, shrimp and sea turtles from
which Maum Betty made pot after pot of her celebrated turtle
soup, with spices unknown even to Margaret, since the plump,
purposeful Betty held her clean, white apron up to hide
every seasoning session.

There was real gaiety again at Hibernia—singing in the evening, occasional dances, excursions on the river, picnics and sailing parties, planned and directed by Tissie, whose heartbreak, whatever caused it, had made her more cooperative, kinder, even with the difficult guests.

Belle entered in, too, especially if there happened to be an eligible young man on the premises and Maggie, now twenty-five, was never far away when Margaret needed her. Frederic was so like his father that people who remembered Lewis—even those who didn't, had begun to call him Colonel Fleming. "They make me sick doing that," Belle complained, and when Margaret asked why, she insisted it was only because *all* Yankees had the dumb idea that all Southern gentlemen were older than they were and had been colonels. "Frederic isn't old and he was never any more than a sergeant!"

Maggie never complained because Margaret insisted upon immaculate grooming and dress-up clothes for them all anytime a guest was in the house. But, Tissie, still part wild colt, even in her new, more subdued personality, did complain off and on and Belle fussed every day. But dress they did and successful they were—more so with the guests of the winter of 1877 than in any other season.

April came with its frail white lilies, like stars carpeting the woods, along with yellow, stiff-stemmed pitcher plants, pink wild orchids and violets that smelled like fresh cucumbers. Wild azaleas bloomed everywhere, and thick along the veranda at the north end of the big house the jasmine blew its heavy fragrance into the air until Belle complained about that too— for being too heavy, too sweet.

Margaret felt that she at last had begun to understand her odd daughter, Belle. Had learned that when Belle complained, it was perhaps a cry for help.

"What do you mean—'help'?" Maggie wanted to know.

"Well, Belle's restless. She always has been. She doesn't like being that way—wants, actually, to be contented as you are."

"Me?"

"Haven't you discovered yet, Maggie, that your baby sister absolutely adores you?"

"Yes, I know she loves me, but—"

"More than that. You're her idol. You could not be more unlike. By nature, Belle will never resemble you—and it angers her. Makes her feel hopeless. I think at times, she'd be terribly relieved if—that jasmine smelled cloying to you, too!"

"I like it," Maggie laughed. "Should I—fib and say I don't?"

"No, dear. But let's make a pact. Let's you and I promise each other that when we can possibly chime in and agree with Belle, we will."

"All right. I'd like to help her. Tissie wants to smack her most of the time. I also understand that, but I promise."

"Good."

For a long moment, Maggie stood smiling at her mother.

"What's so funny, dear?"

"Not 'funny,' Mama. That was a happy smile. It's good to learn new things—even about your own baby sister, isn't it? And—my goodness, you've helped me learn—so much. How can I ever thank you?"

Margaret returned the smile, with all the love in her heart. "Just by—being you and being with me."

Maggie laughed. "Don't worry. I'm never going any place—I'm already here!"

On the hottest November day in Margaret's memory, a letter from L.I. came when the boat brought the Hibernia mail and bills. Margaret made herself sort it all, saving L.I.'s always-cherished pages as a reward for handling her duties as postmistress first. Then, in a rocker on the empty veranda, fanning furiously with a palmetto fan, she began to read L.I.'s letter:

> Jacksonville
> 14 November, 1877

My dear Miss Margaret,

My heart is fighting my pen with every word I write, but it is almost certain that a yellow fever epidemic is upon us here. Frank and his family were among the first to fall ill from the disease. They are quite sick and the doctor informs me that Frank, Lydia and the two children need constant nursing. Mary Evelyn cannot leave our own children and you must not come. At your age, it would be too strenuous for you. So, could Tissie or Maggie come at once to nurse Frank and the others? Let me hear by the first mail. My prayers and my love come to you,

> L.I. Fleming

*   *   *

Maggie, dressed in a brown linen travel suit, her two small tapestry valises beside her on the Hibernia dock, kept hugging her mother, trying to reassure her that she would take the very best care of Frank and be home far sooner than anyone expected.

"Tissie," Maggie said, "I'm trusting you to stop Mama's tears once I'm gone. Promise?"

"She's crying now because it's so hard for her to let *you* go," Tissie said. "I don't see why I can't be trusted to nurse Frank's family."

"Of course, you could," Maggie said.

"So could I," Belle wailed. "But no one ever dares depend on me. Not for anything!"

"Hush, all of you," Margaret ordered firmly. "This is hard enough without a family spat. *Maggie is the one I'm sending.* It's settled. Kiss your brothers good-bye, Maggie. I see the boat already."

"I don't much like to kiss anybody," William said, his eyes on the steamer.

"But I like to kiss you, dear William," Maggie hugged and kissed William and turned to Frederic. "Take care of Mama, Big Brother."

"I will, Little Sister. You take care of yourself."

"Don't worry—as long as I know Mother's all right, I'll be fine. Tissie, I've written down all my daily duties. The list is on your dresser. Belle? I know you're going to be such a big help to Mama with all those guests coming so soon."

The small steamer slowed to move in toward their dock.

"Oh, Maggie," Margaret said, embracing her. "Maggie, Maggie—I'll miss you!"

Frederic helped his sister aboard, William carried on the valises, and they all waved until the steamer was out of sight.

"Maggie can't see us any longer, Mama," Frederic said gently. "We'd better get back to the house. You look tired."

Margaret tried a smile. "No. Not tired. Just—heartache for Frank and his family. And, oh, Frederic—except for my visit to Louisa at the end of the war, I've almost not been away from Maggie in all her twenty-six years!"

There were two short letters from Maggie; in one, she assured them all—"Mama especially"—that Frank, his wife and his children were slowly improving. The second letter, in which Maggie admitted how glad she'd be to get home where she could sleep straight through the night again, came on November 24. On December 1, expecting another group of winter guests, Margaret and Frederic, as always, were dressed and waiting on their dock when the *John Sylvester* arrived from Jacksonville.

On tiptoe, Margaret scanned the passengers gathered around the steamer's railing. Then, through the crowd pushed L.I., his face a mask. The cluster of people parted to allow six Negroes carrying a heavy box to reach the gangplank.

"Mama," L.I. said, jumping to the dock. "Oh, Mama!"

Margaret could only stare at him, her face white.

"L.I.," Frederic demanded. "What is it?"

"It's—Maggie. Maggie's—in that coffin they're—bringing off the boat. Everybody in Frank's family got well. She—saw to that. Maggie died of yellow fever—at my house last night."

All the Hibernia guests agreed to allow Frederic to transfer their reservations to Magnolia Hotel in nearby Green Cove Springs. His mother had collapsed so completely, he saw no other way.

"Why, Frederic?" Tissie kept asking, day after day—weeks after they'd buried Maggie. "Mama was so strong when Papa died, when her mother and George died—when Seton was killed—when Cousin Louisa died." Her eyes filled with helpless tears. "Why—has Mama just taken to her bed like this? I know Maggie was the best of us all, except you, but you've got to tell me. I'm scared for Mama. Do you know it's been almost a month since—Maggie died? I couldn't believe it when Mama didn't even come out of her room for Christmas dinner! Can't we do—*something* to help her?"

Frederic, his face more troubled than Tissie had ever seen it, sat in the spacious, empty parlor staring into a blazing fire. He said nothing.

"Frederic! Answer me."

On a heavy sigh, he said, "Tissie, Mama and Maggie were—so close, her grief alone is enough to make her sick. But—it's more than that."

"Then, what? What, Frederic?"

He took a deep, uneven breath. "Mama—blames herself—that Maggie is gone."

Tissie sank slowly onto a nearby love seat. "Oh. Oh, so that's it. But—she's got to—forgive herself! Mama didn't do anything wrong. She just knew that Maggie would make a better nurse than anyone else. Mama didn't do—anything intentionally. She—just trusted Maggie. Thought only Maggie could really take care of Frank."

"I know. But, try to tell Mama that. I've talked to her until I'm blue in the face and she just turns her head away and lies there. She's either in her bed—or sitting by the window staring at nothing. No matter what Maum Betty sends up, she doesn't eat enough to keep a bird alive."

"But, Mama's the one—who taught me that—sometimes, I just—had to forgive myself!"

"I know. She doesn't seem to—be able to remember any of the things she's taught us all."

Tissie walked to the window, then back to where Frederic sat. "Brother, do you think I—could try to get her to—talk to me, now that you've told me she blames herself about Maggie?"

Frederic gave her a weak smile. "Can't do any harm, I guess."

In the hall by the stairway, Tissie stopped outside her mother's half-open bedroom door and listened—almost unable to believe her ears. Belle was talking, talking to their mother, louder than she meant to, the way Belle always did when she was arguing.

"Mama, you're going to listen to me," Belle was saying. "I'll be twenty-three in May. I've got a right to expect my own mother—at least to listen to me—even if your heart is broken. Mama?"

There was no answer.

"Turn your face this way and look at me," Belle ordered. "Doesn't it matter that my heart's broken, too? Over Maggie— because she was my idol—" her voice broke. "But by now, mostly—over *you*. I'd think you'd make some kind of effort, after all you've tried to teach us for all the years of our lives. I'd think you'd care some that Tissie cries herself to sleep every night—over you. Over the way *you're* acting. We don't even wait for night to cry most of the time. We cry off and on all day. Frederic's heart is smashed to pieces, too. Over Maggie, yes, like with all of us. But our hearts are just about to—burst over you, Mama!" A sob split Belle's voice again. "It's—almost like you're—dead, too! What are we going to do in this big house without you?"

Tissie, still listening intently, could hear only her mother's jerky breathing, as though she were stifling sobs.

"I'd be *ashamed* if I were in your place," Belle cried.

Tissie stared at the half-open door, unable to believe what she was hearing her sister say—and to Mama of all people!

"I'd be downright ashamed," Belle plunged on, "to add to all our grief like this. Do you think you're the only one who loved Maggie? All my life, you've tried to make me believe—things about God and all. And whether you knew it or not, I did try. I used to lie in bed all night and squeeze my eyes shut, trying." Belle stopped, cleared her throat, then said firmly: "Mama, at least tell me one thing. Tell me where—your faith is now? What happened to all that—*hope?* Don't I matter at all? Doesn't Tissie? Or Frederic or William? William just sits out by the barn all day with his head in his hands—over the way you are, Mama. *Don't we matter?*"

From the hall, Tissie could hear the bed creak, but she waited—afraid to take a step either way, for fear Mama and Belle would know she was there. It seemed odd to mind about Belle, but her pesky little sister had suddenly become someone to reckon with.

The bed creaked again, the old familiar sound that always meant Mama was getting up. Still, Tissie waited.

"Mama?" Belle's voice sounded suddenly—almost glad. "Mama! Oh, Mama!"

"Come here, Belle. I want to—kiss you."

Tissie took the first easy breath in weeks and let it out slowly, so relieved her head began to ache.

"There," her mother said in a voice that still sounded weak.

Belle began to cry. "Oh, Mama, thank you—*thank you for—getting up!*"

"Hand me my robe and slippers, Belle. It must be nearly time for dinner."

Tissie, unable to contain herself, rushed into the room and threw her arms around her mother. "Mama, we've—missed you so much. We've needed you so desperately!"

"Thank you, Tissie, I promise you, I'm back." She fastened the soft, woolen dressing gown and gave them both a long, loving look. "I wonder if you'd leave me alone now, both of you. Tell Frederic I'll be out in just a little while. For dinner."

"I'll go to the barn and tell William, too," Belle said, her eyes shining.

"Yes. You certainly *told* me—exactly what I needed to hear. So, I wish you would go tell dear William that—Mama's back."

Slowly, carefully, Margaret began to dress for dinner. Tears streamed down her pale cheeks as she struggled to arrange her hair exactly as Maggie had. Then, corseted, over her head, she let her bottle-green dinner dress fall to the floor, hooked the bodice, pulled it down smoothly over her still firm breasts and took a handkerchief and matching scarf from her dresser drawer. After a deep breath, she walked out into the hall and straight to the front door where she could see the river, turning copper-pink now under a brilliant winter sunset.

The river was there, rolling toward the sea, the same as ever. Her guests were no longer present, so she felt no hurry. For a long time, she stood, watching the river. Finally, alone in the darkening hallway, not minding that the children might be listening, she spoke quietly: "Lord, forgive me—for refusing to forgive myself." Then, with the merest hint of a smile, she added: "And—will You please tell Maggie, Lord, that it was—*Belle* who brought me to my senses?"

AFTERWORD

The three months remaining to Margaret Seton Fleming were evidently buoyant ones. The Hibernia guests returned and at her urging, work commenced again on her little chapel. It is said that in early April, as she lay dying from what was called "sudden heart failure," she smiled now and then at the sound of hammers and saws from the woods across the shady lane from her big house. The first service to be held in the as-yet-unfinished church was Margaret's funeral on April 6, 1878, some four months after Maggie's death. The anniversary of St. Margaret's Episcopal Church—obviously not named for Margaret Fleming, but for a young Christian martyr—is observed still on that date. Of course, Margaret is buried in the church's small, picturesque cemetery.

Her son, Frederic, with the help of his wife, Margot, and his sisters, Belle and Tissie, continued to entertain visitors in the big house beside the St. Johns until Frederic's death in 1917. Tissie died in 1922, Belle in 1934. Both, after unhappy marriages, had returned to live at Hibernia. Frank became governor of Florida and in February, 1889, remembering Maggie's tragic death, called a special session of the legislature to create a state medical board to meet health problems—especially the dreaded yellow fever which had killed his sister. Governor Frank Fleming died in 1908 and is buried in Jacksonville. It is not known when Tina died, but her grave is undoubtedly at Welaka, Florida, the locale of her husband's plantation. William never left Hibernia and died shortly after his sister Tissie, in 1922. In the *Florida Times-Union*, on the day following L.I.'s death—September 14, 1888—there appeared an editorial with these words: "Today, the whole city mourns the passing of one of Jacksonville's most distinguished and best loved citizens." L.I.'s law office is still in existence under another name and is the oldest in the state. In the cemetery behind Margaret's church, markers are there for Margaret, Lewis, his first wife, Augustina Cortez Fleming, his parents, George and Sophia Fleming, Frederic, William, Tissie (Matilda Fleming McRae), Belle (Isabel Fleming Sudlow) and young Maggie. It is almost certain that Margaret's stepson George is there, too, although the marker is gone.

The big house on Fleming's Island no longer stands, but the area is still called Hibernia. New Switzerland, the land across the river once owned by the Fatios, is now called Switzerland. As far as is known, Louisa Fatio is buried there in the old family plot, but even that has been lost to the lush, heavy Florida forest.

It is possible, I am glad to say, to spend as much time as you like in what was once Louisa's handsome guesthouse in St. Augustine. It is located on the corner of Cadiz Street and Aviles Street and is magnificently restored and furnished much as it was when Louisa lived there. Its owners, the National Society of the Colonial Dames of America in the State of Florida, have not only done superb research on the house itself, including extensive archaeological work, but have found much of interest about its various owners—including Margaret's dearest friend, Louisa, who owned the house from 1855 until her death in 1875. With volunteer docents, the Dames keep the house open free to the public at certain times. The St. Augustine Information Center will supply details of when the now famous Ximenez-Fatio house may be seen. I seldom go to the old city without a visit to Louisa's house and, to me, it is almost as though Louisa were there—just in the next room.

Immediately north on Aviles Street is the imposing home of Louisa's colorful, Rebel neighbor, Mrs. Judge Smith. The sign on the house (now the St. Augustine Public Library) marks it as the birthplace of Confederate General Edmund Kirby-Smith.

In this book's accompanying *Diary of a Novel*—my account of the writing of *Margaret's Story*—I have written of my experiences with those close to the story who gave generously of their records and knowledge of everything relevant from family genealogy to steamboats. With one exception, I will here merely list again the names of all the others who supplied information, but because of her generosity which was of so much help in structuring the novel, I especially thank Marion Fleming of Houston, Texas, who sent copies of records pertaining to the actual military orders which evicted

Margaret from her home during the Civil War. Through her, I also had access to Margaret's own petitions to the U.S. government begging for restitution for the dreadful damage done her home while she was forced to be away. The character of Mr. George Causey was drawn directly from his deposition in Margaret's behalf. There would have been a novel without these valuable papers from Marion Fleming, but it would not have been as authentic as I believe it to be.

This book is dedicated to Dena Snodgrass, Jacksonville historian, without whom there really would have been no novel. Dena not only kept me on track throughout the writing, but more than once kept me in good spirits. Directly to me or through her, the following persons have given of their expertise and valued opinions: Dot Barker, St. Mary's, Georgia, Dr. William Hitt, Dr. Haywood Moore, Agnes Holt, George Baker and Miles Baker, of St. Simons Island; Jackie Bearden, Eugenia Arana and Mary Ellen Fabal, St. Augustine Historical Society; N. Clement Slade, Mr. and Mrs. John P. Ingle, Jr. (Elizabeth Fleming Ingle), Mr. and Mrs. Herbert F. Williams (Hester Fleming Williams), Edward Mueller and Norma Lockwood, all of Jacksonville; Mr. Leon J. Barrie, Green Cove Springs, Florida; the Reverend Mr. Bob Libby, Orange Park—rector of St. Margaret's Episcopal Church; Bruce Chappell and Ellen Hodges, P. K. Yonge Library, University of Florida, Gainesville; and from the same university, Dr. John Mahon and Dr. Ashby Hammond, professors of History, and my valued friend Pat Wickman; Dorothy Jean Olson, Mark Fretwell and Claudia Moffet, St. Augustine; Dr. Jarrell Shofner, Professor of History, Central University, Orlando; Luis R. Arana, Historian, Castillo de San Marcos, St. Augustine; Dr. George E. Buker, Jacksonville University; Margaret C. Burgess of the Florida Historical Society; Helen Latrico and George T. Davis of Fernandina Beach; Robert W. Harper III, Associate Director of the Lightner Museum, St. Augustine; Nancy Morris and Kathleen McKee, Hibernia, Green Cove Springs; Kaethe Crawford, Pittsburgh, Pennsylvania; Jim Darby, Director, and Marcia Hodges, Reference Librarian, Brunswick Public Library, Brunswick, Georgia; and once again, I thank my friend Burnette Vanstory of St. Simons Island, for her valuable research on What They Wore. Deep gratitude also to Ann Hyman of the *Florida Times-Union*, whose writer's sense nudged me toward this story and to Margaret's granddaughter, Margaret

Seton Fleming Biddle, whose privately printed book, *Hibernia, The Unreturning Tide*, was often beside me as I wrote. There are no words to communicate my gratitude to Margaret's descendants, who have not only become my encouraging friends and helpers, but who have faithfully read and approved the manuscript—Hester Williams, Dorothy Austin, Jane Rowley and Betty Ingle.

Margaret's Story, along with *Don Juan McQueen* and *Maria*, completes the Florida trilogy and marks the end, for now at least, of one of the most cherished and stimulating experiences of my professional life. Certain areas in the vicinity of St. Augustine will always be Don Juan's or Maria's land, and now, the vast, beautiful, history-rich St. Johns River will be, to me, Margaret's "friend, the river." The tidal river "with a way of its own," the Indians said of the St. Johns. The people who once lived along or near its shores have had a way of their own with me for nearly a decade. I will miss them all.

Eugenia Price
St. Simons Island, Georgia

ABOUT THE AUTHOR

EUGENIA PRICE, a native West Virginian, has lived most of her life in Chicago where she wrote and produced radio and TV programs. In 1954 she wrote her first book, and since then she has lectured in almost every state in the union. Her first novel, *The Beloved Invader*, was published in 1965. As Miss Price devoted more and more time to the writing of both fiction and nonfiction, she has gradually curtailed her speaking engagements. She is now "hooked" on the research and writing of historical novels about real people who lived in the eighteenth and nineteenth centuries along the southeastern coast. Eugenia Price lives in a secluded section of St. Simons Island, Georgia—the setting of her best-selling St. Simons Trilogy, *The Beloved Invader, New Moon Rising*, and *Lighthouse*. She has won numerous awards, including the Georgia Distinguished Service Award. Other books she has written include *Maria, St. Simons Memoir* and *Share My Pleasant Stones*.